# MARSHAL'S OBSESSION

## JM JOHNSEN

Quirled Toes Publishing books may be ordered from your favorite bookseller.
www.quirledtoes.com

Hardcover: 979-8-9921908-1-6
Paperback: 979-8-9921908-2-3
Kindle: 979-8-9921908-3-0

Library of Congress Cataloging Number and Cataloging in Publication data on file with publisher.


Printed in the United States of America
10 9 8 7 6 5 4

To all my friends and family who have supported
my quest to bring these stories to life.

# CHAPTER 1

# THE FIRST TIME

It was late. Most respectable people were already home and asleep in their beds, but he had been waiting. He'd been waiting for her since midnight.

He didn't know who she was, but he knew what she was...a woman of the night. He had often watched her from the apartment window, following men into the alley across the street. He knew what they were doing.

The clipping-clip-clop of a horse's hooves and the clattering of carriage wheels echoed through the deserted cobblestone streets. He faded further into the shadows of the alley, waiting for the carriage to disappear from sight before venturing forward again. The darkness between the two buildings was cold and dank, and the stench of garbage filled his nostrils.

He fidgeted, flexing his fingers and wiping his hands down his pant legs. He didn't have to be afraid. The city had a myriad of streets and dark alleys to hide in. He'd never get caught.

Then he saw her. Alone, the seductively clad woman swayed drunkenly down the street. She was perfect. He trotted across the street, and as he'd seen other men do, he flashed several bills in her direction. She smiled coquettishly and stumbled after him into the alley.

He nibbled at her neck and stroked her soft flesh. She would be his first. She started to raise her skirt, but he stopped her and turned her around. She didn't see the knife.

He had no idea it would be so easy.

Lying at his feet, her eyes and neck both wide open, he admired his work. Watching the blood gush from her neck had aroused him like nothing ever had. Now, it had subsided, and there was only a tiny trickle from the corner of her mouth. He squatted beside her and examined the cut. He had been nervous and, in his excitement, had sliced too deep. It was over too soon. He licked a drop of blood from her cheek and bid her farewell.

He would be more careful next time.

# CHAPTER 2

# 1866 - THE HUNTER

He arrived before dawn and edged through the thick timber. The sharp smell of pine and rotting vegetation accosted his nose and made his eyes water. He looked for a perfect spot to watch for his prey. A shallow ditch at the edge of the woods suited his needs. He settled into position. If he stayed low and quiet, he wouldn't be seen. His heart raced with anticipation as a light flickered in one of the windows. He heard the faint rattling of pots and pans and then silence. The smell of frying bacon wafted to him in the light breeze. *Breakfast time*, he thought.

Waiting for her husband to come downstairs for breakfast, Mila Jacobs pulled her diary from the desk drawer. Will had given her a drawer in his desk for household records and her journal. The drawer belonged to her, and her alone. She opened the leather-bound book to a new page and dipped her pen in the inkwell.

*May 10, 1866*

*I am waiting for Will to come downstairs for breakfast. We have a lot to do today, and I can't imagine what is taking him so long. We have things to get ready for Jake's birthday. I can't believe our little Jake will be ten years old. Time has flown.*

Will kissed the back of her neck, smiling as he looked over her shoulder. "Woman, what are you doodling in that book of yours?"

"None of your business, mister," she said, slapping the diary shut. She stood and turned into his arms for a proper kiss.

"Mmmm, I smell something good." Taking her hand, he led her to the kitchen. Will went to the warmer and pulled out the platter of food. "The way you feed me; I should be round as an apple."

Mila smiled, looking him up and down. His farmer's workday clothing couldn't hide his muscled body or the broad shoulders and narrow hips. She hoped he wouldn't get all soft and round, but she would love him even if he did.

"Ahem."

Her eyes jerked to his face.

"Stop looking at my crotch unless you're serious." His eyes sparkled with mischief, and his grin widened as Mila's face turned red.

"I'm not looking— Oh, sit down and eat your breakfast."

Will Jacobs finished his breakfast and kissed his wife before heading to the barn. Sliding open the barn door, he thought of all the chores to be done. The most important was preparing a stall for his son's birthday surprise.

Mila watched her husband disappear through the barn door and then went to the bottom of the stairs, wiping her hands on her apron. A frown of exasperation wrinkled her forehead. "Jake. This is the third time I've had to call you."

"I don't feel good."

"Nonsense. Your father has already had his breakfast, and you better get down here right now, or you'll be late for school."

"I can't go," he whined. "I have a stomachache." But his mouth watered, and his stomach rumbled at the aroma of fried bacon.

"William Caster Jacobs, get your backside down here now before your breakfast gets cold. I know you aren't sick."

"But Mom."

"I mean it, Jake. Don't make me come up there."

She headed back to the kitchen and straight to the stove, shaking her head. She broke two eggs into the hot bacon drippings and adjusted the damper. The eggs sizzled and popped, edges bubbling in the hot grease.

It's that Watkins boy. That's why he doesn't want to go to school. She poked at the eggs, loosening them from the bottom of the iron skillet. She worried about her son. He came home too often with scrapes and bruises. The Watkins boy was a horrible bully and made Jake's life miserable. She pulled a pan of biscuits from the warmer and slammed it on the table. *Somebody has to do something about that no-good Sam Watkins.* She checked the eggs, flipping them over as Jake sat at the table.

"I'm sorry, Mama. I shouldn't have lied to you about being sick, but I don't want to go to school today. Please, let me stay home."

"Is it that bully again? Is he bothering you?"

"No," Jake said, his eyes focused on his lap.

"Then what?"

"There's that history test today."

Mila wiped the back of her hand across her forehead, pushing back a stray lock of hair. "I helped you study last night, and you know all the answers. You'll do fine. When was the Declaration of Independence signed?"

He answered without hesitation. "The Continental Congress adopted the document on July 4, 1776, and on August 2, 1776, delegates began signing the declaration." He looked at his mother with eyes the same color as his father's. "It's different when it's on a test.

"It's all right, Jake. I understand," his mom said, sliding the eggs onto his plate. But she didn't understand. Mila set the skillet back on the range and stepped away from the stove's heat.

So, it wasn't Sam Watkins, after all, but a test. She didn't understand how taking a test could cause him to get so upset. And why did his mind go blank? Did it have anything to do with his special gift? She studied her son with arms crossed. "Would you like me to talk to Mr. Terrence about—"

"No, Mama, no. Please don't talk to him. I'll do better. I promise." He squirmed in his seat, the bacon and eggs no longer holding any appeal.

"All right. I won't talk to him." She changed the subject, trying to get his mind off the test. "You haven't forgotten tomorrow is your birthday, have you? I'm baking your favorite cake, and your dad says he'll make ice cream. Isn't that exciting?"

"I guess so," he said, trailing his fork through the runny egg yolks, making a pattern against the white plate. His concern over the impending test and the thought of his mother speaking with his teacher had overshadowed any joy a Saturday might bring. Even if it was his birthday and even if there would be cake and ice cream.

He picked at the food on his plate and left for school, his feet dragging. Mila stood at the kitchen window, holding back the red gingham curtain. She sighed, watching her son's slender figure disappear down the lane. She hoped he would do well on the test and wished she could do something to help him.

The hunter also watched.

Mila picked up Jake's unfinished breakfast plate and headed to the barn. Either her husband or their pig, Sylvia, would get the leftovers. Will was cleaning out the stall previously used for storage and preparing it for the new occupant.

Mila's eyes twinkled, thinking about the surprise they had planned. "Is everything ready for tomorrow?"

Will hung his pitchfork between two pegs on the barn wall and took the plate from his wife. "Don't worry, dear. I have everything under control. The stall is ready. And tomorrow morning, I'll ride into town to pick up the mule and the new saddle. I'll come through the back pasture, so Jake won't see me, and I'll leave the mule hobbled there until it's time for our party. I can't wait to see Jake's face."

"The mule? He's gentle?"

"The man at the livery says so, and I've found him to be an honest sort."

"You rode the mule?"

"Yes, I rode the mule. He's gentle as a lamb. And the most striking mule I've ever seen. Black as a crow's wing with four white socks. Jake will love him."

"And you've checked the icehouse."

He laughed at his wife, pushing a wisp of hair behind her ear. "Such a worrier. Yes, my dear, I have double-checked, and there is plenty of ice left to churn the ice cream. I also talked to Daisy, and she promised to provide extra-rich milk in the morning. We'll have the creamiest ice cream ever to put on top of your cake. *Und Du machst den besten Kuchen, meine Liebe.*"

"English, Will. You keep forgetting that we decided to speak only English when we got to America."

"As I recall, you decided that. I think Jake should know how to speak the language of our homeland. What harm can it do?" He wrapped his arms around her, kissing away any further objections she might have had.

Mila pushed her amorous husband away and changed the subject. "I can't believe how old our baby is."

"He'll be a man with a wife and kids before we know it." Will frowned. "And I'll be sleeping with a grandma." Mila punched his arm, making him laugh. "But tomorrow, he's still our little boy, and we'll make it a perfect day for him. After all, a man only turns ten once in his life. Will looked to his right at the mow full of fresh straw. "You have anything on the stove?"

"No, why?"

He fell onto the pile of straw, pulling Mila on top of him.

"Will Jacobs. You stop this. I'm not going to wrestle around with you out here in the barn in a pile of straw." She tried to squirm from his arms, giggling like a schoolgirl. "Wilhelm Frederick Jacobs, you stop this right now. Someone might see us."

He rolled her over, pinning her beneath him. "You worry too much. We're all alone here except for Sylvia and Daisy. No one will see us."

Will was wrong. The hunter watched through the open barn door.

Later, Mila and Will walked arm and arm back toward their house, holding on to one another, still wrapped in the soft glow of their love-making. The heat from the sun warmed their backs, and a gentle breeze lifted Mila's tousled hair. They stopped at the well for a cool drink and soft, gentle kisses, unaware of the watcher.

Will brushed a kiss across his wife's lips. "You were very distract-ing this morning," he said, tugging a piece of straw from her tangled hair.

"And you were very wicked."

He gave her an affectionate smile. "I have work to do, woman, and so do you." He swatted her playfully on her behind as she turned away.

"You'll pay for that, you brute," she hollered over her shoulder as she hurried into the house. She heard his laughter behind her and wondered if there was any way she could love him more.

Uncomfortable after hours of surveillance, the huntsman squirmed and stretched. He'd been so focused on his prey that he hadn't heard the scurrying and rustling sounds of the forest floor around him or noticed the green, long-legged beetle waddling drunkenly down his arm. He brushed the beetle away and settled back down. He had already decided, but he wanted to watch for just a bit longer and enjoy the anticipation.

Mila cleaned up the breakfast dishes, wondering for the hundredth time why Jake didn't fight back when the Watkins boy bullied him. Jake was strong, and even though his slender body might look underfed, she suspected he could hold his own. And why did such an intelligent boy struggle with tests? She cringed, wondering again if it might have something to do with his unique abilities.

Early on, there were clear indications Jake had inherited her family's unusual talents. And coming at such a young age, the signs were significant. Jake would be a powerful seer. Perhaps even more powerful than her grandfather had been. Her grandfather called it a oneness with the Universe…a fearsome responsibility. She would have to talk to Jake soon and teach him how to use and control his powers. She dreaded putting such a burden on his young shoulders, but it was time.

Heading for the garden to pick a mess of green beans for supper, she thought of her handsome son and how he favored his father. He may have inherited her family's gift of vision, but physically, he had inherited his father's looks. They had the same olive-colored skin, thick black hair, and dark blue eyes.

Jake worshipped his father and wanted to be like him in every way. He dressed like him and tried to walk and talk like him. He even tried to comb his hair straight back like his father did, but a cowlick had other ideas. She smiled, wondering how often she had seen him run his fingers through his hair, trying to force the stubborn lock into submission. But the cowlick always won, and his hair fell over the left side of his forehead.

Mila pulled the bottom of her apron up to form a pouch and started down the row of beans. She picked the oldest from each bush and smashed bean weevils as she went. When she had enough for supper, she hurried to the house and dumped them on the kitchen table. She grabbed an empty egg basket and danced her way to the henhouse, humming a spirited song…unaware of being watched.

The hunter squirmed backward along the ground. He had made his decision. He needn't stay any longer. He moved some distance into the woods before standing and stretching. They were the perfect loving couple, and they lived in an ideal location. He would leave for now, but he would soon be back. His pulse quickened. By this time next week, they would be his.

He trotted back to the horse and carriage he'd left beside the road. Earlier, he had pulled overalls over his regular clothes. Now, he shucked them. He wadded them into a bundle and threw them into the back of the carriage out of sight. Walking to the side of his rig, the hunter pulled a burr from his cuff. He was already imagining how he would take his pleasure. They would beg for their lives. They all did. They would die slowly and beautifully, and he would—

He spun, pulled from his reverie. A man in a buckboard approached. Thomas Grant, owner of the Circle G Ranch, reined to a stop.

"Oh, it's you," the hunter said, with a smile.

"What are you doing way out here?"

The huntsman gathered himself and calmly shrugged into his coat, but his heart raced. "I'm on my way home from an appointment in Mapleton. I had to stop for…some personal business."

"Kinda jumpy, ain't you?"

"You gave me a start. I thought I was all alone."

"Well, be careful of them rattlers when you got your britches down out there in the woods. Ain't no one gonna volunteer to suck the venom out of your ass," Grant chuckled. "I'll be at Kat's later. Stop by, and I'll buy you a drink." Grant clucked to his horses, and his spring wagon lurched down the road.

The hunter let out a breath and climbed into his rig. Grant didn't suspect a thing. How could he? There was nothing to suspect. At least not yet. And besides, he thought with a smug smile, he'd been doing this for years and never been caught.

# CHAPTER 3

# 1880 - THE TINKER

Tiny, the tinker, made his way to smaller settlements and isolated homesteads several times a year, bringing them much-needed supplies and the latest news. When hearing his off-key singing and the rattle of pots and pans, the local people would rush to greet him. He was a welcome sight and a cause for celebration.

Tiny, who was anything but, liked to stop in Grant's Crossing to wash down the trail dust and resupply at Wagner's General Store. His first stop was always Kat's Place for a meal, a bottle of whiskey, and to flirt with the owner. Today was no different.

With a snoot full of whiskey and a stomach full of fried steak and potatoes, he waddled happily across the street to the general store. He and Steven Wagner, the owner, had become friends over the years, each knowing how to spin a yarn and always trying to outdo one another.

As he and Steven loaded his wagon, Tiny related a story that needed no embellishments. Tiny grunted, hefting a bag of sugar into his wagon. "I was sitting in the hotel lobby in Clay Springs. You ever been to Clay Springs, Steven?"

Steven shook his head. "Can't say as I have."

"Well, it ain't much of a town, and the hotel is old as dirt. But it's clean, and there is an attached saloon. I was sitting there thinking I'd wander over and have a quick snort or two before supper. As I got up, I overheard some townsfolk talking about it being the first anniversary of a murder that had taken place there. I didn't hear everything but enough to make me curious." Tiny removed his bowler and wiped his forearm across his sweaty forehead. "When I went into the saloon, I asked the barkeep about the murder, and I got way more information than I'd bargained for. The barkeeper had helped the doctor clean up the mess, and he had no trouble recounting all the gruesome details."

Tiny finished his story, and with his wagon loaded, he prepared to leave. "See you next time, Steven."

Steven put a hand out to stop him. "Wait, Tiny, you have to tell the marshal. He needs to know what happened in Clay Springs."

"I'll leave telling the marshal to you, Steven. I got no liking for the law." He hooked his thumbs in his red suspenders. "Had some problems a few years back with an ill-tempered sheriff. Since then, I tend to keep my head down whenever I see a badge."

With a full stomach and inventory restocked, Tiny said his goodbyes. His wagon lurched to the side with a screech as he climbed aboard, puffing and grunting. He waved goodbye to Steven and clattered out of town, singing at the top of his lungs.

Steven charged down the street and into the marshal's office before Tiny was out of sight.

CHAPTER 4

# CLAY SPRINGS

Clay Springs boasted a hotel, two saloons, a barbershop, and a general store that served as the post office and stagecoach depot. Such a town rarely faced any serious trouble, and being sheriff was more of an honorary title. That was why the murders had never been reported. The sheriff of Clay Springs, who also served as mayor and blacksmith, didn't know that such a violent crime should be reported to the Federal Marshal in Grant's Crossing. If it hadn't been for the tinker, Marshal William Jacobs would never have known there were two more murders to add to his tally.

Based on what Tiny had relayed to Steven, Marshal Jacobs' first interviews were with the barkeeper and the doctor. The barkeeper was more than eager to share his bloody story with a Federal Marshal and reveled in the telling. But the doctor provided him with the most detailed information he'd ever had.

The doctor had taken copious notes regarding the condition of the bodies and the surrounding area. He shared his notes and reviewed them at length with the marshal. It came as no surprise to Marshal Jacobs that the details of these murders mirrored those of his parents. As he read and reread the report, vivid memories of the day that changed his life flashed through his mind, and it became harder and harder to remain an objective investigator.

The doctor insisted he join him for drinks and supper at the hotel. "It's the town's favorite watering hole, Marshal."

"I could use a drink. And call me Jake."

"All right, Jake. I'll introduce you around. Maybe some of the locals remember something unusual about that day."

But as always, no one had seen or heard anything out of the ordinary.

## CHAPTER 5

# DEATH REMEMBERED

Marshal Jacobs rode out of Clay Springs as the first rays of sunlight illuminated its dusty, rut-scarred streets. Based on the previous evening's supper, he decided to pass on breakfast. He had stayed overnight in the hotel, thinking it would be better than sleeping on the ground. *Not your best idea, Jake,* he thought. It had definitely been a mistake. The bed was hard, and he had shared his room with another traveler…one who kept him awake most of the night snoring. The man snored so hard Jake would have sworn the window shades rattled.

During the three-day ride home from Clay Springs, Jake had plenty of time to think about the doctor's notes. Even though the information was more detailed than he'd ever had before, it was still a dead end.

He had been pushing back all the ugly memories, but now he embraced them, hoping the doctor's notes might trigger something new. Something he'd missed in the countless other times he'd relived that day.

*The day had started like any other. He had breakfast, kissed his mother goodbye, and went to the barn to saddle Herald. He didn't want to go to school and told his father as much. His father laughed, telling him he had to go. He needed an education. Jake hugged his father and rode away, unaware he would never see his beautiful mother and strong, kind father again.*

*At school, an unexpected quiz had him squirming in his seat. He hated tests. He always choked. He had chewed his pencil down to a stub, searching for answers that wouldn't come.*

"I swear, Drach, I can almost taste the wood and lead from that pencil and feel cold sweat running down my back."

*When the school day was over, he hurried to where Herald was tied, hoping to avoid a run-in with Sam Watkins. But he wasn't fast enough. Sam grabbed him from behind and spun him around. "Where you off to so fast? Running home to Mommy?"*

*"Leave me alone, Sam."*

*Sam grinned and shoved him to the ground. "You gonna cry for us?" Sam sneered and kicked dirt in his face.*

*Jake got to his feet, his jaw clenched, his fists at his sides. Sam was spoiling for a fight, and he wanted to give him one. Sam glared at him, daring him to throw a punch, but Jake swallowed his anger and turned away. He rode off listening to Sam's jeers and laughter.*

"I often regret not standing my ground that day, Drach. It might have been worth the cuts and bruises and a black eye." Jake's mouth twitched into a wry smile. "Funny how time has changed our lives. I couldn't have a better friend than Sam. Except for you, of course."

A trickle of sweat ran down his neck. "It's too hot for this time of year, Drach. We need rain. But there's not a cloud in the sky." The stream, running alongside the road, looked inviting. He patted his horse's neck and reined to a halt. "Come on, Drach. Let's stop here for a spell and enjoy some shade. Jake's icy blue eyes carefully scanned the area for any danger before unsaddling his horse and turning him loose to graze. Jake didn't sense any danger, something he was good at, but scanned the area again before leaning over to bury his face in the cool spring water.

After drinking his fill, he propped his saddle against a tree trunk and settled himself. His mind went back fourteen years to a bright, clear day, much like today. On the ride home from school, he explained to Herald how he hated tests and Sam Watkins. Herald nodded with a mule's understading and whimpered in agreement.

Jake raked his fingers through his dark wet hair; I was so wrapped up in my miseries that I wouldn't have seen a buffalo in the middle of the road that day.

*Jake pictured himself riding into the barnyard and sliding off Herald's back. He followed him to his stall, checked his hay and water, and gave him a quick rub down. Then, started toward the house, thinking there would be time to go fishing if he hurried and finished his chores.*

Jake didn't want to remember anything more, but his mind wouldn't rest.

*He was halfway between the barn and the house when the unfamiliar feeling of terror hit him. He stopped. The hair on the back of his neck stood on end, and his head throbbed. A tingling sensation took hold of his backbone, sending a shiver through his entire being. It had been the first time he'd experienced those feelings. Jake remembered it well. It told him that evil had been there, and its darkness lingered. He didn't have to open the door to know his parents were gone.*

Jake got up and whistled for Drach, who came racing down the creek bank, kicking up his heels. He stopped in front of Jake pawing the ground, ready to go. Jake saddled Drach, talking to him all the while. "It's strange, Drach, while I was standing there between the barn and the house, I didn't hear a thing. Odd, don't you think that I didn't hear the bees or the chickens, or even the birds arguing in the oak tree, but now, I remember all the sounds clear as a bell. It's what makes me think I may have missed something else. It's what keeps me going back and reliving the day." Mounting, Jake headed back for the main road, still thinking about his first run-in with evil.

*He wanted to turn and run but knew he couldn't. He had no choice but to move forward. He stepped onto the porch. The boards bowed under his weight like they always did, and as always, the front door creaked as he pushed it open. His dad had been promising to oil the hinges for weeks. He never got around to it.*

*He took a wobbly step back and grabbed the door jamb with both hands trying to stay on his feet. He closed his eyes, unable to look at the butchery that confronted him. He took several deep gasps of air, almost choking on the metallic stench of blood. When he finally had the courage to look, the sight ripped his heart in two.*

Jake, the marshal, stood in the doorway beside Jake, the boy, forcing himself to reexamine everything his younger self had seen. He struggled to detach himself from his emotions. He could see his dad's hand on top of his mom's in the center of the table, and their other hands rested on their laps, holding their hearts.

Jake shifted in the saddle. He saw nothing new, but the memories tore at his heart and waves of pent-up emotion fueled the anger and hatred that ate at his belly.

Any memory of riding to the Circle G escaped him, but somehow, he did manage to get there. Mr. Grant and two of his top hands, Chris and Pete, rode with them back to his home. After that, all he remembered was the three men burying his folks. He'd chosen a place near an enormous oak tree, close to his mother's garden. It was a spot where they had often picnicked. The swing his father made for him hung from one of the branches and he watched it sway in the breeze.

He'd never forget the eerie shadows cast by the pale moonlight, the sound of shovels slicing through the dirt and sand, or the breeze that ruffled his hair…like his mother often did. Once he was sure he'd felt her hand, but logic told him it was only the wind.

Jake leaned forward and scratched Drach's ear. "Knowing what I know now, I'm pretty sure it was Mom telling me goodbye. I knew back then I was different, I just didn't understand it. Heck, I still don't understand this inner knowing. It's a part of me that can be downright terrifying."

"When we got back to the ranch that night, I remember Lorene fussing over me like I was a newborn pup. You know how she is. They took me to a bedroom on the second floor and stayed with me the whole night. I don't think I slept much, but I remember telling Mr. Grant I was worried about my stock. He said it was all taken care of and we'd decide what to do about such things later, but for the time being I would stay with them. He said the Circle G could always use a good man."

"All those blanks in my memory give me another reason to think I might still remember something important. I guess after fourteen years I'd ought to give it up."

Jake scoffed. "I know Grant wants me to put my search on the back burner. He thinks I've fallen so far down the rabbit hole I'll never get out. He could be right, but I can't get the killer out of my head, and I won't be able to until I've put him six feet under. It's not just about my mom and dad anymore. It's about all the innocent lives he's stolen. I need to find him…I need to stop him."

The stream they had stopped at earlier snaked across the road in front of them and they stopped to drink. Jake's cold blue eyes scanned up and down the riverlet before dismounting. He saw and sensed no danger, but they didn't linger. He had two more days on the trail. He was already tired of eating dust and was eager to get back to Grant's Crossing…back to his friends and the routine that kept him sane.

The rest of the day was spent in silence. Jake committed himself to pushing away the memories of murder and the disgusting creature responsible. He rode till after dark, stopping to camp only when Drach snorted and shook his whole body with displeasure.

"Sorry, boy. Guess I'm pushing a little too hard. We'll cold camp tonight. It's too dang hot for a fire." Jake pulled the saddle from Drach's sweaty back and grabbed an airtight of tomatoes and one of peaches from his warbag. He was tired, and after finishing the tomatoes, he fell into a deep sleep filled with disturbing dreams; dreams of returning to his house the next morning.

He had asked Mr. Grant to stay outside. Jake knew he didn't want to, but Grant honored his request. The hair on the back of Jake's neck stood on end as he started toward the house. He sensed the evil that had attacked his home, and didn't want to go in. He glanced toward his parents' graves. They were standing there, holding one another, smiling at him. He rubbed his eyes and looked again…they were gone. He took a deep breath and, using the back door, entered, turning his head to avoid seeing the kitchen. But the smell of blood and the sound of buzzing carrion flies couldn't be ignored. He steeled himself and entered his parents' bedroom.

Sitting in silence on the edge of the bed, he clenched his father's pillow to his chest. His father's scent clung to it. He breathed it in and held the pillow closer, not wanting to believe his strong, fearless father was gone. He'd never see him again. He'd never feel his powerful arms easily lifting him into the buckboard or hear the rumble of his laughter. They'd never go fishing or hunting again…and they'd never finish the game of checkers they'd started.

How could there be a world in which his parents didn't exist. He loved them and was helpless without them. They were always there… every day of his life. Grief ate into his bones, into the marrow of his being, and as he gently pulled his mother's pillow to his chest, the grief and sorrow hardened into anger and hate.

He trembled as he breathed in the spicy apple scent of her perfume. He could almost see her standing in the doorway with her hands on her hips, scolding him for being in their room. He'd never again feel her hand mussing his hair or hear her squeals of delight on Christmas morning when she opened one of his homemade gifts. He loved her so much.

He pulled the pillows tight against him, closing his eyes tight, and wishing the nightmare would go away. But he knew it wouldn't.

Laying the pillows on the foot of the bed, he went to the wardrobe and pulled a black suede vest from its hanger. His mother had given it to his father on their last Christmas. He folded it reverently and slipped it into the pillowcase. One day he would wear it. He looked up at his father's go-to-church black Stetson on the top shelf. It was out of reach, but he pulled a straight-backed chair from beside the wardrobe and climbed up. He'd done it many times before looking for Christmas and birthday presents. The remembrance stung.

He put on the Stetson, and it fell around his ears. He caught his father's scent once again and tears stung his eyes. He swallowed hard, blinking them away. He pushed the hat back on his head and went to his mother's dressing table. He found the small silver box he was looking for in one of the glove boxes on top of her dresser. He carefully opened the precious keepsake with shaking fingers. He was relieved to see his mother's wedding ring undisturbed, sitting on a puff of pink silk. She hadn't been able to wear it since she broke her finger. He put the box in his pocket, picked up the pillows, and stopped in the doorway for one last look. Then he closed the door and walked away.

After tying the pillows onto Herald's saddle, he went to the shed behind the barn. He returned with a five-gallon bucket of coal oil and methodically poured the liquid around the base of the entire house, soaking the porch and splashing it against the front wall.

He glanced at his parents' graves then back to the house. There would be no more memories made here, and the one that lingered needed to be destroyed.

Mr. Grant who had remained outside, came to stand by him. Grant's hand on his shoulder was comforting and strong like his father's. Grant asked if he was sure and when he nodded, Grant puffed the stub of his cigar to life and handed it to him. He tossed the cigar at the front door and the front of the house exploded in flames that raced around the house, quickly turning it into a roaring inferno.

Standing as close to the fire as possible, he hoped the intense heat would burn away the memory of what he had found inside, but it hadn't. He watched his home burn down to glowing orange cinders and swore to find the monster who had done this. He would kill him. His parents would be avenged.

Jake woke with a start, drenched in sweat, his heart racing. Drach was nipping at his shoulder and nuzzling his neck. "I guess it's time to go," Jake said, letting out a sharp breath and scratching Drach behind the ears and down his neck. Drach melted against his hand for a moment before backing off, shaking his head impatiently and pawing the ground.

"I hear you loud and clear," Jake said. They were quickly on the trail, Jake eating his peaches for breakfast as he rode toward home.

Jake managed to keep his mind focused on what was happening in Grant's Crossing and at the Circle G until mid-afternoon when he spotted carrion birds circling off to the west. He went to investigate and found a cabin at the center of the vultures' vortex. Jake noticed three horses in the corral and figured the owner to be home. He announced himself and waited before he dismounted. He entered the cabin and immediately saw the empty rifle mount over the stone fireplace on the wall across from the door. A narrow cot with soiled covers took up one wall, while a dry sink flanked by open shelves claimed the opposite wall. Flies buzzed noisily around a pile of dirty dishes strewn over a lopsided table in the center of the room.

Jake hurried from the cloistering room, a flashing memory of carrion flies threatening to yank him into the past. He stood quietly in front of the ramshackle cabin that someone called home. A tingle crept up his backbone, and he knew no one was coming home.

He moved toward a broken-down building, which was more of a shed than a barn. He deeply regretted his decision to investigate the source of the vultures' interest. The pigsty on the far side of the building was where he found the farmer and his rifle. The pigs and vultures had done a fair amount of damage to the man's remains, and Jake flinched at the sight.

In the shed, he found a tarp, a pitchfork, and a shovel. Opening the gate, he chased the pigs from the pen and used the pitchfork to roll the remains onto the tarp. He placed the rifle beside its owner, and rolled it up tight, securing it with a length of rope.

Drenched in sweat, Jake leaned on the shovel and looked down at the freshly dug grave and the rough cross made of dead twigs. "This is the best I can do for you, old-timer. Rest in peace."

## CHAPTER 6

# A NOISY HOMECOMING

Jake rounded the bend and saw the lofty white steeple of the Lutheran church gleaming in the distance. He smiled at the welcoming sight, and according to a new marker at the fork in the road, it was only three miles to Grant's Crossing. He was almost home.

Marshal Jacobs and his horse, Drach, were tired and dusty. They'd been on the road for the better part of six days, and the marshal's back-side, along with every bone in his body ached. He shifted in his saddle, thinking about the soft bed waiting for him at the ranch.

Turning onto Bridge Street, Jake squared his shoulders and shoved the memories and darkness away. He loved Grant's Crossing and the people who lived here, and since becoming Marshal, he spent most of his time here.

Jake had grown up in Grant's Crossing and watched it expand from a dozen buildings on Bridge Street to a bustling town growing by leaps and bounds. When he was appointed Marshal, the population had been under three hundred. Now, over a thousand people lived and prospered in Grant's Crossing. The rasping of saws and pounding of hammers never ceased. New businesses popped up overnight, and new families arrived daily. The influx of people made his job challenging.

He couldn't always tell if a man would be an asset to the community or trouble waiting on the porch.

Grant's Crossing boasted all the professional services a person could need or want, and all were prospering. There were more saloons than necessary scattered throughout the town, but most were busy every night. The barrooms were full of rugged men. Some looking for a brief respite from the harsh life of the plains. Some were cowboys wanting a night on the town to get drunk and maybe spend some time with a willing woman. Husbands escaping from nagging wives or squalling kids could be found among the patrons. And, of course, gamblers were always present, trying to make an easy buck, preying on the naive. His town could be rough and rowdy at times, but he and his deputies worked hard to keep it peaceful.

Jake rode down Bridge Street, passing the school where he had learned to read and write and the Lutheran Church where he attended services. The Methodists and the Presbyterians were building churches north of the Lutherans. Groundbreaking ceremonies had already taken place, and stacks of lumber had been delivered. Jake thought Jackson Street would soon become church row, and Sunday mornings on this end of town would be real bellringers.

He rode into Miller's Livery Stable and dismounted, stretching his tall, lean frame and dusting off a cloud of trail dust with his hat. They needed rain, and if the spring rains didn't come soon, many farmers and ranchers would be in trouble.

John Miller came from the tack room, smiling at the sight of his friend. "Marshal Jacobs, glad you made it home at last."

"Me, too. Can you take care of Drach while I check in with Logan and Sam?"

"I'll see to him. Do you want me to bring him over to the office when I'm done, or will he be spending the night?"

"If you wouldn't mind bringing him by the office, I'd appreciate it. I'm headed for the ranch when I get done here in town."

John knew these trips were difficult for his friend. He shouldn't be asking, but he couldn't help himself. "Anything new?"

"Some saddle sores and this beard. And another murder, same as the others." Jake choked, struggling to keep the darkness at bay.

"You'll find him, Jake. I know you will." Seeing the frown on his friend's face, John changed the subject. "See you tomorrow at Winnie's homecoming party?"

Jake's somber mood changed, and his face brightened at the mention of Winnie's name. He slapped John on the shoulder. "You bet, John. Save me a dance."

"You got it, Jake. I'll make it a slow one."

"See you tomorrow, then."

"Oh, and by the way," John chuckled. "I doubt Winnie will think much of your beard."

John stood with his muscular blacksmith arms akimbo, watching Jake walk away. He thought Jake and Winnie would make a perfect couple. Winnie was unpredictable and wild, and Jake was not. He figured they might be tailor-made for one another and prove the old adage that opposites attract.

Jake left the livery smiling, thinking about Winnie and the homecoming party. He rubbed the growth on his chin as he started across the street, wondering if he should keep it, but all thoughts of beards and parties were pushed from his mind. Pressure was beginning to grow at the base of his skull. He rubbed the back of his neck, squinting against the discomfort. He looked up and down the street. Everything looked normal, like any other day, but something was wrong.

The streets and boardwalks were bustling with activity. He headed across the street, quickening his steps, still watchful. The pressure intensified as he neared his office. Someone was in trouble.

Deputy Logan came tearing around the corner as Jake reached for the latch of his office door. "Jake," he hollered, running toward him. "Sam's at the Bent Ear. There's a mean-looking cuss causing a ruckus, and Sam's trying to talk him into giving up."

Jake and Logan bolted toward the Bent Ear Saloon. "He thinks Mal's Faro dealer cheated him. He's looking for his own kind of justice." Logan struggled to keep pace with Jake, his words tumbling out between gasps for air. "He's waving a gun...threatening to shoot the dealer... Dice saw you ride in...I hightailed it to get you."

Several men had gathered around the saloon's entrance but parted to let Jake and Logan through. Dice stood peeking over the saloon's batwing doors along with two other curious men. All but Dice moved away, making room for them.

"Sam got everyone cleared out," Dice said in a whisper. "He's trying to talk this guy into giving up, but he's not having much luck."

Jake eased up and glanced over the doors. U.S. Deputy Marshal Sam Watkins stood about ten feet in front of the troublemaker. He was talking to him in a calm voice, telling him to put down the gun and let the law take care of the crooked dealer.

"No. I'm the one who's going to make him pay. I'll take care of this. Get out of here. This is none of your business." The drunken stranger waved his gun in Sam's direction and shot three bullets into the floor near Sam's feet. Sam's jaw tightened, but he didn't move. Wobbling and trying to keep his balance, the troublemaker jerked his head, motioning toward the dealer cowering behind the turned-up Faro table. "I won't be cheated and made a fool of."

The dealer poked his head up from behind the table, and a thunderous roar of profanity escaped the troublemaker's lips. He turned to take a shot at the source of his anger, but Sam drew and shot the gun from the troublemaker's hand before he could pull the trigger.

Grasping at his hand and screaming in pain, the troublemaker charged at Sam, but he stumbled and staggered, falling to his knees. His breath came in hoarse gasps, and he cradled his mangled hand against his chest as if it were a baby. He knelt, swaying, staring at Sam. He tried to speak, but his eyes glazed over. He toppled to his side with a dull thud, still clutching his hand against his body.

Sam twirled his pistol into its holster and squatted down. "He's alive," he said, pulling the kerchief from his neck and using it as a tourniquet. Sam looked up at the Faro dealer, who had left his hiding place. "You all right?"

"I'm fine, Deputy. Thank you. You saved my life."

Marshal Jacobs pushed through the batwing doors. "Logan, get Coop."

Deputy Logan hurried from the saloon to fetch the doctor.

"Trying to talk him to death, Deputy?"

Sam smiled at hearing Jake's voice and looked up. "You know me. I always prefer a chat to a shootout." Sam tightened the tourniquet and stood as Doctor Cooper came through the doors. "I don't think he's hurt too bad, Coop."

"Well, hurt is best for my business. Drunks, rowdies, and gamblers keep my business booming. Welcome back, Jake," Coop said, stooping to inspect the stranger's injuries.

"He'll live," he said, rolling back on his heels, "but I'm guessing his hand won't be much use." He stood and looked at the three men wearing badges. "When I'm done with him, do I let him go, or will you want to arrest him?"

"We'll check the wanted posters and let you know," Sam said.

Doctor Cooper's head jerked up, and his breath caught in his throat. Sam ignored the knee-jerk reaction, but it reminded him that Coop was a wanted man. A man on the dodge, unaware that he and Jake knew all about him and what he had done.

"Logan, go with Coop and make sure our friend here doesn't cause him any trouble." Sam looked to Logan and got a nod.

Leaving the Bent Ear, Jake and Sam heard Coop and Logan rounding up men to help get the stranger to the doctor's office. "You know, I didn't think about Coop when I talked about looking through the wanted posters," Sam said. "Guess it's a sensitive topic for him."

"I'm sure it is. Maybe it's time we tell him we know he's wanted for murder, and we know his real name is Lloyd Templeton?"

"Might be better if we don't. He's the best doctor we've ever had, and I'd hate to see him light out on us. We need him." Sam grinned at Jake. "You gonna keep the beard?"

"Not sure," Jake said, running a hand over his chin.

"I doubt Winnie will like it."

Jake ignored Sam's comment. "Anything newsworthy happen while I was gone?"

"Four or five fist fights. It wouldn't be a Saturday night if the boys from the Lazy W didn't kick up some dust. This guy was the worst of it."

"Let's stop by the office and thumb through those wanted posters. I'd hate to turn that nut loose if he's wanted somewhere." They flipped through the stack of flyers but found no wanted notices on the stranger.

Walking toward Coop's office and squinting into the glare of the late afternoon sun, Jake asked, "Where is Mal, anyway? I didn't think he ever left the Bent Ear."

Sam pulled his hat low to shade his eyes. "Out of town for a week or so, visiting his sick sister in Lincoln. Word is she's in bad shape."

"He won't be happy when he gets back."

"The way I figure it, broken glasses and a shattered table or two are the cost of doing business for a saloon owner. You ever think about changing jobs and running a saloon?"

"No," Jake said, opening the door to Coop's office.

Logan met them at the door. "Coop's still working on him. No word yet."

Moments later, Coop came from the treatment room, he looked at Jake's respectable, week-old beard and mustache. "Nice beard," Coop said, wiping his hand down the sparse stubble sprouting on his chin.

"I see you're trying again," Jake said with a grin. He had watched Coop struggle time after time to grow a mustache and goatee. Coop thought it would make him look older and distinguished. The way a doctor should look.

"You're an ass, Jake," Coop said with a wry smile. "You look tired."

"I am not your patient."

"The way you look, maybe you should be."

Coop sat at his desk and glanced at Sam. "He lost his finger. Either you shot it off, or it got yanked off when the gun flew out of his hand. Either way, it's gone. His other fingers are minced meat. They'll be useless."

"He won't be drawing on anyone again," Jake said. "Logan, stay with Coop until our troublemaker comes around."

Logan nodded. "Will do, Marshal. I'll bring him to the jail and lock him up when he's able."

Opening the door to leave, Sam turned to Logan. "We'll be at Kat's if you need us for anything. Come on, Jake, let's get a drink, and I'll give you a full rundown on all the exciting things that occurred while you were away."

Kat's Place was one of the largest and fanciest gambling saloons and dance halls west of the Mississippi. Open twenty-four hours a day, seven days a week, and always busy. They crossed the street, dodging horses and freight wagons and discussing the upcoming party.

Kat saw them enter and came from the far end of the long mahogany bar. She crossed the well-worn wooden floor and placed a whiskey and a root beer on the table.

Sam chose not to drink, and although most men wouldn't dare order a soda in a saloon, no one questioned Sam's decision. He had nothing to prove, and no one dared to challenge the tall, well-muscled deputy.

"You were gone too long, my friend. I worried about you," Kat said.

"It's a long way, but I had no trouble. I did hear some howls and growls just outside the light of my fire one night. It set my hackles on edge, but no two-legged varmints were prowling about. At least none I saw."

Kat examined Jake's face. "Didn't pack a razor, I see."

"Nope. And the barber in Clay Springs was ninety if a day. He shook so hard his teeth rattled. I decided to skip the shave and let it grow."

"Winnie won't like it."

"So I've heard."

"You know how she was about her father's whiskers," Kat said, getting up to tend to other customers. "See you tomorrow at the party?"

"You bet. Save me a dance, beautiful."

"You got it, handsome."

Sam filled Jake in on what he'd missed out on during his absence and saw the tension begin to drain from Jake's face and shoulders. He was glad Jake planned on spending the night at the ranch. Time with Grant calmed him. *Grant is our anchor,* he thought...*mine and Jake's.*

Jake looked across the table at his longtime friend, his blue eyes intent. "Today, after I rode into town, I had another one of those headaches. The kind I get when someone's in trouble. It's like an icy chill that crawls up my backbone and wraps around my chest. And the pressure at the back of my head gets so intense, I'm afraid it'll explode. I try to ignore it, to force it away, but it won't give up. At least not until I figure out what it wants. It?" Jake scoffed, "Whatever 'it' is."

"You knew your mom had some healing abilities," Sam said. "Think she could do other things?"

"If she did, she never said." Jake chewed on a matchstick, frustrated by what he didn't understand. "Today, when I rode in, I knew someone was in trouble, but I didn't know who until Logan came running around the corner. Then I knew it had to be you. After that, no chill, no headache."

"You seem to have those headaches a lot more often these days."

A rare smile claimed Jake's face. "Maybe it's because you're getting into trouble a lot more often lately."

Sam smiled back, relieved to hear a lightness in Jake's voice.

"Two murders." Jake knocked back his whiskey. "I'll stay in town tomorrow night after the party and bring you and Logan up to date, but tonight, I'm headed to the ranch."

Jake was getting ready to leave when Steven and Charlie, co-owners of Wagner's General Store and Apothecary, came in talking and laughing. They persuaded Jake to stay for another drink, which turned into two.

His friends and the laughter were better medicine than any tonic in Steven's store, but talking to Grant was what he needed. He pulled himself away from the crazy gossip and stories Steven was famous for and left Kat's. His head down, he pushed through the doors, running into Nate Daniels.

"Sorry, Daniels."

"Marshal. See you tomorrow at the party?"

"Wouldn't miss it."

# CHAPTER 7

# BLOOD STAINS ON HIS SHIRT

The six-hour ride from Mapleton left Nate tired and dusty, and as he rode into Grant's Crossing, his thoughts were on a cold beer. At least, that's what he told himself. He stopped in front of Kat's Place, hesitating to go in. He hadn't stopped to see Kat since she turned down his marriage proposal. He wasn't sure if he wanted to see her. She had stomped on his heart, and it hurt, but she'd been right. It never would have worked. *What the hell*, he thought as he dismounted. *I've got to face her eventually.*

Nate entered Kat's Place, so intent on planning what to say to Kat that he ran headlong into Marshal Jacobs.

When Kat saw Nate, she hurried to his side. "Hi, stranger."

Nate smiled and relaxed. "Hi, yourself."

"You haven't stopped by in a long time. I thought you were angry."

Drinking from the beer mug Bear had placed in front of him, he turned to the beguiling woman at his side. "Kat, I could never be angry with you, but a man with a broken heart tends to stay away from the woman who shattered it."

Kat rolled her eyes and pointed to the dried blood spattered across the front of his shirt. "What happened?

"Cut myself shaving this morning. You worried about me?"

"Of course, I'm worried about you. But it looks like you haven't shaved for a week."

Nate looked down at his shirt. "They were dehorning some steers over at Murphy's ranch. I might have picked it up there." He smiled, changing the subject. "I don't suppose you've changed your mind about marrying me?"

"We've had this discussion, Nate. You can't leave your farm, and I won't leave my saloon. We had a good time together. I care for you, but it would never work."

"I had to try one last time, Kat. You're a hard woman to forget."

Kat changed the subject, thinking the weather would be a safer topic. "Still no rain. You concerned for your crops?"

"I haven't been back to the farm in over a month, so I'm not sure what kind of troubles they're having. I've been on the trail looking for breeding stock and news like I do every spring. I stayed away longer than usual this time, trying to forget about the gal back home."

Kat rolled her eyes, about to scold him.

"I know, Kat, and you're right about it not working out for us. I can't imagine you standing over a hot range making peach preserves or carrying slop to the hogs."

Kat scowled at him. "You'd expect your wife to slop the hogs?"

Nate laughed at the look on her face. "Of course I would," he teased. "Why else would I take a wife?"

"If you remember, we found pleasant pastimes. The kind of dalliances a man and his wife would share."

"We did dally quite well, but Southern gentleman that I am, I shall refrain from speaking any further of such." He took a swallow of beer. "Stopped by to wash down the dust before heading home and to see if you'd changed your mind." He finished his beer. "See you around."

It saddened her to tell him goodbye. If things were different, she thought, it might have worked. He was kind and gentle, but he also had a dark side. She suspected the darkness was rooted in the war. He never spoke of those days, but she had seen the scar that puckered his skin from his shoulder to below his waist.

# CHAPTER 8

# FIRE IN THE HEARTH

Lorene had wanted to go to Grant's Crossing with Tom to make the final arrangements for Winnie's welcome home party, but there had been too much to do.

She went from room to room, checking to make sure everything looked perfect. The parlor and the billiards room were all in order. She glanced into Tom's office and shut the door with a groan. The dining room and the library were spotless. Lorene tarried in the sunroom. It was her favorite place in the house. She adjusted a pillow on the soft burgundy-colored leather sofa. The deep hue of the sofa and matching chairs accentuated the vibrant jewel tones of the elegant Persian Serapi rug that covered the floor.

During the day, sunlight streamed in through the multi-paned windows on either side of the French doors. The doors opened to a stone terrace overlooking the flower gardens. A small brook bubbled through her garden, and a fanciful white bridge led over it to her greenhouse.

In the evenings, the copper sconces crowned with Gillinder's star-patterned shades sparkled on either side of the white-tiled fireplace. Deep blue tiles framed the firepit, a stark change from the white. Watercolors, oils, and charcoal drawings graced the white walls. All depicted birds and other wildlife. She straightened a picture, gave it a critical glance, and headed to the kitchen.

There was a short hallway that led from her kitchen to the back porch. She heard a commotion coming from that direction and went to investigate. She found Stewart, one of the ranch helpers, in the wood room stacking wood. "Sorry, ma'am," he said. "I didn't mean to disturb you, but your supply was getting low. It was a cold winter, and it takes a lot to keep all those fireplaces of yours blazin'. I'll bet you got a dozen of 'em in this place," he said, tossing the last log on top of the pile.

Across the hall from the wood room was the milk room, or what Lorene referred to as her big pantry. The milk was brought here from the dairy. Two separators stood in the corner of the room, and milk and cream cans lined one wall. Egg crates full of eggs and jar after jar of canned goods were stocked on the big pantry's shelves. Two of the kitchen helpers were busy at the butter churns. The swishing and sloshing indicated they'd be at it for a while.

Lorene checked the regulator clock on the kitchen wall, wondering what was keeping Tom. She looked out the window and saw him coming down the lane. She ran to the front door to greet him.

# CHAPTER 9

# GRANT DANCES INTO THE HOUSE

Thomas Grant was returning home from the Carmichael Hotel and Cafe where he'd finalized the details for Winnie's homecoming. But he wasn't thinking about the party as he rode toward home. He was thinking about his daughter. By this time tomorrow she'd be home and he couldn't be happier.

Despite his eagerness to get home and tell Lorene about the party plans, he made his regular stop on Picnic Table Hill. The Hill got its name from a large, flat-topped rock surrounded by three bench-like rocks.

He sat on the rock table with his feet resting on one of the three stone benches. As far as he could see in every direction and beyond, the land belonged to him. His grandfather and father had worked hard and persevered through many hardships and battles to build the Circle G ranch. He was proud of his heritage but understood that no one could own the land. A piece of paper said it was his, but he and the paper were like leaves on the wind. He was no more than a temporary custodian, but the land was forever. The land would endure long after he was gone.

His horse was grazing peacefully in the dappled shade nearby, occasionally stomping to dislodge a fly, and somewhere off in the distance, a cow lowed calling to her calf. The whir of bees dipping into spring flowers and the hum of hovering dragonflies could be heard over the gentle burbling of Raccoon Creek. This was his world, and if you were silent, you could hear it breathe.

Grant watched an armada of fluffy white clouds sail slowly across the bright blue of the Dakota sky. So close, he thought, that if he stretched just a little, he could touch one. The sun warmed his face and the grace of God filled his heart as he spoke to the power above.

*Thank you, Great Spirit, for the beauty of the land and the bounty you have bestowed upon my family. As my father taught me, we honor the gifts of your land, your plants, and your animals. You know what is in my heart, Great Spirit: Bring my daughter home safe, and let Jake find the monster he searches for so he may find peace.*

Mounting, Grant spoke to his horse, "Buck, we need to get home. Lorene was madder than a wet hen that she couldn't come with me, but she gave me plenty of instructions. She always does," he said with a smile.

He reined Buck to a stop on the rise that overlooked his home. The ranch proper was more extensive than some towns. Chris and Pete had jokingly referred to the towpath from the house to the stables as Main Street. The name stuck, and courtesy of their blacksmith, a homemade street sign hung from one of the fence posts.

Grant turned onto Main Street and rode to the hitching rail in front of the large two-story house. He dropped his reins and took the stairs to the portico two at a time. He sped through the doorway, running smack into Lorene. He grabbed her before she fell and spun her into the parlor as if dancing a polka.

"Not bad for an old man," Lorene teased.

His eyes narrowed to slits that sparkled with mischief. "What do you mean, old man?"

"I meant what I said, old man."

"Lorene. I turned fifty last month. Don't you remember?"

"You're lying to me. You turned fifty-five, and you know it."

He spun her around again and kissed her before releasing her.

"Thomas, I swear you are a heathen." Lorene fluffed her apron at him. "Linc wants to see you, and there's a telegram from Texas on your desk."

"Wonder what that's about."

She gave him the I don't know shrug. "Did you get everything set up for the party? You've reserved the cafe for the entire day so we can decorate?"

"Yes, ma'am, and I've reserved the entire hotel. There will be plenty of room for anyone wanting to stay overnight. We don't have to worry about a thing. Lars and Sally have it handled down to the last detail. They enjoy spending my money," he chuckled. "It might have been cheaper to buy the place."

"You told them to make sure there's plenty to eat and drink."

"Yes, I did."

"And what about the musicians, Tom? Are they on their way?"

"They arrived this afternoon on the train from Kansas City."

"And the banner? They have the Welcome Home banner ready to hang up in front of the hotel?"

"Relax, dear. It's all under control."

"They better not mess this up, Tom," she said, giving him a scowl.

"I've got things to do in the kitchen," she said, fluffing her apron in his direction. "Hank and I have it all planned out, but there is still lots to do before everyone gets here for breakfast."

"You're letting Hank in your kitchen?"

"No, he's letting me in his. He's a darn fine cook, and the men are lucky to have him. Now get out of here and let me get back to my business, and don't mess up my house. It's all spotless and ready for Winnie."

"Those things of yours can wait for just a moment," he said, taking her hand and guiding her into his office. He closed the door behind them and wrapped her in his arms. "I love you, Lorene. And I know it hasn't been right how things have been. I've always had other things on my mind. But you've always been there for me and the kids, and I guess we fell into a comfortable companionship. At least I did." He frowned. "Recently, I overheard some comments from the church women, and I've seen the looks. I guess with Winnie, Jake, and Sam all being gone and us alone in this house, it gives them cause for judgment."

"Tom, I don't care what those old bats say. I don't live my life for them, and we are comfortable the way it is."

"Are we comfortable? Are you comfortable, Lorene? I'm tired of sneaking around. I want to hug you and kiss you…and take you to my bed without worrying about who might see us. Lorene, will you marry me?"

"You're proposing? After all these years?"

"I've been wrong to wait so long. Yes, I'm proposing. I'll get down on my knees if you want me to.

Lorene chuckled, "I can't imagine Thomas Grant on his knees for anyone."

"I love you, Lorene. I'd do anything for you."

"It'll change things."

"Yes, it will. You'll have to sleep beside this old man every night for the rest of your life."

Lorene laughed, "I love you, Tom. And yes. Of course, I'll marry you." Grant gave her a kiss that made her want to take the old man straight to bed, but she pulled away. "I have things to do, Tom. And isn't it time you headed to the back porch for your devil whiskey and cigars?"

He laughed as he grabbed the telegram from his desk. "That's a great idea, but with all that devil whiskey talk, you sound like Prudence Purdy."

Lorene rolled her eyes and fluffed her apron, shooing him out of her way with her whole face smiling.

He followed Lorene into the kitchen, where Linc caught up with him.

"Evening, Miss Lorene."

"Evening, Linc. Thank Effie for volunteering to help tomorrow morning. Me and Hank can use an extra pair of hands."

"Effie's always willing to pitch in."

Lincoln James was the ranch foreman. Linc had worked at the ranch for twenty-some years. He and his wife had come to the ranch as fugitive slaves and been given refuge. They'd been with a group of six men and women being taken to Canada, but a relentless slave hunter tracked them down. Linc and Effie managed to get away. The others had not been so lucky.

Linc was a hard worker and smart as a whip. He had quickly worked his way up from cowhand to a savvy foreman and manager. He had earned the respect of the men who worked for him, and Grant trusted him completely.

"Sorry to barge in on you like this, Mr. Grant, but I thought you should know. A man was here today, saying he has a prior claim to that section of ground out past Stinky Mesa. It ain't good for much, but it's a fair-sized piece of land, and several creeks run through there that bring us water. He told me he'd be checking with the land office tomorrow and get back to us."

"He's barking up the wrong tree, Linc. He won't find a thing at the land office in Grant's Crossing. All my deeds are registered and on file in Butte Point. I was always worried about that four-eyed clerk at the land office. Wouldn't surprise me if he could be bribed to misplace certain documents if the price was right. But if that man who came here is looking for a fight, I'll give him one. You know how I feel about this land. My father and I worked hard to build this ranch, and I won't let anyone take it from me. I'd give up everything else. I'd give it all and fight to the death before I'd let this ranch fall into someone else's hands."

"I'd fight beside you, Mr. Grant, and so would every one of your cowhands."

"Well, let's hope it never comes to that."

'I'd better get home. Effie will have supper on the table, and if I'm late, there won't be a thing left." He smiled and shook his head, "Those growing boys of mine could eat a fellow out of house and home."

"Linc, your sons are getting older, and if they want to go to college, you let me know. As much as I'd like to have them riding for my brand, it would please me to see them end up as doctors, lawyers, or teachers."

"Thank you, Mr. Grant. Maybe they'll change their minds, but for now, all they want to do is wrangle cows."

"Maybe you can make the job miserable enough that an education will look more inviting."

"Worth a try," Linc chuckled and headed for the back door.

Grant followed Linc out and settled in his chair on the back porch. A Saint Louis crystal carafe of whiskey and two glasses were on the side table by Grant's chair. He smiled as he settled in. Two glasses…that meant Lorene thought Jake was coming home tonight, too. He poured a whiskey and opened the telegram. It was good news. His purchase of lands in Texas and Oklahoma had been finalized, and he was officially a wildcatter. A wildcatter. He liked the sound of it.

Grant was enjoying his cigar and whiskey, wondering how Winnie would take the news he and Lorene were planning to marry. He snapped back to reality when he heard footsteps coming around the corner of the house.

"I thought I'd find you out here," Jake said.

## CHAPTER 10

# AN ABUNDANCE OF MURDERS

The sun was well below the horizon by the time Jake left Kat's and headed for the ranch, but a full moon backed by a cloudless sky illuminated his way. The eerie moon-drenched landscape reminded him of the night they buried his parents. It called to the darkness in his heart, reminding him of the hate he had for the monster he hunted. The darkness was always close by, and the slightest memory could pull him into its depths. A barn owl flashed silently across the road in front of him. If he hadn't seen the owl, he'd have never known it was there. It traveled silently…not a whisper of a sound. He marveled at its stealth as he watched it swoop down for its supper. The owl's prey had no chance. The yapping of coyotes echoed across the valley, and Jake wondered if they were also on the hunt.

The owl and the coyotes hunted and killed to live. That was how nature worked. They had no conscience and knew no guilt. But his madman was human, and humans should feel. But maybe he had no soul. Maybe he was empty inside. Maybe—

He pushed the thoughts away and buried the demons. He was home now…sheltered and safe. Night sounds surrounded him. An army of crickets called to one another with discordant trills, and bullfrogs living along Raccoon Creek croaked and groaned. Jake thought the frogs sounded a lot like Deputy Logan complaining about his aches and pains. He thought about Winnie and how much she might have changed. He was excited to see her, even a bit nervous. But why should he be nervous? It was just Winnie, he thought with a shiver of anticipation.

When Jake rode into the main stable, the other horses greeted him and Drach with soft nickers. Jake dismounted, eager to speak with Grant, but first, he took care of Drach. He checked his feed and water and brushed Drach's inky black coat until it glowed in the lamplight. Then he checked on Herald. "See you boys in the morning," he said, turning out all the lanterns.

Rounding the back corner of the house, Jake found Grant on the porch, stargazing with a glass of whiskey in one hand and a cigar in the other. "I thought I'd find you out here," Jake said.

Grant motioned to the decanter on the table between their chairs. "Glad you're home, son."

Jake poured a whiskey, the moonlight reflecting off the crystal decanter as he set it down. He took a sip and leaned one hip against the balustrade that surrounded the porch

Grant puffed on his cigar in silence, giving Jake time to enjoy the whiskey and relax.

"It's good to be home," Jake said, taking a seat.

"You gonna keep the beard? Darned impressive for a week."

"Not sure. There was a commotion earlier at the Bent Ear, and I caught a glimpse of my reflection in one of the mirrors behind the bar. I hardly recognized myself, but I could get used to it. It makes me look tough."

Grant chuckled. "Winnie didn't like my beard and mustache. Said it was like being kissed by a goat." Grant blew a smoke ring. "Lorene didn't like it either. That's why it's gone."

Jake downed the whiskey, feeling the warmth spreading through his chest. He poured a second, thinking about how Grant had taken him in, stood by him, and protected him through the worst days of his life. He loved Grant like a father.

"It was a double murder," Jake said, rolling the whiskey glass between his hands. "Some folks didn't want to dredge up memories or talk about it. Those who did talk couldn't tell me much. They heard no screams and saw no strangers. There was nothing unusual. But the doctor took detailed notes. When I read them, it was like I was back on the front porch, staring at what was left of my parents." Jake downed a healthy swig. "It hit me hard."

In the dim light, Grant studied the smoke rising from his cigar. He understood it was difficult for Jake to talk about these murders, and he remained silent, waiting for him to continue.

"It was a young couple, married less than two months. He stole their lives and the lives of any children they might have had." Jake raked his fingers through his hair and looked at the shadowy figure of Grant sitting beside him. "Sometimes I wonder if any of this will ever point me to the killer."

Jake tossed back the whiskey remaining in his glass. "The Clay Springs' murders bring the count to eighteen double murders. Thirty-six people, killed and mutilated." Jake poured another whiskey. "What kind of lunatic is he?"

"I don't know, Jake. He's sick in his mind. He has to be. What drives such a man is beyond human understanding. But I do believe you'll find him. One of these days, you'll find the answer you've been searching for."

Grant thought back to the day Jake's parents were murdered. Grant was standing by the corral with Pete and Chris when Jake rode in and dismounted.

"Jake, what are you doing out here alone?" Then he saw the boy's ashen face and trembling chin. He squatted, grabbing Jake's shoulders. "What is it? What's wrong, Jake? Where are your folks?"

"They're dead, Mr. Grant."

"Lorene, get down here and see to Jake," Grant hollered. "I'm riding to the Jacobs' place to find out what's happened." He motioned to Chris and Pete. "Get your horses."

Jake steeled his chin and mounted Herald. "I'm going with you, Mr. Grant."

Grant saw the determination in the boy's dark blue eyes and relented. "Okay, Jake, we'll ride together."

It was getting on toward evening when they arrived at the Jacobs' home. Dust swirled around them as they rode up to the hitching rail, and dismounted. Only Grant stepped onto the porch and opened the door.

Grant's stomach lurched, and he took an involuntary step back, Jake's mom and dad had been slaughtered and gutted like animals. Blood was everywhere, and their insides were strewn around the room like Christmas garland. Grant backed away in silence, his head spinning, he leaned over the porch railing and aired out his stomach. *What kind of monster could do this?* His heart ached for the young boy who had witnessed this sight, knowing it would haunt him for the rest of his life. He shuddered, knowing it would haunt him as well.

Pete rode ahead into town to get Sheriff Logan, and the sheriff's reaction was much like Grant's. But he gathered himself and entered. He looked for anything pointing to who might have done such a thing. He found nothing, and rode off to check on neighboring farms.

Grant, Pete, and Chris buried Jake's parents under the giant oak tree near the garden and rode back to Grant's place.

\* \* \*

Jake had lived with the Grants since that day.

Jake's voice brought Grant back to the present. "It tears at my gut, Grant. I have to find him. Reading the doctor's scribbles made it all too real. He has to be stopped before he kills again. The monster has to be put down."

"I know you don't want to hear this, but maybe you should back off. I'm not saying to forget about it, but you've had fourteen years of hate building up inside you, and I don't like what it's doing to you. It's time to put this on the back burner and live your life. Find a girl, get married, have kids, and smile, Jake. Life is too short for you to waste it like this."

"I hear what you're saying, and I do understand, but it's springtime. Who will he kill next? I can't stop. Not until he's six feet under."

Grant nodded and remained quiet. Protesting further would serve no purpose. Besides, Jake was right. Whoever was responsible needed to be destroyed before anyone else lost their life.

"I had plenty of time to think on the ride back. The doctor's notes gave me detailed information that I've never had before, and I thought, maybe if I combined everything I knew from all the people I've talked to over the years, I could figure out what it is that drives the man and maybe where to look for him."

"Seems reasonable."

"There's no anger in what he does, and he's skilled in the slaughter. Maybe he's a butcher. Or he might have been a sawbones in the war, a town doctor, or even a vet. It's all about the ritual and the pain he inflicts. He enjoys every cut."

"I believe he plans ahead how he wants to pose the people long before he takes them. I think he watches them." Jake's voice broke thinking of his parents. Had the monster been watching them, planning their deaths? Jake took a breath and pushed back the anger.

"But for all my thinking, I don't know anything I didn't know before."

"You said he might be a butcher or have a medical background. That's something."

"Still, every farmer in the territory knows how to butcher a hog. All I know for certain is he makes two kills every spring. It's always in the spring and always a man and wife. I know of eighteen killings, including my parents. I always figured they were the first. At least, I haven't found any murders dating back before theirs. If you do the math, in fourteen years, he may have murdered as many as fifty-six people." Jake sighed and took a drink. "If my thinking is correct, I'm missing reports on at least a third of his victims."

"The number is staggering. You think there could be so many?"

"More." Jake swiped his hand through his hair and brushed the stray lock from his forehead. "There could be more. What if my folks weren't the first, and what if he makes single kills during the rest of the year? I can't begin to fathom the total count. And why is it always a husband and wife? Why always in the spring?" Jake's voice turned hard. "Why don't they fight back? And why does he play with them, gutting and positioning them like he does? There are too many whys, Grant. Too many whys with no answers."

"You've made headway over the years."

"Not enough."

"You were twelve the first time you disappeared on me, off looking for clues. When you got back, you told me you'd run out of people around here to question and had to widen your loop. I was frantic when you didn't come down for supper. I looked everywhere for you. Then, that cranky old sheriff brought you home. The one from Wood Creek. What was his name?"

"Morse. An unpleasant man."

"Yes, he was. Sheriff Morse raked me over the coals for letting you run loose."

"He roughed me up some before bringing me home. He said if my folks didn't care enough to whoop my ass, he'd be more than happy to do it for them. That was the first and last time I ever felt the sting of a belt."

"You never told me about him taking a belt to you."

"I can't say why I didn't want you to know. I felt like a man, and Morse tried to knock me back down to being a boy. But I didn't cry. Sam took care of me when I got back. He'd taken enough beatings from his father that he knew what to do."

"You should have told me."

"I should have. But he got his comeuppance not long after that. His wife bashed his head in with an iron skillet and got off scot-free."

"Sounds like he got what he deserved. I'll admit, Jake, I wasn't too keen on you riding out alone like you did, but I couldn't figure any way to stop you short of tying you down."

"I'm glad you understood. I was hell-bent on finding the killer and getting my revenge."

"Jake?"

"Yeah."

"You still hell-bent on revenge?"

"Yes." Jake stared at the bottom of his empty glass, feeling the darkness hovering.

## CHAPTER 11

# RANCH BUSINESS

"Enough doom and gloom," Jake said.

As the words cleared Jake's lips, Lorene bustled onto the porch. The grass-green screen door slammed shut behind her with a bang. "I swear you two haven't a lick of sense between you. Out here drinking whiskey on an empty stomach." She placed a tray of chicken, potato salad, fresh-baked bread, pickles, and fresh vegetables from her greenhouse on the table between them. "Jake. You smell like trail dust and Drach. Once you're done with your supper, get cleaned up. And don't even think about coming into my house until you do. And, Jake, get rid of that hair on your face."

Lorene leaned over and kissed his whiskered cheek. "We worry about you out on the trail, but you're home now…safe and sound." She fluffed her apron, a habit she denied when teased about it, and headed for the kitchen. "I have lots to do before tomorrow, and you've already taken up too much of my time." Lorene disappeared through the door and into her domain.

Jake and Grant devoured the cold supper, and Jake turned his attention to ranch business. "Any additional cows missing?"

Grant nodded, thankful that Jake had disconnected from the murders. "Someone's up on the north range helping themselves. Gus says he has the same problem at the Lazy W."

"How many did we lose?"

"Maybe a hundred head. We'll have a better idea after the roundup. It's not a lot, considering the size of our herd, but one cow is too many."

"Any signs of a camp site?"

"Pete and Chris have been up north. They rode in just before you did. They said they didn't see anyone or anything unusual. They did say the herd had wandered down to the west draw. Probably looking for greener grass. We need rain, Jake. Everything is dry as a bone."

"It's the same from here to Clay Springs. Not a drop of rain. I ate enough dust on this trip to plant a crop." Jake popped a crisp, spring radish into his mouth. "Who's with the herd now."

"I sent Roy and Cody out with Trace, the new guy. I figure they can show him how we do things around here. I've never kept a lot of men up on the north range. Didn't figure I had to. But I will from now on."

Jake nodded.

"After Winnie's party, I'm sending Pete and Chris back out with some extra hands. Honestly, I don't know what to expect, and it concerns me that whoever's behind this might come back. I just hope whoever it is doesn't decide to start shooting at our riders."

"Maybe you should make it a dozen men if we can spare them. It's better to be safe than sorry. At least until we know what we're up against. I would hate to see anyone get bushwhacked."

"You're right, but if we have so many men out there, we need a headquarters for them and their gear. I've been thinking about doing something with that old trapper's cabin. Maybe we can fix it up or even expand it? What do you think?"

"It'd be a great place for roundup and a stopover on the way to the lake house. Any ideas who you want on the project?"

Grant studied his empty fork and smiled. He leaned forward as if telling Jake a secret. "I'll put Winnie in charge of the cabin. She'll need something to do when she returns tomorrow, and that will keep her busy and out of mischief for a while." Grant chuckled. "God knows what she'll come up with. Would you be interested in working with her?"

"I wouldn't mind," Jake said. The corners of his mouth twitched to form a soft smile.

"I'll count on you to make sure we don't end up with a castle and moat."

The thought of Winnie back on the ranch had Grant smiling. He was excited about his daughter's return. She had been gone for the better part of two years, and he wondered if he'd been right to send her away. But it had been a last resort.

Grant's wife, Sarah, died shortly after Winnie's birth. The loss had shattered Grant. He couldn't take care of himself, let alone his infant daughter. A lady from church recommended he contact Lorene Cable. She told him Lorene had recently been widowed and could use the money. But she would also be a kind and caring nanny. Grant hired her, and with single-minded determination, Lorene invaded and took over his ill-managed household. She had everyone whipped into shape in no time. Grant often commented that an army would lose no battles if she were in command.

Despite Grant and Lorene's best efforts, Winnifred Elizabeth Emma Grant never outgrew being a tomboy. By the time she turned twelve, she could outride and outshoot every man on the ranch. The ranch hands didn't mind having her around except for the questions, but they respected her—not only because she was Mr. Grant's daughter but also because of her intelligence and an all-in attitude. Even though she was spoiled, she would do the dirtiest chores without a single complaint.

But Grant didn't want a ranch hand for a daughter. He wanted a partner who would one day run his entire operation. Winnie was intelligent and fearless, but she had been sheltered and had much to learn about the real world. And what decent man would want a spoiled tomboy for a wife? That had clinched his decision. She needed to know there were more things in life than cowboys, horses, and guns.

He glanced at Jake, thinking how happy he'd have been if Jake and Winnie had fallen in love. He'd never have to worry about his daughter's future or the ranch if they were married, but he'd seen no sparks between them.

On her seventeenth birthday, Grant sat her down for a heart-to-heart. "I'm sending you to Boston to Miss Minerva's Finishing School and then to Europe. Miss Minerva will train you how to be a lady and teach you some business skills. Then you'll go to England for a visit with your aunts and uncles. They will show you a whole new world."

Winnie had thrown a tantrum, but he stood his ground and gave her a look that Winnie referred to as the Grant glare. He was adamant, and she had no choice but to calm down and listen. He warned her that he would suffer no nonsense. If it took years, she would remain at Minerva's until she graduated. Winnie was still livid two days later when she was packed off to Miss Minerva's Finishing School for Young Women with her arms crossed and a scowl puckering her face.

"Grant?" Jake's voice cut into his reverie.

Grant chuckled. "Sorry, Jake, I was thinking about the day we sent Winnie off to Boston. She was so riled, I thought sure she was gonna explode."

Jake remembered the day well. He mostly remembered how pleased he felt that the pesky tag-along would no longer be underfoot.

Grant puffed on his cigar. "I still question if I should have sent her off like I did. It could have been a mistake. She might be too highfalutin for us now, Jake. Guess we'll find out tomorrow."

Jake stood with a stretch. The cold plate Lorene had fixed for them was wiped clean, and a soft, warm glow from the whiskey warmed his body. "Guess I had better head to the bunkhouse and get cleaned up before I fall asleep in my chair. It's good to be home," he said again as he stepped off the porch.

Grant remained a while longer, mesmerized by the sky's vastness. He didn't want to go in, but tomorrow would be a long day. By this time tomorrow, his little girl would be home, and he couldn't wait to see her.

## CHAPTER 12

# THE NEW GUY

Jake strolled toward the bunkhouse, thinking about Winnie. Would they have anything in common? What would they talk about? What had they talked about before? Would she spurn his attention? He grunted. Why did he care so much? Did it have to do with the inner knowing he possessed? Is that how he knew she was the one for him? Was she the one? Would he even like her?

Still some distance from the bunkhouse area, the soft strumming of a guitar could be heard. *Colby,* Jake thought. Colby liked to play before bedtime, and no one discouraged him. Smoke from the roasting pits near the kitchen hung in the air, making Jake's mouth water. Tomorrow, Hank would serve the men a meal that would have them groaning and loosening their belts.

Jake passed the kitchen and chuck house and entered the courtyard, which was situated between the two long buildings that housed the ranch hands. Dotted with benches, tables, and fire pits, the courtyard was often a busy place. Tonight, a lamplit Poker game was in progress at one of the tables, and Colby was at another, with his guitar.

"Evening, Jake. How goes the marshaling business?"

"Fine, Colby. How goes the guitar business?"

"Fine," Colby said with a chuckle and a thrum.

Colby walked with Jake to the washroom on the west end of the bunkhouse. "Colby, you know anything about this new guy?"

"Trace?"

"Yeah."

"Who's asking? Rancher Jake or Marshal Jacobs?"

Jake shook his head. "Rancher Jake."

"Don't know much. He's been here for maybe two weeks. Keeps himself to himself. Said he was from Oklahoma. The Panhandle area, near Sanford, I think he said. Why?"

"Just curious."

The washhouse was busier than usual, with cowhands getting cleaned up and ready for tomorrow night's party. The room was filled with chatter and laughter and steaming heat from the boiling kettles of water on several potbellied stoves. Jake had grown up around most of these men and, like Grant, knew each of them by name. They always gave him a bad time about wearing a badge, but when he came to the ranch, he left the tin shield behind.

He saw Otto and Heinrich. They came from the same village as his parents and had worked for his father. Otto, a gruff-looking German, was pinning a pair of frayed long johns onto a clothesline. He mumbled a greeting to Jake through the wooden clothespins clamped between his teeth. Heinrich, Otto's brother, climbed from one of the dozen claw-footed bathtubs lined up against the wall and asked Jake what he was doing in the bunkhouse washroom. They spoke in German, Jake telling him Lorene had refused him entry. He was too dirty to use the ranch house accommodations. They laughed and chatted as Heinrich got dressed. They talked of the old days but avoided any mention of the murders.

A shower opened up, and Jake grabbed his turn. Pete and Chris came in as Jake emerged from the shower with a towel wrapped around his waist. "Welcome home, Marshal."

Jake walked to one of the mirrors on the wall, towel-drying his hair. He hung the towel around his neck, pushing the stubborn lock of hair from his forehead. Jake studied his reflection, rubbing his hand over the growth on his chin. He looked different with the beard…older and grittier. He bared his teeth and growled. He looked mean. He wanted to keep it.

"Gonna keep it?" Pete asked.

"Thinking about it."

"What did Lorene say."

"She told me to get rid of it."

Activity and chatter in the bunkhouse picked up as men came in and prepared for bed. Jake studied his reflection. How many times had he heard the words Winnie won't like it? He made his decision and, with a sharp sigh, stropped the straight-edged razor and lathered up.

## CHAPTER 13

# THE DRAGON

Jake stopped by the stable on his way back to the house to check on Drach and Herald. His two mounts were as different as night and day. Each had a unique personality and capabilities, and when he was on the trail, his life depended on their abilities as much as his own.

He rubbed Drach's soft muzzle and ran his hand down his neck. He had caught the horse around the same time he was appointed marshal and had worked with the animal week after week, trying to win his trust. The spent time and the cracked ribs were worth the effort.

The first time Jake caught sight of Drach was a cold spring morning. Drach was showing off, bucking and pawing the air. Jake thought he looked like a smoke-breathing dragon with his breath misting and hanging in the air. Drach's head reared up, and he looked straight into Jake's eyes. He had sensed his presence. He wheeled and galloped away with his tail in the air. Jake hollered after him that he'd be back for *Der Drache*, the dragon.

He left Drach's stall and checked on Herald. As agile and strong as Drach, Jake often chose Herald when he'd be traveling over rough terrain or mountainous trails. Drach had the heart to do it, but Herald had the inborn ability. It was almost like riding a mountain goat. Jake brushed Herald's dark coat, telling him about Sam's run-in with trouble and about Winnie's homecoming. Jake and Herald had a strong bond, and as always, Herald whinnied and nodded or shook his head in proper response to Jake's comments.

Jake checked that all the lanterns in the barn were out and the stall doors secured before heading for the house. His talk with Grant, the whiskey, and the supper had put him in a better frame of mind. And after the shower and time with the horses, he was relaxed. Every muscle in his body was limp with exhaustion, and his bones ached with it.

Trudging toward the house, his thoughts were on Winnie. He couldn't stop thinking about her. When she left, he was glad to get rid of her. But now, he couldn't wait to see her. He missed her and wanted— What did he want? He didn't know, or maybe he did know and didn't want to admit it. He was ill at ease with these new feelings.

Winnie had been five years old when he'd come to live with the Grants. She'd been a nuisance from day one, always underfoot and in his way. Looking back, he realized she had provided a distraction from his grief and sorrow. Looking forward, he was sure she was his future.

## CHAPTER 14

# NAUGHTY WORDS

The moon lighting the way, Pete and Chris left the bunkhouse and headed for their cabin located near the apple orchard. "It'll be a welcome change to be at home with a roof over our heads. I get tired of sleeping on the ground every night. It can get dang cold up on the north range."

"We'll be in the lap of luxury when they get that cabin finished," Chris said with a chuckle, fiddling with a loose button on his shirt and hoping Effie would have time to fix it. "I always liked riding the north range. It's quiet, but this time, I kept feeling sorta skittish. I've never felt that way before."

"I felt it, too, Chris. I figured it was 'cause I knew there could be rustlers about, but even the horses were on edge."

"They probably picked it up from us. I don't know what's going on, but Jake and Grant will figure it out," Chris said. "Jake's parents would be right proud of him. Too bad they couldn't a lived to see what a fine man he turned out to be."

Pete shivered and shook his head, "Jake was lucky to have Grant."

Chris stretched and yawned. "So were we. We'd be cooling our heels in prison if it hadn't been for Grant. Don't know why he thought we might amount to something."

Pete returned the yawn. "Can't wait to see Winnie. It's been powerful peaceful around here since she left."

"It has for a fact."

"When Grant put us in charge of keeping Winnie out of trouble, I hated it. I didn't want to be a kiddie wrangler, but it wasn't so bad. It seems funny that she's all grown up now."

"She was so darned cute," Chris said. "And smart. Those green eyes didn't miss a thing. We taught her to ride and to fish and—"

"—and we taught her some inappropriate words that got us into hip-deep trouble," Pete finished for Chris with a chuckle. "I'd liked to have seen Grant's face when those words came flying out of Winnie's mouth in front of his dinner guests."

"Dinner guests that included the governor. We were lucky Grant didn't skin us alive."

"I've been thinking," Pete said, opening the door to their cabin. "I'd like to have a family."

Chris followed him inside, collapsing into a soft leather chair. "I've been thinking along the same lines myself. But if that's what we want, we'd better get after it." Chris lit a store-bought cigarette. "You going to see Belle tomorrow at Kat's?"

"I hope so," Pete said, going to the stove and peering into the blue enamel coffee pot. "Want coffee?"

"Wouldn't say no."

Pete scooped coffee into the pot and pumped water to fill it. "I asked her to stop working at Kat's, but she won't. How can I court her? There's no privacy there."

"Have you told her how you feel? That you're serious about her?"

"Yeah, but she's downright mulish about not wanting to leave her job." Pete went to the corner bookcase and pulled a dime novel about the James boys from behind a bottle of whiskey on the bottom shelf.

"She's a fine-looking woman, Pete, and I'm sure she makes a decent living working at Kat's. Maybe she's afraid to give up the security."

"I told her I can afford to buy us a place of our own, but she still won't let me call on her. If I want to see her, I have to pay for dances and drinks like any other man."

"Have you asked her what she wants? Maybe she doesn't want to live in the country. She is a townie, after all." Chris hesitated, not wanting to interfere in his friend's love life. "Why don't you ask her to come with us, I mean with you, to the party tomorrow night? I doubt Kat would mind if she were gone for a while."

"I like that idea. I'll ask her tomorrow when we get into town." Pete smiled and sat in the chair across from Chris, opening the book. "And here I thought you'd be jealous."

## CHAPTER 15

# PEEK-AND-RATTLE ROUNDS

It was a brisk spring evening in Grant's Crossing, and Deputy Marshal Sam Watkins was preparing to start his rounds. It was his habit to go out around dusk and again before midnight to ensure the town was buttoned up and secure. On Saturday nights or if there were rowdies in town, he would make extra trips. But tonight, everything was peaceful. The only sounds were laughter, piano music, and the clinking of glasses.

Sam checked his revolver and grabbed his hat. The sun had drifted below the horizon, and he stepped out into a star-studded twilight. He headed down the street, rattling doorknobs and peeking in windows. These were what he called the peek-and-rattle rounds. During the day, they were like social calls. Everyone wanted to visit, and it took twice as long to make it across town.

Laughter drifted from the General Store as a last-minute shopper with a parcel under his arm came charging out. Sam nodded to the man hurrying for his horse. "Evening, Eric. How's it going?"

"Everything's great, but if I'm gonna keep it that way, I've got to get home to my wife and pronto. I forgot her birthday. Thank God the store was open," Eric said, heeling his horse into a gallop.

Still smiling from his encounter, Sam entered the store where Steven and Charlie were finishing up for the day. "Sounds like you may have saved Eric's life."

"Yes, we did," Charlie sang out. "A life saved and a penny made, and now, we are done for the day."

Charlie shook his head at the exuberance of his partner. "After we close up, me and Steven are heading to Kat's for a drink…a little tipple before supper. If you're of a notion to join us, we'll buy.

"Sounds good. See you over there."

Sam finished his rounds and stopped at Kat's Place. He seldom drank, but he enjoyed the company of his friends and listening to their stories and gossip. Steven and Charlie were two of his favorite people, and Steven's yarns could make anyone smile except for Prudence Purdy. She was the sourest curmudgeon in the territory. Some wondered if she had ever smiled at anything in her entire life.

He entered Kat's, the swinging doors flapping noisily behind him. He stopped, surveying the room; he didn't see Steven or Charlie. Kat stood at the far end of the bar, talking to Bear. She tolerated no nonsense in her establishment, and Bear guaranteed it. Sam nodded to them and headed for a table.

He looked over at the Poker game in the corner. It had been going nonstop for five years. There was always at least one player, sometimes several, waiting to buy in. Gamblers from all over the country came to play in what had become a legendary game. Kat claimed they wouldn't miss a deal, even if the place caught on fire.

Steven and Charlie came in and headed for Sam's table. "Wonder if Eric survived? Charlie asked as he pulled out a chair.

"Well, he did buy her an extravagant bonnet for her birthday," Steven said, plopping down in the chair beside Charlie. "How could she be mad?"

They all sputtered with laughter, knowing exactly how mad she could get. They had seen her wrangle Eric home from the bar on many occasions.

Kat came to the table with two glasses of whiskey and a soda for Sam. "On the house, gentlemen." She nodded at their thank you. "You men are always laughing about something. What is it this time?"

Steven couldn't wait to tell Kat of Eric's plight, and of course, he added some dramatic embellishments. Making them all laugh again at poor Eric's marital woes.

Kat changed the subject to Winnie's homecoming. "I'm excited to see her, and I'm looking forward to one of Grant's legendary parties. He does know how to shake the timbers." They nodded in agreement and shared stories of the wilder parties Grant had thrown in the past.

Steven brought the topic back to Winnie. "Sam," he said. "Everyone thinks you and Winnie would make an adorable couple. I heard tell you might be planning to court her?"

Sam frowned, surprised by the question. Then he realized he was being ribbed. "Steven, I believe everyone is you. And no, I do not plan to court Winnie. We're friends. Besides, Jake is all in a stew about her coming home. He's been counting the weeks and the days." Sam looked at them, shaking his head and laughing. "You guys are terrible."

The swinging doors slammed open. It was Eric, and he headed straight for the bar. "Bear, I need a whiskey."

"Guess it didn't go so well with the Mrs.," Charlie said stone-faced, and they burst into laughter.

Still smiling, Steven and Charlie got up to leave, and Steven couldn't help but comment. "I still think you and Winnie would be an adorable couple."

Charlie saw the scowl on Sam's face. "I think we should leave, Steven, before Deputy Watkins shoots us."

Sam turned to Kat. "I should be going, too. Thanks for the soda."

Kat put a hand on his arm. "Wait, Sam."

He sat back down.

"About Winnie. Are you sure you have no feelings for her other than friendship?"

He shook his head. "No. I've missed her, and I look forward to seeing her, but that's all. And even if I had the kind of feelings you're talking about, I wouldn't act on them. Jake's the one who's got a bad case of calico fever for her. What brought this up anyway?"

"Experience, I guess, and men in general. I care about you, and I don't want you to make a mistake and miss out on the love of your life. If you have feelings for Winnie, let her know. Don't fold your hand because of Jake. Let Winnie decide who she wants."

"I get it, Kat, and I do love her, but as a friend...a sister. Besides, Winnie might not want either of us when it's all said and done."

He smiled and squeezed Kat's hand. "Thanks for your advice and the soda. I'll be at the office tonight if you need me."

CHAPTER 16

# BUTCHER, PREACHER, AND A MURDER MAP

Sam returned to the marshal's office and sat behind the desk, thinking about Winnie and Jake and his discussion with Kat. *I'd know if I were carrying a torch for Winnie, and I'm not. But even if I were, I'd never go against Jake, and that's the end of it.*

Sam glanced at the territorial map hanging on the wall. From Fargo to Deadwood and north to the Canadian border, it was the territory he, Jake, and Logan were responsible for. It was vast, wild, and sparsely populated. Jake had covered most of it, traveling thousands of miles in the last fourteen years, looking for answers. At first, Jake had kept his inquiries close to home and focused on his parents' murders, but as he grew older and his loop widened, Jake found many others who had been murdered the same as his parents.

Wherever they went, it was the same story. The murders were in isolated areas, and no one saw or heard a thing. The killer left no solid evidence, only mysterious clues left intentionally to mark his kill. Jake often questioned why the sheriffs hadn't done more to try and track the killer, but in most small prairie towns the office of sheriff was more of an honorary position. Someone to tend to Saturday night drunks.

Sam was worried about his friend's obsession with finding the killer. He agreed wholeheartedly that the monster needed to be found and put down, but Jake was in too deep. Every time he found another killing, Jake relived the brutal murder of his parents, and the hatred stirred. It was a vicious circle that consumed Jake, and the only way to break it was to find the monster.

Staring at the map, Sam wondered if it could hold the answers they needed. They had often studied the roads, paths, properties, forests, and waterways, trying to locate where a particular murder had occurred. They had even put pins and marks here and there on the dimpled and worn paper. However, they hadn't noted all the locations. Sam got out a box of pushpins and started marking the rest of the similar heinous slaughters. So far, they had found only one other killing further away than Clay Springs. The murder was outside Sioux Falls, South Dakota, over 400 miles away, and one of the oldest they knew about. That was the first pin pushed into the map.

After marking several more murder sites, he stopped, deciding to wait for Jake. He couldn't be sure, but even with so few pins in the map, he thought he saw a pattern emerging. It wasn't much, but it looked to Sam like the murders were fanning out from Grant's Crossing. He put down the box of push pins and returned to the desk, still staring at the map. Tomorrow, he would show Jake what he'd found, and they would mark the rest of the murders together.

Sam got up from his desk several times, returning to look closer at the map, tempted to mark the rest of the murder sites but talked himself out of it. This was Jake's hunt. He paced back and forth and decided to leave on his rounds. Maybe a walk would clear his head.

The streets were dark and almost deserted. Two men sitting on a bench in front of Rankin's Gunsmith Shop were having a spirited conversation about politics. He nodded to them as he passed. Could one of them be the killer?

A couple standing on the hotel porch caught Sam's attention. They were taking in the evening air, holding each other close. Could that man be the monster they were looking for? Could such a man be married and living a normal everyday life right here in town? Or could they be a team? Working together. They'd always consider it to be one killer, but could he have a partner?

Had they lived alongside evil all these years and not known? Of course, the devil they were hunting had no horns or pointy tail to identify him. Not even the lingering smell of brimstone. No, this monster looked like any other man on the street. He could be anyone.

The butcher, locking up his shop, waved to Sam from across the street. Sam waved back. He wondered if the mild-mannered Carl Faversham could be a killer. He had the strength and the tools for the job. He shook off the image of Carl with a meat cleaver in his beefy hands and a wickedly toothsome smile on his pudgy face.

And what about Jake's abilities? Wouldn't he experience one of his headaches if he were sitting across the poker table from the killer, or standing next to him at the bar, or passing him in the street? How could he not sense it?

A cowboy hurried past him, headed for Kat's.

But maybe Jake's senses only warned him when someone was in trouble or in physical danger. He had shown up more than once to help him out of a spot. Maybe it had to be someone close to him or someone he cared about who was in danger. If that was the case, Jake could play cards with the devil himself and not know it. A chill ran down Sam's spine. Perhaps he already had.

"Deputy?"

Sam didn't know how long he had been standing there, wrapped in his thoughts, but Bart Story from the Lazy W brought him back to reality. "Deputy, there's a fight up at the Schooner. Some guy is waving a knife around and says he's gonna start taking scalps. He's after Klaus."

Sam turned and ran to the Schooner. The minute he entered the man with the knife turned on him and lunged with the knife extended. Sam sidestepped and knocked him to the floor. The man with the knife was a local cowhand, known as Toot, who had a nose full of rye. Toot got up from the floor, sawdust clinging to his face.

"What happened?" Sam asked

"Klaus can get mouthy when he drinks, and he insulted Toot's manhood. In a number of ways," Bart answered.

"Get Klaus home and tell him he's not to show his face in town till after the weekend."

"But Sam. The party? He'll miss the party."

"All right, but I'm warning you, he'd better not cause any trouble."

Sam took Toot by the scruff of the neck and hauled him to jail. "You can get your knife and gun back in the morning." Sam turned the key in the lock and left to finish his peek-and-rattle round.

His thoughts returned to the murders. Who among the citizens of Grant's Crossing might have committed the murders? Sam and Jake didn't know the exact dates, and some had been years ago. There was no way anyone would remember who had been in or out of town.

What about the people who passed through? The circus came through, but not every year and not always in the spring. The revival ministry was a possibility. It came every spring and stayed for two weeks or longer, depending on the turnouts. And what about the medicine man who wandered the countryside selling his potions? And the tinker? Could he be a brutal killer?

They had questioned all these people, but had they asked the right questions? Did they miss a connection? And what about Pastor Emil? He traveled all over creation, looking for stray lambs to add to his flock.

Sam returned to the office, snorted, and shook his head. *Do you really think the pastor did it?* He stretched out on the cot and fell into a fitful sleep, thinking of maps, murders, and a butcher with meat cleavers and bloody knives.

# CHAPTER 17

# STEVEN WAGNER

Steven and Charlie left Kat's and walked to Minnie's Wishbone Cafe for supper. The cafe was as comfortable as home, and the food was as belly-warming and delicious as anyone's Mother could make. When they finished eating, Charlie suggested they take a short walk before heading home.

Steven patted his paunch. "Charlie, we have to quit eating so much, or I won't be able to fit in my clothes. Maybe we should start eating at home."

Charlie laughed at the idea of either of them cooking. "After a day at the store, you want to go home and pluck a chicken and peel potatoes?"

"Heavens, no. You're right. I'd be too tired to cook. And after the fire we had last year, I don't want you near the stove. I guess we continue to let someone else do the cooking."

Charlie and Steven climbed the outside stairs leading to their apartment over the store. "I swear these steps are getting steeper every day," Steven said, pausing to catch his breath on the landing outside their door. "My forty-nine-year-old knees complain every day about having to climb this mountain."

Charlie pushed open the door to their apartment, and Steven entered ahead of him. Steven hung his jacket on the coat rack near the door. "Sam says Jake is all worked up over Winnie. How is it I didn't notice?"

"As a general rule, Jake doesn't say much."

"He doesn't, does he?" Steven brushed his hand across his thinning hair. "He and Winnie would make a striking couple," he said, settling into his chair.

"Not adorable?"

"No, Jake and Winnie would not be adorable." Steven threw a pillow at Charlie, missing him by a mile. Then his boyish round face broke into a smile. I can't wait to see Winnie. She'll have such marvelous stories about lords and ladies. And castles and knights.

Charlie laughed. "Me? I'm excited about one of Grant's parties." Charlie rubbed his hands together in anticipation. "Tons of food, barrels of whiskey, kegs of beer, and music and dancing. That's what I'm looking forward to."

"Grant does know how to throw a shindig," Steven said, selecting a pipe from the smoke stand. "I love my friends, Charlie, and this town. I can't imagine what might have happened to me if it hadn't been for one crazy piece of luck. One trifling decision that changed my life. I decided to eat at Kat's Place instead of the hotel."

"You've never told me how you came to be here," Charlie said, rolling a cigarette.

"It was the war that drove me here. I don't like talking about it." Steven removed the lid from the humidor and poked a rich-smelling tobacco into the bowl of his pipe. "Or thinking about it. Virginia wasn't the same after the war, but I guess no place was. Everything I loved was destroyed. Safe streets became dangerous. My business partner was shot walking home from our store. He wasn't bothering anyone, but we'd had problems. We didn't support or cooperate with the northern scum who had drifted into town."

Charlie leaned forward, listening intently. Steven had never talked about his life before coming to Grant's Crossing.

"I thought burying my friend was the worst thing anyone should have to endure, but entire families had been wiped out by the war. Compared to them, my loss was hardly worth mentioning."

Steven struck a match and held it over the bowl of his pipe, sucking the flame to the tobacco. "A week after burying my friend, someone set fire to my store." Steven held the match, staring into the flame. "No fire brigade came. I stood alone, watching the last remnants of my life go up in smoke." Steven blew out the match and watched the smoke rise in a swirl. "Come morning, nothing but cinders remained, and I knew it was time to leave. I lost everything except my life, and I feared for that. I climbed aboard the first train heading west, all my worldly possessions in a tattered valise with a broken lock. I had no destination in mind and no plan other than to escape the insanity."

He dropped the match in the glass ashtray and, puffing on his pipe, went silent. His mind wandered back to the day he met Kat. His westbound train had stopped in Grant's Crossing that day to load freight and livestock. He had stepped from the passenger car, thankful for a respite from the train's jostling clatter and his seatmate's incessant chatter. His seatmate was an enormous woman named Ebba Stang, who seemed to never run out of words.

Standing on the depot platform, he rolled his shoulders and wondered if he could find a decent meal in such a backwater town. When asked, the station master suggested either Kat's Place or the hotel. "Kat's Place is the better of the two," he'd said. "But a bit further to walk."

Ebba lumbered toward him with a wide smile that sat above two jiggling chins. "Are we going to get something to eat?" she asked.

He nodded and told her the station master had recommended either the hotel or a saloon up the street. Holding out his arm as a polite invitation to join him, he told her he'd decided on the saloon. She scalded him with a look and turned, waddling toward the hotel, mumbling something about a palace of sin. Kat's Place had definitely been the right choice.

Strolling along the boardwalk, he was impressed by the town's cleanliness and the citizens' politeness. The bustle and activities of the street were laced with laughter and the buzz of friendly conversation. Everyone was welcoming, and he liked the feel of the town.

It was late morning when he entered Kat's Place. It was clean and inviting. A quiet game of Poker was in progress at one of the felt-topped tables, and several cowhands leaned against the bar, sharing a bottle of whiskey with a comely dance hall girl.

An attractive and impeccably dressed woman greeted him from behind the bar. "Will it be food or something to drink?" she said, smiling as she approached.

"Both, please. I'm thirsty and hungry as a bear. My bones are rattling from riding on that clickety-clackety, smoke-breathing behemoth they call a train. It'll take several drinks and a good meal to settle me down."

Kat smiled at the man, who looked nothing like a bear. "The menu is limited right now, but we can whip you up a thick, juicy steak with fried potatoes, or a bowl of chili, or both." She paused with a smile. "If you're returning to the train, I wouldn't recommend the chili."

"I'll take the steak, well cooked with fried potatoes, please, and a whiskey while I wait." Steven hopped onto a barstool. "You run this place?"

"Owner, operator," Kat said, pouring him a glass of whiskey. "First one is on the house."

"Thanks, Miss. This is a nice place you got here, and the town has a friendly air about it." He took a sip of his drink. "Have you always lived here?"

"Name's Kat Masters, and it's been a spell since I got off the stage here in Grant's Crossing. A friend told me once that there wasn't a better place to live. Said she never should have left. I was looking for a fresh start, so I headed in this direction. I've never regretted putting down roots."

"I'm Steven Wagner, by the way, and I guess you could say I'm looking for a new start myself."

She poured him a second drink. "So, what do you do when you're not bouncing around on a train? Are you traveling on business?"

"No," he said with a pleasant smile and paused. "I was going to tell you that I'm running away, but I'd prefer to think I'm running toward something. Something better than what I had."

Bear placed an epic-sized steak with fried potatoes and onions in front of him. Kat smiled at his surprised expression. "If you're still hungry after that, we've got apple crumble." She liked Steven, and while he ate, she told him about the town. And between bites, Steven told her about the aftermath of the war and how he had feared for his life.

"Take a walk with me," she said to Steven as he pushed aside his empty plate and rubbed his belly. "There's something I want you to see."

They walked across the street to the opposite corner, dodging freight wagons and half a dozen cowpokes hurrying to her saloon. Kat stopped on the boardwalk in front of a large, empty building. "This was our general store until several months ago."

They entered the building, greeted by a stale, dusty smell. Steven looked the interior over as Kat continued her story. "Our storekeeper wasn't much of a businessman and didn't know a button from a button-hole, but he did okay until he married. She turned out to be a handful and fond of fine trappings. She spent money faster than he could make it. His business went bust, and when the money dried up, she headed for California. He followed her, leaving us desperate for a store and a storekeeper."

Kat watched Steven inspect the open spaces and the numerous empty bins, display cabinets, and shelves. "So, Steven, what do you think?"

Steven turned to her with a smile on his face. He'd found his new home.

*** 

"Ahem, Steven?"

"Oh, uh, What?"

"Are you still thinking about Virginia and what happened?"

"I'm sorry, Charlie. No, I was thinking about my first day in Grant's Crossing. How I met Kat. And then she introduced me to you. What a string of luck." Steven tapped the ashes from his pipe, replacing it in the pipe stand.

Charlie was disappointed that Steven hadn't finished the story, at least not out loud. In time Steven would tell him. He just had to be patient. He picked up his newspaper and scanned the front page...a bank robbery, cattle rustled, a town shot up, and a body found. What was the world coming to? He flipped to the second page. "Steven, there's an article in the Butte Point Gazette about Winnie coming home tomorrow."

"What's it say?"

"Says she's coming home tomorrow," Charlie said with a mischievous twinkle in his eyes and tossed Steven the paper.

## CHAPTER 18

# AN ANTLER ABOVE THE REST

It was after midnight, and Kat's Place was busier than usual. Kat stood at the far end of the bar, surveying the large, open barroom. All was peaceful. She stifled a yawn, thinking it was time to call it a day. Bear and Morgan had things under control behind the bar, and there were plenty of girls circulating to keep the late-night partiers entertained and drinking.

She thought about the stack of paperwork she'd been ignoring and was justifying putting it off a little longer when her thoughts were disrupted. Mamie Howard burst through the shiny oak batwings, brandishing a double-barreled shotgun. Her tousled strawberry-blonde hair framed a face contorted with anger, and her dark, crazed eyes searched the crowd intently. "Where are you, you two-timing piece of cow dung?" she bellowed, her voice a mix of frustration and fury carried to the back of the room, drowning out every other noise.

Everyone froze, watching the wild-eyed girl frantically swinging the barrels of her hacked-off scattergun from one side of the room to the other.

Kat knew Mamie was looking for her fiancé, Dutch Kinney. Kat saw him moments earlier, sitting at a poker table with Calico Cathy perched on his lap. Kat glanced over, relieved that Callie had slipped away and Dutch had slid under the table.

Kat had no doubt that in her current frame of mind, Mamie wouldn't hesitate to pull the trigger. She couldn't say she blamed her. Dutch was the worst kind of bounder, but that scattergun would take out more than Dutch. Everyone at the table or nearby would be killed or injured.

Sam had already checked in on his midnight rounds, and Kat briefly wondered if he was still out prowling the town. *I wish you were here, Sam,* she thought as she slowly rounded the corner of the bar. "Bear," she whispered. "I'm going to get between her and Dutch. You try to get behind her."

Men bolted for the door, scrambling past her to get outside and to safety. Mamie's face was mottled red, and her eyes blazed with anger as she scrutinized each one. With Mamie distracted, Kat and Bear moved in her direction.

Dutch cowered under the table as the room cleared out. It was only a matter of time before she saw him. "Mamie," Kat said quietly. "Please, put down the gun. We can sort this out."

She turned toward Kat. "I'm going to sort things out all right. I'm going to kill that stinking jackass." Then she yelled, "Dutch Kinney, show yourself. I know you're in here, and I know you've been courting LouAnn Muller behind my back. Did you think you could string us both along? How many others are there?" she screamed, tears rolling down her cheeks.

Thankfully, most of Kat's customers had made it to safety. However, a large number remained just outside, peering over the top of the batwing doors, eagerly waiting to see what would happen when Mamie spotted her target.

Bear was still too far away from Mamie to grab the gun. Kat knew he needed more time. "Mamie, we can—"

At that moment, Mamie's eyes honed in on Dutch Kinney. She swung the barrels in his direction and, putting the stock to her shoulder, let out an unearthly, high-pitched squeal.

"Now, Bear," Kat yelled.

Bear lunged at Mamie, knocking the gun barrels toward the ceiling as the hammers dropped. The blast was deafening, followed by the musical tinkling of shattered crystals raining down from the destroyed chandelier above.

Bear pulled the weapon from Mamie's hand and tossed it to Morgan, who was still behind the bar. Shards of Italian glass crunched beneath her feet as Kat rushed to help Bear.

Mamie struggled against Bear's hold...trying to pull away. He tightened his grip. When she tried to bite him, he held her tighter. "I don't want to hurt you, but you need to calm down," he growled. "Quit fighting me, and I'll let you go."

Kat put her arms around Mamie, smoothing her hair and talking to her as a mother would to a heartbroken child.

"Careful, Kat," Bear said, releasing his hold. "She ain't lost any steam."

"She's fine, Bear. Haul Dutch out from under that table and kick his ass out of here."

At Kat's words, Mamie struggled. "Don't hurt him," she begged, tears streaming down her face.

Kat clutched Mamie closer. "He's not worth it, Mamie. You're too good for him. You deserve better."

"But I love him," Mamie sobbed, melting into Kat's arms and the soothing tone of her voice.

"I know, baby, I know, but in time, you'll forget him. Don't let that bounder ruin your life. There's a kind, handsome young man out there waiting for you. One that will treat you right. He'll steal your heart and show you the true meaning of love. And when you find him, you'll be glad you left Dutch behind."

"But I love Dutch," Mamie said, stirring in Kat's arms. Kat held her tight. "He's your past, Mamie. One day, he'll be nothing more than a bad memory, and you'll wonder why you cared so much. You have an exciting future ahead of you. Don't let a worthless two-timer like Dutch spoil it. Let LouAnn have him."

"Have you ever been in love, Miss Kat," Mamie sniffled.

"I thought I was, but no. I never have been." Kat smiled and looked into Mamie's teary eyes, "Guess I'm waiting for that special man who'll steal my heart."

"You really think there's another man out there waiting for me?" Mamie said, the fight leaving her.

"Mamie, you're a beautiful young woman," Kat said, releasing her hold. "I expect there will be more than one once they know you've tossed Dutch to the dogs." Mamie gave her a weak smile.

"Morgan," Kat said with a wink, "please escort Mamie home."

"Glad to," Morgan said, charging from behind the bar with a wide grin. He took Mamie's hand and led her outside.

"Morgan will have his hands full if he decides to court that gal," Bear grinned.

"He will, for a fact," Kat said, gazing at the shredded chandelier. One lonely, tear-shaped crystal hung defiantly from its center, catching the light and reflecting a rainbow of colors.

"I'll fetch a broom," Kat said with a heavy sigh and headed for the supply closet at the back of the room.

As she passed by the never-ending Poker game, she stopped briefly to watch the deal. "Still going?" she asked.

"Yes, Ma'am. No one even flinched."

"Yeah, it'd take more than a shotgun-wielding woman to stop the game."

She didn't recognize any of the players, but that wasn't unusual. Players came from all over the territories to sit in the game. It wasn't a game for a poor man, but there were always two or three men on the ante-up list, waiting for a seat to open.

It was rumored that Bat Masterson, Buffalo Bill, and Soapy Smith had sat in at one time or another, but Kat hadn't seen them and wouldn't confirm. She had, however, seen Poker Alice at the table just the week before, her low-cut blouse and deep cleavage successfully distracting the other players.

Denny had returned to his piano, and the regular din of the barroom was picking up as the men who had previously left the saloon trickled back in. Denny was practicing a song for the new review as Kat walked by. "Will you be ready for next weekend?" Kat asked.

"I'll be ready, Kat, and so will the girls. We've been rehearsing like the dickens."

"Kat, there's someone here to see you," Bear yelled across the crowded barroom.

Turning from the stage area, Kat crossed the dance floor. Klaus Redding and Bart Story were seated at a table next to the wall that was covered with antlers and spurs. They both stood at her approach. "I hear we missed some excitement," Klaus said.

"You did for a fact," Kat replied, motioning them to their seats. "Thankfully, my chandelier was the only casualty. You boys in town early for Winnie's welcome home party?"

"Yes, ma'am," Klaus said. "Only a fool would wanna miss one of Mr. Grant's parties. We figured to stop here tonight and prime the pump a bit."

"And Klaus wanted to check on his spurs," Bart taunted with an evil grin.

"I'm not ashamed," Klaus said, scowling at Bart and motioning to the wall covered with spur-decorated horns and antlers. "Mine were the first ones up there. It was the first time I danced with Belle, and I like to make sure they ain't been knocked down. It's kinda special."

"Well, you boys have fun," Kat said, chuckling as she left their table and headed for the bar where a young woman awaited. "I'm Kat. How can I help you?"

"My name's Regina Vaughn. I'm looking for a job," she said, wringing her hands.

Kat frowned at the woman, trying to gauge her experience. "You ever worked in a saloon before?"

"Yes, ma'am. In Butte Point."

"The Sailor's Inn?" Kat asked, her jaw tightening. She knew how they used their women. When she was younger, Kat had experienced life in a parlor house and didn't want any working girls in her place. And she didn't want any women working for her that had that inclination.

"I worked at the Red Ribbon," Regina replied. "Delivering drinks and singing. Some say I have a sweet voice."

"I could use another waitress. Let's see what kind of a singer you are. Come with me." She led Regina back to where Denny played the piano. Kat motioned to the stairs leading to the stage. "Show me what you've got, Reggie."

"Now?" Regina said wide-eyed.

"This is as good a time as any," Kat said, moving to one of the tables bordering the dance floor.

"What shall I sing?"

"Your choice, Reggie."

Reggie sang *Molly Malone*. Her voice was sweet and clear, and the men gathered around. Diners dropped their forks, and gamblers deserted their games as her voice floated melodically across the room. Reggie finished the song to rousing applause and shouts for more.

Kat pushed through the crowd of men who had gathered around and pulled Reggie away. "You have a job if you want it," Kat said.

Reggie smiled. "When do I start?"

"Tomorrow night. I'll have Denny show you the ropes, and he'll include you in the rehearsals for the show next weekend. You have a place to stay?"

"I have a room at Hal's."

"That'll do for now," she said, leading her back toward the piano and Denny. "I don't allow my girls to work the sheets or do drugs. If you do, you're fired. The women here are waitresses and dancers, the games are honest, the food is exceptional, and the liquor isn't watered down." She squeezed Reggie's hand. "I'm sure you'll do fine. Just keep the men drinking, gambling, and dancing." Kat stopped by the upright piano. "Take care of her, Denny. She's our new lead singer."

"Henry is not going to be happy," Denny said with raised eyebrows.

"I'll break the news to Henriette tomorrow," Kat said with a scowl. After leaving Reggie with Denny, she headed back toward the bar. Bear had swept up the area, and business was returning to normal. Kat slipped behind the bar to help Bear until Morgan returned.

Thirty minutes later, Morgan returned, a smug smile on his face as he lifted the bar gate and joined Kat and Bear behind the bar. "Mamie's feeling much better. We had a long talk, and I convinced her she is very desirable. She agreed to let me escort her to Grant's party. That is if I can have tomorrow night off."

"I'll let you and Bear work it out," Kat said, casting a sorrowful glance at the remains of the chandelier.

Bear nodded to Morgan. "I'll be fine on my own...won't be much of anyone here anyway."

"I'm going to get a bowl of soup and head upstairs. See you in the morning," Kat said, starting toward the kitchen. Weaving through half a dozen green felt-topped tables, she waved at Swede, the dealer handling the new roulette wheel. The clattering of the ball bouncing as it looked for a pocket made her smile. Her games were honest, but the odds were always in her favor. She saw Dice leaving the Chuck-A-Luck table. "How's the vet business?" Kat asked.

"Doing great," he said. "Better than this stinking dice game. I thought you said you put that bell on the cage for good luck."

"I did. I just didn't tell you it was for my good luck."

"Nice," he said with a smile and headed for the bar.

Kat stopped momentarily to watch her new Faro dealer, Stella Reeves. Stella seemed to be on the up and up but had provided no references. However, she did have an impressive bosom that kept men jostling to get to her table to buck the tiger.

Pushing through the kitchen doors, Kat greeted Tank, her cook. "Got some soup left for me?"

"Sure thing. Saved you some." Tank stopped what he was doing, pulled a bowl out of the warmer with a towel, and handed it to Kat.

"Where's Archie?" Kat asked. "He should have been here an hour ago helping you prepare for the breakfast crowd."

Kat had barely finished speaking when a young man came barreling through the kitchen doors. "Sorry, I'm late. Evening, Miss Masters," he exclaimed in a clipped British accent and a slight sassy bow in Kat's direction.

"Who was she?" Tank asked with a knowing smile.

"Never you mind, old man," Archie said, giving Tank a cheeky grin and a wink.

Kat left smiling. Her kitchen was in experienced hands. She climbed the steps of the open stairway, pausing for a moment on the balcony to look across the enormous barroom below. Her heart filled with pride. She worked hard to make Kat's Place one of the best dance halls west of the Mississippi. She intended to make it even better... beginning with a new chandelier.

## CHAPTER 19

# HORSES, KIDS, AND PINS

"You have any needle and pin work today?" John Miller asked his wife as he tossed their youngest in the air, making her giggle.

"Just a few alterations for Miss Purdy," Mary replied, setting breakfast on the table."

"Is she coming here or meeting you at the shop?" John asked, tickling his daughter into gales of laughter.

"John, stop that. You're getting her all stirred up. Then you'll go to work, and I'll have to deal with her." Mary rolled her eyes at her husband. "Prudence won't go to the shop. Ever since she ran into one of the girls from the Slipper, she won't go to my shop. She doesn't want to chance being that close to a sinfully tainted woman again. I'm surprised she lets me alter her store-bought dresses."

"Don't let her scare the children," John said, making a face and growling at the five children seated around the breakfast table. He glanced at his wife and grabbed a fresh-baked breakfast roll with a wink and a smile. "I need to get to work," he said, taking a big bite of the sticky roll. I've got a busy day at the livery. Bart and Klaus from the Lazy W brought in two wagons for repair. Bart said old man Weisenberger wants them ready tomorrow night so they can take them home after the party." John took another bite of his sticky roll. "Let me know if old Prudie breaks into a smile while she's here."

"Now, John, you know she's had a lonely life. She never married, and her parents died when she was young. She's lucky they willed her enough money to maintain that big old mansion for all these years."

"Wish we had that house. There's a dozen bedrooms in that place," he said, putting his hands gently around Mary's swollen belly, feeling the kicking baby inside her.

"Six is enough, John. If I ever figure out what's causing this, I'll stop it immediately," she said, her eyes twinkling with her smile.

John felt a solid kick and looked at his wife, his eyes full of love. "Mary, I have absolutely no idea what could be causing this." John laughingly pulled her into his muscled, blacksmith arms and gave her a kiss that left no doubt what he was longing for.

"I thought you had to get to work," Mary said with a smile, reluctantly pushing him away.

John sighed as he released her. He kissed each of his children goodbye and met Mary's mother at the door as he was leaving.

"Morning, Mom," John said, giving her a hug and a sticky kiss on the cheek. He knew she didn't like him calling her mom.

"Good morning, John." Her smile didn't reach her eyes. She had never approved of him. "I thought you'd be at work by now mucking out the stables."

"On my way, Mom." His mother-in-law had never cared much for him, but they had become good at subtle barbs, pretending they cared and avoiding each other whenever possible.

"I don't know what you ever saw in that man," Mary's mother said when John was out of earshot.

"Don't start, mother. I love John, and nothing you say will ever change that. Please, just watch the children so I can get busy on Miss

Purdy's alterations. I want to have all my work finished so I can meet Winnie's train tomorrow."

"Fine, I'll take the children outside. We'll all walk with Mark and Peter to school."

As Mary put the finishing touches on the dresses, Prudence knocked on her door. Mary struggled to get up and waddled slowly to her front door.

Prudence greeted her with a scowl. "I don't have all day. Are my garments finished as you promised?"

"Yes, ma'am. Please come in, and I'll get them for you."

Prudence looked around as if she expected a dancehall girl to jump out at her. It annoyed her that Mary made dresses for those evil, soiled girls, and she often told Mary as much. She also told her she doubted she would know how to make a respectable dress for a decent woman.

Mary brought her garments and handed them to Prudence with a hesitant smile. "They are exactly as you requested, Miss Purdy."

"They better be, or you will get them back."

"Yes, ma'am, I even ironed them for you."

"Well, I would hope so. Put these on my bill." And Prudence Purdy was gone in a huff of judgmental righteousness.

Mary shook her head and returned to her sewing room to tidy up. Her mother hadn't spoiled her good mood, and neither would Miss Purdy.

# CHAPTER 20

# OPEN WIDE

Quintin Ivanov was born into a wealthy family in New York City, where they lived in an elegant mansion in an elite part of town. They were catered to by a butler and a vast array of servants, wore the finest clothes, and dined in the finest restaurants. They wanted for nothing.

Quintin was an intelligent and creative young man. Everything came easily to him. He graduated from high school before his sixteenth birthday and was the youngest graduate to give the commencement speech at the graduation ceremony. Despite his age, he was mature beyond his years, and was treated as a peer by his classmates. Handsome, charming, and wealthy, it was no surprise that he was popular with all his classmates.

Quinn, as he preferred to be called, didn't know what business his father, Artem Ivanov, was in. After graduation, Quinn was eager to join in the family business, but his father always told him he was too young. He would be called on soon enough, but in the meantime, he should enjoy his youth and freedom. "Have fun. Chase the girls and spend time with your friends," he'd said.

Quinn and his mother may not have known what kind of business Artem was into, but they did know whatever it was, it had gotten him killed.

It was late evening when the policeman came to their door. His somber face and solemn manner portended bad news. "Mrs. Ivanov?" he said, removing his helmet-shaped cap. He was nervous, he'd never before delivered a death notification.

"Yes."

"Ma'am, I'm afraid I have some bad news for you. I'm sorry to report that your husband's body was found a block down the street. Can you tell me if he would have been on his way home or had he just left? Do you know where he was going?"

Mrs. Ivanov concentrated on the double row of shiny brass buttons on the front of the officer's long coat, giving herself time to absorb the news. "I'm sorry. It can't be," she said, looking up. "There's been a mistake."

"There is no mistake," Mrs. Ivanov," the young officer said, shifting on his feet.

"How did it happen?" she said, her hand on her chest, her eyes filling with tears.

"It's better you don't know the details, ma'am," he said, with a shake of his head.

"How did it happen?" she insisted, pulling a lace hanky from her ruffled sleeve and dabbing away the tears

"He was shot in the head. It appears to have been an execution." He rested his hand uncomfortably on the billyclub hanging from his belt. "His eyes were removed."

She swayed, grabbing onto the doorjamb for support, her sobs becoming wails. "I - I'm sorry, officer," she managed to say, "I can't do this right now. Could it wait for morning?"

"I'm sorry. Of course. A detective will come around in the morning. Again, my condolences for your loss." The officer hurried from the door, relieved his job was done.

Quinn was at the door with his mother. Grief-stricken at the news, he comforted his mother, waiting for the policeman to leave. As soon as the policeman turned his back and the door was closed, she brushed him away.

"Hurry, Quinn, we must leave immediately. Get whatever cash, valuables you have in your room, and some clothes. Choose wisely. We won't be coming back. Meet me at the back door."

She ran to call for the stableman to hitch up her carriage, stopping only long enough to instruct the cook to prepare a basket of food. Then she hurried to her husband's den.

Quinn, shocked at his mother's abrupt change and overwhelmed by sorrow stood like a statue watching her. He couldn't comprehend her words or her actions.

Mrs. Ivanov finished emptying her husband's safe and desk of all valuables and was on her way to her bedroom to gather her jewels and clothing. As she rushed from Artem's den toward the stairway, she saw Quinn standing, unmoving. "Quinn! You must hurry." Then in a softer, breathless voice, "We'll have time to grieve later, but right now, we must act. We're in danger. Your father told me that if anything ever happened to him, we should run for our lives."

She shoved him toward the staircase, and in a daze, he climbed the stairs and went to his room. He pulled a valise from the closest shelf and clumsily gathered his valuables. He looked in his closet. "What clothes should I select? What does one wear when running for one's life? Should I choose something black for mourning my father's passing or something—?" The laughter started low in his belly but grew in proportion until he was doubled over with the power of it. The laughter turned to sobs and tears streamed from his eyes.

His mother grabbed him from behind and pulled him away from the closet. Slapping him with a force she didn't know she had, she screamed. "We haven't time for this. Grab some clothes and a coat and meet me downstairs. Now."

As instructed, a large basket of food had been placed at the back door. Before picking it up, she stopped, telling the cook to gather the other servants and let them all know they should leave the house as quickly as possible. Then she grabbed the basket and went out the back door with Quinn behind her.

Quinn and his mother packed their few belongings into the back of the carriage and climbed in. She clucked to the horse, slapped the reins on his back, and the carriage lurched down the dark driveway.

The horse's hooves sounded unusually loud Quinn thought as he turned his head to take one last look at his home. It had been less than fifteen minutes since the policeman had knocked on their front door changing their lives forever.

"Where are we going?" Quinn asked his mother as the lights of New York City faded behind them.

"We're going to Philadelphia. Whoever murdered your father will try to find us, but Philadelphia is large enough for us to get lost in. If we melt into the background, we should be safe there."

"I'm not leaving," Quinn told his mother. "I'm going to find the man who killed Father and make him pay. I want vengeance. Father would expect it."

"You are not staying here. You don't know the kind of men your father was associating with and what they are capable of. The Whyos killed your father and they'll kill us and think no more of it than swatting a fly. Forget about avenging your father. We're both leaving, and that's the end of it."

The loss of his father was heart-wrenching, and the grief left him empty inside. His mother's cold-hearted detachment made him even angrier, and he barely spoke to her as they traveled toward Philadelphia.

Mrs. Ivanov kept the horse at a steady pace, not wanting to hurry and draw attention to them. A shotgun tucked under her lap-robe provided her with a sense of security, and she hoped she was ready for anything that might befall them.

On the evening of the third day, the lights of Philadelphia appeared in the distance. "We're almost there," she said, pointing to the glow on the horizon. "We'll camp here for the night. There's still enough food in the basket to tide us over. It'll be a sparse meal, but it will do."

They ate in silence, ensconced in a secluded grove of cottonwood trees. It seemed safe among the trees and close to a bubbling creek. "You've hardly said a word to me since we left New York."

He glared at his mother, wanting to scream and yell at her. He wanted to run away and go back to New York, but he doubted he would survive without her, which made him even angrier. He grunted out an answer, "I have nothing to say, Mother. Nothing."

"I know you want to go back, but we can't. The Whyos have eyes all over the city; they'd find us. We'd be no match for them rogue Irish bastards."

When they got to Philadelphia, Quinn's mother rented a filthy one-room apartment on Arch Street under the name of Mrs. Emma Sumner, thinking if anyone came looking for them, she would make it as difficult as possible.

Quintin stood in the doorway in disbelief. "We're going to spend the night here?"

"We're going to live here until it's safe. Your name is now Quintin Sumner."

"My name is Ivanov," Quinn said with fists clenched at his sides.

"It was, but it isn't anymore. I'll let you keep the name Quintin, but you need to get used to the fact that all we knew is in the past."

"And this is our future?" Quinn said with a disgusted laugh

"Only for the time being. It won't be forever."

"One night is too long," He snarled.

"Get over it, Quinn," she said, throwing the lap-robe from the carriage over the filthy mattress hanging over the edge of the narrow cot.

"There's only one cot. Where will I sleep?"

"You can sleep here with me or on the floor. Your choice."

He was disgusted that she would suggest he sleep with her. He looked at the rickety kitchen table and the two splintered chairs on either side of it. There was no way he could piece them together to make anything that would serve as a bed. He looked out the cracked window above the table and cursed his mother.

"I'll sleep on the floor," he said, setting his valise on the table. But the floor was hard, and when the lights went out, the roaches and the scurry of rats quickly changed his mind. Embarrassed and humiliated, he crawled quietly onto the cot beside his mother.

He found it impossible to believe what was happening to them. They had run from a carefree life in a stately mansion with servants catering to their every whim. Now they were living in filthy, rat-infested squalor, listening to neighbors argue, babies cry, and the smell of boiling cabbage thick enough to cut with a knife. He was ashamed of their current condition and blamed his mother for the whole situation. They should have stayed in New York.

The next day, Emma Sumner sold her horse and carriage, hocked her jewelry, and found a job. She figured they had enough money for several years if they each got a job and were frugal. And it was a good idea to appear poor and needy to avoid drawing any unneeded attention to themselves.

Two weeks later she came home from work to find Quinn staring out the cracked, filthy window. "You need to get a job."

"You want me to go to work?" he asked not looking away from the hum of activity in the street below.

"Yes. For two weeks I've been telling you to get a job. I know this is a nightmare, but you're not the only one who lost someone you love, and not the only one who was yanked out of an easy, carefree life. Do you think I like getting my hands dirty? Well, I don't, but we don't have a choice, Quinn…contribute or get out."

She was sad for her son's grief, but he needed to accept the realities of their new life. She knew he hated her for her coldness and lack of grieving, but she feared if she let sorrow and grief take over, she would crumble and be useless to herself and her son. One day, it would be safe to grieve for the man she loved. One day, she would release the scream and wail for her loss, but not today. For now, she had to be strong.

After his mother's ultimatum, Quinn went to a local pub where he had noticed a "help wanted" sign in the window. He walked in and looked around, wondering what the customers were like and what his duties might be.

He was about to ask about the job when several college students came in, laughing and talking about their day in class. "Did you see how Professor Ludlow was looking at his assistant?" one student said and all six of the boys chuckled. "He looks that way at all the girls," another said. "Ludlow's eyes never leave her breasts," yet another student said, and they all laughed as they ordered a round of drinks.

"He's not a bad teacher. He just has trouble staying focused on teeth," one of the students said paying the waiter as he placed drinks in front of them.

"How could he focus on teeth when he has bouncing Betty leaning over his desk. A man could get smothered in that bosom."

"But what a way to go."

Quinn couldn't make out all the conversation but was intrigued by what he heard. He approached their table, offering to buy them a round of drinks, and asked if he might join them. They talked about school, the classes they were taking, and how they were all going to be wealthy one day. They shared story after story, mostly about cute little bouncing Betty and how they would like to get to know her a whole lot better.

Later that evening, when his mother came home from her job, he told her he wanted to study dentistry. It took some convincing, but eventually, based on the return on the investment, she agreed and Quintin enrolled in college.

Like his other schooling, he excelled and graduated at the top of his class. He was Doctor Sumner before he turned eighteen and on his way to regaining his pride and status.

A severe bout of pneumonia the second winter in Philadelphia almost killed Emma and she was never quite the same after that. Quinn blamed her for stubbornly insisting on remaining in that filthy, heatless room until after he graduated.

"We're going to Arizona," he announced immediately after the graduation ceremony. "They say the dry climate will be good for your lungs, and I can open a practice there as well as anywhere."

They arrived in the spring and enjoyed the dry, sunny weather. Quinn opened a dental practice but had trouble getting it up and running. One of his patients threatened to kill him if he wasn't a painless dentist as his shingle promised.

He befriended a local Shaman who taught him how to ride and how to use many different weapons. The Shaman also taught Quinn how to track his prey and how to clean, and prepare the animals that he killed. Quinn enjoyed the hunt and was out early every morning, rain or shine, to practice with his weapons. He became proficient with guns, knives, and even the bow but always preferred using the knife.

Quinn also learned about herbs and cacti and what each was used for. The strength and potency of the innocent-looking plants amazed him and he knew the knowledge the Shaman shared with him was priceless.

But after two years, Quinn's mother pulled him aside. "I hate the summers here, Quinn, and the violence. And the weather hasn't helped my lungs at all. Can we move away from here? Somewhere cooler."

He hated to admit it, but he was having trouble building a profitable practice. No one seemed to care much about their teeth and he also hated the weather and violence. The only downside to leaving was saying goodbye to the Shaman. There was still so much he had to learn and so many questions he wanted answered.

Quinn and his mother traveled to Kansas City and spent several days considering their options. They considered settling there, but the hustle and bustle of city life didn't appeal to either of them.

The Shaman once told him that one must wait quietly, and the answer will come on silent feet. Sitting in their hotel room one evening, reading the paper, the answer came to him on tiptoes. Quinn had folded up the paper and was about to toss it in the trash when he caught sight of an ad on the back page. A growing town in the Dakota Territory needed a dentist. It intrigued him. Out West, he would have plenty of room to hunt and grow his gardens. With a smile, he hurried to the telegraph office.

# CHAPTER 21

# QUINN'S PARADISE

Leaning against the veranda railing of his plantation-style mansion, Quintin Sumner looked out across his massive gardens. A slight spring chill hung on the evening air. It was a time of new life and of creation. He was happy here in Grant's Crossing. Happier than he'd ever been.

Upon his arrival fourteen years earlier he purchased ten acres of land east of Mill River, giving him plenty of room for his gardens. He immediately began planting herbs and specific trees for their bark and foliage. He also constructed a greenhouse on the south side of his house and raised a dozen varieties of cacti. All his plants flourished and his gardens were productive and beautiful.

Quinn's reverie was interrupted when Carol, his mother's newest caregiver, wheeled Emma onto the porch and parked her wheelchair close to where Quinn stood.

"Your mother was getting anxious and kept calling for Artem. I thought perhaps some fresh air would help. Do you mind if we join you?"

"You may leave Mother here, but I'm sure you have duties inside to perform."

"Yes. Of course, sir. I'll get supper ready."

"Where's your father?" Quinn's mother asked, looking up at her son. "I thought he would be home by now."

"He'll be home soon, Mother."

"I miss him."

"I do, too." Quinn smiled down at her. "Father would be proud of how you saved our lives. We probably would have died that night if it hadn't been for your quick thinking. I hated you on that trip to Philadelphia. I wanted to run away...to return to New York. But even then, I knew you were my strength. As you always have been. Even after we reached Philadelphia I wanted to run, but knew I would never survive without you. Those were rough years, but we survived and they paid off."

She still had good days. Days that made a person wonder if she wasn't cured. Her mind was clear, and her brain forced her legs to put one foot in front of the other. But it happened so rarely anymore.

"Artem," she said, looking up at her son with a coy smile. "I'm glad you're home. I've missed you. We didn't live in Philadelphia, did we?"

Quinn sighed, taking his mother's hand in his. She was having a bad day, and it was always worse in the evenings. He sat on his heels beside his mother's chair. "We only lived there for a while. I barely remember it myself."

He stood, leaning his hips against the veranda railing. He looked at his mother's gray hair and frail form. She would soon leave him.

"Quinn, did they ever find those boys?"

"What boys?"

"Those two classmates of yours that disappeared...the police suspected foul play."

"The police said there had been a scuffle, and when they found the boys' wallets on the pier, they figured they'd been robbed and thrown into the river. I wonder if they ever found their bodies."

"Is Artem home yet?"

"Yes, Mother. He's washing up for supper." Quinn's eyes misted. His mother's mind and body were disintegrating in front of him. She barely ate enough to keep a bird alive, and her gaunt, ashen face was a constant reminder that her death was near. He loved her and would always care for her as she had cared for him.

"When are you going to get a job? You should be at work, not lazing around at this hotel. I sold my jewels and my thoroughbred horse, and I'm waiting on rich bitches and snobbish whores in that stinking department store." His mother's bony fingers clamped around his arm. "Why did I send you to college? You still can't find a job."

Quinn sighed. "I have a thriving dental practice, Mother. I've worked hard and have become successful and well-liked in Grant's Crossing. Remember Mama? I am an elder of the church and was elected to the town council."

"Of course you're successful. There isn't another college trained dentist within a thousand miles in any direction. And don't you forget that it was my hard work and sacrifice that paid for your education."

It seemed the older and more senile she became, the more she found it necessary to remind him of all she had sacrificed. He resented the harping, and it rankled him that she never acknowledged his hard work or accomplishments. Only she had made sacrifices. She paid for his education. He wished just once she would give him a word of praise or a pat on the back and tell him how proud she was of him.

"I've worked hard, Mother, and I've built up a very successful practice."

"Yes, dear, you have a fine practice, but how are you paid? You're paid in loaves of bread or peach pies. What did Mrs. Torrington pay you with today?"

Quinn laughed, "She gave me a dozen eggs and a squawking chicken which Carol is preparing for our supper tonight." Quinn looked at his mother with kindness and love reflecting in his dark eyes. "It's all they have to give. Sometimes I don't take what they offer because I know they'll have to go without. We have so much, and it's only right that we share. It makes me feel good to help these people."

When he first opened his practice in Grant's Crossing, people came to his office only if the pain was unbearable. The horrors of the dentist's chair were well-known in stories and firsthand experience. But he was slowly changing how people perceived him and his profession. He kept up with the newest procedures and had the finest, top-of-the-line equipment. He used nitrous oxide or ether to alleviate the pain associated with dental procedures and kept his instruments sterilized. Everything, including himself, was as clean as possible.

"I'm planning to make one of my trips out of town soon," Quinn said to his mother, excited by the prospect. The trips were exhausting, but it pleased him to be helping so many people. "I wish you were well enough to go with me."

"I can't go," she said, her eyes hazing over. "I must be here when Artem returns. I've missed him, you know."

"I know, Mother." Quinn patted her hand. "I'll miss having you there as my helper. You always do such a wonderful job handing out the toothbrushes and wooden chew sticks."

"Giving them away, you mean. You don't charge the rabble even a cent. At least you charge something for the toothpaste samples. You need to charge more."

"Yes, Mother."

Patients usually came to his office in Grant's Crossing, but several times a year, he hitched up his carriage and went into the backcountry and surrounding towns. He performed simple procedures using the tools he carried with him, but for more delicate operations, he asked patients to come to his office. Sometimes, they did, and sometimes, they waited until the pain was stronger than their fear of the dentist's chair.

With his mother in such poor health, Quinn decided not to travel far from home this time, Emma was failing fast. If something happened, he needed to be close by.

"Winnifred Grant will be coming home soon," Quinn said, changing the subject. "I'm going to ask Tom Grant for her hand."

"Such a wild child. She will not make you a suitable wife," his mother snorted.

"She has a natural beauty that pleases me, and she reminds me of you. She's strong like you. Besides, I'm sure I can mold her into a satisfactory wife."

The thought of seeing Winnie made his heart race. He needed to mate with a superior woman, and that woman was Winnifred Grant. She was strong and fearless like his mother once was, and she would provide him with the sons he desperately wanted.

He was about to ask Mr. Grant for permission to court his daughter when Mr. Grant unexpectedly sent her off to finishing school and Europe. It was a setback, but he believed she would return more sedate and proper than when she left.

"It's getting late, and we haven't had supper yet," he said, rolling his mother back into the house. "I'll get an early start in the morning and make it a short trip, so I'll be back in time for Winnie's homecoming party." He pushed his mother's wheelchair up to the table, and they had a lovely chicken supper courtesy of Mrs. Torrington's wisdom tooth extraction.

After supper, Quinn watched Carol wipe gravy from his mother's face and hands and carry her up the stairs to her bedroom. He didn't like to look directly at Carol. She was bankrupt of even fair looks, but she was strong, kind to his mother, and had the largest breasts he'd ever seen. Fascinated by the shifting, bouncing mounds of flesh, he seldom looked at her face.

Quinn waited for Carol to get his mother tucked in. When Carol came down the stairs and disappeared into the kitchen, he went up to say goodnight to his mother. Entering her room, he found her frantically trying to get out of bed. Seeing Quinn, she settled back against her pillows.

"Artem? I'm so glad you're home. I was so worried about you."

"Yes, Emma, my love, I'm here," Quinn said, climbing into bed and taking her in his arms.

Later, when his mother had calmed and was sleeping soundly, he climbed from her bed. He leaned down and whispered, "I love you, Mother." Then kissed her cheek and smoothed her hair before retiring to his own room.

As he prepared for bed, there was a gentle tapping on his door.

"Dr. Sumner?"

"What is it, Carol?"

"Will you need me for anything else?"

"Nothing tonight, but I'll want an early breakfast."

"Yes, sir. Goodnight," Carol said, going to her bedroom at the end of the hall.

Quinn hired Carol Grover a few months earlier as part-time help to care for his mother when he wasn't there. As his mother continued to fail, he asked Carol if she would consider being a live-in helper, and she gladly accepted the job.

As he crawled into bed, he thought of Winnie. He would see her soon, and she would soon be his wife.

## CHAPTER 22

# MUST BE THE BEAVER

Nate Daniels took three or four weeks off from farming every spring to visit nearby ranches and towns, searching for breeding stock and catching up on the latest news. This year, he had stayed away a little longer than usual, trying to forget about Kat and his broken heart. Luckily, he had a manager capable of running the farm in his absence.

His trips were all business, except for the last few days when he would stop in Mapleton before heading home. Gigi, a French woman who worked at the Painted Pony, pleasured him in glorious and delightful ways. Between Gigi and the opium den in the cellar, he could briefly lose himself, and the pain from his wound ceased to exist. He couldn't recall much about his time at the Painted Pony, except he was free of pain and all his desires satisfied.

As he rode in, his manager and a couple of his workers came out to greet him. He was tired and covered with trail dust.

"Glad you're back, boss," one of the men said, taking the reins from him and leading the horse to the barn. Nate motioned for the manager to follow him into the house. Everything was exactly as he had left it. It smelled stale from being shut up for so long, but it was home.

"How was the trip?" his manager asked.

"Picked up some fine-looking stock over in Montana Territory. We'll have to send some men out to get them."

The manager smiled. "And the stop in Mapleton?"

"Always the best part of the trip. I feel amazing the whole time I'm there. But too much of a good thing can be bad. I always have to fight a hankering to stay."

"You need to find yourself a woman, boss."

"Thought I had for a while."

"Well, it's good to have you back. But it might be a while before we can free up any men to pick up the new stock. A couple of the men quit last week, and with the new place you bought, it's been a struggle to keep up with the planting and the chores. There's also a problem with one of the irrigation canals. Don't know what's wrong, haven't had time to ride out and see to it, but we'll be needing water soon."

Nate rubbed his eyes and looked at his manager with a weak smile. "It's the same everywhere. There wasn't a drop of rain. Look, I need to get the trail knocked off me. I'm headed down to the creek for a wash, and then I'll have a shot of whiskey and a long night's sleep."

"You look tired."

"I am, but a solid night's sleep should do the trick. I'll ride out in the morning to check on the canal. It might be that dang beaver I chased off last spring. I should have shot the varmint."

"You're too soft."

"I doubt everyone would agree with your evaluation," Nate scoffed. "Whatever you plan on doing tomorrow, have it done before noon. We're going to town to rustle up some men, and then we'll hit Grant's party. You deserve a night off for holding down the fort, and nobody throws a better wingding than my old friend. We can talk about the rest on the ride into town."

"You got it, boss. Welcome home."

Nate snorted. *Yeah, welcome home,* he thought as he calculated how long it would take him to ride back to Mapleton and sweet oblivion.

It was a short hike to the creek, and on the way, his mind wandered. Would he find any decent men in town looking for a job? Men who would last past their first payday. And what could be wrong with the canal? Probably the dang beaver again. And he thought about Gigi and the packet she had sent home with him. Something to help with the pain, she had said. He wanted some right now but knew he shouldn't. In the war, there were men so addicted to painkillers and so desperate they stole from the doctors, leaving the wounded men to suffer. Nate figured they would have killed their own mothers if need be, and he thought about Grant's party. He and Grant had been friends for years. He had bounced baby Winnie on his knee and had watched her grow up wild and free. He wondered how her trip back east and abroad might have changed her.

The stream ran close to his house, and there was a wide, shallow spot perfect for bathing. As he approached the bank, he could make out the outline of an exposed sandbar, looking like an island in the middle of the creek. It was usually covered with two or three feet of water. He shook his head and shucked his clothes. *We need rain,* he thought as he splashed into waist-deep cold water.

He saw the washouts under the creek bank, some extending back, deep underground, like caves. He had caught catfish around those holes before the water went down, and he wondered where the fish had gone. Where could he drop his line when he was hungry for a mess of fish?

He toweled himself dry as he returned to his house. Rotating his shoulder and feeling the pain, he wanted to take some of the *medicine* Gigi had sent with him. It would relieve his pain, but he walked past his saddlebags and went straight to bed. He was tired enough to sleep like the dead without it.

# CHAPTER 23

# AHHH, SPRINGTIME

If someone had heard their screams, maybe he could have been stopped. But no one heard, and no one came.

Over time, he found that explaining in detail what he was going to do to his prey created a wellspring of terror. And that was what he was doing now. He talked to them the whole time, telling them how important they were to him and how he had watched them before deciding they were the perfect pair. He explained how significant today was. It was his 200th kill, and it was a celebration.

He watched their faces as he tortured them, cutting into them and stealing their lives. The hunter saw fear, anger, and sorrow…sometimes even defiance in their tear-streaked faces, but he wished he could be inside their minds and know the horror firsthand. He had created it. It belonged to him. He wanted to feel it.

He usually worked with the woman first so her husband could watch, but today, he left the woman till last. She would have the special honor of the day. He extolled the virtues of a sharp knife as he cut and sliced into the man. Each cut of his knife was like an artist's brush. The woman's screams and the desperate struggles of her husband, helpless to stop what was happening or to protect his wife, were aphrodisiacs to him. Listening to them beg, he rubbed the man's blood over his body and stroked himself to a climax. Then he turned to the woman.

Perfection was in the detail, and he had worked slowly, taking extra time with each of them. He wanted today to be perfect. He laid his knife aside. They were still alive, but barely. He watched them, his face blank of expression, mesmerized by the blood draining from their bodies. When they took their last breaths and gave in to death, he moved their bodies, adjusting them into various positions, looking for the proper effect, the perfect nuance. He arranged and then rearranged them in slightly varying positions, like dolls at a tea party. He was creating a meaningful story, a tableau of death.

He stood back to critique his work, absentmindedly stroking himself. He had created a dramatic statement honoring this special occasion. He squatted beside the woman, admiring her face. Such incredible bone structure, he thought. He pushed the corners of her mouth into a smile. Now, she was perfect. His vignette was a perfectly horrendous abomination.

He surveyed the scene one last time before enjoying a well-earned repast. The couple sat facing each other at the kitchen table, their eyes wide open. Sad, he thought they could not see each other and how incredible they looked. Each held the other's heart, and their entwined entrails formed the shape of a heart around them. He had outdone himself, but then, this was a special occasion.

He raided their pantry and made a sandwich before taking a seat at the kitchen table like a guest, sharing a friendly meal and a drink. He chatted about the weather and politics and asked how their crops were doing.

He wrapped his bloody fingers around his sandwich and took a big bite. He told them of his early years and how he had been insatiable. "My first was a streetwalker. That was over twenty years ago. I was young and nervous, but it was so easy. After that, well, I don't mean to brag, but I killed no less than ten a week. It was a slaughter," he said proudly with a chuckle. "My exploits were front-page stories, and in the taverns, the killings were all they talked about. I liked being famous, but, as with all young men, I was arrogant and cocky, and I got careless. I was almost caught on more than one occasion. After two months of slashing and tearing folks to ribbons, I was bored and knew if I was going to avoid the law, I needed a calmer approach," he said as he took another bite of sandwich before continuing.

"I taught myself to be patient and slow and to choose my prey carefully. And as you can see, it has developed into an art form. You are proof of that. Now, the anticipation and, of course, your starring roles in the event make it ever so much more enjoyable than simply slashing someone's throat. Don't misunderstand…I still kill when I feel the need. But in the springtime, I release my imagination and am inspired to create art," he said with arrogance, as he wiped his hands on his bare chest.

"What, you don't believe that I've scored two hundred kills. How can you doubt me? Hmm, let's see if I can justify that number. But you are dead, so I don't know why I bother. I've been at this for over twenty years. So, on average, that's just ten a year. Four souls in the spring, and a few scatter through the rest of the year as needed. As needed," he chuckled. "Sounds like a prescription, doesn't it? Get it? Of course, you don't; you're dead." He took a drink of milk, looking thoughtfully into the distance. "When I'm upset or agitated, the number of *as-needed* tends to increase substantially."

He bit off a chunk of his sandwich, chewing noisily. "What's that you say? Why haven't I been caught? I'm too clever for the law, and I hardly have to worry at all around here. The marshal's been looking for me for fourteen years and has no idea we cross paths every day. And his deputies? They are equally inept. I'm right under their noses, and they haven't the vaguest idea," he laughed, spitting bits of sandwich from his mouth. "Perhaps I should write the marshal a letter or send him a souvenir. What do you think? That might be fun."

When he finished eating, he poured each of them a glass of whiskey and stood for a toast. He nodded to each, thanking them for their cooperation and generous hospitality. He saluted them and downed his whiskey.

His work was complete, and it was time to go. He scanned the room, enjoying one last lingering look. He wanted to remember his 200th kill. He wished he had someone to share it with. Then inspiration struck, and a cocky smile of satisfaction split his face. He moved toward the man, apologizing profusely.

When he had collected his prize, he wandered into their bedroom, searching for a suitable receptacle. He found a wooden jewelry box on top of the dresser, dumped the cheap bobbles onto the bed, and replaced them with the man's essential parts.

The hunter looked down at his crimson-stained body. It was late, and he still had to get cleaned up. He gazed back, hating to leave, but he had to get on the road before someone came along and spotted him. Getting caught would not be a satisfactory way to end such a glorious day.

He washed off in the nearby creek and put on the clothes he had removed earlier in the morning in anticipation of his celebration. Tucking his shirt into his trousers, exhaustion hit. It was a long way home, and he wished he could stop somewhere for the night. But he didn't dare. He needed to put as much distance as possible between himself and his creation. And he wanted to be home in time for Winnie's party. He had to keep moving. But on the trip home, he would relive every moment and savor every detail of this extraordinary day.

## CHAPTER 24

# WINNIE ARRIVES

"Checking the clock won't make the time go by any faster," Gertie laughed. "We can get you ready from hat to slippers in less than an hour, so we have plenty of time."

Winnifred Emma Elizabeth Grant and Gertie, her traveling companion, sat at the gaming table in the center of the railroad car, playing *Old Maid*. Winnie had trouble concentrating and looked at the clock every few minutes. "I'm tired of the clattering, the whistles, the bells, and the whooping steam. This would have been intolerable if Dad hadn't sent his private car for us."

"Better than a stagecoach," Gertie said, cocking an eyebrow.

Winnie smiled. "It is for a fact."

Gertie glanced at a green dress hanging on the closet door. "The dress you chose for today is perfect. It's simple but elegant. It will turn heads."

Winnie smiled wistfully. "There's only one head I want to turn."

"Well, the dress is a beauty, but once you put it on, you can't sit down, or it will get all wrinkled."

"It's your turn to draw," Gertie said, picking up the forgotten cards. "I know you're nervous, but you'll do fine. They might even recognize you."

Winnie shot her a look.

"I'm sorry. You haven't changed all that much," Gertie laughed. "Still, you have changed in a lot of ways. What I'm trying to say is you are still a free spirit inside, but now there is a proper lady on the outside. Sort of a wolf in sheep's clothing."

Winnie laughed. "I don't know whether to snarl or curtsy. Come on, let's play cards," Winnie said, drawing a card from Gertie's hand and placing a pair on the table.

"I was angry with my father for sending me off like he did, but he did the right thing. I found out just how big the world is. I'm just sorry I took my anger out on you." It embarrassed Winnie to think about how she had treated Gertie the first time she saw her. Her first words to her were disrespectful and insulting. She wished she could take them back.

"I'm made of stern stuff, Winnie. But you had worked up a righteous anger when I met you at the train station. You told me I looked like a prison guard and had as much hair on my face as your dad. Your scowling face was downright scary, and the thought of being responsible for you in Boston and abroad was frightening. If I hadn't needed the money, I would have cut and run."

Winnie looked across the table at her friend and smiled. If Gertie had been hurt or displeased, she hadn't let it show. She had simply looked Winnie up and down and let out a harrumph of displeasure.

Winnie's face flushed, "I still regret my words."

Gertie laughed. "Winnie, your father paid me handsomely, and he did warn me you were a handful. He told me I'd earn every dime he was paying me. And he was right." Gertie drew a card from Winnie's hand. "What bothered me was you calling me Gertie. I didn't like it at all…at first. Now, I'm kind of used to it."

Winnie looked a little sheepish and corrected her posture, looking extremely ladylike. "I have changed. I know how to say please and thank you and how to hold a teacup properly. And my insults are far more subtle, but I still won't call you Gertrude," Winnie said with a smile.

"By the time we got to the hotel, you had simmered down and were much nicer."

"I had accepted my fate by then, and everything was so exciting."

"When we arrived at the hotel, I was in awe of where we were staying. I thought it must surely be a mistake. Our suite was so elegant, and I felt so out of place. I should've been a maid, cleaning up after rich people, not enjoying the comforts of such a luxurious room. And then, when we entered the dining room, the Maître D knew my name. Not just the Grant name, but my name, too."

Winnie smiled at her with the mischievous grin Gertie had become familiar with.

"We were escorted straight to a reserved table, and the waiter showed up immediately with a basket of warm rolls and butter. No one had ever waited on me. You, of course, took over and ordered an enormous dinner. I think you ordered everything on the menu. I was speechless and when—"

"Now, Gertie." Winnie interrupted, laughing. "Tell it the way it was. As I recall, you were anything but speechless. You scolded me soundly for ordering too much food and for being wasteful. But we did clean up everything on every one of those fancy plates. It was so delicious—we stuffed ourselves!"

"After you ordered and the waiter left the table, I received your lecture on how we would proceed. I recall your diatribe verbatim. I had started to say I prefer you not call me Gertie when you butted in."

"You grabbed a roll from the basket and began buttering as you told me you preferred to be called Winnie, but if Miss Winnifred made me happy, you'd *allow* it. However, you would not call me Gertrude. It was going to be Gertie, and that was that," she said with a grin.

"A bit of butter dripped down your chin as you explained that you knew your father had hired me to keep you out of trouble, and you agreed to *allow* it. You admitted to a tendency to get into trouble, but since your father made it abundantly clear if he received any bad reports from the school or me, you would remain at Miss Minerva's until you could behave. You swore to me that you would work hard, excel in every subject, and graduate with the highest honors. I doubted you," she said with a giggle.

"But the best part was after supper, when we were back in the suite, I almost doubled over with laughter when you told me, and I quote. "You know, Gertie, I am quite charming enough. I don't understand why my father is sending me to school and torturing me like this."

"And you told me I was not the least bit charming, and my father was wise in sending me off to learn how to be a lady."

"The next morning, you *allowed* me to escort you to Miss Minerva's School for Young Ladies." Gertie winked at Winnie, "Surprisingly, you did graduate with the highest honors."

Winnie laughed, "How did you ever manage to put up with me? I was an arrogant, obnoxious brat."

"We did have a good time, Winnie, but you spent way too much money, and buying me a whole new wardrobe was the topper."

"You looked beautiful in your new clothes, and besides, I couldn't be seen with a raggedy old woman as a traveling companion, now could I? Besides, you earned it. Anyway, in case you hadn't noticed, my dad has plenty of money and doesn't mind me spending it."

"You have been blessed with a loving family and a lifestyle few people could even imagine."

"I know. I'm very fortunate, but my dad has worked hard for what he has, and he's made some wise investments. He'll be the first to tell you he's been unbelievably lucky and blessed. Angels at work, he says."

Winnie looked at the clock. It seemed the hands were frozen in place. "I can't wait to see what kind of party he has planned for me. He gives some of the best parties in the Dakota Territory. He spares no expense. But he is also a kind and generous man who loves to share his abundance. Sometimes, it's as simple as a few extra supplies for a hard-luck family."

Winnie looked at the clock again. "Is it time?"

Gertie chuckled. "Not unless you want to stand up for an hour."

"Then I'll keep talking about how special my dad is. I've got a great story to tell you about what a soft heart he has. About five years ago, a few days before Christmas, Dad was in town and heard the little Drummond boy asking his papa if Santa could bring him a mule for Christmas. His papa told him Santa couldn't bring him a mule, at least not this year, but there would be a fruit basket for them all to enjoy. They would sing carols around their Christmas tree, and the family would be together safe and warm."

Then the little boy asked his papa if Santa was mad at him. He'd been a good boy. He did his chores and hadn't played hooky from school.

"Dad said when the little boy asked if Santa was mad at him, it broke his heart. The little boy's disappointment was more than he could stand. On Christmas Eve, a mule was tied to the hitching post in front of the Drummond's home. And there were burlap bags filled with all kinds of food and gifts for the whole family."

"Dad persuaded Chris and Pete, a couple of our ranch hands, to help him get everything together, and they had the time of their lives picking out toys and special treats for the children. They didn't forget Mama and Papa Drummond either. When the shopping was done, they tied a strip of sleigh bells to the mule's halter, loaded all the goodies on his back, and led him out to the Drummond farm. They tied him up and scurried for cover behind some rocks and brush, waiting for them to hear the sleigh bells and come outside. They didn't have long to wait. Dad said the looks on the children's faces warmed his soul. Every year since then, those three elves have helped one or more families."

"Your father sounds like an extraordinary man."

"It's not always money or gifts. Sometimes, it's respect and a helping hand. Dad is always a softie when it comes to helping a stray of any kind. He's helped many people turn their lives around by giving them a second chance when no one else would."

Winnie frowned at Gertie. "I know it's selfish, but I wish you weren't returning to Denmark. Are you sure your fiancé won't come over here?"

"No, he has a job he likes. He wants to be close to his family, and I'll get to be with my family, too. We can raise our children with grandparents, aunts, uncles, and cousins close by to spoil them and look out for them. My father can give me away at my wedding." Gertie's eyes misted, and Winnie came around the table to hug her.

"I'm going to miss you, my friend."

Gertie looked at the clock, blurred by the tears in her eyes. "It's time, Winnie. We'd better get you dressed. Are you ready?"

Winnie nodded. She had picked her attire carefully. She wanted her father to be proud of her and Jake to notice her. To wear the dress she had chosen, she would need to wear a corset, cinching her waist tight.

"Gertie, isn't it tight enough?" Winnie gasped. "I don't think I can breathe." Gertie continued pulling, occasionally stopping to measure her waist.

"Well, Miss Winnifred, you may have had one too many crumpets with your tea." Gertie laughed, giving one last superhuman pull. "This should do it, but you don't dare take a deep breath. If this corset bursts, it could kill someone."

"Very funny," Winnie said, gasping for air. "Let's get me into my dress before I pass out."

The emerald green dress accentuated her narrow waist and made her bosom appear larger. She hoped Jake would notice.

Her hat was a work of art. Over the crown, a fine netting was subtlety interwoven around ostrich feathers and pulled to the back, forming a bow. Winnie placed the hat on her head and was about to secure it with a pin, but Gertie stopped her. She moved it slightly to the side and pinned it in place. "It gives it a jaunty look that suits you much better," she explained.

Gertie stepped back, looking at Winnie with approval and admiration. "You are going to knock all of them off their feet."

With squealing brakes and smoke pouring from its sides, the engine slowed. Winnie ran jerkily to the window, trying to keep her balance. "Look, Gertie. There's a welcome home banner on the front of the depot office." She turned her attention from the banner and tried to see who was on the station platform, but they were still too far away for her to see clearly. Winnie bounced up and down with frustration, and Gertie warned her not to dislodge the hat or put too much strain on the corset.

When the train finally came to a stop, she saw Sam. His height always gave him away. She saw Lorene and her dad. "My dad shaved his beard and mustache. I don't believe it."

There was Pete and Chris, and then Mary came charging up to the front of the platform, waving an enormous white hanky and hollering, "Welcome home, Winnie. Welcome home."

There was Kat and Steven. But there was no Jake. Her shoulders slumped. She had been so excited to see him and so sure he would be here to greet her. Maybe Jake hadn't missed her as much as she missed him.

But when she looked again, Jake stood next to Sam with his hat pushed back on his head. He was here. She smiled, relieved and excited. The thought of him had her heart racing and goosebumps zinging up and down her spine.

Gertie was looking out one of the other windows. "I see your Jake and Sam. They would be hard to miss in any crowd. Both are handsome enough to make a girl's knees weak."

Taking a deep breath, Gertie gently hugged Winnie, afraid of wrinkling her dress. "This is where we part company, my friend. This is your day." She furtively brushed away a tear.

"Ooooh, Gertie. We promised no tears. I wish you could stay for the party?" Winnie said, wrapping Gertie in her arms.

"I have connections to make and tickets to Denmark, but I promise I'll write. Thank your father for letting me travel back to New York in his private car. Remember, don't take any deep breaths, and stay calm." She hugged Winnie and stepped back, her gray eyes misty."

The porter came to open the door, and they hugged one last time. "Now, go and knock them off their feet." Gertie turned to the window and watched Winnie step onto the platform, her natural beauty and grace casual and effortless. Gertie held no envy in her heart, but she couldn't help but wonder how one person could be blessed with so much.

Winnie paused, remembering how a lady was supposed to hold herself, and then she walked out to meet her family and friends. She was a vision, but it lasted for only the blink of an eye. The facade of being a lady crumbled when she saw her dad and Lorene. She ran to them with hugs, kisses, and joyful tears, blurring her vision.

Grant wrapped her in his arms. "I missed you, Winnie," he said, his eyes bright with tears. Embarrassed by the tears, he said, "Go greet your friends while Lorene and I take care of getting your trunks and luggage sorted out. We'll talk later. We'll have lots of time. Welcome home, sweet pea."

Before Winnie could hug Lorene, Mary came running up and wrapped her in a hug. Winnie looked at her wide-eyed, feeling the bump between them, which was definitely another baby. "Again?" Winnie asked.

"Yes, and we are so happy. John said to tell you he would see you later at the party. I love your hat, and I'm so thrilled you're back. You look magnificent, Winnie. I haven't had anyone to talk to in ages, and your dress is beautiful. Such a striking green. I swear it will take us months to catch up on everything. It matches your eyes. I have to run. Mom said she could only watch the kids for a few minutes. John and I will see you later."

Winnie turned toward Lorene, but Kat snagged her and pulled her into a hug. She took Winnie's hands in hers and leaned back, critically eyeing her. "Gorgeous, simply gorgeous. Where did you get that dress and the hat? Stunning." She pulled Winnie into another hug. "I'm glad you came home to us. Winnie. I was afraid some prince would steal your heart, and we'd never see you again. See you at the party." And she was off in a flurry of satin and petticoats.

Steven rushed up as Kat whirled away. "You are a vision, Miss Winnie. I don't think I have ever seen anyone more beautiful, and I know you made your daddy proud today. Me and Charlie drew straws to see who stayed to watch the store…he lost…but we'll both be at the party."

"Thank you, Steven. I missed you, too."

Pete and Chris greeted her with awkward but exuberant hugs and then headed for The Carmichael to help Lars and Sally finish setting up for the party. There were last-minute details that needed to be finalized.

"I don't feel much like partying," Pete said as they headed toward the Carmichael, "but I'd do anything for Miss Winnie."

Pete had invited Belle to the party, but she had refused him, saying she had the night off but had other plans. "I thought Belle cared for me, Chris. But I was just another cowboy buying her drinks and dances." His voice broke. "I was just a dollar sign."

"Good thing you found out before you got wrapped up any deeper," Chris replied. "Look on the bright side, you'll be able to drown your sorrow with free whiskey tonight."

Sam and Jake had stayed in the background while Winnie was greeted by her other friends, but now they approached her smiling. Winnie wanted to take a deep breath to calm her racing heart, but the corset digging into her body objected, and she thought she might swoon right at their feet.

"I missed you guys," she said as Sam picked her up and spun her around. When he sat her down, she stood on tiptoes to plant a quick kiss on his cheek. "Good Lord, Sam. Are you still growing?"

Sam laughed. "Good Lord, I hope not."

She turned to Jake and gave him a lingering hug and a quick, awkward kiss on the cheek. "I missed you, Jake." Surprised at the breathy sound of her voice, a blush crept up her neck.

He took her hands in his and said quietly and just to her, "You are a vision, Winnie. You looked so beautiful standing there on the platform. You took my breath away."

She was surprised and overwhelmed by the range of emotions surging through her at the sound of his voice and his gentle touch.

He released her hands and moved back a step, speaking in a normal voice. "Sam and I have some business to take care of, but we'll be at your party. You know us growing boys," he said, looking at Sam, "we don't miss a meal. Save me a couple of dances."

Seeing her friends had caused a chaotic whirlwind of emotion, and several times, she had to stop herself from crying with joy, but now she wanted to spend time with her dad and Lorene.

She finally got to hug Lorene.

Winnie walked between her father and Lorene, holding their hands, as they headed for the hotel. "We'll have plenty of time to talk before people start showing up," Grant said.

"The welcome sign on the front of the depot is so huge it took my breath away. I didn't expect so much to do about me coming home."

Grant chuckled. "Wait till you see the hotel."

Clark appeared with a buckboard and pulled up in front of them. Grant pointed to the trunks on the depot platform that were to be taken back to the ranch house and put in Winnie's room.

Winnie greeted Clark and asked if he would please drop off the green humpback trunk at Mary Miller's house.

"Welcome home. Of course, Miss Winnie. Be glad to." Winnie smiled at the old-timer she had known all her life and thanked him. Clark clucked to his mule and flipped the reins on her back. "Hy-yah, Beulah. That mostly looked like Miss Winnie but didn't sound like her one bit. Please, Clark. Thank you, Clark?" He shook his head, spit tobacco juice over the side of the buckboard, and wiped his mouth on his shirt sleeve. "Whatcha think, Beulah? Yeah, I agree, didn't sound like her at all."

# CHAPTER 25

# FRIENDS HELP FRIENDS

At the café door, a smaller "Welcome Home" sign greeted Winnie, and inside, colorful pennants hung from the beams amid streamers and balloons. Another brightly colored welcome banner hung over a row of tapped beer barrels and whiskey kegs. A waiter was busily twisting beer mugs into a large tub of ice.

Grant took Winnie's hand and led her into the hotel lobby. Three clowns lounged on the sofa, one with his oversized red shoes resting on a hassock. The wide toes pointed to the ceiling. A juggler dressed in a jester's costume nonchalantly tossed three apples into the air, easily catching them. He tossed one over his shoulder and caught it behind his back without a miss. A small, round, mustached man sat in an over-stuffed chair with an accordion on his knees and a monkey perched on his shoulder, its tail wrapped around the man's neck.

Winnie looked at her father, her eyes bright with questions.

"It's entertainment for the kids," Grant said with a big smile. "The monkey does all kinds of tricks. They'll love it. Did you see the Castellet in the corner?"

"No," Winnie said, turning to where her father pointed.

At that moment, a puppet popped up. "Welcome home, Winnifred Grant. Ain't you one fine-looking piece of calico," the marionette shrilled. Then, he lowered his voice, "Wanna meet me later…in my room?"

"Thank you, but no," Winnie said politely.

"Damn," the puppet said, pounding his head noisily on the miniature stage.

Winnie looked at her father with a grin. "Where's the elephant?"

Lorene laughed, "Don't give him any ideas, Winnie. He thinks up enough on his own."

"Let's find a table out of the way where we can talk," Grant said, leading the way toward the back of the café.

Luscious aromas coming from the kitchen reminded Winnie that she hadn't eaten since breakfast, and she was starving. She sat back with a deep sigh and looked about the brightly decorated room. "I can't believe all the trouble you've gone to," Winnie said, smiling at her father with loving eyes. "I never expected such a homecoming."

"Tell us about your trip," Lorene coaxed.

They talked for over an hour. Lorene listened intently, letting father and daughter do most of the talking. Winnie told how Aunt Gracie Louise Brown had hurried them from the coast and across England to a hunting lodge that had been in her husband's family for generations. "It was humongous, cold, and beautiful, but not as beautiful as our ranch," Winnie said.

"When we arrived at the lodge, we barely had time to get changed from our traveling clothes before guests started arriving for a clay pigeon shoot. I don't know why they call them pigeons. They look more like cow pies. Uncle Chester was kind enough to lend me a gun so I could join in the shoot. I ended up winning the match. Uncle Chester didn't say as much, but I think he regretted allowing me to participate."

Grant laughed, "I know he regretted it. He told me so in a wire he sent. He said you carried yourself well and made them proud. Except for outshooting the entire gun club."

"Did he tell you they tried to even the score by giving me a brute of a horse to ride in the fox hunt? That beast was a handful, but we came to an understanding. Boy, could he jump." Winnie grinned, "The clothes were outlandish…not the least bit practical for a hunt, and that little saddle was quite uncomfortable. Best part of the day was that the fox got away."

"Did you go to any dances?" Lorene asked. "Did you meet the queen?"

"I didn't see the queen, but I went to lots of dances and social events. I danced with a prince and all kinds of young men proudly sporting titles. Some seemed to think their titles gave them permission to act inappropriately. I had to give a couple of those soft lordlings a sharp lesson in Dakota manners." Winnie unpinned her hat and tossed it on top of the upright piano in the corner. "Before I forget, Aunt Gracie told me to be sure and remind you that you are nothing but a regular old peon."

Grant laughed. "I don't know how she ever got that count to marry her, but I couldn't be happier for her. I miss both my sisters. Too bad they settled down so far away."

"I think Aunt Rita and Uncle Phillip had fun escorting me to countries outside Great Britain. We traveled by boat, by train, and in fancy carriages with coachmen in matching uniforms hanging from the back. I can't imagine who built the gigantic cathedrals we saw or how they managed it. And the ruins in Italy were amazing. I even learned a few new words." She smiled at her dad. "Thank you, Dad. It was quite an experience."

Grant took Winnie's hand with a gentle squeeze. "It was thoughtful of you to make sure Gertie got to Denmark to visit her family. She was reunited with her parents and her boyfriend, and now she's returning home to marry and build a new life. You did a kind thing."

"I'm going to miss her," Winnie said. "She asked me to thank you for the use of your private car. I should say thank you, as well. It made the trip home tolerable."

The guests would be arriving soon, and the waitstaff was bringing out the food. Tables set up just outside the kitchen door were laden with platters piled high with steaks, pork chops, roast beef, fried chicken, and catfish. There were giant bowls of mashed potatoes, candied carrots, and sweet potatoes, along with potato salad and fried apples. A dozen gravy boats were scattered about, along with platters of grilled onions and slices of freshly baked bread. A dessert table was loaded with pies, cookies, sticky rolls, and sweets of all kinds. Canisters of ice cream, freshly churned, sat ready in ice-filled tubs.

The aromas were enticing and reminded Winnie of her hunger. "I think I'll run up to my room and change right quick before people begin arriving." She leaned close to Lorene's ear with a giggle. "I'm starving, but with this corset digging into me, I doubt I could eat a thing. I can barely breathe."

As Winnie started toward the front desk to get her key, Mary flew into the room, blue satin and lace whispering around her. She pulled Winnie toward a table and collapsed into a chair. Winnie sat down next to her. "I missed your drama and enthusiasm," Winnie said, looking down at the bump. "I'd ask what you've been up to while I was gone, but I guess the answer is obvious. I can't believe you're having another baby. That will make six, right? You didn't sneak in another while I was gone, did you?"

"No, silly. This is number six, but you were gone long enough that I could have squeezed out another one."

Winnie blushed at her friend's casual comment and asked her about each of her children. Mary loved to talk about her family and any random thing that popped into her head. Mary was talking a mile-a-minute when the Wilkinson family came through the café door.

"Excuse me, Mary. I should greet the guests. We'll talk later."

"Miss Winnifred," eight-year-old Alice Wilkinson said, running up to her. "You look like a princess. Mama says you're stunning."

"Thank you, Alice. Let me look at you. You are beautiful and I can't believe how much you've grown."

I've missed you in Sunday School, Miss Winnifred. You were the best teacher ever. Now we've got Mrs. Kent. She's an old—"

"Alice," her father warned. "Be nice."

Winnie greeted the other four Wilkinson girls and their parents. After the Wilkinson family, there was a continuous line of friends and acquaintances coming through the door. Winnie went through the motions of greeting each of them, but her thoughts were on Jake, and her eyes searched the line for his face.

Kat came through the door in a cinnamon-colored gown that made her blonde hair glow with copper tones. She hugged Winnie and whispered in her ear, "I hope no one is offended by my presence."

"I don't care if they are," Winnie said with a silly smile.

"Good, then I'll stay long enough to eat and annoy the good Christian women of Grant's Crossing."

Steven and Charlie were right behind Kat and, after paying their respects to Winnie, hurried to join Kat. Pete and Chris, along with at least two dozen cowhands from the Circle G, jostled through the door, ready to party. "You boys clean up good," Winnie said, surrounded by their jubilant greetings. These men were the core that kept the ranch going, and she knew each of them by name. Whooping and hollering, they headed for the kegs. Things were about to get noisy.

Grant introduced Pastor Emil Larsen and asked him to bless the celebration and the food. Everyone turned toward the pastor and bowed their heads as his voice boomed above the growing din. Pastor Emil kept it short and sweet, something no one would have expected, and his amen was greeted with cheers and hoots.

Grant turned, motioning to the musicians. He was about to introduce them when squeals of joy, cheering, and uncontrolled giggling turned everyone's attention to the hotel lobby, where the children were being entertained.

"What's his name?"

"Millie."

"That's a stupid name for a boy."

"It's short for Milford."

"Can I pet him?"

"No."

"Please."

"No, he's very high-strung."

"He looks soft."

"I said, no petting."

"But he's so cute."

"No. Stop. Don't do that."

The monkey shrieked, and the children laughed as Millie ran from the lobby into the party. The children scrambled to the lobby door and watched the small agile simian leap onto one of the tables.

Chittering, Millie ran the length of the table, leaving a path of destruction behind him. Women screamed, and men jumped back, chair legs scraping the floor as they tried to escape. Glasses were knocked over, spilling their contents, and mischievous little hands sent silver-ware and China tumbling to the floor.

"He won't hurt you. Don't shoot him. He's just scared. He won't hurt you," Millie's owner shouted, chasing after him.

Ross Meadows, the owner of the saddlery shop, and Vance Ramsey, Grant's attorney, stood just inside the doorway watching the chaos unfold. After ransacking two tables, the monkey dashed toward the food table. Lars and his waitstaff grabbed chairs, holding them clumsily in front of them, prepared to bravely fend off the wild creature. But Millie stopped short of the goal and instead leaped onto the upright piano. He snatched Winnie's hat and, with both hands, held it on top of his head. He stretched his small body to its full height and beamed at the crowd, smiling, proud of his prize. He bowed and scampered back toward the lobby with his owner still two steps behind him.

"Sorry about that, folks," Grant said. "We'll have things cleaned up in no time. There's plenty of food and drinks, so help yourself and enjoy the lively music of these wonderful musicians. Please welcome the Kansas City Brass."

With the monkey under control and the waitstaff rapidly cleaning up the results of his high jinks, the crowd was returning to their seats. The talk was all about Millie and his antics but soon turned to other things. Winnie could hear bits and pieces of their conversations.

"Goodness, Ralph, you screamed like a six-year-old." "Did not."

"I've never seen the like." Leave it up to Mr. Grant to make things memorable."

"You screamed like a sissy boy, Dominic." "I did no such thing.

"I'm still hungry." "How much do you think that hat cost?"

"When is the dance supposed to start?" "Wonder what it cost to ship in those musicians."

"That monkey was a cute little critter." "I hope the children are safe."

"Have you seen Earl?" "I need more beer."

"Wonder how much that green dress set her back." "Can you believe the nerve of that Kat Masters showing her face among respectable people?"

"There's ice cream." "Where's the whiskey?"

Winnie toned it all out. Gus and Sylvia Weisenberger, four of their children, and a dozen men who rode for the Lazy W were next through the door. She greeted Bart and Klaus by name and asked Sylvia Weisenberger if their oldest son, Matt, would be coming later.

"Matt said to tell you he's sorry to miss your party. He wanted to see you, but one of his prize breeding mares is about to foal."

"Tell him I missed him," Winnie said with a wistful smile.

Carl Faversham, owner of the butcher shop, shook his head as he took her hand in his. "Miss Grant, if you ain't the prettiest woman in all of the territory, God's a possum."

Winnie thanked him and watched with a smile as he hurried to the food tables. When she turned around, Jake was standing there in front of her, smiling. His blue eyes were filled with a heat that warmed her to the core. He saw her reaction, and his smile widened. "Welcome home, Winnie."

Sam and John Miller were right behind Jake. "Come on, Jake," Sam said with a chuckle. "You're holding up the line. The mayor and the town council are behind us.

"Good to have you back, Winnie," Sam said, pushing Jake out of the way. "We'll find a table and save you a place."

When no one remained in line, Winnie finally turned away from the door and looked around the crowded, noisy room. The rumbling hum of dozens of conversations nearly drowned out the raucous hoots and laughter from the back of the room, where the bar was located. She was overwhelmed by the number of people who had turned out to welcome her home. But she knew it wasn't all about her. It had a lot to do with Grant's reputation for throwing the best parties west of the Missouri. She looked around the sea of familiar faces and saw Jake and Sam sitting at a table with John, Mary, Mr. Terrance, Coop, and Jenny.

She hurried over and slid into a chair across from Jake and Sam. Coop was discretely holding Jenny's hand under the table, and Mr. Terrance was returning to the table with a cold, sweaty beer mug grasped between both hands. "You missed the entertainment, Winnifred," he said, taking a sip and wiping the foam from his lips. "There was a one-man band, a vocalist from St. Louis, and a banjo player who twanged the heck out of that...he slurped a sip of beer...banjo. And, of course, there was that wee simian who had everyone ready to flee." Mr. Terrance smiled and chugged down half the beer.

Winnie smiled at her ex-teacher. He was tipsy, and that was something she never thought she'd see. The others had finished eating, and she'd forgotten about being hungry. They asked her about her trip, and she told them some funny stories she thought they might enjoy. She was intently aware of Jake and Sam watching her as she spoke. It was disturbing, and she was becoming uncomfortably warm. She looked between the two men and wondered which of them made her heart beat so erratically. She was sure it was Jake, but Sam was an exceptionally fine-looking man.

As usual, their conversation turned to bygone school days. The stories had been told countless times, but they still laughed and groaned. They particularly enjoyed teasing Sam for  having been such a bully and Jake for his incredible speed, especially when Sam was chasing him.

"I can still outrun any one of you," Jake said with a scowl.

Sam stood and excused himself. "I need to get going. Welcome home, Winnie. You were missed. Goodnight all. As always, it's been a pleasure hearing about my ill-spent youth." He doffed his hat and headed out the door.

"Sam. Wait," Winnie said, jumping up and following him outside.

He turned as he reached the boardwalk, watching her descend the stairs. She stopped and stood on the bottom step directly in front of him, still not at eye level, but closer than usual.

"What is it, Winnie?"

"I thought you'd stay for the dance. I saved one for you." Winnie smiled up at him.

"Well, I'm not much of a dancer, so your toes should be thankful. Besides, I saw all three Weisenberger girls looking at me like I was a hunk of chocolate cake." He looked down at Winnie with a chuckle. "I figured I was safe until they started putting the food away, but after that—"

Winnie laughed and looked into Sam's eyes. *Such beautiful brown eyes*, she thought, jealous of his long lashes. "Sam, I missed you so much."

"I missed you too. Life was pretty dull around here without you."

"Sam, I want to ask you something."

"Sure, what is it?"

Winnie hesitated momentarily, then reached up, put her arms around Sam's neck, and pulled his face close to hers. "This," she said, placing her lips on his in a tentative and clumsy kiss. Sam was surprised but grabbed her around the waist and, breaking off the kiss, whisked her into the shadows at the side of the porch.

"Winnie, what the heck?" he asked, setting her down gently.

"I wanted to know what kissing you would be like. I've not been kissed before, not a real kiss anyway."

"Never? Not even by a handsome prince?"

"One tried but didn't like the results."

"I thought maybe Matt had stolen a kiss or two."

"No."

"And?" Sam couldn't help but smile at her.

"What? Oh," Winnie grimaced. "Well, I expected something more. It wasn't much of a kiss, and frankly, I'm disappointed."

Sam laughed. "I agree with you, but you kissed me. Would you like me to kiss you?"

Winnie frowned, doubtful but curious. "There's a difference?"

"Oh, yes," he said, running his hands down her back and pulling her against him. The heat of his body pressed against hers, and his warm, firm lips brushing over hers made her tingle. He kissed her thoroughly but gently. He could feel the shiver run through her body, and her arms tightened around his neck, and he broke off the kiss.

Leaning back slightly, he smirked, "Better?"

"Oh my, yes," Winnie gasped, looking at him intently. "Were there fireworks?"

"Fireworks?"

"Yeah. You know. Fireworks. Bright lights, explosions. Bang, bang."

"Winnie, what is this all about? I sure didn't mind kissing you, but spill it. What's going on?"

"Well, crossing the ocean takes an awfully long time." Winnie hesitated. "And when I complained about not having brought enough books with me, one of the passengers gave me some of his books to read, and as it turned out, one of them was…um…extremely educational."

"Educational?"

She looked up at him sheepishly. "All right, they were naughty and unbelievably specific and detailed about…a man and a woman."

Sam laughed a rumble of a laugh and pulled Winnie into his arms, giving her a bear hug. "Yep, it was boring around here without you."

"Sam, you rotten egg, don't you dare laugh at me," she said, trying to hide a smile.

He looked down into her face in all seriousness and gave her a long, lingering kiss…one he enjoyed way too much. He released her with a sigh. "You have become a beautiful woman, Winnie, and I imagine you could get almost any man all stirred up and feeling frisky, but we're friends. It wouldn't work for us any other way."

Winnie contemplated his words. "You're right, and you always seem to know what to say. I'm glad we're friends, and I'm glad you were my first real kiss. It was…quite splendid."

Sam still had trouble believing she'd never been kissed. Maybe he and Jake had been too protective of her. Over the years, they had chased off an army of young men hanging around too close. Matt Weisenberger had been the worst of the bunch. He never wanted to give up.

Sam put his arm around Winnie's shoulder. "We had better get you back to your party. How was it that man gave you such a book?"

"He gave me a stack of books, and it was sandwiched between two of them."

"Well, however, you came by it, if you want to try something out or practice, give me a holler. I would be more than glad to help you." Winnie punched his arm playfully and rolled her eyes.

Sam continued unabashed. "Friends help each other whenever possible, no matter how horrible the task." She punched him again, harder this time, but he only chuckled.

"You, Jake, and I have a special friendship. We grew up together. All for one and one for all? Like the musketeers?"

Winnie smiled at the reference, remembering when she was young and Jake was always sad. They sat under the trailing willow fronds by the creek, and Sam read to them. She could almost feel the breeze on her face and hear the gurgling of the water meandering past them. The story of the valiant musketeers had enthralled them completely, and they decided they would be the three musketeers and blood brothers…a pact they swore to.

"You only included me because you needed someone to be the third musketeer," Winnie chided with a pout spoiled by a giggle.

"True, but you were always underfoot anyway, so it didn't make much difference." Sam laughingly dodged another punch as Winnie chased him out from the shadows and directly into the path of Pastor Emil, nearly knocking him off his feet.

Sam and Winnie stood before the pastor like errant children, struggling to control their laughter. To Pastor Emil, they seemed guilty… of something. A severe, judgmental glare blazed from under his bushy black eyebrows as he took in their disheveled appearance.

Sam spoke, trying to break the stare, "Are you all right, Pastor."

"You should both come to church on Sunday and ask the Lord if you are all right in His eyes," Pastor Emil's voice thundered. Then, before walking off, he said in a less judgmental, more scolding tone. "The party is inside, and that is where you should be."

Sam and Winnie ran up the steps to the hotel's front door, holding hands and laughing. Sam kissed her gently on the lips. "I do have to go. I have rounds to make and some reports I need to finish for tomorrow's mail. I work so that Jake may play. Give him my dance."

He started down the steps, then turned back with a waggish smile. "Glad I could help with the kiss, and remember, I am always available if you want to try any of the naughties in your book. I will gladly volunteer."

"I wish I had something to throw at you," she yelled at his back.

## CHAPTER 26

# AIN'T A PARTY WITHOUT A FIGHT

The sound of the musicians warming up was joined by the racket of tables and chairs being shoved across the wood floor as Sam walked away. He was glad Winnie was back. If Jake was the one she wanted, he was a lucky man.

Winnie caught her breath and returned to the party, thinking she had to get out of the corset. She had intended to excuse herself and go to her room to change, but the dance was already in full swing. And when she approached the table where Jake was seated, he rose and took her hand, leading her to the crowded dance floor. She would have sworn her heart skipped a beat at his touch.

Jake took Winnie in his arms, having trouble maintaining control and keeping her at arm's length. All his senses were heightened and intense as he pulled her close. Closer than he should have, but every ounce of his flesh and every nerve in his body wanted to feel her against him. He tried to concentrate on other things with little success.

John and Mary were dancing nearby, watching them. "Do I need to get the hook and ladder to put out the fire?" John laughed as they danced closer.

Pete and Chris were drinking and laughing with a couple of Gus's Lazy W ranch hands. They had known each other for years and developed a friendship. They were telling stories and lies and taking full advantage of the free beer and whiskey.

Klaus Redding was whispering about the girls at the Stable Saloon and how cooperative they were no matter what you asked them to do. Bart Story, Klaus's partner, scolded him for not being able to keep his horn in check. "You're always on the prowl for a willing partner to take you in." They all chuckled at Bart's innuendo and laughingly extolled and exaggerated Klaus's lustful desires and exploits.

"Well, a man has gotta be a man sometimes, that's all I can say, and the women at the Stable are more than willing to let ya."

"But you have to pay for their services," Pete slurred.

"At least I'm getting more for my money than you do. Over at Kat's, you buy Belle drinks and pay for dances, and for what? Maybe you can steal a kiss or nuzzle her ear. But when she's working at the Stable…Klaus leaned across the table to emphasize his point…she'll do anything."

Pete reared up. "You take it back, Klaus. That's a lie. Belle wouldn't work at the Stable."

"Well, Pete, let's take a stroll down there right now. She's working tonight. I could treat you to an hour with her. Or better yet, we could share her. As I said, she'll do *anything*."

Pete lunged across the table at him. "You filthy liar." The table collapsed, with bottles, glasses, and plates clattering to the floor along with Klaus and Pete.

Bart grabbed the half-full bottle of whiskey just before the table collapsed.

"Good reflexes, Bart," Chris said with a nod.

Bart handed Chris the bottle, and they stood back, watching their friends settle their differences.

"What's wrong with Pete anyway?" Bart reached for the bottle and tipped it back, taking a long draw. "If she's working the sheets down at the Stable, she's nothing but a cheap whore, not worth his time."

"What do you mean, what's wrong with Pete? There ain't nothin' wrong with Pete."

Bart was holding the bottle while poking Chris with his forefinger. "Well, I would say he is stinkin' stupid not to see how Belle is, and that's for true."

"Pete ain't stupid," Chris said, sucker-punching Bart in the gut and grabbing the whiskey bottle out of his hand as Bart crumpled to the floor. "My partner is not stupid. You crooked-eared jackass." Chris took a long pull on the bottle and turned to see the rest of the LazyW ranch hands closing in on him.

"Oh, shit," Chris said, dropping the bottle.

Jake had been watching from the dance floor, hoping the dispute would be settled without his interference. However, it was about to become a full-blown brawl, and he needed to stop it before any more of Grant's men joined in.

"Excuse me, Winnie. I need to go to work for a few minutes. You men break it up," he hollered.

Chris was about to swing at one of the cowboys closing in on him when Jake's voice rang out. He dropped his fists to his sides, but the cowboys headed in his direction did not stop. One landed a punch to Chris's midsection, sending him sprawling on the top of the collapsed table alongside Pete, Klaus, and Bart.

Jake pushed his way through the drunken melee. "Break it up, break it up, or I'll put all of you in jail." The word jail was the magic word, and the group quieted. He elbowed his way into the middle of the chaos, where there was still some shoving and grumbling. "I said to break it up. The fight's over. Go back to your tables and mind your manners, or get out."

Chris was on top of the pile, and Jake pulled him to his feet. "Who started this?"

Chris nodded at Pete and Klaus and helped Jake get them to their feet.

"I don't know what went on between you, and I don't care, but it's done. Shake hands."

When they hesitated, Jake added. "Make nice, or you'll both go to jail for a week."

"A week?" they slurred simultaneously and clumsily shook hands. "Come on, Klaus, let's get us a drink, but don't talk bad about Belle no more."

"I'm sorry 'bout what I said. Hey, that was some fight. Too bad Bart and Chris missed it."

Bart and Chris watched them walk to the bar arm in arm, helping to hold each other up.

Bart was rubbing his gut. "You know I owe you one, right?"

"Yeah, I know," Chris said, heading for the bar. "Come on, let's join them."

Walking back to his dance partner, Jake ran his hand through his hair, pushing it back from his forehead. "Sorry," he said with a soft smile that warmed Winnie's heart and melted every bone in her body.

## CHAPTER 27

# I CAN'T BREATHE

The party was back in full swing, and after a few dances, Winnie was feeling warm and faint. Between the fight, the dancing, the closeness of Jake, and the corset digging into her midsection, she was breathless and lightheaded. She doubted she could make it up the stairs to her room to change. "Jake, can we step outside for some air?"

"Sure, you look awfully pale." Jake wrapped one arm around Winnie, and held the other hand firmly as they exited the doors into the starlit night.

"That's better," Winnie said as she held back her head, stretching and carefully breathing in the cool evening air.

Jake leaned against the porch railing. "I told myself I wasn't going to ask. I mean, well, it isn't any of my business, but what was the thing with Sam earlier?"

"I wanted to kiss him."

"You wanted to kiss him?"

"Yes."

"That's all, just yes."

"Yes, that's all. I wanted to kiss him."

Jake looked at her with a frown, then pulled her into his arms and kissed her. It was soft and gentle but flared into a passionate, demanding kiss, leaving no doubt what was on Jake's mind. Both were lost in the moment, not wanting it to end and wanting more.

Winnie roughly shoved him away, frantically gasping for air. Jake was startled by her reaction and started to apologize. "I'm sorry. I…I shouldn't have grabbed you. Winnie, I'm so sorry, it wasn't right. Can you forgive me?"

Winnie was still struggling for air. "Shut up, Jake. My corset is too tight. I can't breathe."

She thought she might faint, but after a few deep breaths, she could stand upright. "I have to get out of this thing," she gasped. "I can't breathe."

Jake stared at her in utter confusion and then burst into laughter. "And here I thought I had taken your breath away."

"Oh, you did. Don't you dare go anywhere. I'll be right back."

Winnie stopped at the front desk to get the key to her room and waved to Mary. Mary trudged as quickly as she could up the stairs behind her. She helped Winnie out of her dress and unlaced the corset from hell.

Winnie sighed with relief as she peeled it from her body and threw it on the bed. Rubbing the deep gouges at her waist and around her ribs, she looked at the lacy white garment. "It looks innocent lying there on the bed, nothing like the implement of torture it is. It should be hanging in the dungeon of some castle."

Mary found a simple, but elegant dress, one fancy enough for a dance but comfortable enough to allow Winnie to breathe. Winnie hurriedly pulled it over her head and wiggled into it. "Jake's waiting for me on the porch, or at least I hope he is." She rushed down the stairs with Mary lumbering close behind.

While Winnie was upstairs changing, Sally had managed to slip onto the porch, where Winnie found her making a move on Jake. Sally was Lars' wife and the biggest flirt in town. No man who booked a room at the hotel was safe from her advances. Being married didn't stop her from shopping around, and her husband couldn't control her.

Sally had Jake pushed up against the railing, leaning into him with her hands on his chest. Winnie came up beside her. "Excuse me, but I believe your husband is calling for you."

Sally turned to Jake with a sultry promise. "See you later, Marshal."

Winnie stared after her with eyes that could scorch, and then she said to Jake, "Hope I didn't interrupt anything."

"You know Sally. She's always on the prowl. I managed to avoid her until now, but I was out here, waiting for you, and she cornered me." He smiled at her, his blue eyes twinkling. "Can you breathe now?"

"Yes, I can breathe now, and I'm glad you waited for me."

"Of course I waited for you," Jake said softly, taking her hand and pulling her close. He put his arm around her shoulders, and they stood together quietly.

Winnie spoke softly. "Jake?"

"Hmmm."

"I kissed Sam because I wanted to know what it would feel like, and I wanted to know if I had any feelings for him." She paused and moved closer to Jake. "I love Sam, but as a friend and nothing more."

"And?"

"He does have sweet kisses," she teased.

Jake turned to face her with a questioning look. "And?"

Winnie looked up at him. "Oh, you mean your kiss? Well, I'm not sure. It got interrupted. Perhaps we should try again."

He had intended the kiss to be light and gentle. But his emotions were raw, and his newfound passion for her ran too close to the surface.

The kiss, like the last one, wanted, needed, and demanded. Winnie's lips were soft and yielding, and he pulled her close. He was rapidly losing control and pulled away. Touching his forehead to hers, he motioned to a window behind them where he could make out Mary's smiling face. "I hope no one else bought a ticket to the show."

"I don't care," Winnie said breathlessly, stretching up to touch her lips to his.

"I can't," he whispered in her ear. "I can't. Besides, this isn't the time or the place for this. Later, Winnie, we'll have plenty of time, but right now, I have to leave. I'm meeting Sam. I'll see you tomorrow."

Jake hurried down the stairs, knowing he had to put some distance between them. He turned, walking backward, and waved to her. "Tomorrow, Winnie, I'll see you tomorrow."

"I hope you and Sam have a delightful evening together," she shouted, glowering at him as he turned his back and trotted down the street.

She looked after him, weak-kneed, tingling all over, and confused. Why was he walking away from her?

Mary burst out onto the porch. "Dang, but you got Jake all fired up."

"Not enough to keep him here," Winnie huffed.

Mary snorted. "Winnie, he was too fired up to stay."

## CHAPTER 28

# THE FUTURE MRS. SUMNER

"Good evening, Miss Grant, Mrs. Miller," Quinn Sumner said, coming regally up the porch steps, nodding politely to each woman. "I know I'm late, Winnifred, but I wanted to welcome you home."

"Thank you for coming, Councilman Sumner. There's still food left inside and plenty to drink."

"I would be most honored if you would save me a dance, Miss Grant, and please, call me Quinn."

With Jake leaving, her dance card was empty. "I'd be glad to dance with you, Quinn, and please, it's Winnie." She smiled and let him escort her inside and onto the dance floor.

Quinn was an exceptional dancer. He had a light touch and a gentle way of leading. He was in charge of the moves, but they were partners. She had learned the proper way to waltz while in Europe and now had a chance to show off her skills with Quinn. They were so graceful together everyone cleared the dance floor to watch.

Several dances later, laughing and winded, he asked if she would like to take some air. "We could step out on the front porch for a few moments if you'd like." His offer seemed gracious and lacking in guile.

The evening had cooled off, and he put his arm innocently around her shoulders in a protective manner. "Tell me about your travels. What was your favorite site? Is it true you can't tell where the water ends and the sky begins when you're at sea?"

They talked for some time, standing there on the porch. People entered and left the party, all stopping to chat with her.

Winnie thought it odd that she was so comfortable with this man and even attracted to him. She hardly knew him, and he was so much older…old enough to be her father. Yet she found him strangely irresistible. He was charming and an old-fashioned sort of gentleman.

She took hold of Quinn's hand and gracefully spun away from the arm around her shoulder. "I need to get back inside. I enjoyed dancing with you, and perhaps we will dance together again sometime."

"I would like that," he said, sure they would dance together many times, including at their wedding. He would be kind and gentle with her, and she would see how much he loved her. If she didn't love him now, she would learn to love him in time. How could she not? He would convince her.

Before they entered the hotel, Quinn impulsively pulled her into his arms for the briefest kiss. "I'm sorry, Winnie, that was terribly forward of me, but I've wanted to do that all evening. I simply couldn't resist any longer."

Winnie looked at him wide-eyed. "That was entirely out of line, Doctor Sumner." She was about to stomp away, but then, surprising herself and him, she leaned in for another kiss. It was a pleasant kiss, and it made her blood race.

He had a powerful gentleness about him that mesmerized her. His arms encircled her. He didn't hold her tight as Sam and Jake had. She could pull away if she wanted to, but she didn't want to. She wanted the kiss to linger, and she pressed against him.

Sumner pulled away with a smile, and they stood looking at each other. Winnie pulled her hands away from his, wondering what had happened. Sumner was about to kiss her again but was interrupted by several of Grant's cowhands charging out the door. Seeing Winnie, they stopped to welcome her home.

"Winnie," Quinn said softly when they were alone again, "I know I'm older than you, but I want to call on you. I want to get to know you. We have a strong connection. I know you felt it, too." He pulled her into his arms and kissed her again with a passion that surprised Winnie. It surprised her even more that she didn't want to pull away. She should, but she didn't want to.

"Quinn," she sighed breathlessly, finally pushing away. "I don't know what to say. I can't lie, I feel a strong attraction to you, but we can never be a couple."

"No hope, even after that kiss?"

Winnie smiled. "Even after that kiss. It was nice, but I have deep feelings for someone else."

"Then I shall joust for m'lady's hand," he said with a deep, sweeping bow.

She laughed at his chivalry, and he was sure he saw wavering doubt on her face. "Tell you what, how about we meet for lunch and talk? You'll feel more comfortable once we get to know each other. I promise you will find me irresistible, and I will have the privilege of being seen escorting the most beautiful woman in town. Maybe I can change your mind about you and the old guy being a couple. I'm wealthy, Winnie. You could have anything you want, anything."

"Your money means nothing to me, Quinn. I already have everything I could want. But we can have lunch and talk. The next time I'm in town."

Quinn left the hotel, practically dancing down the steps. He had worked up the courage to kiss her, and she had kissed him back. It was more than he had hoped for. She admitted she was attracted to him and had kissed him with an innocent passion.

He loved how she danced, and his loins stirred, thinking of her kisses. He had wanted her before, but now she had lit a fire in him, and he vividly imagined what it would be like to hold her and make love to her. She had strength and grace, and their lovemaking would be a beautiful dance. She would make him an excellent wife and bear him many sons.

## CHAPTER 29

# LOOK WHO TURNED UP

Winnie went back inside to join her dad and Lorene. She wondered who the man sitting with them was, with his back toward her. When he turned, she was delighted to see Nate Daniels smiling up at her.

He rose from the table. "Winnifred. You look more beautiful than ever. Grant, would you mind if I asked your daughter to dance?"

Grant shook his head.

"Miss Winnifred, it would be my honor?" His voice retained a bit of a southern drawl even though he had been in the territory for many years. It was a warm, pleasant voice.

She accepted his outstretched hand with a smile and an almost imperceptible curtsy. He led her onto the dance floor and swept her into his arms.

They chatted about her trip and his farm as they twirled around the dance floor. He was an excellent dancer, and the evening went by quickly.

Nate had lost his wife and daughter during the war. He came home to find them buried in the orchard. No one knew how or when. It just was. He had told her a long time ago his daughter would be about her age if she had lived, and the look on his face had broken her heart.

She wondered why he hadn't remarried. He was handsome, charming, and doing well, but he stayed to himself most of the time. She figured her dad knew him as well as anyone.

When the last dance was announced, she excused herself. "Nate, the last dance is for Dad." With a slight bow, he watched her walk into her father's arms and return to the dance floor.

She had become an exquisite woman, and he couldn't help but wonder what his daughter would have been like if she were alive. He shook it off and asked Lorene to join him for the final dance of the evening.

## CHAPTER 30

# I HAVE AN IDEA

Winnie wanted to stay up and talk with her father and Lorene, but exhaustion slammed into her like a locomotive. It was late, and Winnie watched the last few stragglers stumble through the doorway. She hugged her father and Lorene. "Thank you for this grand party. I am so glad to be home. I'll see you in the morning, but not too early," she said with a tired smile.

Most of the folks were heading home or taking the hotel stairs to their rooms, but some men would be heading off to Kat's or one of the other saloons in town to extend the celebration.

Chris had enjoyed the party, drinking and dancing with all the girls, but Pete had spent most of the night sitting in the corner by himself, drinking and pouting. He'd been hurt by Belle's rejection and what Klaus had told him about her.

When he got up to leave, he told Chris in a drunken slur he was going to the Stable Saloon for a drink and to enjoy Belle for an hour or so. "She can't turn me away if I've paid for her."

Chris was beside him as he wobbled to the door. "You can find a woman there if you got the money, but this is not one of your better ideas. It would be best if you didn't go looking for Belle. It will only cause trouble."

Pete kept moving down the street, wavering from side to side. He was hell-bent on going to the Stable Saloon. Chris was trotting right behind him, trying to reason with him. He took hold of his arm, trying to pull him back, but Pete shoved him away.

Chris's words of reason were not sinking in, and as a last resort, Chris took a flying leap onto Pete's back, taking him to the ground. "There will be another girl for you, Pete. Someone who appreciates you, but at the Stable, the women are after your money, and who knows what you might catch from the bed-maggots they got working there. Besides, if you cause trouble at the Stable, you'll likely get a knife stuck between your ribs."

"Well, I can't go back to Kat's, not with everyone laughing at me, thinking I'm a fool," Pete mumbled.

Sitting in the middle of the street, Chris slung his arm around Pete's shoulders. "Listen to me, partner. No one is laughing at you. Belle is the one folks are laughing at. She turned down a kind-hearted man with a steady job. A man who would have protected and loved her for the rest of her life. You tell me, who's the fool?"

Pete was swaying back and forth, smiling lopsidedly at his friend. "I guess you're right. But," his eyes misted a little, "I thought she was the one, and it hurts my heart."

"Come on." Chris got up and held a hand out to Pete. "Let's get out of the street before we get trampled. We can stop at the Bent Ear or the Schooner for a couple of drinks. Or we can get a bottle and take it back to the hotel. We could have a nightcap on the front steps."

Pete took Chris's outstretched hand and got up, wavering slightly. "No. By jiggers, we are going to Kat's. Guess it's kind of like getting back on the horse what threw ya."

Chris was relieved his friend was coming to his senses. As they walked along to Kat's Place, he asked Pete what he thought about advertising for a wife in the Eastern papers. There weren't many available women around Grant's Crossing to choose from, and he had heard several success stories of men who had advertised. It might solve Pete's problem, and Chris didn't mind the thought of having a wife and family himself.

"I like your idea, Chris. Let's get a drink and chew on it." Pete was still stumbling over his words and wobbling back and forth, but at least he was calm and sensible. After a drink at the bar, they took a bottle back to the hotel and sat on the front steps, discussing how they should word the ads. They wanted to attract the proper type of woman.

## CHAPTER 31

# HE COULD BE DANGEROUS

As Winnie climbed the stairs to her room, she couldn't help but wonder why Quinn had affected her as he did. She vaguely remembered him as the guy who had pulled a baby tooth that refused to let go. He was older than her by twenty years, but he was attractive and successful. He was on the town council and a friend to anyone who was anyone in Grant's Crossing and across the territory. There was a raw power and determination under the gentlemanly exterior. A power that made him desirable and maybe a little dangerous.

She hoped agreeing to meet him wasn't a mistake, but she wanted to get to know him better and explore the attraction. What harm could there be in a friendly meeting?

As she got ready for bed, Winnie thought about Gertie and how much she missed having her around. She had been no more than a room away for the last twenty months, and tonight, Winnie wished she could run next door to talk to her about what had happened at her party. But Gertie was well on her way back to Denmark.

Winnie fell into bed thinking about Jake. She could still feel his lips on hers and the warmth of his hands. He was the man she loved and wanted to spend her life with him. At least, she thought she did. But if she wanted only Jake, why had she reacted to Quinn the way she did?

She fell asleep and dreamt of dancing a beautiful waltz with Quinn while Jake stood watching.

## CHAPTER 32

# THE MURDER MAP

When Sam left Winnie on the hotel's front porch, he headed straight to the office. He figured it might be a while before Jake showed up, so he decided to make the rounds without him. As he rattled doorknobs and peeked in windows, he smiled, thinking about his conversation with Winnie. Fireworks and naughty books, he thought, shaking his head.

By the time he got back to the office, Jake was coming up the street. Sam waited outside. "All is secure. Can we talk?"

"Sure, but if it's about Winnie, she told me there is nothing between you. You're just friends."

"Did she tell you everything? About her new book?"

"Yes, she did," Jake said, feeling an unexpected surge of jealousy and wondering what he meant by her new book.

"Honestly, Sam, I'd like to light into you, but I know you don't deserve it. Besides, you can still beat the crap out of me."

"Hey, take a swing if it makes you feel any better. You can still outrun me."

"I'm not mad at you, Sam. I have no claim on Winnie, but I am crazy in love with her."

"We're all right then?" Sam asked.

"Yeah, we're all right. Anyway, how could I be mad at you? I'm crazy in love with you, too," Jake gave Sam a silly grin and shoved him toward the door. "But no more kissing on my girl."

Sam shook his head with a chuckle. "You got it, Marshal Jacobs."

They walked into the marshal's office and found the retired sheriff, now Deputy Marshal Logan, waiting for them. He had been a sheriff most of his life, and most of that had been in Grant's Crossing.

It was Sheriff Logan who went to the Jacobs' home to investigate the murder of Jake's parents. Grant had warned him, but he hadn't expected anything so horrible. He had seen a lot in his time, but this sent him running to the porch to settle his gut. Ever since that night, he had helped Jake look for the monster, and when Jake was appointed Marshal, he stayed on as his deputy.

Logan hadn't married, but he occasionally enjoyed a woman's company. He stood about five-foot-five and weighed 190 pounds. Lately, he was dismayed to find his stomach inching its way over his belt and stressing all the buttons on his shirts. He blamed it on the home cooking at Murphy's Boarding House, where he lived. The boarding house was convenient for him, and the Widow Murphy was the woman whose company he occasionally enjoyed.

Sam told them what he'd found, and the three lawmen finished putting the last few pins on the map, including the dates if known. They stood back, analyzing the murder map, and saw the hint of a pattern.

Sam squinted at the map. "This indicates our killer lives in town or nearby. It isn't enough to predict where he might strike next, but it does indicate a general area. Based on this, the next killing could be east of town somewhere."

Logan was looking intently at the map. "I agree. Unless something disrupts how he chooses his targets or his murder sites?" Logan rubbed a crooked forefinger back and forth across the bottom of his chin. "I think you're right about the son-of-a-bitch living here in Grant's Crossing or nearby. Hell, we probably know him."

A knock on the door pulled their attention from the map. "What you law boys up to?" Coop asked as he entered.

"There's coffee if you're interested."

"Nah, I saw the light and stopped by to see what was going on.

There was another tap on the door, and Calvin came in carrying a package. "Sorry to intrude, but I found this on the bench outside the depot on my way home from the party. It didn't come by post, so someone must have left it there."

He handed it to Jake. It's addressed to you, Marshal." It was a wooden box wrapped with a red ribbon. Under the bow was a folded piece of stationery. *To Marshal Jacobs* was written in fancy script.

"Thanks, Cal."

"Anytime, Marshal. Goodnight, all."

"Odd it wasn't posted," Jake said, carefully removing the ribbon and unfolding the paper. He read out loud:

> *"Dear Marshal Jacobs. You can add two more to your tally. If correct, your count should now total two hundred. I've enclosed a small memento for you in honor of the occasion. The woman is so beautiful. She is my Mona Lisa. And the man, so virile, or at least he was. Too bad you can't see my artwork. Oh, that's right, you have—your parents. You'll never catch me, but please keep trying. It amuses me. Best wishes always."*

Jake's temper flared. "Two hundred!" Jake said, slamming his fist on the table, causing everyone to jump. "He's bragging about two hundred murders?"

Logan squared his shoulders. He had seen up close what the man was capable of doing. "What do you suppose he means by memento?"

"There's only one way to find out," Jake said, holding his hatred and anger in check as he flipped the latch on the box. Tension hung in the air as Sam, Logan, and Coop watched him slowly lift the lid.

"Oh, dang." They all flinched away except Coop, who calmly inspected and verified the contents. "It's a penis. And the scrotum and testes as well. It's the whole dang shootin' match."

Jake slammed the lid shut. "God almighty, I hope he was dead when this happened."

"Pretty sure he was," Coop said. "Not much blood. He was already drained, good and proper, when this happened. Before you slammed the lid, I noticed it looked like a clean cut. It wasn't jagged, but then I guess, if what he says is true, he does have some experience with a knife."

"Coop, is there anything you can tell from…this?" Jake motioned to the box.

"I doubt it, but I'd be glad to take a look and dispose of it for you."

Jake shoved the box across the desk in Coop's direction. "Thank you."

"I'll see you in the morning," Coop said, putting the box under his arm and leaving the three marshals to ponder what had just happened.

Sam broke the silence. "He's taunting you, Jake. This could be his first big mistake. He thinks he's too clever to get caught, but he's asking for attention."

Jake combed his fingers through his hair, trying to ignore the reference to his parents. "Guess this confirms our suspicion that he lives nearby."

"Wonder where we'll find the bodies, or if we ever will," Logan said thoughtfully to no one in particular.

Jake shook his head and leaned back in his chair, letting out a sharp breath. "We were thinking he'd strike east of town. Maybe he did." Jake sat forward. "It's been a long day, but let's get wires out to all the sheriffs east of town. Logan, go shake Wade out of bed, and we'll meet you at the telegraph office."

"No point, Jake," Logan said with a wide yawn. "There won't be anyone in those small-town offices till morning. Heck, even Wade won't man the key around the clock."

"You're right," Jake growled. "And we're not even sure he'll hit east of town. It's just a hunch."

Sam gave Jake a side look, one eyebrow raised. "A *hunch* hunch?"

"No, more of a guess," Jake said, his voice edged with frustration.

Sam motioned to the map. "Then let's notify all the sheriffs within a hundred-mile radius. We can get the telegram ready to send and get Wade on it first thing in the morning." Sam picked up a pad of paper and a pencil. "What do you want to say?"

"Keep it simple, Jake," Logan said, leaning back in his chair, stretching, and trying to ignore the stressed buttons of his shirt. I'd keep the details to a minimum. Don't want folks getting all riled up for nothing."

"He's never struck in a town that we know of. Only remote and isolated homesteads. It's those folks who'll be in the most danger," Jake said.

"Sadly, it'll be impossible for the sheriffs to check on everyone," Sam said, tapping his pencil on the desk.

"New Frankfort is a good piece past the hundred-mile loop, but we ought to let that sheriff know what's going on. He's a stickler for the law and has never given up on the hunt for this maniac. He'll do his darndest to make sure every one of his sheep are in the dry. How long you known that man?" Logan asked.

"Better part of five years," Jake said, looking at Sam.

"Yeah, we met him when we were following up on a rumor about a murder out his way. I was with Jake on that trip," Sam said.

"He's experienced the same troubles we've had. No one saw or heard anything unusual. He wires me every now and again, asking if we've made any headway," Jake said.

"Logan is right. We should send him a separate wire with the details. He'll be interested in the souvenir you received and what we found out from our map."

"It's kinda nice knowing someone else is looking for this madman besides me."

Logan laughed. "What are we, Jake, chopped liver?"

Jake scowled and pushed the lock of hair from his forehead. "How about this? *Check on your out-of-town and isolated folks. Stop. Make sure they are all right. Stop.*" Jake looked at Sam and Logan with a shrug. "Should I say more?"

"Well," Logan said, bringing his chair upright with a bang. "I don't think you should provide any details."

Sam agreed. "That's probably enough said. Informing them a sadistic killer may be in their area could cause a frenzy and get innocent people killed."

Let's wrap this up for tonight," Jake said. "I'm tired, and after that, I doubt I'll be able to focus on anything."

Sam and Logan nodded their agreement.

"Sam, get to the telegraph office first thing in the morning and get Wade busy sending those wires. Logan, you take the morning rounds. And we'll meet at Kat's for breakfast." Jake started for the door. "If you need me for anything, I'll be at the hotel."

Sam nodded. "I've got some paperwork to finish, and then I'll head home."

Logan looked at the map in deep thought, then turned away, shaking his head. "Goodnight, Sam. See you at breakfast." He grabbed his hat and headed for the door. "I hope one of us can dream up an answer to this nightmare."

## CHAPTER 33

# BELLE'S A WORKING GIRL

Before going to Kat's the following morning, Jake met Grant in the hotel cafe for an early coffee. "Everyone was gone by the time I got back last night. I had hoped to see Winnie, but she must have been tired after a long day of travel and the party."

"Yeah, she was. We all were. I was so proud when she stepped off the train. All I could think was, that beautiful woman is my daughter." Grant chuckled, "Had to check to make sure I hadn't popped any buttons."

"She is beautiful." Jake smiled.

"It's uncanny how much Winnie looks like her mother. I used to tell Sarah she was my breath." Jake saw the sadness dull Grant's eyes. "Loving her was the best thing that ever happened to me, and losing her was the worst. But life goes on. Even when we think it shouldn't or couldn't possibly go on, somehow…it does."

Grant let out a sigh and changed the subject. "So, how'd you sleep last night?"

"Great. Thanks for the room."

"No late-night visitors?"

"No visitors. I hitched a chair under the doorknob to be sure." Jake chuckled and rubbed the back of his neck. "I can't believe you're bringing that up."

"So, Sally couldn't get to you this time, huh? Bet she was disappointed."

"Grant, you can't imagine how unnerving it was to wake up being groped. I was about to throw her across the room when I realized who it was. She could have gotten herself hurt, maybe killed. Plus, she's a married woman, and I was naked as a jaybird. Lars could have shot me, and no one would have blamed him."

Grant laughed. "Everyone, even Lars, knows what she's like. Especially where you're concerned. Although Sam is in the running, I've seen the way she looks at him."

"He has more to worry about from the Weisenberger girls. Last night, they were looking him over like a Sunday ham."

Grant chuckled and yawned. "So, you riding north with Winnie today?"

"I had planned on it, but something's come up," Jake told Grant about the package and the taunting note he'd received.

"What kind of maniac?" Grant shook his head. "How many times have we asked that question?"

"Too many," Jake said.

"What's your plan?"

"Sam's at the telegraph office. We've got Wade sending wires to all the sheriffs within a hundred-mile radius, and Logan is making the morning rounds. Then we're meeting up at Kat's for breakfast before riding out to check on the nearby settlers and ranchers. I got a hunch we won't find anything, but for the first time, I feel like the end is in sight."

Grant nodded. "Those feelings and hunches of yours pan out more often than not." Grant cradled his coffee mug between his large, rough hands. "Listen, I've got half a dozen loafers in the bunkhouse, and if I don't figure out something to do with them, they're gonna get restless and mean. Checking on the out-of-towners would give them something to do and keep them out of trouble. I can send them out when I get home, and don't worry about the ranch business. I'll still have plenty of men to keep an eye on the herd and get things ready for roundup. We can't put it off any longer."

"I'll gladly accept your offer of men, and I'm glad Pete is heading out of town." Jake half shook his head. "He's pretty broken up over Belle, but he's lucky he didn't get too involved."

"Know what those two are up to now?" Grant said with a wide grin. "They're putting ads in some Eastern papers looking for ladies who want to come out West to get hitched."

Jake chuckled, "I have no idea what to say, except it could get interesting. At least it gives Pete something to think about besides moping over Belle. She's not worth it. I saw her the other night working at the Stable Saloon. When Kat finds out, Belle will be out on her ear."

"You haven't told Kat you saw her?" Grant was surprised. "That's what the fight was about last night. Klaus told Pete he'd been at the Stable, spending some quality time between Belle's legs."

"I didn't know that's what the fight was about, but I didn't tell Kat because I didn't want Pete to find out. I figured I'd wait until he was out of town before I said anything." Jake sighed, "Kat will not be happy with me." He grabbed his hat and, settling it into place, moved toward the door. "If what we are working on doesn't pan out, I'll see you late tonight or early tomorrow."

"If you can, I'd sure like you to go with Winnie, but Clark is our best carpenter, and he'll know what to do. I'll just have to warn him to keep Winnie in check.

"Like he could," Jake said, leaving to meet Sam and Logan. Grant went upstairs to see if Lorene and Winnie were ready for breakfast. As he turned into the hallway, Lorene came out of her room.

"I was just about to knock and see if Winnie's ready. I heard her moving around." She tapped on her door. "Winnie? You ready?"

Winnie opened the door, dressed to the nines, and smiling from ear to ear. "I thought I would give the satin and lace one more outing before packing them away," she said with a graceful twirl of blue silk. Then, she whispered in Lorene's ear, making Lorene smile. "I hope Sally is working this morning. This is all for her."

After breakfast, Winnie turned to her dad. "Would you mind terribly if I spent the morning at Mary's? I'd like to see her, but I don't know when I'll be back in town. John will lend me a horse from the livery, and I promise I will be home early. I can't wait to sleep in my bed."

"Of course, we don't mind. Have fun, but don't be late. You remember how to get to the house?" Grant chuckled.

"Yes, Dad. I remember."

## CHAPTER 34

# THE BAD MR. SMYTHE

Jake walked from the hotel to Kat's to meet Sam and Logan. It was a cloudy morning, and a light breeze was blowing. The street was dusty and still mostly empty, but Steven and Charlie were opening up the General Store. He waved in their direction.

Kat wouldn't be happy with the news about Belle, but he had to tell her. He was surprised she hadn't already heard, but then again, maybe no one wanted to be the one to tell her. He walked through the swinging doors and headed straight to where she stood.

"Good morning, handsome." Kat greeted him with a smile. She enjoyed being the cause of the disgruntled look he shot her way.

"Good morning, gorgeous," he countered.

"You know Jake, I love being called gorgeous. Especially by such a handsome man. Whereas you get all upset and flustered when I call you handsome."

"Good point, but you are gorgeous."

"And you are handsome. So what's up?"

"You aren't going to like it."

"Spit it out, Jake."

"I saw Belle a few nights back working at the Stable Saloon."

"And you're just now telling me about it?"

Jake raised his hands in a defensive position. "I would have told you immediately, but I wanted to wait until Pete was out of town. Plus, I was out of town for several days myself."

"Not much of an excuse, Marshal Jacobs," Kat said, steaming.

"I don't allow my girls to work in any of those other places, and you know it. They agree to it when I hire them. I pay them well enough, so they don't have to. I hope that slimy Arnold Smythe wants to hire her full-time because she's done here."

"Sorry, Kat. I knew you were going to be upset. I can't imagine why she ever went there."

"I can, drugs. Smythe gets them all drugged up and does whatever he wants to them. I saw it before in a different life. Get the girls hooked on drugs, and they will do anything for more. And I mean anything." Kat shook her head in disbelief and disgust. "I noticed a difference in Belle, but I thought it was about Pete. As much as I hate throwing her to the wolves, I won't tolerate drugs and whoring."

"You ever have any trouble with Smythe?"

"No, but he is a horrible man." She lowered her voice. "He breaks in all his new girls to ensure they're properly trained for his *high-class* clientele." Kat's voice dripped with sarcasm. "I've heard horror stories about what some of those men are willing to pay for. You might be surprised at what some men want to do to a woman."

"Do I need to look into what's going on there?"

"He hasn't done anything illegal. At least not according to law books. But morally, it's despicable."

"Well, illegal or not, I don't like what you're telling me. Drugging his girls is enough to concern me. I'll tell Sam and Logan to keep an eye on the place."

"Be careful. Smythe is a man who will sneak up behind you and slide a knife between your ribs."

"If I remember correctly, he has been here for about three years. Do you know where he came from?"

"No. I don't know much about him, but I would bet the farm he's on the run from something in his past."

"We'll check the wanted posters."

Kat turned from Jake. "Bear, watch the place. I'm taking a walk."

"Whoa, there, Kat. Where do you think you're going?" Jake said, stepping in front of her.

"I am going to talk with Belle right now. I don't want her coming anywhere near my place if she is on drugs and working the sheets at the Stable."

"It's a little early to go busting down doors, don't you think?"

She gave him her best butt-out look. "No time like the present."

"Kat, if you wait, I'll walk with you. I don't want you running into any problems."

"I can take care of myself. I'll be fine."

"No, you won't. You will wait for me, or I will cuff you to the bar."

Kat's eyes flew open. "You wouldn't dare."

Jake laughed at her dismay. "Yeah, I would."

"Why you miserable—"

"Ah ah ah, Kat. Look, I wouldn't have thought much about it until you told me about the drugs and how he treats his girls. If Smythe is the lowlife you described, you need someone to watch your back, and I am going with you. That's the end of it. Besides, I need to let Mrs. Murphy know what's happening. She does not allow any funny business in her boarding house."

With a deep, frustrated sigh, Kat backed down. "Let me know when you're ready to go, Marshal."

Sam and Logan came through the swinging doors as Kat stomped away from Jake. "Wow, did we interrupt something?"

"We had a slight disagreement on whether or not she could walk down to Murphy's without an escort."

Jake filled them in on what was going on at the Stable. "We need to keep a closer watch on that place."

The three men settled at their regular table, and Bear brought their usual breakfast plates. Setting the dishes on the table, Bear smiled at Jake. "Ain't seen her that mad at anyone in a long time. At least no one who lived to tell about it." Bear walked away from the table, shaking his head and chuckling.

Sam spooned gravy over his fried potatoes. "Wade's busy sending the wires. Said it would take a while. I was thinking, it's too bad we aren't looking to stop something, not just searching for victims."

Jake nodded. "I had coffee with Grant, and he's sending us some men to check on the folks outside of town. Says he won't need them till roundup. Looks like we'll miss roundup again this year, Sam."

Logan rolled the ends of his mustache between his fingers. "Sure wish you'd get one of those gut feelings of yours. You know, one of your hunches."

"Yeah, me too."

"You know your mama healed me once." Logan shook his head, remembering the pain he had been suffering. "I know an earache doesn't sound like much, but between the earache and the ringing, I was ready to fold my cards. I thought about putting a gun to my head. That worthless, no-account doctor we had back then told me he didn't know of anything that would help but said I might try Mrs. Jacobs. He said she had some herbal cures or something. He didn't make it sound too promising, but I figured it couldn't hurt. By then, I was ready to try anything."

Logan shook his head. "When I got to your place, it was like she already knew I was coming. She sat me down under that old oak tree and then sat in front of me. She smiled, closed her eyes, and started whispering something in German. Then she blew ever so gently in my bad ear and covered my ears with her hands. She whispered more words I didn't understand, and when she took her hands away, there was a pop. The pain and ringing were gone. Your mama saved my sanity and probably my life. She was a fine woman. All she wanted in payment was for me to keep it to myself."

Jake smiled at Logan, but there was only sadness in his heart. "I'm glad you told me. She was an amazing mother, and I miss her and my father every day." Jake took a deep breath and blew it out. "If it wasn't for this maniac we're chasing, they might be alive today. Let's get him and stop the killings."

## CHAPTER 35

# WALKING THE KAT

"Logan, want to help me escort Kat to the boarding house?" Jake said. "I'm afraid I may need a bodyguard."

"Sure, I'm heading that way. Home sweet home, you know."

Kat was leering at them, waiting for the escort Jake had insisted on giving her.

"You ready, Kat?"

Kat looked at them in disgust and pushed past them to the door. Jake and Logan smiled at each other and followed her through the swinging doors, hurrying to keep up as she hustled around the corner and down the side street toward Murphy's Boarding House.

She was about to open the front door to Murphy's when Jake reached out, grabbing her hand to stop her. "Wait, Kat. Let me and Logan take the lead. We don't know what's happening, so please, let us do our job."

Kat scowled at him but nodded and stepped back. Both men drew their guns. Jake looked at Logan, who nodded that he was ready. Jake entered first, checking in both directions.

"Kat, get Coop over here, now," he yelled over his shoulder.

Mrs. Murphy was lying in a rag doll heap at the bottom of the stairway. Logan bolted past Jake and ran to her side. He picked up her hand and held it to his cheek. "Rachie, talk to me. Please, please talk to me."

Jake took the steps two at a time. At the top of the stairs, he turned toward an open door and inched along the wall until he could see that Belle's room was empty. It was evident there had been a struggle.

Checking the rest of the rooms, he found only a couple of the residents at home, but no one had heard or seen anything. He headed down the stairs and saw Coop tending to Rachel. She was sitting up, leaning against the wall.

"How is she, Coop?"

"She'll be fine. There's a fair-sized knot on the back of her head but no broken bones. She'll need someone to stay with her and keep her awake for the rest of the day. She'll have a humdinger of a headache and might need some help doing her regular chores for a while." Coop chuckled, "I had to have Kat take Logan outside. He was absolutely beside himself."

"Can I talk to her?"

Rachel Murphy chimed in. "Hey, I'm right here, mister, and yes, you can talk to me, Marshal Jacobs."

"How's your head?"

"It hurts like a son-of-a-gun, but Coop says I'll be fine."

"Can you tell me what happened?"

"I was back in the kitchen. It's right under Belle's room. I heard shouting, and something crashed to the floor. I came out to see what the ruckus was all about, and when I got to the top of the stairs, two men were dragging Belle out of her room. I told them to leave her alone and get out. The one guy told me to mind my own business and shoved me down the stairs."

Coop stood and motioned to the front parlor. "Jake, help me get her up and over to one of those  chairs."

Kat and Logan came in just as they settled Rachel in  a cushioned chair. Logan went to her side and knelt beside the chair. "Rachie, how are you?" Concern was etched on his face as he put a lap-robe over her knees.

"Don't fuss, Eddie. Coop says I'll be fine. Nothing's broken. You need to help the marshal."

"Eddie?" Jake raised an eyebrow.

Logan shot Jake a look and returned his full attention to Rachel.

Jake sat on his haunches next to Mrs. Murphy's chair. "Can you tell me what the men looked like?"

"You bet I can, Marshal." She nodded and then grimaced at the slight movement. "The man who shoved me had greasy black hair combed straight back, a filthy black mustache, and a nasty scar on his—" She paused to decide which side. "Left cheek, and he was wearing a raggedy red shirt with a black vest."

"That sounds like Smythe's number one thug," Kat said, recognizing the description.

"Did you see the other man?" Jake said, shifting his gaze back to Mrs. Murphy.

"I only saw his back, but he had a sweat-stained tan hat with a braided leather hatband and a dark blue shirt. Maybe he had brown hair, but I can't say for sure."

Kat frowned. "Neither one is Smythe, but I doubt he'd do his own dirty work. What do you think they want from Belle? Why would they kidnap her?"

"Mrs. Murphy, you have been a great help. Kat, can you stay here with her while *Eddie* and I go down to the Stable?"

"Watch your back, Jake. You know what I told you," Kat said.

Jake nodded and started for the door.

Logan looked after Jake and then back at Rachel.

"Kat will be with her. She'll be fine," Jake said, soothing Logan's concern.

Coop took another look at his patient before leaving. He patted her on the hand, telling her she would be fine in a day or two. Then he followed on Jake and Logan's heels. "Want me to go along in case there's trouble?"

"No, Coop. I don't want to put you in danger. Be ready, but stay in your office and clear of any mix-ups."

By the time they got to the marshal's office, Sam was coming up the boardwalk. "What happened?"

Jake gave him a quick rundown. "We're headed for the Stable to see if we can find Belle."

# CHAPTER 36

# BELLE AND BULLETS

When they got to the Stable, all seemed peaceful. They stood on either side of the door straining to hear. The low rumble of men's voices, the shuffling of cards and an occasional outburst of laughter indicated business as usual, but they couldn't take any chances.

Jake put his finger to his lips, then he pointed to himself, then to Sam and Logan, indicating the method of entry. They went through the doors quickly, eyes alert, scanning for any bushwhackers. The floor was covered with sawdust, and the air was bitingly sour with the smell of smoke, stale beer, and the sweat of hundreds of trail-weary cowboys who had passed through the doors.

There were two tables of drinkers. Jake recognized a couple of the men at the one table and was surprised to find such respectable, church-going men in this dirty hole of a saloon, especially now that he understood the full extent of the services offered here. He figured he wouldn't look at them quite the same after this.

He walked up to the bar while Logan and Sam stayed back, taking positions on either side of the entry. The barkeeper glared at Jake. "We don't need no law dog down here east of the river," he said, turning his back on Jake and fussing with some glasses on the back counter.

Jake stretched across the bar, reaching out and grabbing the bar-keeper's collar. He pulled him back against the bar hard, choking him. "Now, we can do this the easy way or not. Your choice."

Jake heard chairs scratching across the floor and the bang of one falling over. The mirror behind the bar gave him a clear view of the barroom. The respectable men were hastily leaving. The men at the other table had not moved. He figured they were on Smythe's payroll.

Jake jerked on the barkeeper's collar. "What's your name?"

"What's it to you, law?" he choked out.

Jake pulled him harder against the bar. "Wrong answer. Try again."

When he got no response, Jake pulled him over the bar and planted a solid punch to the man's midsection. The bartender doubled over with a wheeze.

Jake grabbed him by the front of his shirt and shoved him against the bar. "Seems we got off to a bad start, but I'm willing to let bygones be bygones if you are. We're looking for a dancehall girl by the name of Belle. I know that you know her. I saw her in here several nights ago, and you were working. Do you know where she is?"

"I haven't seen her since."

"Where might your boss have taken her?"

"I have no idea."

Jake knew he was lying and threw another punch, landing the bar-keep flat on the floor. He turned his back on the man and approached the table of three drinkers who had remained seated quietly observing him.

"The barkeeper lied to me, and I don't like being lied to. Do any of you men know where Belle is?"

They all shook their heads. One answered, "We don't know any Belle."

"Hmmm, I see," Jake said, walking around to the side of the table and facing them squarely. "What if your boss wanted to be alone with someone? Where would he take them?"

They looked at one another, shaking their heads. "We don't know what you're talking about."

"Sam, cuff the barkeep with no name to the brass railing," Jake said, and turned back to the three men at the table. "I'll take your guns."

"I don't give my gun up to no one, Marshal, and you ain't got the grit to take it."

Jake smiled. "The man standing by the door with a shotgun pointed at your head says differently."

Seeing Logan cock and aim the canon in their direction changed the men's attitudes. Jake collected their guns and placed them on the bar. Sam had cuffed the barkeep and returned to his position by the door.

"Sam, keep an eye on these three. Logan, you're with me."

They went up the open stairway to check out the second floor. Two or three scantily clad young girls were in each of the four dark and filthy rooms. They smiled and beckoned them to enter. There was no Belle.

They went downstairs and headed to the back of the saloon, where the office was most likely located. Jake was reaching for the doorknob when it opened, and he was face-to-face with a man he assumed to be Smythe.

"I hear you're looking for Belle," the man said, trying to push Jake back into the barroom. "She isn't here and hasn't been for several nights. Sorry, we can't be of any help."

"I need to look around your office and the back of the saloon," Jake insisted, pushing past him.

There was a sudden thunderous hailstorm of gunfire behind them. The sharp cracks of pistols had Jake and Logan rushing to the barroom, but it was over as quickly as it had begun. A cloud of gun smoke hung in the air. Four men were sprawled on the floor, and another bent forward over the table. Sam stood by the door untouched.

He pointed to the men lying face down on the floor not far from him. "Those two came in laughing and joking like they were drunk, then turned on me and drew. The men at the table pulled guns from somewhere. I can't figure out where they could have come from. It happened so fast."

Jake looked at Sam and the splintered wall behind him. "You okay?

"Yeah, I'm fine."

"Logan, keep that shotgun trained on Smythe, and don't be afraid to shoot."

Jake looked again at the bullet-riddled wall behind Sam in disbelief. "You're sure you're not hit?"

"No. Thankfully, they were all bad shots."

Sam and Jake collected the guns and checked to see who was still breathing. "Looks like we've got one dead and the rest wounded. The two who came in last are alive, and they're the ones I want to talk to. They fit Mrs. Murphy's description to a T. Let's get them cuffed and up in the chairs."

Logan's shotgun was pointed directly at Smythe's back. He gave him a hard poke. "What do you want me to do with this pond slime?" he asked Jake, jabbing the man a couple more times for the plain orneriness of it.

Jake figured no one would talk as long as Smythe was anywhere nearby. "Logan, escort Mr. Smythe to a jail cell. He'll be much more comfortable there. Search him and remember he likes knives. If he gives you any trouble, don't hesitate to shoot him. Once he's locked up, let Coop and the undertaker know we have customers for them. Then check in on Mrs. Murphy."

Sam kept his gun trained on Smythe while Logan searched him and tied his hands behind his back. Logan shoved him toward the door with the shotgun at his back. "Let's go, you steaming heap of donkey dung. I can't wait to slam the cell door on you. The only thing I'd like better is if you were to twitch just one little hair on your head so I can blow you in half." Logan poked him again, knowing how much it angered the man.

"Be careful, Logan," Jake said as Logan left the saloon.

Jake pulled a chair out from the table where the wounded men were sitting and swung it around, straddling it, his arms resting on the back. He was face-to-face with the two handcuffed men.

He looked them over, assessing their condition. They were wounded, but not seriously. Still, they had to be hurting. He stared at them, letting them stew.

"I have you guys dead to rights on kidnapping and assault. You will see the inside of a prison." Jake paused to let it soak in. He looked from one to the other. "But if Belle dies or is already dead, we add murder to the charges, and you hang. With that in mind, do you have anything you want to tell me?"

"Yeah, we need a doctor." The man with the scar sneered.

"And you shall have one as soon as I find Belle."

"You can't do this to us." The man with the scar groaned, holding his side.

"Deputy Watkins, what do you think? Can I do this?"

"Yes, you can, Marshal Jacobs. You most certainly can."

"I thought so. Now, one last time before I have to hurt you, where's Belle?"

There was no answer. The man with the scar was stubborn, but Jake could tell it wouldn't take much for the man with the sweaty hat to crumble. He got up from his chair, put his hand over the wound on Sweaty Hat's arm, and squeezed.

"There's a shack out back where—"

The man with the scar cut off Sweaty Hat. "Shut up. You fool."

"The old carriage house," Sam said, already on his way out the back door while Jake continued questioning them.

"I'm not hanging for Smythe. He ain't done anything for me," Sweaty Hat said to the man with the scar. He turned to Jake. "He takes his girls out there sometimes."

"Why did he kidnap Belle?"

"She stole drugs and money, and he wanted to teach her a lesson. Wanted to make an example of her so the other girls wouldn't get any ideas. You'll remember I told you what you wanted to know. I don't want to hang."

Jake shook his head and started for the back door. Sam was helping Belle as she shakily navigated the alley. Her dress was torn, and her face was bruised and bloodied.

"She says she's not hurt, and I didn't find any deep wounds, but she's out of it. She has no idea what's happening." As Sam spoke, she smiled at him and collapsed. Sam carried her into the saloon and propped her up in a chair.

Coop and Bones came through the door, and Jake motioned to Belle. "Coop, you want to take care of Belle first, then take your pick of these guys."

Kat came in a few minutes later, going straight to Coop's side. "How's Belle?"

"Nothing life-threatening. She should be fine." Coop looked around and saw Bones hauling one of the bodies out the door. "I'd better check and make sure that guy Bones is loading up is dead. He can get a little over-eager sometimes."

Kat inspected Jake and Sam for any damage. "I heard the gunfire, and then Logan showed up and told me what happened. I tried to get him to come back with me, but I couldn't pry him away from Rachie."

"Kat, there are some girls upstairs that are going to need help. From the looks of it, they've been drugged and badly abused. I don't have a place for them at the jail. All I know is I can't leave them here."

"I'll go up and see what shape they're in." Kat thought for a minute. "Maybe Pastor Emil and his wife would take them in? We could set up cots in the social hall. After I check on the girls, I'll talk to the Pastor."

Kat hurried upstairs and gathered the dazed girls, talking to them and finding them clothes to wear. Ten young girls came down the stairs, followed by Kat. "This is all of them, and you're right. They have been drugged and abused." She paused, disgusted by the whole thing. "One of the girls is twelve. I hope that bastard gives you a reason to kill him."

Kat grouped the girls around one of the tables in the corner of the room, and went to find Pastor Emil. She returned about fifteen minutes later. The Pastor and his wife Adah had brought a wagon to take the girls to the church and safety.

Jake went behind the bar and poured two glasses of bourbon. He motioned for Sam to join him at one of the tables. "Here, drink this. You look a little green around the gills."

Sam took a drink, grimacing, "I can't believe I'm alive. It happened so fast I didn't have time to think." Sam rubbed his hands over his face. "At least we saved Belle. She got hooked on a bad situation and couldn't find a way out. And all those other girls, I'm sure none of them bargained for what happened to them."

Jake thoughtfully drizzled what was left of the whiskey he had poured for himself into a pile of sawdust on the floor. "That is some nasty stuff."

"It sure is," Sam said. "I'd rather have a steak."

"Almost getting riddled with bullets hasn't spoiled your appetite," Jake said with a raised eyebrow.

It was a little past the noon hour when Bones left with the men who hadn't survived the shootout. Coop was tending to the man who had been slumped over the table. Jake left Sam to join him. "These guys all need to go to jail. Let us know when we can move them."

"Those two who are cuffed are ready to go right now. The bullets went straight through soft tissue; there's nothing more I can do for them. The other one needs the bullet removed and will be out for a while. Jenny's bringing the buckboard for us to move them."

Jenny arrived before Coop had finished speaking, and they loaded the wounded in the back without incident. She headed toward the doctor's office, and Jake and Sam rode along on either side of the wagon, guarding against any trouble.

She stopped at the marshal's office to unload the men with minor wounds before heading to Coop's. Jake and Sam escorted them to a jail cell. It was not a happy reunion between them and Smythe.

After the men were secure, Sam and Jake walked to Coop's to wait for the results on the third wounded man. These were dangerous men, and they didn't want to take a chance of leaving Coop unprotected.

Twenty minutes later, Coop came out holding a bullet between his fingers and smiling. "Got it, and he should be fine. He'll need a couple of days to heal."

"When can we take him to jail?"

Coop blanched and sputtered. "Well, he can't be moved. I told you, not for a couple of days. You'll wreck my handy work, and it might kill him."

"Coop, he's dangerous. We can't leave him here without someone to guard him and you around the clock. You would make my life much easier if we could move him to a cell."

"Tomorrow night," Coop said, shrugging in defeat.

"Well, guess that will have to do. Sam, you want to eat now or later?" Jake asked.

"You go ahead. I'll stay here with Coop and go when you get back."

Jake walked across the street to check on Mrs. Murphy and to let Logan know what had happened. Then he went to Kat's for a bite to eat.

When Kat saw him, she went to join him at his table. "As soon as Belle is able, I'm sending her to a sanatorium in Kansas City for recovery. I know they'll treat her right, and I'll make sure they do. How's Sam?"

Jake sat back in his chair. "He'll be fine. He's had close calls in the past, but nothing like this. I can't believe he didn't get a scratch. He's a lucky man."

"Thank you for saving Belle and those other poor girls." She squeezed his forearm. "If you can believe it, the pastor has talked Miss Purdy into boarding all of them until they're well enough to set out on their own."

"You're right. I don't believe it," Jake said, shaking his head.

"Pastor appealed to her charitable nature and promised to pay her."

"Even so, Miss Purdy with a house full of drugged-up prostitutes? Doesn't seem possible."

"Pastor says she can use the money. The funds her folks left her are almost gone, and it takes a lot to support that enormous house. What will happen to Smythe?"

"He'll most likely go to jail with the rest of them for kidnapping, attempted murder, and assault. I can't imagine Judge Taylor not throwing the book at them. Probably a life sentence."

"What about the Stable?"

"I asked Zeke to go down and board the place up and put a closed sign on the front door."

"Good. I'm glad that place is out of business."

Jake ate a quick meal and, with a wave to Kat, headed out the door on his way to relieve Sam. He looked up and down the street and caught sight of Winnie heading in his direction—a treat he hadn't expected.

## CHAPTER 37

# WHAT A TOAD

Grant and Lorene took Winnie to Mary's after breakfast. Their carriage hadn't pulled to a complete stop when Mary came waddling down the porch steps. She grabbed and hugged Winnie and, waving to Grant and Lorene, pulled her into the house.

"I'm so glad you came. We have so much to talk about. I had Mom take the kids for the day, so we'll have plenty of time to talk uninterrupted. You can see my little darlings another time."

"Slow down, Mary, take a breath." Winnie laughed at her friend's enthusiastic greeting.

"I'm just so glad to see you. I missed our talks and all the fun we had." Mary hugged her again and pointed her toward the parlor. "Let's sit in there."

Mary was a sprite of a woman, a ball of energy and mischief. She usually went at top speed and was interested in everyone.

"Tell me everything," she begged. Her high-setting ponytail bounced with every turn of her head.

"About what?"

"About the kiss, you ninny. What else?"

"Which one?" Winnie teased.

Mary was quiet for a moment, which was not a usual occurrence. She looked at Winnie and then squealed. "What do you mean, which one?"

"It's a simple question, Mary. Which kiss do you want to know about?"

"You kissed someone else? Who else did you kiss?"

"Sam."

"What? You kissed Sam?" Mary pretended to fall from her chair in a faint.

"I did, and I kissed Quinn."

"So, how was . . . What? You didn't. Quinn Sumner? The dentist? That relic of a man? Winnie, what were you thinking? He's old enough to be your father. Ew."

Mary was struck silent for the second time, but it only lasted for a moment. After three blinks of her long eyelashes, she erupted.

"Oh my God, Winnie. That had to have been like kissing the backside of a butchered chicken. Ewwww." Mary, comically and with unfettered exaggeration, wiped the back of her hand across her mouth.

Winnie laughed at her theatrics. "I can't explain it, but there is something about him."

"Well, I suppose he has a certain dignified appeal. But those eyes of his are dark as night and sinister. Hmm, maybe it's the tinge of danger that appeals to you?" Mary drummed her fingers on the arm of her chair. "On the plus side, he has to be experienced at his age. I'm sure he's been around."

"Oh, Mary. You're terrible. I can't say what it is, but there is something persuasively charming about him."

"So, three men? I can hardly breathe thinking about it." Mary said, placing her hand over her heart, her mouth agape. "Sam and Quinn, huh?"

"Ooooohhhh. What about Jake? I saw that kiss, and it was a dandy." Mary fanned her face.

"It was, but then he left me for Sam."

"Winnie, he had to leave. His blood was boiling, and the dam was about to burst." Mary leaned forward in her chair. "And all it took was one kiss."

"Whatever his problem was, I hope he and Sam had a wonderful time together."

"You have to tell me more. What about Sam's kiss? He is so handsome, and those lips of his look so inviting."

Winnie couldn't help but laugh at her friend. "You should have been on the stage. So dramatic. Sam's kisses took my breath away, but there were no fireworks."

"If I weren't married, I'd be after Sam. But what about Quinn? Was it like kissing the backend of a plucked chicken?"

"No, silly. Quinn's kiss was pleasant, but it was Jake who set my world on fire, and then he walked away." Winnie sighed. "I missed Jake terribly while I was away, and I guess I somehow expected more from him on my first night back."

Mary looked at Winnie with a quirky smile. "I know for a fact that he missed you, and I know he's yours for the having."

Winnie smiled at her friend. "I hope you're right because he's the one I want." Winnie stood up and changed the subject. "Did you get a chance to open the trunk Clark dropped off for you?"

"I had Clark put it in my sewing room out of the way. I didn't want the kids crawling all over it, and I didn't want to open it until you were here."

"I'm here, so let's see what's inside that steamer. I packed it so long ago I'm not sure what we might find."

"Sam, hm-hm-hmmm. Breathtaking, you said? I sure would like to kiss those sweet-looking lips of his. Of course, I wouldn't tell John that. John is the one who sets my world on fire, but Sam has those beautiful brown eyes and those broad shoulders. Lots of women would like to climb that mountain of a man," she said, feigning a clumsy swoon as she lumbered down the hall to her sewing room.

She opened the trunk with a gasp. It was packed to the brim with bolts of exotic fabrics and notions. "Winnie, these are beautiful. I - I can't accept all of this. It's too much."

"Nonsense. Besides, I'm thinking of a trade-off. I'd like you to make a couple of garments for me. Some riding outfits that I saw in England. They need to be toned down a bit for around here. I have some pictures from a catalog."

"Anything, Winnie. I love to sew for you."

They talked about clothes and the fashions in Europe and back East, and by noon they had every piece of material strung across Mary's sewing room.

"I made lemonade and pig sandwiches. Will that be enough?"

"Sounds marvelous. I'm starving."

Mary's pig sandwiches were ham, bacon, and a fried egg between thick pieces of homemade bread slathered with butter. She pulled some pickles out of a crock and poured the lemonade.

They ate silently, but Mary started in again as Winnie helped clean the table and put the lunch items away. "Hmmm, I still can't believe you let Quinn kiss you, and you said you're attracted to him."

"I wouldn't say I'm attracted to him, but there is something about him. He's interesting. He said he wants to court me."

"Are you kidding? The nerve of that old toad," Mary said, then grabbed the side of her stomach with a gasp. "Don't look so alarmed,

Winnie. It was just a kick. This one is going to be a real scrapper. Here, give me your hand."

Mary put Winnie's hand on the side of her stomach and watched the amazement on her face as the kicks and punches continued. "Won't be long now. Thank the dear Lord. I'm getting real tired of this."

They talked for a bit longer before Winnie stood to go. "I need to head for home. Next time, I will expect to see the whole brood."

"I hate to see you go. We still have so much catching up to do."

"We have lots of time, Mary. I'm not going anywhere."

Mary walked with Winnie through the pasture to the edge of town, talking the whole way. She hugged Winnie and turned for home, and Winnie walked up the boardwalk toward the Livery. She saw Jake come out of Kate's place and broke into a smile.

"I was going to the marshal's office to report a crime," she said with her biggest smile.

"Well, let's step inside, and you can tell me all about it."

Jake closed the door and put his arms around her. "This is a pleasant surprise. I figured you'd be home unpacking all those trunks I saw stacked up on the platform yesterday."

"I did do a little shopping while I was away, but one of the trunks was for Mary. That's where I've been."

"And what did you and Mary talk about?" Winnie loved to hear his voice, and when he held her close, the rumble of his chest gave her goosebumps.

"You're interested in our girl talk?"

"I'm interested in everything about you." Jake looked down at her with such intensity that it melted her heart and weakened her knees. He leaned down and covered her mouth with his for the briefest moment, but it took her breath away.

"So, what did you talk about?"

"You, of course."

Jake pressed her against the door and kissed her until they were both breathless. He wanted to take her to bed but instead took her by the hand and led her outside. A cot in a jail cell or the cot that he shared with Sam and Logan was not where he wanted to make love to her.

Sitting on the bench in front of his office, her hand in his, he told her about the morning's events.

"Sounds like Sam was more than lucky. What will happen to those poor girls you found? I can't imagine what they must have been through." She looked at him with dreamy green eyes. "While I was laughing and gossiping with Mary, you saved those young girls. You should be proud."

They had been talking for an hour when Winnie sighed and stood. "I don't want to, but I have to go. I want to get home early or at least before dark. I'm glad I got to see you, and I'm glad you didn't get hurt." She hugged him and started across the street.

He watched her until she disappeared inside the livery. When they were together, everything seemed right. Then, groaning, he remembered Sam in Coop's waiting room. He was supposed to be relieving him. Sam would be mad and hungry, and that was a bad combination.

Jake hurried up the street, thinking more about Winnie than Sam.

## CHAPTER 38

# MINE FOR THE TAKING

Winnie didn't want to leave Jake but knew she had to. On the ride home, she thought about Jake and about Mary's words. Mary said he was hers for the taking. She hoped Mary was right. She wanted to spend the rest of her life with him.

The ranch proper and its buildings were sheltered in a wide green valley and hidden from view by a copse of trees and a slight rise in the ground. Her eyes misted as she topped the ridge and looked down on her home. She was glad to be back. This was where she belonged.

Winnie wanted to gallop like the wind, run into the house, and jump into her father's arms like she did when she was little. Instead, she sat and lingered, looking at the well-kept buildings and the corrals, the houses and the bunkhouses, and Lorene's garden. It was bigger than ever.

She rode slowly down the incline toward the main house, taking in all the smells and sounds of home. She heard the ca-clang of the black-smith's hammer, a cow bellowing, and men hooting and hollering.

Maybe a dozen men were gathered around one of the corrals, watching someone attempting to break a new horse. She saw him take a nasty spill and flinched. It reminded her of the terrible falls Jake had survived while trying to break Drach. She was relieved to see the man get up. He walked gingerly to the fence but nodded to the others that he was ready to ride again.

The smell of Hank's cooking drifted to her on the breeze. He was always cooking up something. Feeding the men on the Circle G Ranch was not an easy task. There could be anywhere from 150 to 200 hands on the ranch at any given time.

She smiled at the metal sign identifying Main Street as she dismounted in front of the large white house. Lorene and Grant came out on the front porch and greeted her with hugs and kisses. Their girl was home.

"Welcome home, sweet pea," Grant said, "I'm in the middle of a meeting with our attorney, but it shouldn't take long—some last-minute details regarding the ranch in Texas. You and Lorene go on upstairs and unpack the trunks, and when you're finished, come find me. There are some things we need to talk about." Grant hugged her and retreated to his office.

"Well," Lorene said, "guess we'll go unpack."

Winnie chuckled, "I guess we will. Still bossy as ever."

Winnie was kneeling in front of the second trunk, handing each item to Lorene, who had set up a triage on the bed—dresses in one pile, pants in another, shirts in another, and so on.

Winnie found what she'd been looking for near the bottom of the trunk…two fancifully wrapped but crumpled packages for Lorene. She sat back on her heels and lifted them up like prize trophies.

She held the packages out to Lorene. "These are for you. I was hoping they didn't get missed. I left packing until the last minute, and Auntie Grace had to help. We were frantic, and Uncle Chester made things worse with his huffing and grumbling about it taking too long and how we'd never get to the ship in time. I think Auntie was about to strangle him."

"Uncle Chester informed me that all women are the same, even the impertinent Yanks." Winnie did a fair job of imitating his droll British accent. "Auntie Grace gave him a look that could scald feathers off a chicken and asked how it was he knew about *all women.* It turned into quite the Donnybrook but ended when Uncle politely asked if it was teatime."

Lorene opened the first package—a silk shirt and soft suede riding britches. "I'll have to save these for going to town. I'm afraid I'd scare the cows if I wore these fancies here on the ranch. Thank you, Winnie. I've never had anything so beautifully extravagant." She hugged Winnie, tears sparkling.

"Open the other one." Winnie was almost bouncing with anticipation. "Open the other one."

It was a small box. Lorene carefully untied the string ribbon and removed the shiny wrapping. The brooch sitting on royal blue velvet was breathtaking. "These gems…are they real?"

"Of course they are. The peacock's body is gold studded with diamonds and the tail is sapphires and emeralds. I went with Uncle to have his watch repaired, and this little fellow kept winking at me from the jeweler's case."

"Oh, Winnie. It's splendid. Thank you. I've never had anything so wonderful. I don't know what to say."

Winnie pinned the brooch on Lorene's shoulder and stood back admiring it. "I'm glad you like it. It's not big or flashy, but sparkly enough to be sassy."

"It's perfect," Lorene said. And so is this beautiful silk shirt." She scooped it off the bed and held it in front of her. It's the perfect blue. I can't wait to wear it."

Winnie was thrilled that Lorene liked her gifts. She loved Lorene as if she were her mother. Sometimes, a twinge of guilt marred her love for Lorene when she thought of the woman who had given birth to her.

She knew her mother only through pictures in an album and stories her father told. Winnie loved her, but that love came from her father's memories, not from her own.

Her love for Lorene came from the times they had spent together and the memories they had made. She was the one who baked cookies with her, dug the splinter out of her finger, helped decorate the Christmas tree, cared for her when she was sick, and comforted her when her heart was broken. Lorene was always there for her, and those were her memories.

"Winnie, your father said he would like to see us when we finish unpacking, but I don't think he realized it might take us a day or two. What do you say we save the rest of it for tomorrow and find your dad? He's probably waiting in the study and wondering what happened to us."

Grant was sitting behind his desk reading through some documents when they entered. He stood and came around to hug each of them. "Let's sit down over here." He motioned them to comfortable leather furniture arranged for informal business meetings or casual conversations.

"Winnie, I'm not sure how to say this. So, I'm going to jump in with both feet. I'm getting married, and I would like to ask for your blessing."

Winnie looked at her father, her eyes wide. "What?"

Lorene cleared her throat, giving Grant a meaningful glance.

"Oh, Sorry. It's Lorene. I thought you knew. I'm in love with Lorene and I've asked her to marry me."

Winnie sat back in relief. "Dad, you had me worried for a minute. Of course, you have my blessing. What took you so long?"

Winnie got up, hugging each of them. "When's the big day?"

"We haven't decided for sure, but soon. Maybe in two or three weeks, enough time for us to make the arrangements."

"I'm so happy for you," Winnie said, choking back tears of joy.

# CHAPTER 39

# BREAKFAST

Winnie came down the stairs to breakfast with a yawn and a stretch. Grant was at the table with a newspaper and an empty plate in front of him. "Washington is a mess," he complained. "I can't believe how those ring-tailed Congressmen can get away with wheeling and dealing the way they do. And God only knows who they'll end up nominating for president. We have no say, no vote, but what they do back East rolls across the plains." Grant folded the paper and tossed it on the table. "Clark left a list of supplies he would like you to pick up for him."

There was a stained piece of scratch paper by her plate with writing on both sides, barely legible. She carefully folded the list and put it in her pocket. "Guess I'm going to town. Where's Lorene?"

"In the vegetable garden. She wanted to get out and hoe the weeds before it got too hot."

"She should have hollered. I would have helped her."

"She likes doing it. She says it gives her a chance to get out all her aggression. And I say better on the weeds than on me."

Winnie laughed. "Lorene is the sweetest, gentlest person I know."

"She is, for a fact, but she could tame a mountain lion with one arm tied behind her back if need be. Don't you ever doubt it."

Winnie nibbled at a piece of bacon, washing it down with a swallow of milk. "She tamed you, didn't she?" she laughed, getting up and hugging her dad. "Love you, Dad. I better get a move on. I've got a whole bunch of shopping to do. And since when did I become Clark's lackey?"

"Have fun, Winnie," Grant said with a chuckle, ignoring her question.

# CHAPTER 40

# OUT OF LAUDANUM

Winnie had completed most of her shopping before noon. She had chatted with the different business owners and figured she was all caught up on the local gossip.

Leaving the harness shop, Ross Meadows, the owner, was hot on her heels. He was a few years older than her, single, and clumsily asking her to join him for supper.

He wasn't a bad-looking man, polite and respectful, with a pleasant way about him, but she had her cap set for Jake and wasn't interested in anyone else's attentions. "I'm sorry, Ross, but I'm meeting the marshal for supper," she lied. But if she stopped by Jake's office, maybe it could be the truth.

Quinn stood at his office window, watching Winnie with Meadows. He wanted to know what they were talking about. It didn't look like business. When she headed up the street to the General Store and disappeared inside, he bolted from his office and across the street.

Standing outside the doors to the General Store, he smoothed back his hair and caught his breath. He entered slowly, ignoring her, then feigned surprise at finding her there. "Winnie. What a lovely surprise running into you like this."

"No teeth to fix this morning?" Steven sneered.

"I, uh…need some laudanum for a nervous patient, and I'm completely out."

He turned to Winnie. "Careless of me, but a most propitious error on my part, I ran into you. A true delight."

Winnie laughed at his uneasiness.

Steven was watching Quinn and thought he looked like a cat about to pounce on a mouse. Jake's mouse. "Ahem," Steven said, setting a bottle of laudanum on the counter with a thud.

Quinn looked at him blankly. "Oh, yes, of course," he said, tossing several coins on the glass display case and putting the bottle in his pocket.

There were other customers, and Steven was pulled away, but he kept one eye on the man he could tell was trying to rustle Jake's girl.

"You promised me dinner after our dances and those memorable kisses on the porch. I don't suppose you could make time today?"

Winnie hesitated. She had promised to meet him, and he was so charming. "I don't know. I still have quite a bit of shopping left to do," she lied.

He looked hurt, and she relented. It was, after all, innocent enough, and she thought it would be interesting to get to know him. "How about I meet you at the Wishbone in an hour?"

"Make it the Carmichael Cafe, and we're all set."

"The Carmichael's it is."

Quinn hurried back to his office, his heart pounding with joy and longing.

Winnie was already at a table when Quinn entered. He sat across from her with a soft smile, showing off his perfect white teeth. "I am so glad you accepted my invitation to meet me."

"Everyone has to eat, right?" Winnie smiled and took a tiny sip of water, uncomfortable under the crushing scrutiny of his intense dark eyes.

"So, Winnie, what has been keeping you busy since you got back into town? Anything exciting?"

She told him a little about rebuilding the old trapper's cabin and her shopping trip for supplies but couldn't think of anything else to say.

Quinn changed the subject, hoping she would relax and open up. "What did you miss most while you were away?"

"My family and friends, of course, but I missed the sky. The sky here is…big. It stretches on forever. Everywhere I went, the sky was small. Even out on the ocean, it was different somehow." His eyes were mesmerizing, and she looked down at her half-eaten meal, trying to avoid his gaze. She was like a trapped animal and wanted to escape. She was trying to figure out how to get away without hurting his feelings. She didn't want to make a scene.

"One day perhaps I will be able to enjoy such a wonderful trip, and it would be even better if you were at my side. Perhaps on our honeymoon. You could show me the sights and we'd have a wonderful time. I have heard the palace gardens in London are breathtaking. That would be my first stop. My feeble attempt at gardening would pale by comparison. Did you get a chance to visit the gardens?"

"Winnie," he said sharply, dropping his fork noisily on his plate.

She jumped, looking up from her plate. He was talking to her, but she hadn't heard him and hadn't responded.

"It's polite to look at someone when they're talking to you."

"I know. I'm sorry," she said, rising from her chair. "I…I was thinking about everything left to do on my list. I need to get busy. Maybe another day when I don't have so much on my mind?"

"Please, sit down." It was more of a command than a polite request.

Winnie looked doubtful but sat on the edge of her chair. "Quinn, this is not going anywhere, and I don't want you to think I'm encouraging you."

"But the dances and the kisses?" he said, his countenance changing. A frightening blaze of anger flashed through his eyes.

"I'm sorry if you misunderstood, but I told you I have feelings for another, and we couldn't be a couple. That hasn't changed." She stood and hurried away, wondering what had possessed her to accept his invitation in the first place. But she knew the answer. He was devilishly handsome and captivating. His eyes were fascinating and impossible to ignore, and she feared she could fall prey to his charms, but he was not what she wanted. She had to stay away from him.

Watching her walk away, he seethed with anger. He wanted her, and there was nothing he wouldn't do to have her. Nothing.

## CHAPTER 41

# THE MARSHAL'S OUT

Winnie hurried up the street and into Jake's office, but only Logan was there.

"You look like the devil himself is after you."

"Maybe he is. Is Jake in town?"

"Nope. He rode out with Sam a bit ago. A young kid was complaining about some men trying to chase him down. I didn't think they both needed to go, but I guess they were tired of listening to me complain. Want me to give him a message?"

"Just tell him I'm sorry I missed him."

Winnie finished her shopping and headed home, her buckboard brimming full. It was late when she reined in by the barn.

Silas and Walt, old-timers on the ranch, hurried out to meet her. "You hauling this stuff north in the morning?"

She nodded. "Have them hitched for me first thing. I'll want to get an early start."

"Consider it done."

Winnie thanked them and went inside. She made a sandwich and poured herself a glass of milk. She hadn't eaten much, and her stomach was growling in protest. A piece of bacon at breakfast and a couple of bites of pork chop at noon were not enough. She sat at the kitchen table, eating slowly and rehashing the day's events.

Her father and Lorene were in the den having a spirited conversation about something. Perhaps their upcoming wedding plans, or maybe, her dad was still ranting about Washington. She waved and said goodnight as she hurried past the door and up the stairs to her room. She changed quickly and jumped into bed, fluffing her pillow until it was exactly right. She closed her eyes and drifted off to sleep, thinking of Jake.

*His touch was gentle as he cupped her face in his hands. It was as if he were worshipping her. His eyes held hers, his gaze melting her self-control. She wanted him to kiss her, and when his hand went to her breast, she allowed it. She wet her lips and whispered his name. His mouth took hers, ravaging it with his kiss, his hand kneading her breast. Her body was flooded with warmth and a need that throbbed so intensely that it was excruciating.*

*"Has your marshal ever made you feel this way? Has he held you like this, kissed you like this, made you want him the way you want me? Jake is too tame for a woman like you. You need mad, passionate love. The kind of love only I can give you. A man's love, not a boy's." His hand tugged at her skirts, pulling on them, and she didn't resist when he slid his hand up her bare thigh to—*

*"Winnie?" Jake stood looking at them in disbelief. Then turned away.*

*He had seen her with Quinn, and she wasn't resisting him. She wasn't fighting him off. "Jake. No. Jake, come back. I love you. Jake." She whimpered. "Please, please come back."*

She sat up in bed, drenched in sweat and panting for air. It had been so real. Her body still ached and throbbed with a need she couldn't understand. But she knew one thing for sure; she wouldn't go any-where near Sumner ever again.

No one but Jake would have her. And if he didn't want her, she would die a virgin. Maybe join a convent.

## CHAPTER 42

# THE BOUNTY HUNTER

Graham Bryson rode into Grant's Crossing midmorning on a cloudy, windy day, his slicker billowing behind him. Gusts of wind whipped up dust devils in the street, and dark clouds promised the rain the whole territory needed.

He stopped in front of a building with a large sign announcing to the world that it was Kat's Place. Dismounting and stretching, he looked up and down the street, assessing the town. He tied off his horse and removed the slicker he had put on earlier in the day to ward off the damp chill of the spring morning. He tied it over his bedroll and saddle.

Walking into Kat's, he stopped just inside the swinging doors. With thumbs hooked in his gun belt, the tall, muscled man scanned the room. It wasn't a subtle glance, it was an inspection. He checked out the customers and the location of windows, doors, and stairways. Once he was comfortable with the layout, he strutted to the bar and ordered a rye.

Kat was at the far end of the bar and came up to him with her usual greeting for a stranger. "First drink is on the house for a new customer," she said, smiling. But even before he spoke, Kat knew she didn't like him.

"Thank you, ma'am." But his eyes didn't say thank you, they said, stay out of my way.

The way he'd said ma'am rankled her. "Name's Kat," she said with emphasis. Then, she pulled back her defensive attitude and asked nicely, "You passing through or planning on staying a while?"

He looked her up and down with stone-cold gray eyes. "Well, I'm not sure, *ma'am*. It depends." He drained the glass of rye Bear had placed in front of him and slammed the glass on the counter, blatantly staring at Kat as if challenging her to say something.

"Sorry, I wasn't being nosey," Kat said innocently. "I was going to recommend the Carmichael Hotel if you're here for a short stay, but Widow Murphy's boarding house would be a better option if you planned a longer stay."

Stone-cold eyes locked with hers, sending chills down her spine. He smiled derisively and ordered another rye. Carefully removing a crumbled-up piece of paper from his breast pocket, he methodically unfolded it. Laying it on the bar, he pressed it out several times using the side of his hand until it was smoothed to his satisfaction.

Kat looked at the creased and tattered wanted poster with a picture of Lloyd Templeton. "The only thing I need from you, *ma'am*, is information," his voice reeked of contempt. "You ever seen this guy?"

"You're a bounty hunter," Kat said, looking up from the dodger.

"His dead eyes glared at Kat. "I've been trailing Lloyd Templeton for over a year and followed him here to Grant's Crossing. I intend to cash in on the reward of $5,000, dead or alive."

"He murdered someone?" Kat asked.

"That's what it says on the dodger, but I don't care what he did. He's worth $5,000, and I'm only interested in the money." His eyes darkened, and a sneer distorted his whiskered face. "And no one had better get in my way."

Kat shuddered inside. The image on the wanted poster was Doctor Franklin Cooper. Their Doctor Cooper, Coop. She pretended to study the picture for a moment and then commented. "Well, he's an average-looking guy. Can't say if I've seen him or not." She paused, still looking at the picture. "No, I don't think so, but there are several other establishments in town you might try."

It was a struggle for Kat to keep her voice steady as she spoke. "Sorry, mister, but I didn't catch your name." Asking the question was a gamble, but he could only sneer or slam something. She wasn't too worried, and Bear had her back.

Bryson looked at her with those cold, gray eyes. *Like tombstones*, Kat thought. "Bryson," he answered. "Name is Graham Bryson."

"Well, Mr. Bryson, pleased to meet you," she said as sincerely as possible, "but I have some work to do. Bear will be glad to help you if you need anything else."

Kat walked back to where Bear stood at the far end of the bar. "We got us a heap of trouble, Bear. I'm going out the back way to get Jake and Sam. Keep an eye on him, but don't mess with him."

Bryson was playing a game of intimidation with her. She'd seen it before but had never seen it so well played. She was sure she had maintained her poker face, not indicating to Bryson that she knew the man on the wanted poster. It was a shock. The man she and the whole town knew as Doctor Franklin Cooper was wanted for murder.

She strolled toward her office nonchalantly, talking to customers as she went. When she was out of sight, she rushed out the side door and across the street to the marshal's office.

All three of the town's lawmen were in the office looking intently at a map when she burst in. They turned to the door, but she didn't give them a chance to speak. "We have a problem. There's a bounty hunter named Graham Bryson over at my place with a wanted poster for Coop. But it isn't Coop. It's a picture of him, but the poster says his name is Lloyd something or other, and he's wanted dead or alive for

$5,000. This has to be a mistake. It can't be Coop on that poster. And that Bryson is a bad one. A gunman with nothing but contempt for the world. I've seen his kind before." Kat stopped for a breath. "It can't be Coop on that poster."

The three men exchanged looks. "Well, we always knew this could happen," Jake said, combing his fingers through his thick dark hair.

"Only a matter of time," Logan agreed with a grunt.

"Well, let's head over and see what kind of trouble we're looking at. Logan, you find Coop and take him somewhere safe. Stay with him, and don't let him take off. Keep him close, and Logan, make sure he doesn't do anything stupid. It's too late for him to run."

Kat looked between the men, not wanting to believe what she was hearing. "You knew? You knew he was wanted?"

Sam turned to her. "We did. We were all set to arrest him when he first showed up in town, but we decided we liked him and we needed a doctor. We've been tearing down his wanted posters ever since."

Jake stood at the door. "Coop made a mistake back east, but I can't imagine Coop murdering a man. From all I've seen of him, he's a dedicated doctor and an honorable man."

Kat still couldn't believe Doctor Cooper was a wanted man, but Jake and Sam were right. They needed him, and she couldn't imagine him murdering anyone.

She followed them out and stopped, watching the two men walking side by side across the street. She thought Coop couldn't have any better men on his side. She ran across the street and back through the side door.

"You want me to go in with you or stay outside?" Sam asked as they walked across the street.

"Let's both go in and see what this looks like. Maybe if he knows there are two of us, he'll simmer down a bit."

They walked into the saloon with idle chatter and smiles. Kat was already back at her usual spot, and Bryson had returned to the bar after showing the wanted poster to Kat's customers. Most of them had scrambled out the front door after meeting with the intense bounty hunter.

Jake and Sam walked up to the bar to where Bryson was standing... their badges in plain sight. Jake spoke first. "You're a stranger in town."

He paused for a response. There was none. The man didn't move. "I'm United States Marshal Jacobs, and this is Deputy Marshal Watkins. I haven't seen you around here before."

He waited again for a response, but again, there was none. "I'm curious about your business here and how long you plan to stay."

Graham Bryson looked up slowly, brazenly scrutinizing Jake and Sam with open contempt. "I'm Graham Bryson, bounty hunter. I'm looking for Lloyd Templeton. I've been trailing him for some time now, and this is where the trail ends. I'm staying here for as long as it takes to find him or to make sure he's moved on to another town."

He raked his eyes over the lawmen. "No one in here admits to seeing him around. How about you? You know this man?" Graham showed them the poster.

Jake and Sam glanced at the poster. Jake's eyes were ice blue as they locked with the glare from Bryson's cold gray eyes. "I heard this guy was captured up around Wallace Bend last fall. Most of the posters have been pulled."

Bryson's glare didn't waiver, and neither did Jake's. "I could find no official record of him being captured or killed. I believe someone is covering up for him, protecting him. That wouldn't be you boys, would it?" He chuckled, "If he's here, I'll find him. I'll find him, and I'll kill him." He smiled smugly. "Just a reminder, Marshal, the reward is dead or alive. It'll all be legal-like. I prefer them dead if it's an option. They cause fewer problems for me that way."

His eyes were still fixed on Jake. "I see you wear your gun tied down, Marshal. Like a real gunslinger. You fast?"

"Still standing," Jake answered.

Then Bryson turned his attention to Sam and smiled. Sam didn't flinch under the scathing stare.

"Keep your pistol holstered, Bryson, and there won't be any trouble. We don't tolerate gunplay in Grant's Crossing." Jake paused. "We understand each other?"

Bryson's glare returned to Jake. "Oh, yes sir, Mr. Marshal, sir, I understand completely...*sir*." The sneer on his face and his cold gray eyes were bone-chilling.

"Good," Jake said, and as he and Sam turned to leave, neither showed the dread they felt.

Once they were on the other side of the street, Jake took a deep breath and blew it out. "That was one impressive display of intimidation, but it ain't all bluster. Kat's right. We got ourselves a problem."

Sam nodded. "He doesn't appear to be one who will back down," Sam said, looking across the street, "and sooner or later, someone will let it slip, and then what?"

"I wish I knew." Jake pushed his hat back. "But you're right. One wrong look or response, and Bryson will be on it like a mad dog... probably sooner than later." They went into the office. "I wonder if Logan found Coop?"

As if on cue, Logan came in the front door. "Coop's out at the Humphrey place. Grandma took a turn for the worse overnight, and he rode out this morning to see her. According to Jenny, there isn't much he can do but make her comfortable. He should be safe for the time being."

Sam let out a sharp breath and looked at Jake. "It's time we told him we know who he is. Let's get him someplace safe and let him know about Bryson. I hope we can convince him it's too late to run and safer to let us handle it."

Jake nodded. "I hope you're right...about us being able to handle it."

He turned to Logan, "Can you keep an eye on Bryson while Sam and I ride out to the Humphrey place? We'll take Coop straight to the ranch. He'll be safe there, and Grant will watch him."

"I'm your man, but be careful. You might want to take the back way out of town. Guys like Bryson are cunningly smart. If he suspects you know Templeton and are covering for him, he'll be watching and hoping you'll lead him to his target."

"Thanks for the warning. We'll make sure we're not followed. You be careful, too. Don't go and do anything to get yourself shot."

Jake and Sam headed to the livery for their horses and left by the back door. They cut across behind the schoolhouse and road through a thicket of timber to get to the main road. If Bryson was watching the street for them, he was out of luck.

Now, they had to get to Coop and tell him a killer had come calling.

# CHAPTER 43

# I KILLED A MAN

Lloyd Templeton, aka Dr. Franklin Cooper of Grant's Crossing, was passionate about helping people. It was this desire that inspired him to attend medical school. He wasn't a brilliant man, but his determination was unshakable.

In college, he found some of the classes harder than others. Cutting up and exploring the innards of dead creatures, large or small, always made him nauseous. He had thrown up more than once to his classmates' amusement and his professors' dismay. But he stayed with it. He studied harder than anyone else and got excellent grades. He was a natural, and his hard work paid off. He graduated at the top of his class.

He was excited about his future and all the challenges it held. He had an offer from a thriving practice and would soon be married to a beautiful young woman he loved more than life itself.

Student Lloyd Templeton was engaged to a vivacious young girl, Cora Spencer. Cora was cute as pie and flirted shamelessly with all the men. Lloyd had always tolerated his fiancée's flirtations as being innocent. He reasoned that if she flirted with everyone, how could it be serious? It was part of her charm.

But after he graduated and was around her more, he found that his fiancée had been seeing another man and still was. She had betrayed him, but it was his fault. He had neglected her. His studies had kept him busy, and she had become bored. But Cora hadn't complained once about being ignored and was always loving and attentive during the few hours he could find each week to spend with her. They discussed their wedding plans, where they would live, and how many children they would have. They were happy, or at least he had thought they were.

One evening, not long after graduation, a former classmate and friend, Doctor Whitney Chadway, invited him to meet at a neighborhood tavern for drinks. He and Lloyd had been friends throughout their schooling, and Lloyd looked forward to the evening.

"Two beers," Chadway told the bartender as Lloyd hopped on the stool next to him. "Good to see you, Lloyd. Have you accepted the position with Doctor Thomas?"

"I have," Lloyd replied as the bartender sat two mugs of beer in front of them.

"You lucky upchucker. I can't believe you got the best offer of all of us," Chadway said with a shake of his head.

"I got the top offer because I graduated top of the class," Lloyd said, poking back at Chadway.

"By what, a tenth of a tenth of a percent," Chadway scowled and took a swig of beer. "Hope Thomas doesn't plan on using you in surgery."

They both laughed and after several beers, their conversation became philosophical. They talked about life and death and their futures. Then, Lloyd confided to Whit that Cora was cheating on him.

Whit looked at Lloyd for a moment, wondering what to say and how much to tell him. "Move on, Lloyd. You deserve better. Find yourself a girl who appreciates you. Cora is using you and always has been."

"But I love her," Lloyd said, studying his half-empty beer mug. "Maybe she will come around now that I have more time to spend with her."

Whit stalled again and then decided to tell him everything about his sweet little Cora. Lloyd needed to know what every other student in their graduating class already knew. "Lloyd, she's a whore."

Lloyd turned to look at him. "How can you say that?" he said with more force than he intended.

Whit didn't know how to break it to Lloyd, so he blurted it out. "Cora has slept with almost everyone in our graduating class." Seeing the hurt and anger in Lloyd's eyes made him wince, but he was going to tell him everything. "You were so smitten with her. We should have told you about her, but we were afraid it would ruin your studies, and you had worked harder than any of us."

Lloyd slammed the mug on the bar, splattering beer on himself and Whit. He could barely believe what he had heard. "Did you…?"

"Yes, I'm sorry to say. I was with her." He decided to tell Loyd everything, even if it hurt their friendship. "I had her more than once, and sometimes there would be more than one of us at a time. She said she liked it that way. She liked women, too."

Templeton's eyes glazed over. Cora and his friends had betrayed him…made a fool of him. He was only partially listening as Whit continued.

"She didn't drink, so you can't blame it on her being drunk. Not that we didn't try to get her drunk. She would laugh and tell us alcohol made her do crazy things." He took a swallow of beer, almost choking on it. "Most of the time, she…uh…brought us to your apartment."

Lloyd was sick with jealousy and disbelief. "My apartment?" he yelled, drawing the attention of nearby drinkers. "She took you to my apartment and used my bed?" he said in a lowered voice

"I'm sorry, Templeton. But you needed to know."

"I don't know who she's seeing now, but I'd like to lop off his cock and give it to her with a bow tied around it."

"She has an uncontrollable hunger for sex, and it's a problem. She'll ruin your life, Lloyd, and your reputation."

Chadway got up and patted him on the back. "I have to go. Sorry to leave you with this, my friend, but you needed to know before you married her. Don't do anything you'll regret. Please, just walk away. She won't change, and you'll always wonder who she's with when she's not with you."

Lloyd Templeton returned to his apartment, hurt and angry. He sat in the dim light from the open window, staring at his bed, imagining Cora entertaining Chadway and his other classmates. How many others besides himself had made love to her in his bed? He was disgusted and repulsed. *Oh my God, Cora, how could you do this to yourself and to me? How could you bring them to my bed?* He sat in silence, a storm of hate and jealousy brewing in the pit of his stomach.

He was mortified at how naive he had been. He'd been a besotted buffoon, ignoring the signs of her infidelity. Cora told him earlier that she was staying home with her parents this evening. He wondered if he went to her parent's house if he would find her there or if she was out carousing with another man. Anger raged through his body, and he thought he might be sick. There was nothing he could do. Chadway was right. He needed to get on with his life. But how and where?

A moment later, his thoughts were interrupted by Cora's giggles and a man's deep laughter as she unlocked the door. They fell into the room in a wild, swirling embrace. Lloyd's common sense failed him, and the fury growing inside took over. He ran full force into the man, knocking him to the floor. Lloyd was sitting on the man, swinging wildly at his face. Some punches landed, but most missed or were blocked by the considerably larger man. Lloyd wasn't a fighter.

Cora screamed and screamed as the man knocked Lloyd off his chest and rolled on top of him. Lloyd felt a gun barrel pressed into his side and knew he had to react fast or die. He grabbed the man's hand with both of his, trying to bend it back and away from him, but he wasn't strong enough. They struggled, and Lloyd felt the barrel of the gun poke into his ribs with force. He was no match for the other man, but he held on to the gun tenaciously as they rolled back and forth across the floor.

He wouldn't quit fighting. The man would kill him if he did, and he didn't want to die. His feet connected with the wall, and he used all his strength to shove away from the man. They rolled into the bed frame with a hard thud, and the gun went off.

Lloyd thought he was dead, but he didn't feel any pain.

The man on top of him groaned and went limp. Lloyd felt blood drenching his shirt, and he struggled from under the dead weight lying on top of him. Lloyd checked to see if the man was alive; he wasn't.

Cora was cowering against the wall, weeping and whimpering, "You killed him. You killed him." She had worn herself down, but when the policeman came to the door, she flared up again, "He killed him, he murdered him. Murderer," she screamed at Lloyd.

Lloyd could only imagine that the man's hand had been twisted somehow when they hit the bed frame.

Cora kept screaming as Lloyd explained to the policeman what had happened. The policeman was polite and told Lloyd he would need to come with him to the police station to make a statement.

"He murdered him, he murdered him," Cora screamed as the policeman tried to calm her down. It took a while, but she finally quit screaming. "Ma'am, you need to come with us. You are the only witness to this murder, and you'll need to make a statement telling what you saw. Can you do that?" Cora nodded tearfully and glared at Lloyd.

Lloyd thought that when they got to the station, he could explain what had happened, but the realization of his situation sunk in. The policeman said *murder*. His heart was racing, and he was breathing hard. He was going to be arrested and tried for murder. His body tensed at the horrifying thought of hanging or spending the rest of his life in prison. And with Cora as the only witness to the fight, there wasn't a chance in heaven or hell that he would be found innocent.

Panic rapidly replaced common sense as fear closed in on him. But he needed to remain calm and keep a clear head. He amicably agreed to accompany the officer to the station to get everything taken care of. Since he was so agreeable and friendly and was only a string bean of a man, the police officer didn't put him in handcuffs. A mistake he wouldn't make again in his career.

Lloyd took the first chance he had to make a run for it. He heard whistles, a policeman yelling for him to stop, and his sweet Cora, still screaming at the top of her lungs, "Murderer. Murderer." He ran for all he was worth.

When Lloyd's, or rather, Franklin Cooper's train, stopped in Grant's Crossing, there had been a shooting at one of the saloons. He volunteered to help and missed his outbound train. He found Grant's Crossing to be a friendly town of decent people. The town needed him. The people needed him. It was time to stop running, and hopefully, it was far enough away to be safe.

## CHAPTER 44

# GOODBYE GRANDMA

Jake and Sam rode up to the Humphrey homestead and saw Coop harnessing his horse, ready to head back to town. He stopped to watch them ride in. He looked up at the men on horseback, shading his eyes against the sun. "What's going on? Is someone hurt?"

"We need you to come with us to Grant's."

"Sure, give me a minute. I want to say my goodbyes and check on Grandma one more time."

Seeing a frown on Jake's face, Sam said, "What's wrong?"

Jake looked up slowly to a spot above the cabin roof. "She's gone now, but I saw Grandma Humphrey floating over the cabin, all misty-like, and Sam, she winked at me."

Sam looked above the cabin and back at his friend. "That's a new one, the first time you've ever claimed to see someone who's died. Maybe your gift is changing."

Coop came out of the cabin just then. "Grandma passed. They plan to bury her in the family plot here on the farm, so there's nothing more for me to do here."

Mrs. Humphrey's son and daughter-in-law came out on the porch. Her son put his hand on Coop's shoulder. "My mom had a long life, and except for the last few weeks, she enjoyed every minute of it. She had a knack for living. Thank you for being here with her and easing her pain. She liked you, and I know it meant a lot to her that you were here at the last."

Coop shook hands with each of them. "I'm sorry for your loss. To live ninety-five years is a miracle. She was a remarkable lady and feisty to the end."

Sam and Jake expressed their condolences to the family. "Okay, Coop, it's time to head to your next patient," Jake said, motioning Sam to take the lead. Coop followed him, and then Jake brought up the rear. They were sure they hadn't been followed but still kept a close watch all the way to the ranch.

Grant came out to greet them, and Jake pulled him aside for a quick explanation. Grant nodded and led them to the formal dining room, closing the ornate pocket doors behind them.

Coop looked around for his patient. "Who am I here to see? Is someone hurt?"

"I'll see to it your horses are cared for, and Coop's carriage will be in the back barn," Grant said, leaving the dining room and closing the doors.

Sam sat at the dining table; his hands folded in front of him. Jake sat beside him and motioned for Coop to sit across from them.

"We know who you are," Sam said. "We know that you are Lloyd Templeton and that you are wanted for murder back East. I knew who you were the first time I saw you."

Coop tensed, his eyes darting back and forth across the room, ready to make a run for it. But realizing he had nowhere to go, he slumped in his chair.

Grant rejoined them as Jake spoke. "We recognized you from the picture on your wanted poster. It's a perfect likeness and leaves little doubt about who you are. We were going to arrest you, but we needed a doctor and decided to wait and see how things turned out."

Sam leaned forward. "Ever since, we've been tearing down your wanted posters and telling all the sheriffs in the territory you were captured, somewhere around Wallace Bend."

Coop cocked his head. "You've known all this time and didn't say anything?"

Grant nodded. "Until today, only the three of us knew who you were, but that's changed."

Sam locked eyes with Coop. "A bounty hunter named Graham Bryson rode into town today. He's showing your wanted poster around, and your picture is a perfect likeness. He's smart, Coop. He checked the official records and knew the Wallace Bend Story is a fake. When we left town, no one had identified you as yet. But it's only a matter of time before he finds someone who gives you away. Maybe not on purpose, but he'll know you're here."

A panicked Coop jumped up and started for the door. "I have to get out of here. He can't find me. He'll take me back to hang or to prison. Where's my horse?"

"Coop, sit down and take a breath. It's too late to run. You must realize this guy won't give up. We need to face this now." Jake leaned back in his chair. "He's already informed me that he intends to take you back dead, so you don't need to worry about hanging or prison time."

Coop groaned in disbelief as he returned to the table. "I thought I was safe. I thought I had run fast enough and far enough that he would quit looking." Coop held his face in his hands. Then he looked up. "What do I do?"

"You do nothing. You stay right here and out of sight. Let me and Sam handle it. The guy on your trail is a professional killer who won't hesitate to shoot you in the back. Unfortunately, it would be legal because of the wanted poster. But regardless, legal or not, you'll be dead."

Sam saw the despair on Coop's face. "Trust us, Coop. We'll fix this. Don't run off half-cocked and get yourself shot. Give us time to devise a plan that doesn't get anyone killed, and in the meantime, you stay here at the ranch and enjoy Lorene's cooking."

Jake sat forward, leaning on the table. "I don't know what happened back East, and I don't care. The man I know wouldn't kill unless he had a damn good reason."

Coop was a young-looking twenty-four-year-old with a scraggly goatee and skinny as a bean pole. He was gentle, unassuming, and did not look or act like a killer.

Coop looked at the three men and shook his head. "It means a lot that you have faith in me, but this is my mess. I can't fight Bryson and couldn't live with myself if any of you got killed because of me. So, I'll take my chances and leave town."

Jake shook his head in exasperation and looked at Sam. "Deputy Watkins, I thought Coop was a smart man. He does seem to be smart, doesn't he?"

"He surely does appear to be smart, Marshal Jacobs."

"And didn't I tell him he'd most likely get himself killed if he ran?"

"You did tell him that, Marshal Jacobs."

"And did you hear me tell him to let us handle it?"

"I most certainly did, Marshal Jacobs. You were fairly adamant about it."

Jake looked at Coop. "It's our job to protect the law-abiding citizens of Grant's Crossing, and that includes you. If I have to, I'll handcuff you to the back porch and have you watched twenty-four hours a day. I'm serious, Coop. You need to let us handle it."

Coop nodded and looked down at the table. "How did my life ever get so messed up? How can I ever repay you?"

"It ain't over yet," Jake said, "but we'll do our best to get you out of this tangle and not get anyone killed."

Jake and Sam got up to leave, with Grant following them to the front door. "Is there anything I can do to help?"

"You're doing enough keeping Coop safe. If Bryson figures out he's out here, you could have your hands full."

"I'll notify the men to be alert for any strangers, and I won't let Coop out of my sight. He'll be safe here. You two, be careful. If this guy is as bad as you say, don't take any chances."

They walked out onto the porch and started down the steps. Jake turned back to Grant. "We'll be careful, Grant, but this guy won't go down easy."

Grant waved and disappeared into the house.

"Come on, Sam. Let's get back to town and find out what Bryson is up to."

CHAPTER 45

# THE MAYOR AND THE COUNCILMAN

It was getting late when Jake and Sam rode into town. They went straight to Kat's Place, but Bryson was long gone. Only a dozen drinkers were scattered throughout the saloon, and five Poker players were hunched over a gaming table.

"I'm glad that man is out of here. He's bad for business," Kat fumed.

Sam nodded. "I reckon he is at that. Do you know where he was headed when he left?"

"He stopped across the street and shared his lovely disposition with Steven and Charlie. The last I saw of him, he was swaggering up Jefferson, probably headed for the Bent Ear. But I've heard he's spreading his joy all over town."

"Come on, Sam. Let's go on our rounds as usual. Maybe we'll run into him."

When Sam and Jake left Kat's, they saw Mayor Richards and Councilman Sumner standing in front of the marshal's office, having an intense conversation.

The mayor saw them. "Just the men we were looking for," he shouted across the street, waving them over to join them.

The four men entered the office, and before the door closed, Mayor Richards was in Jake's face. "We want to know what you are doing about this bounty hunter who's terrorizing our town. There have been plenty of complaints, and you need to do something."

"Well, Mr. Mayor, we were about to go on our rounds when you waved us over. We thought we might catch sight of him and find out if he's causing any trouble."

"Causing any trouble?" The mayor's eyes seemed to pop out of their sockets as he blustered, "Let me be perfectly clear, Marshal Jacobs, this has to be resolved, and soon. And where have you been? You should be here protecting the town." The mayor waved his arms like a bird about to take off. Then, as if he thought perhaps he'd overstepped, he glanced at Sumner for validation.

"Mr. Mayor, I appreciate your concern, but I'm responsible for the entire territory, not just Grant's Crossing. What I do or where I go is of no concern to you. We'll take care of the bounty hunter. He's walking a thin line, but so far, he hasn't broken a single law, so there isn't much I can do except watch him."

Jake turned to Sumner. "Anything you would like to add, Mr. Councilman?"

"Only that you spend too much time looking for this…killer of yours and not enough time taking care of business. You're using this office to carry on a personal vendetta and have proven inept at catching the killer or performing your basic duties. Duties you were sworn to uphold. You can be recalled, you know." Sumner glared imperiously at Jake. "Get this bounty hunter taken care of, or there will be consequences. Folks are getting nervous, which isn't beneficial for any of us, but it's especially not beneficial for you. Tend to your business, Marshal, or suffer the backlash."

Quinn turned on his heels and left the marshal's office with the mayor right behind him, still sputtering.

"What the heck was that all about?" Jake asked as the door closed behind their visitors. "The mayor hasn't bothered about us before, let alone with a councilman in tow."

"If you ask me, it was the councilman who had the mayor in tow," Sam said with a shrug.

"You think so?"

"Yeah, I do. Sumner has a hard-on for Winnie, and you're in his way."

"I was seriously thinking about hitting the arrogant bastard, and now I wish I had. He'd better stay away from her if he wants to live to pull another tooth."

"I'm glad you held back. Hitting him would have only given them more ammunition to use against you when the time comes. And I get the idea that Sumner would like nothing better than to see you hung out to dry." Sam chuckled, "We could be in for a real shitstorm."

He removed his hat and ran his fingers through his hair. He settled his hat back on his head and looked at his deputy with a smirk. "Come on, Sam. Let's tend to business as the councilman suggested and find us a bounty hunter."

# CHAPTER 46

# WHERE'S THE DOCTOR

Bryson had been in Grant's Crossing for over a day and had made little headway…until this morning. He had stopped at the Wishbone Cafe for breakfast and heard a conversation between two old-timers at a nearby table.

"Where the heck do you suppose the doctor got to? No one's seen him since he headed out to see Grandma Humphrey."

"Maybe he's making other calls outside of town."

"But he usually lets someone know. Even Jenny doesn't know."

"Jenny is a sweet girl. Think her and Coop play doctor when they're alone?"

"Wouldn't blame him none. She's a fine-looking young woman and kind. Make him a good wife."

"Good thing she was in the office this morning, or Zeke might have bled to death."

"Come on, let's mosey down and see what's happening on the other end of town."

"Yeah, them rockers out front of the saddlery ain't gonna rock themselves."

The conversation confirmed his suspicion that the man he hunted was nearby. Templeton had stopped running. Most hunted men did, eventually.

Bryson finished his breakfast and left the Wishbone, thinking he wanted to meet the doctor's lady friend. With the right kind of persuasion, she might remember where the good doctor was hiding…and he could be very persuasive. Looking up and down the storefronts. Bryson saw the doctor's office across the street and up a few doors. A wicked smile split his face. He could feel it. He was getting close.

He hurried across the street, dodging two freight wagons and a buckboard. He arrived at the doctor's front door as Jenny was locking up. Her back was to him.

"Ma'am," he said softly.

Jenny turned with a start. A man with a ragged beard stood too close to her. "What do you want?" she said, taking a step back against the door.

"I want to see the doctor," he said touching his meaty hand to her cheek.

Jenny flinched away. "He's out, and I don't know when he'll be back." She tried to push past him. "Excuse me, I have an appointment I need to get to."

"You're not going anywhere until you tell me where Doctor Cooper is," he said, shoving his forearm against her neck and knocking her head against the door.

"I'm telling you, I don't know," Jenny rasped as two cowboys came out of the Schooner Saloon next door. "Help me," she managed to choke out before the pressure on her throat increased, cutting off her ability to speak.

"Hey, what's going on here?" one of the men asked.

Bryson whirled to face the two cowboys. "This ain't none of your business. Move along."

"I'm getting the marshal," one of the men threatened and both hurried away.

"Please do. I'd like nothing better," he hollered after them and then returned his attention to Jenny. "Now, where were we?" he said, releasing some of the pressure from her throat.

"I can't tell you something I don't know," Jenny gasped out, trying to squirm away, but he held her tight and again leaned heavily against her throat.

"Get away from her," a voice shouted. At that moment, Jenny thought she'd never heard anything sweeter than Sam's voice.

Bryson released her and turned to face Sam. Sam had a gun trained on him. Bryson smiled. The deputy was taking no chances. Smart man.

Jenny rushed to Sam and stood behind him. "You all right? Sam asked.

"Yeah," Jenny replied.

"We were just having a friendly chat, Deputy." Bryson's cold gray eyes locked with Sam's.

"It didn't look friendly to me," Sam said, unimpressed by the glare. "You want to press charges, Jenny?"

"No," she whispered her throat still hurting.

"You sure?" Sam asked with a frown, keeping his gun aimed at the bounty hunter.

"I'm sure."

Sam motioned with his gun for Bryson to move along. "You got lucky, Bryson. There's nothing I'd like better than to lock you up. If you cause any more trouble of any kind, I'll lock you up for breathing."

Sam and Jenny watched Bryson swagger down the street. "I'd like to see that man strut right into hell," Jenny said, rubbing her throat.

"You sure you're all right?" Sam asked.

"I'm fine. Honest."

"You should have the doctor look at that," Sam said with a smile.

"I would if I knew where he was. Tell me he's safe, Sam. Tell me Bryson can't get to him."

"He's safe, Jenny."

## CHAPTER 47

# DON'T NEED A REPUTATION

Bryson headed for the far end of town and the Bear Paw Saloon. He needed a drink, and he needed to do some serious thinking. The young marshal and his deputy were not intimidated by him, and he didn't like it. The law usually backed off and cowered somewhere in a corner until he decided to leave town.

Jacobs was an unknown. He had a flashy custom-made rig and wore his pistol like a gunfighter, but he hadn't heard of him. He was sure if Jacobs had a reputation, he'd have known about it. Was he an impostor, wearing the fancy gun leather for effect? Bluffing? He didn't think so.

He wanted Templeton bad, five thousand dollars' worth of bad. He was sure the law was protecting him, and if that was the case, they wouldn't give him up without a fight.

Bryson shook his head as he lumbered down the street. A fellow would be a fool not to see that the marshal and his deputy were dangerous men. They were young, and youngsters were hard to predict. One of them was bad enough, but the two together created a whole different set of circumstances. And then there was Deputy Logan. He might be a little long in the tooth, but he didn't dare underestimate him. The more he thought about it, the more cocksure he was that they were going to cause him a whole lot of trouble, and they all had to go.

He was edgy, and he didn't care for the feeling. He didn't care for it at all. It was that dang marshal and his deputy, standing toe to toe with him without batting an eye. But what bothered him the most was not knowing how fast Jacobs was.

He was tempted to call him out, but that would take all of the fun out of it. No, he needed a way to find out just how fast he was. And he wanted to play with him. To get him to come looking for a fight, all mad and flustered. Maybe the chat he'd had with Jenny would bring him out for a showdown.

He pushed through the swinging doors into the Bear Paw Saloon, pausing to survey the filthy doggery of a bar. He didn't care. A bottle of whiskey and a plan were all he needed to make him happy. He wished a plan was as easy to come by as a bottle.

The Bear Paw was a drinking saloon. The service was poor, and the whiskey was watered down but cheap. There were no gaming tables and no dancing girls. Everything was beaten up and patched up from the many fights that had taken place there. The silent, broken-down player piano setting lopsided against the wall was a sad reminder of better times.

But it wasn't the piano that caught his eye. It was the man slumped over on the bar who had his full attention. He looked the man up and down. It was him. It was Russel Fitz.

Several years ago in Missouri, he had run into Fitz on one of his hunts. They had shared a bottle of whiskey and told tall tales of bar brawls and gunfights. Russel Fitz was a shootist, a professional gun for hire, and one of the best—the fastest he'd ever seen. Bryson smiled. He couldn't believe his luck.

Bryson walked up and stood beside him at the bar. "Fitz? How the heck are you? Let me buy you a drink."

Fitz raised slightly and turned his torso toward the man, studying him. "Do I know you?"

"Barkeep, we need a bottle over here," Bryson said, thumping the bar. "We met last October in Missouri. I was hunting an escaped bank robber, and you had just beefed a man. I've never seen anyone faster than you."

The barkeeper nodded and brought a bottle. "Let me see your money."

Bryson gave him his best glare and threw the money on the bar. "Come on, let's sit over there." He grabbed the bottle, and Fitz followed it to the table.

"Bryson?" Fitz said, finally recognizing his benefactor. "Well, I'll be go to hell. I didn't recollect it was you at first. You're looking good."

"Can't complain. You?"

"Been better, but then I've been a lot worse," Fitz cackled and coughed.

"What are you doing in this backwater town?"

"Just passing through," Fitz said, pouring another drink and tossing it back. "What about you?"

"I'm closing in on a bounty. Then I'll be moving on."

"Thought I'd land here and rest up for a few days, but that uppity marshal was on me the minute I rode into town, inviting me to leave. I've kept a low profile and managed to avoid him, but I'm riding out in the morning. He runs a tight town, too tight for my liking. I was aiming to have some fun."

"You got as much right to be here as anyone," Bryson huffed, pouring him another glass of whiskey and snickering under his breath. He couldn't believe how easy this was going to be. He would learn everything he needed to know about that arrogant young marshal courtesy of Russel Fitz.

"That cocky law dog is just plain asking for it," Bryson growled. "He hassled me when I rode in, too. I wanted to teach him some manners, but I hear he's real fast with that fancy pistol he carries. Faster than me, but I bet he's not faster than you, Fitz. You're the fastest I ever saw. Unless, of course, you've slowed down."

Fitz tipped back another whiskey and studied the bottom of his empty glass. "I'm as fast as ever," he said, looking from the chipped glass to Bryson. "Now and again, I have to put some young cock-a-doodle-doo in the ground to prove it. They keep coming, looking to take my reputation. Another reason for me to keep a low profile."

"Low profile? You? Not Russel Fitz. You used to ride into a town tall and proud, daring any man to give you grief. You took nothing from nobody." Bryson leaned forward across the table. "It's a shame that young buck has you skulking around and hiding in the shadows like some no-good varmint."

By the time they finished the bottle, Fitz's ego had kicked in. "Who does he think he is, talking down to me like that? Telling me to leave town. He ain't so high and mighty. I got my rights."

Bryson goaded him. "You could take him. You could call him out and put him down. That would show them all how fast you are and that you are not to be messed with." He paused, "Unless, of course, you don't think you're fast enough."

"I already told you, I'm fast as ever. I can put that snot-nosed pup in the ground in a heartbeat."

Bryson couldn't lose, no matter what happened. If the marshal outdrew Fitz, he'd know he was dang fast and would be a worthy opponent. If Fitz outdrew the marshal, it would spoil some of his fun, but that was all right. He'd still have two other lawmen to toy with.

"I'm gonna do it." Fitz stood and adjusted his gun belt. "I'm gonna call him out. He ain't gonna kick me out of town." He checked his gun, nodded to Bryson, and walked through the doors, letting them flap noisily behind him.

Russel Fitz strutted out of the Bear Paw, looking up and down the boardwalk. He couldn't believe his luck. There he was. The marshal was strolling down the other side of the street, coming right toward him. It had to be fate. Bryson was right. Someone needed to teach this overbearing pup a lesson, and he was just the man to do it.

Bryson hung back, well behind the batwing doors of the Paw. He did not want to be seen. He smiled at his cleverness and peered over the double doors. He had a ringside seat to the gunfight. No one would know he was watching or that he had been the one to set fate in motion.

"Marshal," Fitz yelled.

Jake stopped and looked across the street. "I thought I told you to keep moving. This isn't your kind of town."

"Nobody tells me where I can and can't go. I'm staying, and I'm gonna do whatever I want in this town, and you or no one else can stop me. I'm Russel Fitz and I'm gonna learn you some respect, Marshal. I'm calling you out."

Fitz stepped into the street, and Jake followed suit, watching closely for any indication he was about to draw. "Let's talk about this, Fitz."

"Ain't nothing to talk about. Draw."

It was over in the blink of an eye, and Russel Fitz lay dead in the street. Jake took a deep breath to steady his heartbeat. It was beating so fast he thought it might explode.

Bryson walked off, knowing just how fast Jacobs was. This was going to be so much fun. He was going to kill the man who outdrew Fitz. But now he had to hurry. The marshal's office wasn't far, but he didn't have much time to implement the second part of his plan.

Sam was at Jake's side almost before Fitz hit the ground. "Jake, you okay?"

"Yeah."

Sam kicked the gun away from Fitz's hand and squatted beside him, checking for a pulse. He looked at Jake, shaking his head as he stood up. "He's dead. What happened?"

"He's the one I told you about a few days ago. I told him he was welcome to get a drink and a meal, but he needed to move on." Jake took another deep breath. "He came out of nowhere, Sam, and yelled that he was calling me out."

"You know who he was?"

"He said his name was Russel Fitz. You know him?"

"No, but I know of him. He's a professional gun with a reputation as one of the fastest. Dang, Jake, be careful who you outdraw. You don't need a reputation."

"I know, but I didn't see as I had much choice. I did try to talk to him, but he wasn't interested."

A crowd had gathered around the body, muttering about the marshal and how fast he was. Sam walked over and motioned to a group of several men. "You men get that body off the street and over to the undertaker."

There were still people milling around and talking. "Time to clear the street, folks. Go on about your business. There's nothing more to see."

As the last stragglers finally moved away. Jake took his hat off and ran his hand through his hair. "Sam, what the hell?"

Sam looked at him and shrugged. "You got called."

"Let's finish our rounds and stop at Kat's for a drink. I could sure use one." He hadn't killed anyone before, but he had always known it was bound to happen sooner or later. He took a breath and tried to shake it off. Maybe by the time they finished their rounds, his heart would stop pounding against his ribs.

Kat's Place was abuzz with stories about the gunfight and how fast Marshal Jacobs was. Like lightning, they said, no one faster. He had faced off with Russel Fitz and outdrew him. Kat's Place was noisy and busy, just the way Kat liked it. She was delivering drinks and chatting with customers when she saw Jake and Sam come in.

"Jake, you have caused quite the stir."

"Not intentionally," Jake said, looking around at all the people in the barroom.

Kat squeezed his shoulder. "I need to get back to work. Nothing like a gunfight to bring out the drinkers."

"You seen Logan? It's not like him to miss out on a ruckus," Sam asked.

Kat shook her head. "He hasn't been here," she said as she dashed away to tend to her customers.

## CHAPTER 48

# WHERE'S LOGAN

They left Kat's and hurried across the street to the office, wondering if Logan was taking a nap. They found him on the floor, badly beaten and covered in blood.

Sam grabbed a folded blanket from the cot and put it under Logan's head. He tried to assess the damage. "It's bad, Jake. It looks like he got bushwhacked. There's a goose egg on the back of his head and a stab wound in his side. Whoever it was messed him up good."

Jake grabbed a dipper of water from the bucket and dribbled some on Logan's lips. Then he wet his kerchief and dabbed it on his forehead.

Logan's eyes flew open. Coughing and gagging, he grabbed his side in pain. "I didn't tell him. I didn't tell him anything, but I think he knows," Logan said in a whisper. "He knows Coop's at Grant's." Logan wheezed. "Get to Coop. I'll be okay. Let Kat know I'm here, and she'll take care of me."

"Ride for the ranch, Jake. I'll go get Kat and be right behind you." Sam was out the door and running across the street.

Jake went outside and was about to hop into the saddle when he remembered Logan's earlier warning about how clever Bryson was.

Maybe this was a ploy to get them to rush out for a doctor. "Clever man," he whispered in Drach's ear.

Jake was still standing at the hitching post when Sam and Kat came rushing across the street. Sam looked questioningly at Jake, surprised to see him standing there. "What's wrong?"

"I believe we're being played. Let's go see what we can do for Logan."

Kat got on her knees and felt along Logan's ribs, making him flinch. "He needs Coop," Kat said as Sam helped her up. "But I'll go see if I can find Jenny. She can do more for him than any of us."

She returned shortly with Jenny Young. Jenny dropped to her knees beside Logan and spoke quietly as she ran her hand along his ribs.

"Looks like you got a bad beating, Deputy Logan, but I know what to do until Coop gets here. We're going to move you onto a stretcher so that we can carry you to the office. It'll hurt some when we move you." Logan looked like he was about to say something, but Jenny took his hand and stopped him. "Deputy, you be still now and save your strength." She winked at him and squeezed his hand. "We'll have plenty of time to discuss exactly what this winking and handholding thing means."

Once Logan was on the stretcher and on his way to the doctor's office, Kat went across the street, leaving Jake and Sam alone.

"I'm sure Logan didn't tell him anything, but I am concerned about Grant and Lorene. Winnie is at the cabin with Clark, so I know she's safe. But if Bryson finds out about our connection to the Grants, he could guess that's where we've stashed Coop."

Sam leaned his arm against the door jam, looking out at the street. "Bryson comes into our town threatening us and going from business to business terrorizing everyone he's come into contact with. Then he attacks Jenny, and now, this. He's pushing for a fight, Jake, but why."

Jake looked at Sam with a frown. "Interesting that he was beating on Logan while the main event was happening down on Washington Street...in front of the Bear Paw."

"Are you thinking he orchestrated the gunfight somehow?"

"I don't know. Maybe. Let's take a walk down to the Paw."

Striding down the dimly lit street side by side, they appeared confident and unshakable, but the unease they felt had their senses on alert. Their eyes scanned the street, searching every shadowy alleyway, and they had to fight the urge to respond to every unexpected noise.

"That was a long walk," Sam said as they pushed through the saloon doors.

Several men were playing cards and quietly drinking at one of the tables, and a single cowpoke at the bar was chatting up the barkeep.

Jake and Sam went to the bar. The cowpoke nodded to them and edged away.

"Texas," Jake said, and Sam nodded to the man behind the bar.

"What can I do for you?"

"We have some questions."

"About the shooting? That was something, Marshal. Outdrawing Fitz the way you did. That was truly something."

"Was Bryson or Fitz in here earlier, before the gunfight?"

"They sure was. Sitting right over there at that table, sharing a bottle. Bryson was talking up a storm, and Fitz was hanging on every word." He paused, trying to decide if he should go on or not. He glanced around to see if anyone could hear and lowered his voice. "Marshal, I couldn't catch what was said, but that bounty hunter had Fitz all riled up about something. He was pleased with himself, grinning like a jackass when Fitz left. Marshal, don't tell him I said anything. I'm sure he would kill me without blinking an eye."

"Thanks, Texas. I won't say a thing. I owe you one."

Jake and Sam walked cautiously along the nearly deserted street. A sense of unease still hung over them and apparently over almost everyone else. Some businesses had hung closed signs in their windows, and the few brave souls on the street were hurrying to their destination.

When they got to the jail, Jake leaned against the building, his thumbs hooked in his gun belt. "Where do you suppose he is?"

"I wish I knew," Sam said, resting a hip on the hitching rail, "but apparently, he wants a showdown with you. I don't understand why he doesn't call you out like Fitz did."

"I was going to the ranch in the morning, but I guess that's on hold until this Bryson thing is resolved."

"The mayor and the councilman would be glad to hear you say that."

"I suppose they would. Wonder what they think about the shootout?"

"Probably wishing it was Bryson instead of Fitz that went down. But then again, Sumner might have preferred it was you who bit the dust. It's one way of eliminating the competition for Winnie's attention."

Jake scowled at Sam. "He's no competition, but I'm concerned about her fascination with the man."

"Well, one thing's sure, Bryson isn't done yet…and neither is Sumner."

Jake was momentarily silent, "Why do you suppose Bryson goaded Fitz into fighting me? Was it a distraction to give him time to attack Logan and get whatever information he could out of him?"

"Maybe. Or it could be that he thought Fitz would kill you and get you out of his way. But I think he's trying to get you riled enough to come after him. Then again, as you said earlier, maybe he did think we'd run for the doctor and lead him straight to Templeton."

"None of it makes sense, Sam. I'm beginning to think he's making a game of it."

"If so, it's a dangerous game," Sam said.

"And we don't know the rules."

## CHAPTER 49

# A ROW AT KAT'S PLACE

They rose early the following morning, fixing coffee, shaving, and making the usual early morning conversation.

"Think I'll have steak and eggs with a heaping pile of fried potatoes," Sam said, pulling a comb through his hair and turning from the mirror. "I got a big empty spot behind my belt buckle."

Jake was about to comment on Sam's eating habits when a pain shot through his head like a lightning bolt.

"Kat's in trouble. Bryson!" The pain left him as it always did when he acknowledged the message.

They ran from the marshal's office, checking their weapons, and stopped one on either side of the door. They entered slowly and saw Bryson holding Kat. She struggled against him as he jerked her arm behind her back, pulling a derringer from her clenched fingers.

Bear had the shotgun he kept under the bar aimed at Bryson but was afraid to shoot for fear of hitting Kat. Bryson pulled Kat in front of him and fired on Bear, putting him down.

Jake and Sam drew their guns.

"Don't do it," Bryson yelled. "I'll shoot her. You know I will." He rubbed the barrel of his gun down her cheek and neck. "Holster your guns. I would hate to have to shoot your Miss Kitty Kat. It'd be a real shame."

Sam knew there were several shots he could take, but with the cocked gun pressed against Kat's neck, any move he made could get her killed. He couldn't risk it.

Bryson eyeballed Jake. "You wear that fancy gun leather of yours all serious like, and it made me wonder just how fast you are." He shoved the gun harder against Kat's neck, making her flinch.

"Let her go," Jake said. His voice sounded more authoritative than he felt.

"Thanks to Fitz's sacrifice, I know how fast you are. That was quite a show." He eyed Jake, a wicked smirk on his face, and yanked on Kat's arm, causing her to scream.

Jake and Sam both took a step forward.

"Stop where you are, or she dies." He smiled smugly. "Are you worried about how fast I am?" He paused for effect. "You should be. I will say one thing, sonny, you don't rile easy. It was hard getting you mad enough to come for me. I could have called you out, but this has been more fun."

"Fun? You think this is a game?"

"It is a game. Life is a game, Marshal, and I have no rules cluttering up my life. Oh, by the way, sorry about Logan. He's a tough old bird. I couldn't get him to give up a thing about Templeton. Maybe, if I'd had more time with him, he would have talked, but I was in a bit of a hurry."

"Let Kat go, Bryson. This is just between you and me now."

"You are right, Jakie boy, it is just between you and me, and it's time. It took a lot to bring you out to play. But I figured, you being an honorable man and all, that a lady in distress would get you riled enough to come for me." He laughed, poking her harder with his gun and twisting her arm, causing her knees to buckle. "Are you her knight in shining armor? Riding in to save the day?" His laughter rumbled through the empty room.

Kat was hurting, but she had to do something. While he was distracted with Jake, she thought she might be able to get to the knife in her pocket. But Bryson sensed her muscles tensing and savagely twisted her arm. He grunted, hoisting her limp body tighter against him, never taking the muzzle of his gun away from her neck.

"Enough talk, Jakie. It's time. It's been delightful chatting, but we got business to tend to. Kat and I are going to move out into the street, and I'm gonna find a spot to my liking. I'll be waiting for you. It's time for you to die."

Bryson looked in Sam's direction, turned his gun, and fired. The bullet hit Sam in the chest, sending him to the floor. "Sorry, Deputy, but I didn't want any problems or interference from you."

Jake started to move toward Sam, but Bryson cut him off. "He'll be fine…or he won't," he laughed. "Either way, me and Miss Kat will be waiting for you outside. Kat says you shouldn't make us wait." He winked. "For her sake."

Bryson exited the saloon, dragging Kat with him. Jake ran to Sam's side. He was breathing, but he was losing too much blood. Bear crawled to them, his shirt soaked crimson with his blood. "Go, Marshal. I'll tend to Sam."

Jake hesitated. He wasn't sure Bear could take care of himself, much less anyone else.

"He'll kill her, Jake." Bear groaned as he pulled himself to Sam's side.

Jake stood, checked his gun, and adjusted his gun belt. As he walked toward the door, he heard Bear. "Don't let him in your head. Remember to breathe and don't panic. You're faster than him, and you're smarter."

Jake's heart was pounding as he slowly pushed through the batwing doors. Bear's voice rang in his ears. He took a deep breath. Bear was right. He had to stay focused. If he got flustered or distracted, he'd be dead. With Fitz, it had happened so fast he hadn't had time to think, and Fitz hadn't been in his head. Jake took a deep breath and put fear and thoughts of anything else behind him. He knew what he had to do.

The street and boardwalk were deserted, but every window of every building was crowded with curious faces. A trickle of sweat ran down his back, and the heavy beating of his heart echoed in his ears. *If I do have an inner sense, I sure could use a hand right now. I'll take anything you've got.* Jake's eyes darkened and then as quickly lightened. His breathing returned to normal, and his heart calmed.

The bounty hunter watched Jake step from the boardwalk. Bryson threw Kat to the ground and holstered his gun. "Glad you could make it," he sneered. "Kat and me was getting worried."

Bryson stood with the sun behind him, but as Jake stepped into the street, clouds moved in, taking away the bounty hunter's advantage. Jake stood ready, his eyes fixed on Bryson, waiting for the sign that signaled he would draw. He didn't have long to wait…it was in his eyes.

Jake drew and fired. The sting of a bullet sliced through his left arm as he twisted to the right and fell to the ground. Ignoring the pain, he rolled up with his gun pointed toward Bryson.

Bryson had fallen next to Kat and wasn't moving. Holding his left arm, Jake hurried to where they were lying and kicked Bryson's gun out of reach. Kat was unconscious but breathing. The bounty hunter was dead.

He heard Logan. "You got him, Marshal, straight through the heart."

Jake's head was spinning, but he kept moving. He knelt by Kat, patting her face and talking to her, trying to wake her up. Jenny put a hand on his shoulder. "Marshal, let me look at your arm. You're losing too much blood."

"I'm okay, Jenny. Sam and Bear need you. Bryson shot them. Logan?"

"I'm here, Jake."

"Stay with Kat."

Logan helped him to his feet, and holding his left arm against his chest, Jake followed Jenny into the saloon. His insides knotted at the thought of losing Sam, but Sam and Bear were both alive. Sam had lost a lot of blood, but Bear had staunched the bleeding by pressing bar towels against the wound and leaning on them with his elbow.

Bear looked up at him with a strained smile. "We've both got through and through wounds, Marshal. At least that quack of a doctor won't have to go digging around in our innards searching for a bullet," Bear laughed, flinching with pain.

Jenny looked at his wound. "I'll tell him you said that, Bear."

"You won't have to, Jenny. I heard it all." Coop was standing at the door with Grant at his side. "Jenny, we need to get all the wounded to my office…even Bear." Logan and Grant helped Bear onto a stretcher. "Looks like you saved Sam's life. Good job, Bear," Coop said, smiling down at him. "John," Coop said, his eyes searching the gathering crowd. "And Ross, get over here and help me get Sam on a stretcher."

Jake's knees were weak, and everything was beginning to swim around him, but he shook it off. Everyone needed to be taken care of. "Coop, did you check on Kat?"

"Yes, she's shaken up and has a broken arm, but she'll be fine. We have to go, Jake. Jenny is getting Sam ready for surgery. Logan tied his bandana around your arm, but you've lost too much blood. We need to get it stopped."

Jake studied the tourniquet wrapped around his arm, concerned at the amount of blood trickling down to his fingers and dripping onto the floor. "I'm fine, Coop," Jake said, but he didn't feel fine.

"You're still losing too much blood...and you are not fine," Coop said.

"What are you doing here in town?" Jake asked as they hurried up the street. "You had specific instructions to stay put at the ranch."

"I decided I couldn't hide while you fought my battle. Not when you might need me. I couldn't let you face it alone."

"Shouldn't you be with Sam? You did say he's going to be okay?"

"I told you Jenny is getting him ready for surgery, and we're on our way to my office, and yes, he should be fine."

"I don't feel quite...right," Jake said as he sank to the ground on Coop's doorstep.

## CHAPTER 50

# TOO MUCH

The hunter made himself as small as possible so he wouldn't be seen. Cowering in a recess in the cavern wall, he closed his eyes and hugged his knees to his chest. He imagined himself the size of a tiny dot, getting smaller and smaller until he disappeared. He was hiding but he couldn't remember why. Who was hunting him?

A searing, red-hot pain shot through him as razor-sharp teeth and claws ripped and tore at his body. There was so much pain. He looked down. He was covered in blood and holding his innards in his hands. He swallowed a scream, as he heard the animal roar. Tears poured from his eyes and snot bubbled from his nose. "Don't kill me. I don't want to die," he whispered to his drugged-distorted mind. He passed out and fell into blessed oblivion.

He woke confused and cold. He saw through blurred eyes that he was in his workroom. He didn't know how long he'd been crouching against the wall, curled up in the fetal position, but he could barely move his legs. He didn't remember coming to the workshop. He felt strange.

As his mind began to clear; he remembered a pounding need for a woman to ease his tensions. He had made only two kills so far this spring and the need to hunt was strong. He was beginning to remember.

He'd gone to the Scarlet Slipper. But he didn't go in. He had waited outside for one of the soiled ladies. A whore who no one would miss.

With a sudden gasp of horror, he looked down at his stomach. His body was covered with dried blood, but his belly wasn't slit open, and there were no teeth or claw marks. His stomach lurched and dry heaves racked his body. It must have been the drug. He'd taken too much.

He stood slowly, shaking his legs to get the blood circulating, and walked to his worktable. It was covered in dry blood, and a scalp of long blonde hair was draped across it. His senses and memories came flooding back, along with the feeling in his legs. Drag marks lead from the worktable to an underground stream that flowed through his cavern workshop. A bloodied axe and a saw lay nearby. At least he had disposed of the body.

He splashed into the stream and scrubbed away the dried blood, smiling as more memories returned. He needed to check his journal. He would have recorded the drugs he'd given his guest and her reactions. He hoped he had detailed everything, but it would have to wait. He had an important meeting to prepare for.

He found his clothes where he always left them, neatly folded on his cot. He dressed and quickly climbed the stairs to the hatch and looked around to make sure he was alone before climbing out. He dropped the hatch into place making sure it was disguised with grass and twigs. He pulled his gold watch from its pocket, checking the time. He snapped the watch shut. He had time. It was a meeting he didn't want to miss.

## CHAPTER 51

# WHAT ABOUT COOP

The morning following the gunfight, Jake, Logan, Kat, Grant, Coop, and Jenny gathered in the room shared by Sam and Bear. They were the only ones who knew Coop was a wanted man.

Sam pulled himself up in bed, and Jenny helped arrange the pillows behind him. "Coop says I'll need a couple more days of bed rest before he'll even think about turning me loose. And the way I feel, I'm inclined to agree with his assessment. I'm just glad to be alive. Thank you, Bear."

Bear scoffed. "Don't know why I bothered saving you. You're one of our worst customers."

Kat laughed and voiced her agreement.

"Guess I am at that," Sam said, trying hard not to laugh.

Jake stood at the foot of Sam's bed. "We're here because we need to make sure no one ever comes after Coop again. Our story is and always will be that he is a dead ringer for Lloyd Templeton. No matter what happens, that's our story."

Jake took a deep breath, his shoulders drooping. "I feel responsible for this mess. I should have dealt with Bryson sooner. If I had, maybe he wouldn't have gone to such extremes. I put everyone in this room in danger."

Coop butted in. "If anyone is responsible, it's me. I brought this mess with me."

Logan sounded off in his gravelly voice. "Jake, you can't second guess yourself. You did what you thought was right, and no matter the circumstances, that's all you can do. I doubt any lawman would have handled it any different. And as for you, Coop, we chose to protect you. I don't remember you making us do anything we didn't want to."

Logan eyed each of them. "The only person to blame is Graham Bryson, and he's dead. Quit your caterwauling, and let's solve this problem."

Jake nodded. "Sam says he may have a solution. It's your idea, Sam, you tell them."

"Coop woke me sometime during the night, hauling a body down to the cellar to keep it cool. He intended to have Bones pick it up this morning. I asked him to wait until we had a chance to talk." Sam nodded to Coop. "Why don't you tell them how you came by the body."

"The Ramsey boys came tearing in here around midnight. They'd been fishing on the river just south of the bridge and had found a body snagged on some rocks and tree roots."

"They were rattled at finding a dead man and afraid of what their dad would do to them for being out so late. After they showed me where the body was, I sent them home. I told them their secret was safe with me. I wouldn't tell their dad or anyone else about the body."

"It was a struggle getting that dead weight up on the bank by myself, but I managed. It's been in the water for a day or more and got mangled, bouncing into rocks, and being gnawed on by predators. There's no way I can tell who it is, but I do know it was a man." Coop looked at Sam and nodded for him to take over.

"I was thinking that we could bury that body as Lloyd Templeton."

Logan ran his thumb and forefinger down his mustache. "How do we explain where the body came from, and how could we know it's Templeton if it's so mangled?"

"We make it look like Jake tracked him down and killed him. Doctor Cooper signs the death certificate, and Jake and I file all the necessary reports detailing his capture and death. In the eyes of the law, Templeton is legally and officially dead and gone."

Grant commented. "You know it isn't unheard of for someone to dig up a coffin, legal or not, to confirm a death. Is there anything that belonged to Templeton that can be placed on the body?"

Coop nodded. "I have a family medallion that I - that Templeton always carried in his vest pocket. I'll put it in one of his pockets."

Logan frowned, narrowing his lips. "It just might work. As far as I know, we haven't had any missing persons reported in the last few days. So there shouldn't be anybody stirring up a stink."

"I haven't heard of any either," Jake said. "This guy could be a saddle tramp or a drifter that no one will ever miss."

"What about Bryson and Fitz?" Grant asked.

Jake walked to the window and looked toward the train station. "Bryson is returning to Oklahoma later today at his family's request. He's packaged up and ready to board the southbound, and later today, Bones is escorting Fitz to Paupers Field."

"So? It's decided? We bury this poor soul as Lloyd Templeton, file the necessary documentation with the courts, and no one will be the wiser," Jake said.

"Who'd ever know but us?" Logan said.

"Yeah," Jake said, looking at Logan. "That's the question. Who'd ever know?"

"I can't let you do this." Coop's voice cracked. "If anyone ever found out, you would all be ruined. Maybe end up in jail. I'm going back to face the music. That will solve everything."

Grant spoke with a shake of his head and a snort. "Coop, that's just plain nuts. After what we've gone through to save your hide? You are doing no such thing. We have a story, and we have a plan. The story is that it's unfortunate you look so much like Lloyd Templeton. It caused quite a stir, but mistaken identity is all it was. You're going to grow old here and maybe one day tell your grandchildren how you looked so much like a wanted killer that a bounty hunter rode into town, causing all kinds of commotion. But for now, we bury the dead and ride away. If we all stick to the story, there will be no danger of Coop ever being found out."

Sam looked at Jake. "We need to stage Templeton's capture. You up to it?"

"I can do whatever needs to be done," Jake said, trying to sound convincing.

Coop scowled at him but knew protesting would do no good.

"You need to go searching for Templeton and then return with his body. A body for everyone to see."

"And how do I do that, Deputy Watkins?"

"Well, Marshal Jacobs, it seems obvious…you take the body with you, of course."

"That doesn't sound like the best idea I've ever heard."

"You found him out by Eagles Pass, chased him, and he stumbled and fell from that rock cliff into the creek. It took you until the next day to find him and fish him out. If anyone gets too snoopy and wants a close look, that should explain the body's condition. What do you think, Coop? Realistic enough?"

"It's near enough to the truth to sound plausible. A warning, Jake, that body will be ripe by the time you get back. He's in the cellar keeping cool, but once the heat hits him, it'll get ugly fast."

Jake winced. "If I'm taking our unknown friend for a ride, I'll have to use a carriage. I can hide the body in the back where it will be covered and out of the sun. And if it's a stinking mess by the time I get back, no one will want to get too close." Jake rolled his shoulders with a grimace. "A carriage would probably be the best for me anyway."

Sam looked at the group. "We all have to keep the story straight and stick to it. Coop looks so much like Templeton that Bryson was fooled and wouldn't give up. Jake hunts down the real Templeton, who is buried in Paupers Field. Coop's medical report will document his death and the condition of the body, and Jake and I will file the appropriate forms and reports. Don't explain or volunteer any information to anyone unless asked, and then keep it simple." Sam paused and looked from person to person. "Do we all agree with the plan?"

Everyone did.

Bryson caught the two o'clock train back home to Oklahoma, Bones escorted Fitz to an unmarked grave in Pauper's Field, and Jake prepared to leave on his search for Lloyd Templeton.

CHAPTER 52

# THE HUNTER HUNTS

He always went to church on Sunday. He liked watching them.

In his sermon Paster Emil Larsen of the Lutheran Church extolled the bravery of the lawmen of Grant's Crossing and how they made their growing town a safe place to live. A place where a man could settle down with his family.

He wasn't listening. If he had been he'd have laughed. He thought the law in Grant's Crossing was a travesty. He'd been evading them for years.

He was watching Jake and Winnie from across the aisle. They were seated in the Grant family pew with Mr. Grant and Lorene. Jake's arm was on the back of the pew behind Winnie, his hand on her shoulder.

Such a loving couple. And what an interesting idea. He'd already dispatched Jake's parents. He smiled at the thought of having their son under his knife. *Amen and hallelujah.*

## CHAPTER 53

# NATE'S ADVICE

Winnie was back in town running errands for Clark and her father. She had snuck covertly into town, wanting to avoid any encounter with Quinn Sumner. Seeing the closed sign on his office door, she breathed a sigh of relief. Without him in town, she could go about her business without having to sneak through the back alleys like a thief.

*I know I'm being silly sneaking about, but I can't deal with a confrontation with him, and that's what it would be. I wish he would leave me alone and recognize that I'm not interested in him.* She left the post office, wrapped up in her thoughts and flipping through the mail, not paying attention to where she was going. She walked into a solid wall of a man, and her first thought was of Sumner. She was afraid to look up.

"You need to watch where you're going, Winnifred." The man's voice held an edge of humor, scolding, and the slightest hint of a Southern accent.

"Nate."

"Sorry, I startled you. I stopped and thought you would notice me before you plowed into me."

"I - I thought you were someone else," Winnie said, a flush climbing up her neck.

"I figured as much. Listen, I was just over at the feed and grain putting in an order, and it will be a while before it's ready. I thought I'd go to the Wishbone for a bite to eat while I waited. Don't suppose I could talk you into joining me?"

Winnie frowned. The last time she accepted an invitation from a man, it had not gone well. But this was different. Nate was a longtime friend of her father's and a gentleman. She was starving and couldn't be safer if she were with Pastor Emil. The thought of a plate of Minnie's fried chicken at the Wishbone made her mouth water.

"I would love to," she said, cramming the letters into her bag and taking the arm Nate offered.

"You've been home for over a week now. Have you re-acclimated to the wide open, wild West?"

"From day one. I was so glad to get home and see nothing had changed."

"What brings you into town?"

"Errands. Somehow, I've become Clark's assistant."

"How did that happen?" he said, laughing as he opened the door to the Wishbone.

"We're fixing up that old trapper's shack. You know, the one about halfway to the lake."

"I remember, although it's been years since I was at your lake house. You must have been five or six."

"Hmm, that sounds about right. I remember you quacking like a duck for me."

"I only quack for children up to age six. After that, I growl like a bear." He smiled, mesmerized by her sparkling green eyes. "So, what is the purpose of fixing up the cabin?"

"Well, it started as fixing it up for the crew up there and has ended with rebuilding and enlarging it for roundup as well as the riders on the north range. It'll also make a perfect stopping place on the way to the lake."

"Grant doesn't do anything halfway, and I suspect you may be a lot like him."

Winnie chuckled. "I have heard that before."

"Why aren't you dining with one of your girlfriends?"

"Mary has fittings scheduled for the rest of the day, and Kat is working behind the bar. And, of course, Jake is somewhere saving the world…when he should be in bed."

"Kat's bartending with a broken arm?" Nate asked.

"She's short-handed. Bear can barely move after getting shot, and Archie didn't show up. She's concerned about him. She told me he's late half the time…but always gets there."

Winnie and Nate placed their orders.

"And who is Jake saving?"

"I have no idea, Nate, but Logan said he would be gone for four or five days," she sighed. "I don't know why he's out running around the countryside. He was shot and should be resting. Whatever is going on, he's never here when I need him."

"It would appear that you have hung your shingle out with Jake's name on it. If that's the case, you had better get used to him being away."

"I know, but a woman does need some attention now and again."

"My wife would have commiserated with you on that topic. I was away too much, sometimes for months at a time. The last time, it was over a year before I could return home."

"I suppose I shouldn't complain," Winnie said.

"A word of advice, Winnifred, from an older and wise friend… don't make him feel guilty. It won't help, and it could drive a wedge between you. If he is the man you want, his being gone comes with the territory."

Winnie scoffed, "Yeah, the whole Dakota Territory."

Pushing away empty plates, they left the cafe, and Nate walked her back to her buckboard. "Winnifred?"

"Yes."

"I hope you realize what a beautiful woman you've become. Any man with a pulse could get lost in those beautiful green eyes. And, well, what I'm trying to say is, be careful. You seem to be unaware of how you affect men."

"Are you saying I'm naive?"

"I was trying to avoid that word, but yes. Winnifred, you are naive. You are as alluring today in a cotton shirt and riding britches as you were in satins and lace. You are open and friendly, and some men might take it wrong. Some might take it as flirtatious and an invitation to… well, to other things. Men can be dogs."

"You included?" Winnie laughed.

"Absolutely, Winnifred, me included. I'm no saint. And that is why I know you need to be cautious."

"Jake and Sam will take care of me. They always have."

"But as you said, they are not always around. Pay heed and keep your wits about you."

"Okay, Dad," Winnie said, smiling at her friend.

They said their goodbyes, and each headed home. Winnie thought about Nate's advice, and Nate thought about how enticing Winnifred was and how much he would like to take her to bed.

## CHAPTER 54

# THE PAIN OF WAR

On the ride home, Nate could not get Winnifred out of his mind, and his thoughts were anything but gentlemanly and entirely out of line. He knew his thoughts were insane, but he had been bewitched by her green eyes and musical laugh. He was old enough to be her father, but there was something about her. He couldn't help but smile when he thought of what Grant would do to him if he knew the salacious thoughts he was harboring. Grant would probably shoot him, and it would be deserved.

A stabbing pain shot through his chest and shoulder, doubling him over in the saddle. His old wound was acting up. *Maybe it's time I had some of that medicine Gigi sent home with me.* He rubbed his hand over his chest, feeling the roughness of the scar through his cotton shirt. He tried to massage away the pain, but the pain and scar were always with him, rekindling vivid memories of the war and the bloody battles. It was a time he didn't want to remember, but the memories clung to him like burrs. Even when he was with Gigi at the Painted Pony, his men could still find him. Their dead eyes…empty, staring, and accusing.

He wiped the sweat from his forehead as the pain and memories refused to be ignored. They pulled him back into another time.

* * *

Commander Nathan Daniels lay quietly, his anger building. Yankee forces had annihilated his command. Gunshots, explosions, and screams had filled the air for hours. Even nightfall hadn't silenced them. He had lost hundreds of men. Old and young, they were men he was responsible for and some of the bravest soldiers he had ever known.

In the dim moonlight, he could make out the bodies of men and horses strewn across the field in front of him…the ground muddied with their blood. Random gunfire and cries for help broke the unnatural quiet of the night. He squeezed his eyes shut. *This has to be a nightmare. How can it be anything else?*

What was left of his command was pinned down, and he could see no way out. By morning they would be killed or captured. Considering how fiercely they had fought, he figured none of his men would surrender or let themselves be taken. Tomorrow, they would die.

He was desperately trying to figure out how to get what was left of his command out alive when he saw two heads pop up a short distance from him. His two newest and youngest officers scuttled up to him in a crouched position. Each had been promoted to colonel as their leaders had fallen. When they got to him, they flattened themselves beside him. Commander Daniels looked at the boys. No, after today, they were men.

Breathless but with an unbelievably confident voice, one of the men spoke. "Wilson reporting, sir. Approximately two hundred men are still capable and ready for tomorrow's fight. Seventy are severely wounded and are being tended. We heard several moans coming from out there." The young officer motioned past the stone wall they were using as cover. "Don't know if they are our boys or Yanks. You want us to send men out to check?"

"No. It could be a trap, and I don't want to risk losing one more man."

"What do we do, sir? We do seem to be in a bind."

"I've been studying on it. Haven't decided."

"If I may, sir," the other man spoke up. "Wilson and I were talking, and it looks like we have just two options. One to surrender and the other to stand and fight. We all agree on making a fight of it. We won't survive the day, but they'll know what we're made of, and we'll take plenty of Yanks with us."

"Actually, Colonel, I am considering a third option. Still trying to figure out just how to pull it off."

"Sir?"

"I want to get you and your men out of here, and I think I may have a way."

He explained his plan, and Wilson spoke, "Sir, we cannot allow you to do that."

Nate smiled at the brash new colonel. "It wasn't a request, Wilson, more like an order. You will do as I've instructed. If we have to, we'll fight the Yanks like rabid dogs, but if my plan works, we won't have to. You need to hurry, and you'll need to be quiet."

"Don't you think they'll know what we're doing, sir?" Wilson whispered.

"No, not really. After all, they are Yankees, aren't they? Now move."

Keeping low to the ground, Nate collected firewood and made a good-sized fire at the far end of their position, far away from the ridge line of scrubby trees his men would use for cover. He sat ten of his men around the fire, propping them up against trees and logs. Then he dragged a dozen or more of his dead soldiers to the rock fence they had been using for cover and set them with rifles poking over the wall. His troop of dead were ready.

When he finished, he sat, exhausted, looking from man to man. He knew most of them by name. He talked to the men, asking about their families and recounting the day's battle and how the war was going. He laughed and made noises to attract the attention of the remaining Union forces, distracting them from the actions of his retreating forces. He was exhausted but wanted to give his retreating men every chance.

He looked around at the macabre scene he had created, the lifeless eyes of his men staring... accusing. He'd had his orders and had followed them as any well-trained soldier would, but he had led his men into an untenable situation. He hoped there was a larger plan in play... one worth the sacrifice of so many. He toasted his men with an empty coffee mug and fell into a deep sleep.

It was dawn when he woke to the sound of the first shots. He saw several dead bodies jerk as bullets slammed into them. Then, a searing pain in his chest sent him to the ground. His last thoughts as he drifted into oblivion were of his wife and daughter. Would they ever know how and where he had died?

When he woke several days later, he was in a Southern hospital. The doctor explained that he had been exchanged for an important Union Officer.

Nate knew he was not important enough for such a trade. His father had called in some favors, and it was his clout that had saved him. Several weeks later, Commander Daniels found out that his men had made it to safety and had joined up with other regiments. He prayed they would survive.

It was over a month before his wounds healed enough for the doctor to release him from the hospital. He was declared unfit for duty and headed straightaway to his home, where he found that raiders had murdered his wife and daughter. Someone was kind enough to bury them and had carved a wooden cross to mark their graves.

He sat on the steps of his burned-out home, holding a scorched doll in his hands and staring at the grave markers. He toyed with the idea of rebuilding, but he couldn't. It would never be the same. He needed to get away. He needed a new start, far away from death and sorrow.

# CHAPTER 55

# AVOID THE BEAR PAW

Mark Wilson had recently hired on at the Lazy W. After the war, he wandered the country working various jobs, looking to find his place. He found his place working as a ranch hand. It gave him the freedom and open spaces he preferred. He liked it, and he liked riding for Gus. He was a decent boss, and even the foreman was tolerable. Most of the men riding for the brand were Northerners. He was the only one who had fought for the South.

One night, playing poker in the bunkhouse, Klaus Redding asked him where he had fought. "I try to avoid talking about the war. It causes considerable discomfort for some folks knowing I fought for the South."

"Don't bother us none," Klaus said, looking at two pairs in his hand and raising five matchsticks. "Nate Daniels, a farmer south of town, was some big bug in the Confederate Army. No one seems to care."

Mark was surprised to hear Nate's name. "I served under Commander Daniels. Funny that we ended up in the same town all the way out here. I sure would like to run into him some time. I'd like to shake his hand and thank him for saving my life. He was a hero, you know."

The following morning, the foreman came into the bunkhouse to hand out the day's assignments. "Wilson, I've got a bridle and several harnesses that need repair. Drop them off at Meadow's Harness Shop and wait for them."

When Mark got to town, Ross Meadows, the shop owner, looked at the harnesses in the back of the wagon with a frown. "It'll be at least three or four hours before I can get to them and probably another three hours to fix them. Bring them inside and toss them in that first bin. It could be tomorrow before I can get them finished."

Mark had a long wait in front of him, and he knew what he wanted to do. He hadn't seen much of Grant's Crossing when he first passed through, so he decided to explore. And the first thing he wanted to explore was a woman's body. He asked Meadows where he might go for that kind of exploration, and amid stuttering and stammering, a red-faced Ross directed him to the Scarlet Slipper.

After a romp with one of the Slipper's finest, Mark stood at the bar chatting with Pitt, the man behind the bar. "You know Nate Daniels?"

"Sure do. He comes in now and again for a business meeting with Slippery Sue. She's his favorite, but I haven't seen him lately. He's been seriously wooing Kat Masters."

"Kat Masters?"

"Yeah, she owns Kat's Place up on Bridge Street."

"Has she got a line of girls?"

"No," Pitt said, grinning at the youngster, "and she doesn't work the sheets either. Except maybe for Daniels, but that's personal."

"Thanks, mister. I may be back later for a drink and a meeting with your Slippery Sue."

"Wilson, I recommend you avoid the girls next door at the Paw. Not the cleanest place in town." Pitt chuckled as he picked up the dirty glass and returned the bottle to the shelf. Sue was one of the Slipper's favorites, but perhaps he should tell the young lad about Frenchie when he returned.

## CHAPTER 56

# MAYBE YOU SHOULD LEAVE

Wilson bypassed the Bear Paw, as Pitt had suggested, and turned up Bridge Street. He walked past the fancy Carmichael Hotel and a nondescript City Hall and stopped at the barbershop. He could use a haircut and figured now was as good a time as any.

Angus Wilkinson was a short, wiry Irishman. He wore round slightly tinted wire-rim spectacles and a clean white apron. But most importantly, he had a steady hand. He chatted amicably during the entire shave and haircut.

Since Wilson was a stranger, Angus felt it was his responsibility to fill him in on the town and everything about it. He told him how the Grants and Millers were the first settlers, how it got its name, and how lucky they were to have such a fearless marshal and his deputies to keep them safe.

Angus stopped snipping at his hair and put up his scissors. "It's a shame what happened to the marshal's folks. He was no more than a tad of a boy, and he was the one who found them." Angus filled in all the gory details as he stropped his straight-edge razor.

Wilson left the barber shop with the description of what happened to the marshal's family echoing in his brain. Daniels couldn't have done it. Yet he had to tell someone. But before he did, he needed more information. He owed Daniels too much to put him in any jeopardy.

He entered Kat's place and wasn't surprised to find she was more an elegant lady than a saloon hostess. "First one's on the house for a newcomer," Kat said, approaching the young cowboy. She figured Angus had just gotten done with him. Few cowhands smelled like roses.

"Got a name, cowboy?"

"Mark Wilson, ma'am. Been riding for Gus Weisenberger…almost a month now."

"Well, I'm pleased to meet you, Mark Wilson. You're always welcome here." She started to walk away.

"Ma'am, I would like to talk to you if I could. I know you're a lady, so it ain't nothing improper, but I need some advice."

"Well, okay, but we'll have to talk while I work. One of my bartenders is laid up, and one didn't show up, so I am on bar duty. What can I help you with?"

"It's about Nate Daniels, ma'am."

Kat's head jerked. "Nate?"

"Yes, ma'am."

"Well, if we are going to have this kind of a conversation, I suggest you stop calling me ma'am. Please, call me Kat."

"Yes, ma'am."

Kat scowled at him. "What about Nate?"

"I understand you knew him quite…well, and I was wondering if you thought he would be capable of killing someone."

"Look, I have no idea where you're going with this, but I don't like it. Maybe you should leave."

"I served with him during the war. He saved my life. He was an honorable man and a brave soldier, but sometimes war can change a fellow. I thought I knew him, but…maybe I didn't."

"Look, Mr. Wilson, Nate Daniels is a friend of mine. You had better spit out whatever it is you're chewing on."

He explained what had happened during the war and what Nate did to save his men. And he told her how Angus had filled him in on what happened to the marshal's family. "I wouldn't say it was Nate who done it, but the similarity is troubling. You know him, ma'am. Do you think he could do something like that?"

Kat knew Nate had been severely wounded and was still tormented by the pain and memories. He never gave her any details, and she hadn't asked. But now she knew the source of the darkness she had seen in him. It frightened her. Still, she couldn't believe he was the killer Jake was hunting.

"I've upset you, ma'am. I mean Miss Kat and I'm truly sorry, but I didn't rightly know who else I could talk to."

She shook her head, "There is only one thing you can do. You need to tell the marshal. It's for him to handle. I don't think Nate could do such a thing, but if he is guilty…well, let's not even think about such a thing. The marshal is out of town, and Deputy Watkins is at the doctor's recuperating from a gunshot wound, but Deputy Logan should be there. Tell him your story, and he'll let the marshal know."

No one was in the marshal's office, so Mark returned to the harness shop to check on the repair work. The owner was in the back of his shop arguing with a customer about an order. The shouting continued for some time and ended with the customer throwing up his hands and stomping past Mark and through the door. The repair work for the Lazy W was on the workbench but untouched.

Ross looked at Wilson with a scowl. "I suppose you were expecting a miracle as well?"

"Uh, no sir, I was wondering if you'd had a chance to get it done, but I see it's going to be a bit longer."

"I'm sorry, I need to find a helper. You interested?"

"No, sir, only interested in getting the harnesses."

"It'll be done tomorrow, around noon. It's a promise."

## CHAPTER 57

# JAKE WON'T LISTEN

Wilson stayed in town overnight, spending most of it at the Slipper. The following morning, he went to the Wishbone for breakfast and then stopped at the marshal's office. When he entered, there was a man with a head full of white hair and an enormous mustache napping with his feet on the desk. Mark cleared his throat and banged the door shut.

Deputy Logan jumped from his chair, sputtering about people trying to give him an apoplexy. Once he calmed down, Wilson told him the same story he'd shared with Kat.

Logan had trouble thinking of Nate as a killer, but he couldn't help but wonder. Daniels had moved in around the same time the killings started. He was strong enough to manhandle the bodies, and he did disappear every spring for three or four weeks. Logan also remembered that he always carried a knife, and the murder map indicated that the killer probably lived in or around Grant's Crossing. All of it, put together, had to make a man wonder.

There was nothing he could do. Jake would have to figure it out when he returned from his hunt for Lloyd Templeton.

Jake returned to town late, carrying what was supposed to be Lloyd Templeton's body in the back of his rig. He stopped outside the undertakers and got Bones to collect the body. The body was in bad shape, and everyone had stayed away as he hoped they would.

"I can't believe some of the messes you lawmen expect me to clean up," Bones grumbled.

"Sorry, Bones. I know he's in bad shape. I was hot on his trail when he stumbled and fell into the river. Didn't find his body until the next day."

Jake traipsed to Coop's office to let him know all had gone according to plan and that Bones had Templeton's body.

"I released Bear this afternoon, and Sam is doing well enough that he can leave in the morning. They both need to take it easy, though." Coop looked at Jake with a critical eye. "You look like you're about to drop in your tracks. Maybe you should stay here tonight. You can share Sam's room now that Bear is back home."

Jake declined the offer and headed for his office. He pushed open the door to find Logan asleep behind the desk. With what little strength he had left, he flopped down on the cot, pulled off his boots with a grunt, and fell onto his side.

"Jake, you're back. I didn't hear you come in," Logan said.

"Hmmm. Let me sleep."

"I would, but there is something you need to know."

"Logan, there is nothing I need to know right now. I am too tired."

"No, you need to hear this."

"Is there anything I can do about it tonight?" Jake mumbled.

"No, I guess not."

"Then it can wait till morning."

## CHAPTER 58

# BETTER THAN YOU

Jake woke to bright sunlight pouring in through the window. He tried to sit up but fell back with a groan. His arm was on fire, and he had stiffened up overnight.

"You sound like an old man. Thought it was Logan asleep over there."

"Sam?" Jake rolled over awkwardly and somehow managed to get to his feet.

"Yep," Sam said, sitting at the desk and looking through the mail from the last few days.

Jake shuffled to one of the chairs in front of the desk and carefully lowered himself. "I couldn't make it all the way to Eagles Pass. I couldn't do it. I stopped at Toad Falls and camped there for two days."

"Anyone see you?"

"Not that I know of. The falls are secluded, and I avoided everyone on the trail. I didn't want anyone getting too close. From the smell, they might think I was hauling a dead body with me. Oh, that's right I was. That was a great idea, Sam. Thanks."

"As long as it works, it was worth it. Right? Sam threw the dodgers on the desk and leaned back.

"How you feeling?" Jake asked.

"Better than yesterday and, from the looks of it, better than you."

"Yeah, well, I haven't been lounging around in bed like you have. I've been on the trail, hauling around a stinking dead body."

"You'll never let me forget this, will you."

"Never. Hey, do you know what Logan was all fired up to tell me last night?"

"No idea. He left to get something to eat."

"Breakfast?" Jake asked.

"It's afternoon, Jake."

"Oh."

Logan returned balancing two covered plates from the Wishbone. "Jake, glad to see you up. We got to talk."

"All right, Logan. You talk and I'll listen. I'm starving."

Logan told the story exactly as Mark Wilson had told it to him, and Jake lost his appetite. He raised his hand to push the hair back from his forehead but the pain in his arm stopped him. "Let's go pick him up," Jake said to Sam.

"No," Sam laughed. "The number one problem is that we have to ride to his place, and I doubt either one of us could make it that far. He doesn't know that we suspect him, so he isn't going to run. Next time he's in town, or when we're in better shape, we can bring him in for questioning."

Jake looked at Sam, not wanting to accept it but knowing he was right.

"Besides, I doubt it's him," Sam said. "War can twist a man, and Nate may have his issues, but I can't see him committing these murders."

Jake blew out a breath. "You're right, damn it. I thought for a minute—"

"Let's do our paperwork and wrap up this Templeton thing. And remember, we have a dance to get to tomorrow night. We can ride out together in the morning."

"No, I'm riding out after we finish the reports."

"Think you can make that two-hour ride?"

Jake shot him scathing look.

"All right. I just thought it would be better to wait till the morning. We'll both be feeling better."

"I'll be fine, Sam. I want to sleep in my bed, and I want to see Winnie."

# CHAPTER 59

# CLOSE, BUT NOT TODAY

Jake rode slowly toward the ranch. He was physically exhausted. Sam was right. He should have waited till morning. He knew he'd been pushing himself too hard over the last week, and now he was suffering the brunt of it. But the Templeton thing was finalized. All the official reports were completed and sent to the appropriate government agencies, and a stranger's body was buried under a marker with the name Lloyd Templeton carved into it. He was glad it was behind them and figured the outcome could have been much worse.

He kept thinking about Daniels. It wasn't much, but there were indications that he could be the killer he'd been pursuing for years. Was his hunt over? Could it end so simply? He didn't think so, but he needed to talk to Grant. Grant knew Daniels better than anyone, and Jake needed his perspective.

The other thing he couldn't help but think about on the long ride was the two lives he had taken. There had been no choice, but still, it weighed heavy on him.

As he neared home, he slumped forward in the saddle, every muscle fatigued, and his arm hurt bad enough to bring tears to his eyes. His stomach rumbled against his backbone, and he wondered what

Lorene had fixed for supper. He couldn't remember the last time he had eaten. Was it this morning, he thought, or was it yesterday? No, it was this morning. Logan had brought him breakfast, but he'd only eaten a few bites.

Jake rode up to the stable, barely hanging on to his saddle. Chris and Pete came running to him. "We got this, Jake. We'll take care of Drach. You get to the house and let Lorene take care of you." Pete looked at him with a frown. "You need a hand up to the house?"

Jake shook his head and let them take Drach's reins. Hell, he wasn't sure if he could make it to the house or not. Pete and Chris watched until they saw Lorene at the back door pulling him inside.

Lorene sat him at the kitchen table. A glass of whiskey and water were set out for him. Mashed potatoes, roast beef, gravy, and green beans with bacon instantly appeared on the table.

"Drink," Lorene ordered. "Knowing you, I'm betting you haven't eaten or had anything to drink since who knows when. Drink the whiskey first," she said, setting down a bowl of gravy.

Jake did as directed and the whiskey went down with a sting. "I'm so hungry." That was all he said as he dug into the mound of food in front of him.

When he finished eating, Lorene shooed him with her apron. "Get to your room before you fall asleep. You need to get your rest." Usually, she would have sent him to the shower before letting him go upstairs, and God knew he needed it, but she figured she would have to carry him.

Winnie came to the kitchen moments after he left. "I missed him? How is he?"

"All tuckered out, been trying to do too much, but it's finished. He's home now, and we'll tend to him until he gets healed up and back on his feet."

Late the following morning, Lorene sent Winnie to Jake's room with a mug of hot coffee to check on him and let him know breakfast was ready.

"Good morning, Jake."

"Winnie?" he said sleepily, lying on his side with a white sheet coving him.

She sat on the bed beside him. "Lorene sent me up to tell you breakfast is ready when you are."

He rubbed his face and eyes with his right hand, trying to focus. "Thanks. Tell her I'll be down a little later."

Winnie was alarmed at how pale he was and how horrible the wound on his shoulder looked. "Does it hurt?"

"A little bit," he mumbled, lying. It hurt a lot. He rolled onto his back with a grimace, the sheet falling to his waist.

"I heard what happened," Winnie said, admiring Jake's bare chest.

He was fighting to stay awake. "Not now, Kat, let me sleep. I don't want to think about it anymore."

Winnie was taken aback. "You called me Kat."

Jake was trying to keep his eyes open enough to focus on her. "Did I? I'm sorry, Winnie. I'm so tired. Let me sleep and forget about everything for a while. Please, let me sleep."

"I understand," Winnie said, "I'll tell Lorene you're not ready to come down yet."

"Thanks, Kat, you're the best."

"Kat is the best, huh?" Winnie huffed. "You called me Kat again."

He didn't indicate hearing her or knowing she was still sitting beside him on the bed, which annoyed her even further. "Talk to me," she demanded, angry at being shut out.

She leaned in, examining his face intently, and impetuously brushed a kiss across his lips. "I wonder if Kat does that for you." She waited, but his eyes remained closed, and there was no reaction. He didn't move.

She looked down at him, studying his handsome face, and ran her hands down his chest, feeling the hair tickle the palms of her hands. Her heart was racing and her anger forgotten as she leaned down for another kiss enjoying the soft, warm, gentleness of his lips. It was a playful, innocent kiss until she was grabbed and pulled on top of him.

Jake held her tightly against him, the kiss turning quickly from playful to passionate. "You wanted me awake. Well, I'm awake now, Winnie."

His hands followed the curves of her body, and, taking hold of her bottom, he pulled her tight against him. The moan from deep in her throat had Jake trembling with want. He took his mouth away from hers, his deep voice coarse with need. "Winnie, we shouldn't be doing this." But it was all he managed to say before his mouth reclaimed hers.

He knew he should stop, but he couldn't. He'd been dreaming about her, about making love to her, and now she was in his arms, warm and responding. He had never wanted anything as much as he wanted her. He wanted to go deep inside her to feel her surrounding him.

Winnie was breathless, lost in his kisses. His hardness pressed against her, and she ached with need.

Jake rolled her over, his lips not leaving hers. He struggled to pull her skirt up to her waist. His hand went between her legs, fingers frantically searching for her entrance. Her gasp became a moan of pleasure, and she opened herself to him. She was primed, she wanted him, and he couldn't wait any longer.

Lorene's voice yelling up the stairs was like a bucket of ice water. He rolled off Winnie with a groan, and Winnie jumped from the bed, flushed and breathing heavily. Her heart pounding, she straightened her dress and smoothed her hair with shaking hands.

Jake lay watching her, enjoying her discomfort but not his. "Winnie? You all right?"

"I think so," she said in a shaky voice. "I guess I had better get downstairs and help Lorene."

As she started to the door, Jake called to her, "Winnie?"

She turned to look at him. "Kat does not do that for me. Only you can make me crazy enough to lose all reason." He rolled over in bed, turning his back to her, looking for a comfortable position for his arm. "By the way," he said. "It wasn't very nice of you, trying to take advantage of me while I was asleep."

Jake drifted back to sleep despite the pain in his arm. He was thinking about Winnie and her kisses. He wasn't sure, but he may have told her he loved her. He had been thinking it.

Winnie could not believe he rolled over and went to sleep after what had happened. She sighed, shaking her head in disbelief. Weak-kneed and shaky, she went down the stairs to help Lorene finalize preparations for the dinner party and wedding celebration.

## CHAPTER 60

# LORENE SUSPECTS

Grant and Lorene had decided not to postpone their marriage any longer. They planned to have dinner in the formal dining room with family and close friends, followed by the wedding ceremony, and a large spring dance in the ballroom.

Winnie joined Lorene at the kitchen table, where she was polishing silverware. Stacks of delicate, gold-trimmed China surrounded them, and dozens of exquisite crystal goblets twinkled at them from the sideboard. Winnie picked up a tarnished knife and a polishing rag.

"Winnie, are you all right? You look flushed," Lorene said, inspecting a shiny serving spoon with a nod of approval.

"I'm fine. It's Jake. He made me mad, that's all." But all Winnie could think about was how he had kissed her, how he had touched her, where he had touched her, and how she wished the lingering ache deep inside her would go away.

Lorene looked at her with a slight frown, but then a sly smile spread across her face, and she chose not to question the real reason for the flushed face. She had an inkling it was much more than simply being mad at Jake.

"I'm glad you and Jake are standing up for us tonight. I hope Jake will be up to it. He's still terribly weak."

Winnie thought he hadn't seemed weak a few moments ago. "I'm excited about tonight, Lorene. Everyone is going to be so surprised and happy for you. I can't believe Dad didn't want anyone to know they were coming to a wedding. I had no clue he could be so, well, so romantic. At least, it's romantic for him."

There was a slight pause before Winnie continued, "Lorene, would you mind if I call you Mom?"

"I'd like that very much," Lorene said, reaching across the table to squeeze Winnie's hand.

"I didn't know Jake was so close with Kat," Winnie said, polishing a second piece of silverware, imagining her grandmother polishing that same knife.

"Winnie, You have to know Jake loves you. You've spent a lot of time together since you got home, and I see how you look at each other."

"I guess what bothers me is that I want to be there for him, but it appears Kat has that job. He called me Kat. Twice." Winnie hesitated for a moment; her eyes bright with tears. "He hasn't told me he loves me."

"Jake is not a talkative man. But the way he looks at you and the way he treats you...that says it all. And as far as he and Kat are concerned, they have been close friends for years. For heaven's sake, you and Kat are friends, too."

"I didn't think they were that close, and I can't stand the thought of them being together."

Lorene laughed. "Trust me, Winnie. They don't have that kind of relationship. If Kat did go after anyone, she'd be more apt to aim her sights on Sam. There's a spark  between those two. Has been for some time, but I don't think they've ever done anything about it."

Lorene looked thoughtfully at the tabletop. Kat's more of a loner. Few men have gotten close to her. Although, Nate Daniels was… Lorene searched for an appropriate word…courting Kat for a while, but it didn't work out."

Hank, the chuck house cook, came through the back door. "Thought you gals would be getting all gussied up and ready for the big to-do."

Winnie looked at the clock and jumped from the table. "Come on, Mom, we have to get you ready for your special night."

Winnie dragged Lorene from the kitchen, still spouting instructions to Hank over her shoulder.

"Lorene, stop worrying," Winnie said, closing her father's bedroom door behind them. Hank is in charge of the dinner, and it couldn't be in better hands. Plus, Dad hired plenty of helpers for him to boss around. All you have to do now, Mom, is get ready."

Lorene's wedding gown was spread out on the bed. Mary had made her a simple, cream-colored dress with sequins sprinkled on top of the shoulders. Mary said it was like pixie dust, for good luck.

"I can't wait to see Dad's face. You're going to knock him off his feet. But first, we have to get you into the gown you're wearing for dinner. We can't have your bridegroom seeing you in your wedding dress before the ceremony."

Lorene pointed to a black dress hanging on the back of the door. "I know it's rather bleak for a celebration, but it's a goodbye to my old life, and when I change, it will be to welcome my new life and a husband I will love as much as anyone ever could." Lorene smiled with a wink. "And Steven tells me that black is quite chic these days."

"You jump in the tub," Winnie ordered, and I'll go slink into my dress."

Forty-five minutes later, Winnie knocked on her father's bedroom door. "Are you decent?"

Lorene opened the door with a big smile. Winnie stood back with a whistle. The black dress looked stunning on Lorene. Winnie smiled, noticing the brooch she'd given her shining subtly on Lorene's shoulder.

"Dad's in the bunkhouse getting ready. And according to Hank, getting ready involves a bath, whiskey, and cigars. You can hear the celebration from the kitchen."

A commotion at the front door and the voices of several men interrupted them. "It sounds like the musicians have arrived," Lorene said. It's the same band that played at your homecoming party. They were so well received that Grant arranged for them to come back and play for the dance."

"As long as there isn't a monkey," Winnie said with a laugh. "Come on. The guests will be arriving at any time now."

## CHAPTER 61

# FINE EVENING FOR A PARTY

Grant joined Winnie and Lorene at the front door. "I saw carriages coming down the hill. Our guests will be here soon," Grant said, looking dapper in a black suit coat and matching waistcoat. Lorene gave him a sidelong glance. "I heard you were soaking up whiskey in the bunkhouse."

"The men wanted to congratulate me, and we had a few toasts. They're a fine bunch. Too bad we can't have them all join us, but they won't go hungry." Grant placed a gentle kiss on her lips. "You are a vision, Lorene."

Winnie kissed her father's cheek and stood beside him, looking regal in a deep, auburn-red gown. A one-of-a-kind dress that was low cut and off the shoulders. A glimmer of lace peaked over the top of the sleeves, a weak attempt to honor Victorian modesty. The cinched bodice looked more like a corset but flared into a full skirt over layers and layers of petticoats. A single teardrop-shaped pearl dangled from the delicate lace choker that adorned her neck, and a jeweled comb held her dark brown hair on top of her head.

Kat and Sam were the first to arrive. Sam looked pale and tired as he shook Grant's hand and hugged Lorene.

"Sam, you look terrible," Lorene said. "You should be in bed."

"I can't say I disagree, but I'll be fine. I wouldn't miss your special evening for anything," Sam whispered in her ear. "Kat gave me a ride in her carriage and promised to only make me dance one dance, and as beautiful as she looks, how could I refuse? And speaking of beautiful," Sam said, kissing Lorene's cheek and, with a waggish smile, brushed a kiss across Winnie's lips. "Jake said there was to be no more kissing on his girl, but I doubt that would count. Where is he, anyway?"

"He hasn't come down yet. I hope he's all right," Winnie said, trying not to frown.

Kat hugged Grant and Lorene, then stopped in front of Winnie. "You have to tell me where you and Lorene find these glorious gowns."

"Come on, Kat," Sam said, heading for the parlor and a chair.

Guests continued to arrive and once they were all present, Grant signaled for Hank to ring the dinner bell and escorted Lorene and Winnie into the dining room, followed by their guests

Grant seated Lorene and Winnie and then took his place at the head of the table. Lorene to his right and Winnie to his left.

It was a fine evening, and the steady buzz of conversation and laughter filled the oversized dining room. The two chandeliers hanging over the extended table glittered with imported crystals, but they couldn't outshine Lorene's beaming smiles.

Winnie looked across the table at the empty chair next to Sam. The chair was meant for Jake. She was about to excuse herself to go check on him when she saw him coming through the doors. She was sure her heart skipped a beat as she watched him shake hands with Grant and kiss Lorene's cheek.

"Sorry, I'm late," he said to Lorene. "It took me longer to get ready than usual."

Winnie looked across the table, thinking Jake was the most handsome man she'd ever seen. The white shirt he wore under his back suit coat set off his olive-toned skin, and his blue eyes sparkled. Jake looked back with a smile, their eyes locking briefly before he turned his attention to Lorene.

When everyone finished eating, Grant stood and tapped his fork against his glass. The room slowly quieted. He looked around the table and held up his glass. "A toast to family, friends, and happy times." There were shouts of agreement and the clinking of glasses.

Grant's tender smile warmed Lorene's heart as he reached over and took her hand, bringing her to stand close by his side. "I'd like to make another toast. To Lorene, who has kept me on the straight and narrow for almost twenty years." Grant waited for their guests to settle down before continuing. "I've finally come to my senses and asked her to marry me. And dang me, I don't know why, but she accepted." His eyes shining with love, he raised his glass to Lorene. "To the love of my life."

The crowd of diners burst into cheers and laughter, and several comments echoed the same sentiments. "About time," and "Can't believe she took you up on it."

Grant was embarrassed by the reaction and speechless. He was seldom at a loss for words, but tonight, it was Lorene who finished for him. "You are all invited to join us in the ballroom for our wedding vows and a lovely spring dance afterward. We hope you all can stay and share our happiness."

Laughter and merriment echoed throughout the house as the dinner guests finished dessert and headed to the ballroom. Shortly, additional guests began to arrive, surprised and delighted to find they were attending a spring wedding.

Winnie grabbed Lorene by the hand, and before she could get side-tracked, hurried her to the bedroom to change into her wedding dress. Giving Lorene a final inspection, Winnie had an idea. "You need to have something old, new, blue, and borrowed to carry down the aisle with you. I saw them do it at a wedding in England."

"Whatever for?"

"The old signifies your life before the wedding, the new is for the new life ahead of you, the borrowed is for good luck, and the blue is for fidelity and purity," Winnie explained.

"It all seems rather silly, but why not? The brooch you gave me is new, and it's blue. I can wear that. And my shoes are old. Do you have something I can borrow?"

"I do," Winnie said, pulling a gold locket from a pocket hidden in her dress and opening it. "There's a picture of you and me on one side, and on the other side is a picture of Dad and me."

Lorene's eyes teared up as she took the locket from Winnie's fingers. "Thank you."

"Lorene, you don't have time to cry. We need to get you to the ballroom and fast."

Jake and Winnie stood with the happy couple as they took their vows from Pastor Emil.

Jake's blue eyes sparkled with happiness as he watched Grant and Lorene pledge themselves to one another in marriage. Winnie had trouble keeping her eyes off Jake; and when he smiled, her heart did a flip. She could still feel his lips on hers and the touch of his hands. Goosebumps raced up and down her body as she tried to concentrate on the ceremony.

After the I do's, the kiss, and the introduction of the new couple, the band played a lovely slow song for the newlyweds, and then the dancing began.

"This is my dance," Jake said, putting his hand on Winnie's back and guiding her to the dance floor. A wave of heat washed through her at his gentle touch and the sound of his voice.

"Sorry about this morning." He frowned, his brow furrowed as if in deep thought. "No, I'm not sorry it happened, but it wasn't the time or place for me to make love to you."

Winnie blushed, thinking about the morning's incident. "I shouldn't have been so forward. It wasn't ladylike."

"No, it wasn't, but then, I'm not sure I want a lady." His blue eyes blazed with playful desire. "I'm glad Lorene yelled when she did. I don't think I could have stopped."

"I didn't want you to," Winnie whispered as a deeper blush crawled up her neck to her cheeks.

Sam and Kat danced close to them, and Sam said in a low voice, "Jake, you might want to pull up on the reins a bit. You're putting off enough heat to catch the drapes on fire." Then he whispered to Winnie, "Looks like you've found your fireworks."

"Kat, I'm only good for one dance. I think it's time you took me home before I collapse."

Kat and Sam stopped to pay their respects to Lorene and Grant. "Sam," Lorene said. "Why don't you stay here tonight? Your room is always ready for you."

"I know, and I would stay, but with Jake here, Logan is all alone. It's the same old story, Lorene," Sam said with a winsome smile, "I work so that Jake may play."

"Get some rest, Sam," Lorene ordered.

Jake and Winnie looked sheepishly around the room to see if anyone was looking their way. Jake stepped back, realizing that he had been pulling her closer and closer as they danced. "What are your plans for tomorrow?" Jake asked as they finished the dance.

"I'm heading to town on a supply run first thing in the morning," Winnie said, sorry the dance was over. "Then straight to the cabin. I'm meeting Clark to review the progress and put together a final list of materials we need. The bunkhouse and cattle pens are almost finished. Everything should be ready for the next roundup."

"Would you mind if I rode along? I want to see what you've done with the place and check in with the men. Plus, I can help you with the supplies."

"That would be great if your arm is up to it. I couldn't believe how angry the wound looked."

"Coop says it's healing fine, but not to do anything too strenuous."

"What about your lawman job? Can you be away?" Winnie asked with a smile.

"Sam is up and around, and Logan is on the job." A serious look clouded Jake's face. "Besides, it will give us a chance to talk. And, well, I am sorry about calling you Kat."

"I thought maybe you and Kat were—"

"No, Winnie, there is only you. Look, I'm tired, and if I'm going with you in the morning, I had better get some rest." Then he smiled and winked. "Resisting you is exhausting. See you in the morning."

Jake waited until he returned to his room to rub the wound on his arm. Coop told him it was healing nicely, but when would it quit throbbing, and why was he so damn tired? He stripped and fell onto the bed.

When Jake left the dance, Winnie went to find her dad and Lorene. Judge Taylor had them cornered, telling them one of his fishing stories. She noticed that his suit jacket fit a little snugly, but he looked as dignified as ever. She didn't recall ever seeing him dressed in anything else and wondered if he went fishing in his black suit.

"Winnie," the judge said, beaming, "you look beautiful. I was telling your dad and Lorene how you had suddenly bloomed into such a lovely young lady."

Winnie gave him her best smile. "Thank you, but I doubt the instructors at Minerva's School for Young Ladies would agree with your use of the word suddenly. They worked hard to get me turned around." They all laughed, and the judge excused himself to continue mingling with the other guests.

The band stopped playing at midnight, and everyone said their goodbyes. Winnie started toward the stairs and heard Grant say to Lorene. "It's just us now, Mrs. Grant, and it's time we went to bed. This time to the same bed."

Winnie turned to say goodnight but stopped. Her father had Lorene wrapped in his arms, kissing her. Winnie turned away quickly. She hadn't considered this aspect of having a new mother and wondered if Dad made Lorene feel the way Jake made her feel. She hoped so, and yet that was her dad and Lorene.

# CHAPTER 62

# CLEARING THE AIR

Winnie was up and out before dawn, wanting to get into Grant's Crossing as early as possible. It was a long haul from town to the cabin, and she wanted to get there before dark.

The buckboard was ready with Herald tied to the back. Jake would need his mount if he were joining the men later. Winnie had heard him stirring, so he was up and should be out soon. She went into the stable to curry Ember while she waited. She greeted Drach as she walked by his stall, and he nickered back a soft greeting.

Winnie was impatient, and Jake was taking too long. She put down the curry comb and was on her way to the house when he came in.

"I'm ready."

"About time. It took you long enough. Let's go." She started past him, but he snagged her arm and pulled her against him. "I would like to kiss you and throw you onto that pile of straw, but a hug will have to do for now."

"Good thinking, Jake," Linc, the ranch foreman, said as he came around the corner smiling. "Do you two need a chaperone?"

"No, we're fine," Winnie said. "We have a busy day ahead of us and no time for nonsense and tomfoolery."

Jake helped Winnie up onto the buckboard and took his seat beside her. "Nonsense and tomfoolery?"

Winnie glared at him and flicked the reins.

The store was already open when Winnie reined to a stop. They worked quickly, getting the supplies together. All the while, Steven gushed about Mr. Grant's wedding. He told Winnie how beautiful she looked and Jake how handsome he was. Jake winked at Winnie, and when everything was loaded, he went inside to sign for the supplies. Winnie circled the buckboard, checking one last time to make sure she had everything on her list.

Jake was taking a long time. She glanced toward the door and saw Jake and Charlie chatting. She couldn't tell which one was telling the tale, but it probably had to do with horses, cows, or drovers. It was a long way to the cabin, and she was restless to get underway. If they didn't leave soon, they wouldn't get there before dark. She stood for a moment with her hands on her hips and then decided to recheck her list before exploding.

With her list double-checked, she was done waiting. *Enough,* she thought, turning to go into the store and fetch Jake. When she turned, she found herself face-to-face with Quinn Sumner.

"Good morning, Winnie."

"Quinn."

"It's a beautiful morning," he said with a dazzling smile. "Sorry about the other day. Perhaps we can try again. I would like to court you, but we can take it slow and get to know each other first. How about riding out this afternoon and I'll show you my gardens? They are quite beautiful this time of year."

"No, Quinn, I'm sorry. I'm sure your gardens are lovely, but I'm working today, and Dad has something lined up for me every day for the next month. And I've told you several times that we will never be a couple, and nothing has changed. You need to find someone else to walk with you in your gardens." She retreated, heading for the front of the buckboard. Quinn followed, putting his hands around her waist and helping her up.

Quinn looked up with a charming smile. "Winnie, I'm not a man who waits for what he wants. I'm a man who makes it happen. You'll see."

"Well, you are not going to make this happen," she said politely but firmly. Then yelled in a demanding tone, "Jake, let's go."

Jake turned from his discussion with Charlie and, seeing Quinn, went out immediately. "Move away," Jake said, his steel blue eyes piercing Quinn with a menacing glare. He jumped up on the seat next to Winnie and ignoring the pain from his wound, he put his arm around her shoulders. His eyes never left Sumner's face as Winnie flicked the reins.

Quinn walked beside her, ignoring Jake. "Another time then," he said as the buckboard gained speed, leaving him behind.

Sumner was getting tired of Jake being underfoot all the time, but there was little he could do about it, at least for now. But the time would come when he could get rid of Jake. He was sure of it.

As soon as they were outside the town limits, Winnie turned to Jake. "What was that about?"

"What?"

"The look you gave Quinn could have melted iron, and the arm around my shoulder? You think this is a date?"

Jake removed his arm, wincing. "I heard about you and Quinn and how you danced together at your homecoming party. I understand the two of you put on quite a show, including some kisses on the front porch."

"Well, if you had stayed around, I might have been dancing with you instead. Quinn means nothing to me, and I don't know why I ever kissed him."

"And I suppose you can't tell me why you shared a meal with him at The Carmichael, either?"

"What? Are you having me followed?"

"Don't need to. Sally and many other concerned citizens couldn't wait to tell me."

Winnie scoffed. "I bet not."

He scowled at the thought of Sumner being friendly with her. He was angry and wanted to scold her for seeing him, but he didn't have the right. No promises had been made. But if he ever caught Sumner anywhere near Winnie again, he would make sure he understood the severity of his mistake.

"Let's take a break at Picnic Hill," Jake said. An uncomfortable silence settled between them.

Winnie was wondering what Jake was thinking about.

Jake and his arm were glad when they finally pulled over for a rest from the jostling and jolting ride. He eased down from his seat and walked to the oak tree. He leaned his right side against the tree, and Winnie sat on one of the flat rocks facing him. She was beautiful, and maybe it wasn't official yet, but she was his.

"I can't believe it's been less than a month since you stepped off that train. So much has happened since then. Right before you came home, I heard of a murder in Clay Springs and took a trip out there to investigate. I thought I was over the worst of it, but memories, hate, and anger came rushing back. Sometimes I feel like it's pulling me into a dark hole. One I'll never get out of."

He turned with a grimace, leaning his back against the tree trunk. "Then there was the incident at the Stable Saloon, and after that, it was Fitz and then Bryson." Winnie started to speak, but he put up his hand. "It feels as if all of my emotions are at war, my feelings for you, hate for the man who killed my parents, guilt because I almost got my friends killed." His voice cracked. "Sam could have died."

He paused and took a deep breath. "I should have faced Bryson before anyone got hurt, but I didn't want to fight him. I was afraid, Win—terrified."

"You'd have been a fool not to be afraid. Anyone in their right mind would have been scared of that man. But you did face him, Jake, and you killed him in a fair fight."

"Fair fight or not, I killed two men."

"Jake, I had no idea what was going on in that head of yours. You've been through a lot. But you are not a coward or a killer. It took courage to face Bryson. You haven't backed down from anything for as long as I've known you. Except for running away from Sam more than once, but you didn't run from Bryson. You stood eye to eye with him even though you were afraid. That was a courageous thing to do." She paused, hoping she was reaching him.

Winnie got up and went to him, wrapping her arms around his waist and resting her head on his chest. "I hear the heartbeat of a hero, Jake, not a killer."

Jake kissed the top of her head. "You might be a tad bit biased."

"Maybe so, but I know of no one who would disagree with me except for you." She looked up into his blue eyes. "Jake, you never did cry for your parents that I can ever remember, and fourteen years is a long time to hold back the tears. Maybe the man you have become needs to cry for the little boy and his loss."

"After I catch their killer, maybe then I can cry." Jake looked down into the eyes of the woman he loved and smiled. "But for now, we should get back on the road if we want to get to the cabin before midnight."

## CHAPTER 63

# THE DENTIST IS OUT

Sumner couldn't believe how he had been rebuffed, but perhaps it was all an act for the marshal. After all, Winnie had to know Jacobs couldn't please her the way he could. She needed a man, not a boy. Yes, she would be back, and she would want him. She would come to him begging for his forgiveness.

Still, the anger persisted. He needed to do something to calm his agitation. A trip out of town for a few days was in order. It was too soon after his last trip, but he would immerse himself in helping the peons of the prairie.

He canceled all his appointments and, within an hour, was on the road.

*Yes,* he thought, *getting out of town is precisely what I need.*

## CHAPTER 64

# FLICKERING FIRE

Winnie and Jake saw the glow of a flickering fire and heard laughter long before they pulled up to the cabin to unload. The evening had turned cold, and the men had laid a large fire. They were drinking and telling stories.

When Jake and Winnie pulled in, everyone scrambled to help. The supplies were soon unloaded, and the mules fed and tucked in for the night. Winnie stood inside the dilapidated cabin, glad the supplies were unloaded and stowed. She shooed the men back to the fire.

Pete stuck his head through the slanted doorway. "Winnie, we knew you were coming, so we put up a lean-to for you. It isn't much, but it will give you some privacy." He motioned to the back of the room, where a blanket hanging on a curtain rod served as a door. "Once the bunkhouse is finished, you can have this luxurious palace all to yourself."

She went to Pete and gave him a hug. "You and Chris did this?"

"We had help from some of the boys who know more about putting nails in boards than me and Chris do. If it had been us, who knows what you'd have ended up with."

"Thank you, Pete. It's perfect."

She closed the door behind Pete and headed to the lean-to, carefully stepping around bedrolls scattered over the floor. "I'll be glad when the bunkhouse is finished," she said to the deer head mounted over the fireplace, half expecting it to wink back. She grabbed a coat from her valise and went out to join the men by the fire.

Jake put his arm out, opening up the blanket he had draped over his shoulders, inviting her to join him and share his warmth. She smiled and scooted up close. He put his arm around her shoulders, pulling her against him. Snuggled close and sharing the heat of his body, a powerful surge of desire raced through her body. Wiggling closer, she slipped her arms around his waist. Her head fit perfectly on his shoulder.

Only the two of them and the fire existed. The talk and laughter of the other men had faded into the background. Cocooned in the warmth of the blanket, they shared an occasional brief kiss, oblivious to anyone around them.

Jake wasn't sure how long they sat there lost in each other, but the fire was down to only glowing embers, and it was getting cold. Everyone had wandered off to bed except for them and Chris.

Chris got up. "Everyone's gone to bed, Jake, and I'm on my way. You two had better call it a night."

Jake looked up at him with a grin. "You go on ahead. We'll be there in a minute, Dad."

Chris chuckled, giving him a doubtful look. "Okay, Jake, but don't be too long."

"We won't."

Chris headed toward the cabin, shaking his head and smiling, wondering if Jake would be bunking in the main cabin tonight or in the lean-to.

A yard from the cabin door, Chris turned. He heard claws, small claws skittering up the trunk of a nearby oak tree. His head tilted, listening, he slowly unsheathed his knife. His eyes searched the branches. The squirrel moved and Chris threw the knife with deadly accuracy. The minute he released the blade, he knew it was a clean throw. Chris heard the rapid whoosh, whoosh, whoosh of the knife as it sailed through the air impaling the squirrel. He smiled bending to pick up his quarry. *Ah, Breakfast.*

\* \* \*

Jake turned to Winnie and pulled her against him, reveling in her softness. He saw desire sparkling in her green eyes and knew he would never love or want anyone else. He leaned down, brushing his lips against hers in a gentle kiss. His lips were on hers for only a moment when he pulled back and whispered, "I want you, Winnie, I need you." He kissed her with unbridled passion, a passion she returned.

He pulled back slowly, putting his forehead against hers. His breath came fast, and his heart beat at a crazy pace. He spoke in a whisper. "We have to quit doing this. You make me crazy."

Winnie's mouth captured his in a kiss that shook Jake's control.

"Winnie, this isn't the time or the place. There's a roomful of ranch hands on the other side of that door." Jake was trying to convince himself as well as Winnie.

His body was fighting with his mind and was close to winning, but he remained in control and said firmly, "You need to go in now. I'll make sure the fire is out before I come in."

He couldn't help but kiss her one last time. It might have been a dangerous thing to do, but he couldn't resist. As his lips met hers, he stood up, pulling her with him. He held her close and softly said the words she'd been waiting to hear, "I love you, Winnie."

"I love you, Jake."

Winnie walked slowly to the cabin door, weak-kneed and light-headed. She turned to look back at Jake. She didn't want to leave him. But he was right. This was not the time or the place. But he loved her. He had said it.

Jake had trouble sleeping. He thought about Winnie most of the night and, for the first time, knew exactly what he wanted. He wanted to marry her and spend the rest of his life with her. It was a scary thought, but it was what he wanted more than anything else. Now, he had to work up the courage to ask her.

# CHAPTER 65

# IT'S FOR NO USE

Early the following morning, Jake tracked Winnie down to the creek. She was sitting on the bank with a fishing pole lying beside her. "You won't catch many fish like that," Jake said. She looked up at him with a smile.

"Winnie, I need to talk to you about last night and the other day." He sat down beside her on the bank. "We've had a couple of pretty intense moments."

He wasn't sure what to say next but forged ahead. "First, I want you to know that I do love you, Winnie."

She smiled at him, her green eyes filled with mischief. "You're starting to grow on me, too."

He smiled, but her intense gaze made him nervous. He hesitated. "If we are going to be together, then we need to be honest with one another." He watched her eyes, trying to gauge her response to his words. So far he thought he was doing all right.

"You know I have always been kind of, well, a quiet sort of a loner. At least where women are concerned, and as much as I want to be with you, I'm afraid of… of getting married. I can't imagine the—"

The soft look on Winnie's face turned to disbelief and then quickly to anger. She cut him off, "What? What do you mean you can't imagine being married to me?" She jumped to her feet. "You're afraid of marrying me? You've practically pillaged me twice, and you said you love me. And that's it. That's where it ends?"

"Yes, I mean no. I mean, yes. I love you, but that's not where it ends."

She was already stomping away before he could finish and make her understand what he was trying to say.

"Guess that could have gone better," he said to the wind. There was no one else to talk to.

Jake returned to the cabin with the fishing pole on his sagging shoulders. He found Winnie in the lean-to, preparing to leave. She wouldn't look at him. "Winnie, I was trying to ask you…"

Her words were like ice. "Marshal Jacobs, right now, at this moment, I don't like you, and I doubt I will like you any better tomorrow. And maybe even less the day after that." Her voice shook the timbers of the decrepit cabin. "We're done, William Jacobs. We're done. Over. Finished," she said, stomping from the room leaving Jake in her wake.

* * *

It took Clark and Winnie only a few minutes to take some final measurements and hitch up the teams. Winnie was in a hurry to get away. She wanted to avoid Jake. He had hurt her, and she didn't want him or Clark to see the tears she was trying desperately to hold back. As soon as the mules were hitched she hightailed it away from the cabin and Jake.

Clark checked the harnesses and lines and climbed onto his wagon seat, ready for a trip to the lumber mill. He looked over at the despondent man standing in front of the cabin. "Trouble in paradise?"

Jake nodded. "Yeah, it would seem so."

Clark took out a plug of tobacco from its well-worn pouch and cut off a quid. He shoved it in his mouth and tongued it against his cheek. He chewed thoughtfully for a few minutes. "You love her?"

"I'm afraid to say it, but yes."

Clark cackled, "Then don't bother trying to figure her out. It's for no use."

He chewed a little longer on his tobacco. He spat to the side of the wagon and wiped his mouth on his shirt sleeve. "You planning on marrying up with her?"

Jake looked at him and smiled weakly at his question. "That was the plan."

Clark cackled again. "Well, if that's the case, good luck, boy. You're gonna need it if you're aiming to tame that filly." He jiggled the reins, and with a he-yah, the wagon lurched off.

Jake thought it would take more than luck to change Winnie's mind. He mounted and went to find Pete, Chris, and the rest of the men.

When he caught up to the men he took some serious ribbing about Winnie and his intentions. He took the needling good-naturedly, mumbling, "You should be so lucky."

With Peter and Chris in charge and several men on watch, Jake decided his presence wasn't needed. He had Winnie on his mind as he rode away.

## CHAPTER 66

# A VISION AND ADVICE

Jake rode cross-country to his family homestead, stopping at his mom and dad's graves. For a moment, he let himself remember how happy they had been. He took a deep breath and moved away, not looking at the spot where the house had stood. For the longest time black ashes had scarred the land, declaring its location, but they were no longer visible. They had been overgrown or washed away.

Jake walked down to the creek bank where he had always come to think. Herald walked slightly behind him, sensing his mood and whimpering with worry.

"Dad and I would have come here to fish that night if…." Jake stopped himself from replaying the past yet again. He sat down and laughed inwardly. The biggest problems in his life back then were Sam Watkins and school.

He watched a leaf floating down the stream and wished he could throw all his problems in the creek and watch them float away. The past week's events weighed heavy on his mind, but at this moment, all he could think about was Winnie.

"I love her, and I want to marry her. I want to spend the rest of my life with her," he said softly to himself. "I thought she understood. If only she would talk to me?"

He watched the ripples of water sparkling in the sunlight, wondering what he should do. The reflection from the water momentarily blinded him, and a chill washed over him.

"She loves you, Jake." He was startled to hear a voice so close to him. He had not heard anyone approach.

He looked over to where the voice had come from to see his mother sitting on the bank only a few feet away in a swirling shimmer of mist. "Mom?" he said in disbelief.

"It's me, Jake. Your father and I are always with you. I wish I could take you in my arms like I used to and tell you everything will be all right."

"You are gone and buried. How is it I can see you?" He thought perhaps he had finally gone over the edge, snapped, crazy as a loon.

"The special gift you have grows stronger and it will serve you well. I wish I could be there to help you and to guide you."

"Mom, I miss you and Dad so much."

"We are with you always and so proud of the man you are today."

"There is no shame in what you have done. The men you killed were evil, and it was their time. What happened was meant to be, it was their journey, and it was also yours. All is well in the world." Her voice and image faded away, and she was gone.

"Mom?" Jake said, looking around, but he was alone.

Sitting with his elbows on his knees, his head in his hands, he had trouble believing what had happened. Had he talked with his mother, or was he going crazy?

A wellspring of emotion swept through him. His mother had opened the floodgates and the pain and sorrow of the last fourteen years poured out. The man he had become wept for the little boy.

The burdens he had been carrying were lifted from his shoulders, and he sent a silent prayer of thanks to the heavens.

He still wasn't sure what to do about Winnie but maybe John could give him some advice. After all, he and Mary had been married for ten years and were about to have their sixth child. They seemed to be happy and still wildly in love.

He got up and climbed the creek bank to where Herald was grazing. He scratched his mule's ears and rubbed his soft, velvety muzzle, and Herald snuffled his approval.

It was late in the day, and he knew John would be at home, so he headed straight to his house. On the way, he played and replayed the brief conversation he had had with his mother and decided he wasn't going crazy. He really had talked to her.

When he dismounted, John, Mary, and all five of their children came rushing out to greet him. Jake was always a little overwhelmed by the flurry of activity with him at the center.

Mary hugged him. "You should be honored, Uncle Jake. They don't greet everyone this way. Can't imagine why, but they sure seem to like you."

John slapped Jake on the back. "So, what brings you to our doorstep? You look serious."

"John, I need to talk to you. I need some advice."

"Sure thing Jake, let's sit at the picnic table. Freshly painted and clean. Nothing sticky. Would you like a drink while we talk?"

"No thanks, I'm fine."

They sat silently for a few minutes before John started the conversation. "I can only assume this is about the fuss you and Winnie had up at the cabin this morning."

Jake looked at him in surprise. "How do you know what went on up at the cabin? It was just this morning."

John laughed, "No secrets among friends. Your friends know everything about you. Didn't you know?"

"Well, no, I didn't. Guess that sort of ruins the whole mysterious, loner thing."

"Only in your mind, Jake, only in your mind. Clark said you and Winnie were doing a lot of hugging and smooching last night by the fire, but this morning she told you it was over and done. So what happened?"

"John, I love Winnie, but I'm afraid of her, well, that's not right, I'm not afraid of her, but about getting married . . . I'm not so sure."

"Well, first off, Jake, I'm glad you're not afraid of the woman you want to marry and spend the rest of your life with. No one should fear their bride-to-be, but on the other hand, it is Winnie we're talking about."

Jake didn't laugh. "Not funny, John. I'm serious. I came to you for advice because I see how happy you and Mary are."

John got serious. "So, what did you do to set Winnie off?"

"I tried to have this conversation with her. I wanted to be open and honest about how I feel about her and marriage."

Mary had popped onto the front porch shaking a rag rug, "If you were no more *eloquent* than you were just now, I can see how it might not have gone well."

John gave his wife a look and reclaimed the conversation. "All right, seriously, maybe we're all a little bit afraid of marriage, to begin with. At least, us men are, but it's a leap of faith. I mean, our wedding night was…."

"John." Mary interrupted from behind him, picking up some scattered toys. "Perhaps you should let Jake talk?"

John blew her a kiss. "Jake, you have a head start due to the fact that you already know Winnie, and she is one of your best friends. You lived under the same roof for nearly fifteen years. You know her moods, what she looks like in the mornings, what makes her laugh, what makes her cry, what scares her, and probably some of her closest secrets. You have all of these insights and you know all of her foibles. And still, you want her in your life. Not because you fancy her or because she's beautiful, but because you love her."

Jake sat for a moment, thinking about what John had said. "I'll take that drink now." John went to the well and pulled up a whiskey bottle tied to the end of a rope. "This keeps it cool and out of the reach of the children. And what Mary doesn't know—"

Mary chimed in through the open kitchen window, "John, you think I don't know about that bottle?"

John laughed, handing the bottle to Jake. "She doesn't miss much. She sees everything and hears everything. She calls her ears Mama Ears. She can hear a gnat fart twenty miles down the road."

Jake looked over at the laughing children playing and frolicking in the front yard. He took a drink. "What about children?" Jake asked, passing the bottle back to John. "What kind of a father would I be? Could I deal with a bunch of children running around? I love your babies. They are beautiful and funny. Then I go home. When they are yours, they are with you all the time."

"They aren't with me all the time, Jake. I only wish they were."

"What about my preoccupation with finding my parents' killer? I realize I'm obsessed with it. I don't know how, where, or if it will ever end." Jake paused and said quietly. "If I don't find him, will I ever be able to let it go?"

Jake ran his hand through his hair. "And my job? A lawman can get killed at any time." Jake looked John straight in the eyes. "That thing with Fitz and the bounty hunter could have gone either way. Bryson got off the first shot. It could have been me lying in a coffin. It would be bad enough to leave Winnie a widow, but if there were children."

"Jake, you know you can't look at life that way. I could get kicked in the head by an ornery old mule tomorrow, but I'm going to live my life and enjoy Mary's love and the love of my children every day. Tomorrow isn't promised to any of us."

"You came to me for advice, and my advice is to go find Winnie and apologize. Beg her for forgiveness. Get on your hands and knees if you have to and, ask her straight out to marry you."

Mary came and sat beside Jake. "He's right. Go find Winnie and propose." Mary looked at him in disbelief. "Jake, you're still sitting here? Go and find her . . . now."

John laughed. "Calm down, Mary. He's a little skittish, and we don't want to spook him."

CHAPTER 67

# WHO DOESN'T KNOW?

Jake left John and Mary on their front porch, waving after him. He had planned on going straight to the ranch, but it was late, and he was tired.

"Herald, we're staying in town tonight." Herald didn't care. He knew that wherever they stopped, hay and a nice rubdown would be waiting for him.

Jake headed for the marshal's office, knowing he would probably find Sam and Logan. He shook his head, wondering what he would do without them.

When Jake rode up, Sam was coming out the door.

"Wanna join me on rounds?"

"I thought you'd never ask. You feeling better?"

"Dog tired and hurts like hell if I move the wrong way, but Coop says it will get better every day. He also said walking will help me heal, so I'm making the rounds several more times a day."

"I wonder if the people notice?"

"By people, do you mean the mayor and Sumner?"

Jake scoffed but didn't give Sam an answer.

"How's your arm?"

"A little stiff, and I get those on and off again pains. But it is better today."

They walked side by side down the boardwalk in silence.

Finally, Sam spoke. "I thought you'd be looking for Winnie."

Jake grunted. "I suppose you know about everything that went on at the cabin, too."

"Clark couldn't wait to entertain us with your problem."

"I figured as much. I was going to find Winnie tonight, but it's late, and I'm tired. Besides, everyone would be turned in by the time I got there. I'll get an early start in the morning."

"You want me to go home and let you have the office cot?"

"Nah, I'll get a room at the hotel."

"Wanna stop by Kat's?"

Jake gave Sam a friendly slap on the back. "One of the best offers I have had all day."

They finished rounds in silence and then stopped at Kat's.

They sat at their regular table, and Kat came from the bar to join them.

"Before you start, I'm going to the ranch in the morning to talk to Winnie and ask her to marry me."

Kat laughed. "There are no secrets. Steven told me all about what happened at the cabin."

Jake shook his head and smiled. "So, who doesn't know about my love life?"

Bear brought their usual drinks to the table and stopped so they could all compare wounds and scars. Sam won.

Jake was a little off-center when he got to the hotel, thanks to the drinks at Kat's. He was tired and couldn't wait to find a bed. He approached the desk and rang the bell expecting Lars but got Sally.

She was helpful and flirtatious, as usual. "Sally, just give me my key, please."

She licked her lips, and a wanton smile graced her pretty face. "Want me to come . . . tuck you in."

"No, Sally, just the key."

When he got to his room, he leaned against the closed door with a sigh. Then he locked it and hitched a chair under the doorknob before falling onto the bed.

# CHAPTER 68

# STILL MAD

The following morning he was off at the crack of dawn. He couldn't wait to see Winnie. He was terrified he would mess it up, but he was going to ask her to marry him. He wanted to do it properly and planned on meeting with Grant first to get his blessings.

When Jake got to the ranch, there was a carriage in front of the house that he didn't recognize. He went in the front door and headed to Grant's office. "Grant, you in here?" Jake called.

"I'm in the office, Jake. Come on back."

As Jake walked to the office, he passed Quinn as he was leaving. "Quinn," he said in greeting.

"Marshal."

"What did he want?" Jack asked as he walked into Grant's office.

Grant's smile of welcome at seeing Jake turned into a scowl at the reference to Sumner. "He asked for my permission to court and to marry my daughter."

The slight niggle of a headache caused Jake to rub the back of his neck. "What did you tell him?"

Grant snorted. "I told him I disapproved—too much of an age difference. Besides, I never really liked the guy. He seemed all right at first, but I've always felt there was something different or odd about him. Anyway, I told him I had no control over her. She's an adult and can decide who she does or doesn't want to see."

"I don't like that guy," Jake said, stretching and rotating his neck against the persistent hint of a headache.

"He had to know I'd never give him my blessing, but at least he was polite enough to ask."

"Oddly enough, that's why I'm here this morning. I want your permission to ask Winnie to marry me."

Grant laughed out loud and came around the desk. "Jake, nothing could make me happier." He wrapped him up in a bear hug and hollered for Lorene.

"Better not celebrate till she accepts. She's awful mad at me right now. I need to find her and make her understand."

He ran to his room, taking the stairs two at a time, and pulled a small silver box from his dresser drawer—a box he had treasured since his parents' death. He put the precious keepsake in his pocket and galloped down the stairs, through the kitchen, and out the back door.

As he flew past, Lorene yelled, "She's out currying Ember."

When he reached the stable door, he jerked to a stop. Quinn was standing in front of Winnie, talking to her. Jake couldn't make out what was being said, but Quinn turned away from her; his face was bright red.

At the sight of Jake, a wave of hatred washed over him. "She'll be mine," he glowered at Jake as he stomped past him. "She'll be mine."

Winnie saw Jake and smiled. "I'm glad you showed up when you did. He was getting a little scary."

"What did he say?"

"Short version, he is going to court me, I am going to marry him, and we will have a blissful life together, and I will give him lots of sons."

"And you said?"

"What do you think I said, you idiot? I told him no, of course, but he was having trouble understanding no, and I asked him to leave. I don't think he had a mind to until he heard you."

Jake wanted to take after Sumner and, if not kill him, at the very least, warn him to stay away from Winnie, but he was on a mission and couldn't be distracted. He'd deal with him all in good time.

He took a deep breath. "I certainly hope I do better than your last suitor. I love you, Winnie, and I have asked your father for your hand. Will you marry me? Will you be my wife?"

"Just like that?"

"Yes, just like that. I'm sorry for the misunderstanding yesterday morning. I'm not afraid of marrying you, Win. I'm afraid of how it will change our lives, but don't doubt for a moment that I love you and want to share my life with you."

Jake pulled the silver box from his pocket and opened it. There was a narrow gold band lying on a soft silk pillow. "This was my mother's wedding ring. I was going to give it to you on our wedding day. But I want you to have it now."

Winnie's eyes were misted. "Oh, Jake, it's beautiful."

"If you ever doubt my love or are mad at me for saying or doing something foolish, feel this ring on your finger, and know I will love you for as long as I live."

Winnie's eyes brimmed with joyful tears. One tear escaped, and Jake wiped it gently away with his thumb. "Yes, Jake, I'll marry you. I love you so much."

Jake slipped his mother's precious ring on her finger, and Winnie wrapped her arms around his neck, kissing him with abandon. She suddenly pulled away from him, a radiant smile lighting her face. "Let's go tell Mom and Dad."

## CHAPTER 69

# GAMBLING DEBTS PAID IN FULL

Seething with anger after returning from Grant's and his discussion with Winnie, Quinn paced the length of the veranda. *How could she dismiss me like she did? And in front of that ignorant and boorish marshal.* "No! She will be mine," he hollered at the full moon.

He took a deep breath. *She'll come around and see the terrible mistake she's making, and she'll beg me to marry her.* Quinn chuckled. *Winnie, you have much to learn and I'm eager to begin teaching you.*

The smell of roasting meat reminded him of his physical hunger. When Quinn went inside, his mother was seated at the dining room table. Carol had everything ready for the meal. He kissed his mother's cheek and sat down to eat.

Carol was doing her best to spoon-feed his mother. Her nasal voice coaxed and pleaded, but without much success. Quinn watched as most of what Carol managed to put in his mother's mouth bubbled out and slid down her chin.

He slammed his fist on the table, causing the China and silverware to bounce and clatter. "For God's sake, Carol, from now on, I'll expect you to feed my mother in the kitchen or in her bedroom. This is disgusting and has spoiled my appetite. Put her to bed. Now."

"Yes, Dr. Sumner," Carol whispered, keeping her head lowered, looking up at him through man-sized dark eyebrows. She knew from his sudden outburst that he would come to punish her later.

Quinn left the table, going back to the veranda to calm himself. A sudden burst of lust shot through his body as his mind went to Carol and the corporal punishment he intended to inflict on her. He was rough on Carol, but she deserved to be punished.

Carol was a large, homely girl. He didn't particularly like her, but she was competent. She seldom spoke or created issues for him. She was kind and gentle with his mother. The house was clean, his mother was clean and well-kept, and Carol was a decent cook. She made his life much easier.

He remembered, with disgust, the day he went to speak with her parents about her moving in as full-time help. "We're pleased that she's working out for you," her father said with a yellow, snaggle-toothed smile. "But I'd like an upfront payment. She does a lot for us, you know, and what with me and the missus getting older and all, we'll miss her help."

"Would five hundred be enough?" Quinn asked.

"Dollars?" her dad exclaimed. "Yes. Yes, of course, that would be fine."

Leaving her parents' filthy shack, he felt tainted and couldn't help but feel sorry for Carol. He had gone to hire their daughter, but it seemed more like he had made a purchase. He could not help but wonder if they had any love at all for the ugly troll they had spewed into the world.

Carol was only fifteen but had unbelievably enormous breasts, which fascinated him, and a wide, plump bottom. Her homely round face disgusted him. So pale and bland it reminded him of mushy oatmeal. Her mousy brown hair had never been cut, and she wore it in tight braids wrapped around her head. Her mouth was small and tight, with her front teeth protruding slightly. Her expressionless, dull brown eyes peered through narrow slits, and her thick, manly eyebrows owned a good portion of her forehead.

He did his best to avoid looking at her, but when he did, his gaze didn't move above her neck. Instead, he focused on her breasts and how they shifted and jiggled with every move.

The transition from part-time to live-in status had been smooth. She put his mother to bed every evening and then, on her way to her room, would gently tap on his door. "If there isn't anything else, Dr. Sumner, I'm going to bed now."

For several weeks his answer was, "No, Carol. Goodnight." Then one evening, when she tapped, he answered. "Come in for a moment, please."

# CHAPTER 70

# THERE'S ALWAYS A FIRST TIME

Quinn enjoyed thinking about the first time he had taken her and how shocked and horrified she had been. Like a timid mouse, she opened the door slowly, peeking around the edge, not entering his room.

"Come in, Carol. I won't bite."

Carol walked to within three feet of where he was sitting. "What can I help you with, Dr. Sumner?"

He rose slowly from his chair so as not to frighten her. "I'm curious," he said, and without warning, he reached out and grabbed her. He backed her up against his bed, tearing her smock away, giving him access to her breasts. "I was curious about what you had under your blouse that jiggled so." His hands roughly squeezed her breasts. "As soft and pillowy as I imagined," he said. He sucked an oversized nipple into his mouth and buried his face in the mounds of flesh. When he could no longer restrain himself, he pushed her down and thrust into her hard, shaking with the pleasure of his release. He pulled away from her, turning his back. "Goodnight, Carol."

With shaking hands, Carol pushed herself up and tried to gather her torn smock to cover herself. She had wondered what it would be like to make love to such a handsome and wonderful man. How it would feel to have his lips on hers and his hands caressing her body. He had seemed so kind and such a gentleman. What she had imagined was nothing like this.

"Get out, Carol. Go to your room."

"Yes, Dr. Sumner?" she said, her voice shaking.

Carol ran to her room and sank onto the bed, sobbing. How could she face him tomorrow? Why had he been so rough? She had thought she would be safe here, but he was just like every other man she'd ever known.

Carol knew about men and what they wanted from a woman. Her loving father had given her to his drinking buddies numerous times to pay off gambling debts. They were cruel, telling her how ugly she was and telling her father they weren't sure they would accept her as payment. But dear old Dad explained amidst raucous, drunken laughter that he knew for a certainty she had all the necessary parts. They might not be the prettiest, but all parts worked just fine. Those men had been rough but nothing like Dr. Sumner.

When the tears ran out, she took a deep breath and decided that tomorrow would be another day, like any other. What else could she do? She had no place else to go.

Thinking about that first time made him eager to go to her and fondle her soft, velvety flesh and to nurse at her enormous breasts. He could wait no longer, and there was, after all, punishment to be administered. He smiled as he entered the house, pulling his favorite riding quirt from a peg inside the door. He slapped the short-riding whip against his leg as he climbed the stairs and walked down the hall to Carol's bedroom. He couldn't enjoy his mother, the way he enjoyed Carol. It wouldn't be right. And he couldn't mar Winnie's beauty with the kind of things he did to Carol. He'd keep Carol even after he married Winnie. He liked the idea. He opened the door to Carol's room and peered in with a wicked smile. "It's time for your punishment, Carol."

She was bent over the bed, naked and on her knees. "I see you've been waiting for me."

When he finished, he went down the hall to his mother's room to say goodnight. She was barely breathing, and her eyes were vacant. It had been that way for a long time. If she had any memory at all, she thought Quinn was her long-dead husband.

Quinn crawled into bed next to his mother and hugged her. Her condition broke his heart, but there was nothing he could do but comfort her. He would miss her, but he would have Winnie.

His mother opened her eyes, looking at him with a spark of awareness. "Artem, my love, is it you?"

"Yes, my darling, it is Artem," he whispered in her ear and pulled her into his arms.

## CHAPTER 71

# SOMETIMES YOU NEED A BREAK

Quinn woke in his mother's bed early the following morning, encouraged by the comfort Carol and his mother had given him.

He woke with a plan, and things looked bright in the morning sunlight. He knew what he had to do. He had to get Winnie to his estate. Once she was here, he could convince her of his love and persuade her to marry him. All he had to do was get her away from Jake and her friends. All they needed was time alone. He remembered the kisses and how soft and yielding Winnie's lips had been, and a shudder of lust swept through his loins. He'd kiss her like that night, and she would understand.

He was too agitated to go to work. He could only concentrate on the idea that was taking form. If it didn't go well, it could be dangerous, but Winnie was worth the risk and the danger of it appealed to him.

If this were going to work, he had to be ready to act when the chance presented itself. He needed supplies from his office, and then he would have to wait until Winnie was in town and alone to set his plan in motion. He saddled his horse and headed to Grant's Crossing, playing and replaying every scenario he could think of. Each ended with Winnie falling into his arms and passionately giving herself to him.

He chuckled, talking to himself. "In time, I will shape her into whatever I want her to be. She'll be unable to resist me or my…charms."

He tied his horse in front of his office. As he dismounted, horses galloped by their hooves pounding, throwing dust in the air. He looked around to see Jake and Sam riding hard toward the east. He wondered where they were off to in such a rush.

Then he smiled, realizing Winnie would be alone. Was today the day? Was fate on his side? His hands shook with anticipation as he opened his medicine cabinet, searching through the various vials of painkillers, potions, and herbs. He found the bottle he was searching for. It was a drug he often used on his patients, and knew Winnie would be awake but wouldn't be aware of what was happening. He had always hoped she would come to him freely, but if this was what it took to get her alone, then so be it. She would belong to him and no one else.

He pocketed the drug. Now, he needed to find Winnie. He figured if anyone knew where she was, it would be Kat. And maybe she knew where the marshals were off to in such a hurry. It didn't concern him too much, he had other things on his mind.

People were still eating breakfast when he walked in, but he found an empty table. He was deciding how best to proceed when Kat came up behind him. "Good morning, Quinn. Are you here for breakfast?"

*Perfect*, he thought and turning in his chair, he looked up at her with his most charming smile. "Yes, I'm here for breakfast. Coffee, please, and biscuits and gravy, if it's on the menu this morning."

"Always is. I'll put in your order."

"Kat, why don't you grab a coffee and come join me for a bit? I could use some company. My mom is in bad shape, and I don't think she'll be with me much longer." He hoped he had sounded pathetic enough to appeal to her womanly instincts to comfort him.

"Sure, Quinn, I could use a break."

Kat returned to the table with two coffee mugs and sat across from him. "I am sorry to hear about your mother. You must be close."

"Yes, we are, and I don't know how I will ever get along without her. She's been bad for some time, but lately, she's been failing fast." He coaxed a tear to slide down his cheek. "Sorry, I didn't mean to get all maudlin. I came to town to take care of a few housekeeping chores at the office and to get away for a little while."

"Sometimes you need a break. To take care of yourself."

"I saw the marshals head out of town, stirring up the dust. Must be an emergency of some kind."

"There was a double murder reported east of here, over by Sparkston."

"That's awful," Quinn said, as if bothered by the news. He didn't care. All he cared about was finding Winnie. "Guess Winnie will be lonely today without the marshal riding shotgun for her."

"She doesn't need anyone riding shotgun for her, Quinn. She can take care of herself."

"Of course, she can. I didn't mean anything by what I said. I just figured she'd be alone."

"She's not alone. She's at Mary's house getting fitted for her wedding dress, and I'm meeting them at the Carmichael at noon."

"A wedding dress?" His heart was beating fast. It was for him, for their wedding. She did love him.

"Yes, a wedding dress," Kat said. "Jake proposed yesterday, and she accepted."

"Jake? She's marrying Jake!" Everyone in the room turned to look in the direction of the outburst.

"Calm down, Quinn. Of course, she's marrying Jake. Who else would it be?"

"I'm sorry, Kat. I'm just such a mess…worried about my mother and all. I shouldn't have stopped here. I should have gone straight home." He stood to leave. "How much do I owe you."

He had never lost control before. He took a breath, trying to pull himself together. He wanted to hit something, but he couldn't afford to lose his composure. Not now when he was so close to the prize.

"Don't worry about it, Quinn. Take care, and get some rest. You look like you need it," Kat spoke softly, walking with him to the door. "Let me know if there is anything I can do for your mother."

He nodded his thanks, unable to speak with a civil tongue.

She watched him charge down the boardwalk toward his office, mount his horse, and gallop out of town. Something was off with that man, and Kat wished Jake and Sam hadn't left town.

She motioned to Bear that she was leaving. Pushing through the batwing doors, she headed across the street, dodging three large freight wagons filled with lumber. Logan was in the marshal's office, dozing with his feet on the desk and hands crossed over his stomach.

Kat slammed the door. "Logan."

He flew from the chair, knocking it to the floor. "I'm awake," he said, bending over to pick up the chair. "What's so danged important you have to give me an apoplexy?" he said, sitting down.

"Sorry, Logan," Kat said, with a frown. "I think I may have said the wrong thing. Winnie is at Mary's house this morning, and I may have put them both in danger."

"What are you talking about? What kind of danger?"

"Quinn Sumner came in for breakfast and was acting odd. Odder than usual. He asked about Winnie, and when I told him she was marrying Jake, he went nuts."

Logan rubbed his eyes. "Jake told me Quinn has been pestering Winnie, wanting to court her. You think Sumner would hurt her?"

"I wouldn't have thought so, but you didn't see his eyes." A shiver ran down Kat's spine.

"She's at Mary's?" Logan asked.

"Yes, that's where she should be."

"I'll go check and make sure everything is in order." Logan threw on his hat, grabbed his shotgun, and headed out the door. "I'll let you know if I find anything. Sumner is an odd stick, but I'm sure it's nothing to worry about."

He headed across the Miller's pasture, taking a shortcut and approaching quietly. He searched the outbuildings, and they were all clear. Mary and Winnie sat at the kitchen table with youngsters running around, creating total chaos. Logan knocked on the door and was greeted with squeals of joy from the pack of children.

"Everything all right in here?" he asked from the doorway.

Winnie came to the door and stood beside Mary. "Sure. Why?"

Logan explained Kat's concerns about Quinn.

"He's turned into a real pest, but I can't imagine him being dangerous. He wasn't such a bad guy until he started getting pushy. Maybe he'll leave me alone now that Jake and I are getting married."

"You want me to hang around for a while? Make sure he doesn't show up uninvited."

Mary placed a piece of rhubarb-strawberry pie and a mug of steaming coffee on the table. "Have a seat, Deputy. You have to stay long enough to clean your plate."

Leaning his shotgun next to the door he came to the table, rubbing his hands together. "Thank you, Mary, glad to oblige."

Logan patted his belly and checked his mustache for crumbs. "Thank you, Mary. That was real good pie." Logan stood and headed for the door. "I'll be close by," he said, picking up his shotgun.

"I won't let anyone bother you young ladies." Logan left the house and rechecked the property.

From the hayloft where he was perched, Logan had a full view of the property and buildings. No one had come or gone. When he saw Winnie and Mary leave for the hotel, he waved to them and headed back to the office. He figured Winnie would be safe enough at the Carmichael, and he would catch up with her there.

## CHAPTER 72

# A FRESH ONE

Jake and Sam made it to Sparkston shortly after noon and rode straight to Sheriff Water's office. A young deputy waited for them. He was a young kid, not much older than sixteen.

"I'm Deputy Cambridge," he said, strutting out to meet them with his thumbs tucked into his gun belt.

"I'm Marshal Jacobs, and this is Deputy Watkins. We got the sheriff's telegram late last night and got here as soon as we could."

"What you want to see is on the outskirts of town. The sheriff stayed there all night and hasn't allowed anyone to move anything. He wanted you to see it before they removed the bodies and cleaned up the mess."

"Our horses are out front, Deputy. Let's go." They were inches from the front door when a sharp pain seared through Jake's head. Sam grabbed him and got him to a chair.

Jake leaned forward, holding his head in his hands, breathing through the pain. His mother had said he should listen, but all he heard was blood pounding in his ears. When the pain subsided and he could think straight, he looked up at Sam. "It's never been this bad."

"A vision?" Sam whispered.

Jake stood shakily, grimacing at the remaining echo of pain. "No. It's more of a knowing. Come on, Sam, let's get this over with. We need to get home. Someone's in trouble."

Jake looked at the young deputy, who had been watching them closely. Jake wondered how much he'd heard of their conversation. "I get these horrible headaches from time to time, but I'm fine now. Let's go, Deputy Cambridge."

They followed the deputy half a mile past the edge of town and reined to a stop in front of a secluded but well-kept log cabin. Jake paused, bracing himself for what he would find inside. He couldn't afford to fall apart when he was so close to the killer. The other murders had been months or years old when he learned about them. This one happened yesterday. This could be the break he'd been looking and praying for.

"I'll leave you here," Deputy Cambridge said, looking a little green around the gills. "I was here last night."

Jake and Sam approached the house, pausing outside the door. "I know what you're thinking, Jake, and you're right. This isn't going to be easy, but you can do it. We can do it."

Jake nodded, and they entered, greeting Sheriff Waters. He looked tired, and his red-rimmed eyes were glazed with sadness.

Jake put a comforting hand on the Sheriff's shoulder. "Who found the bodies?"

"The tinker. It was Tiny who found them. I don't recall ever knowing his real name." He took a shaky breath, "Martha always fed him. They'd let him sleep in the barn and rest his mules for a day or so whenever he came through the pass."

Jake left his hand on the sheriff's shoulder. "When did he find them?"

"Yesterday. I came out to investigate and telegraphed you right away. I knew you'd want to know. This is bad, Marshal. I can't believe what he did to them." The sheriff paused to clear his throat. "When you stopped through last fall, telling me about all the killings you'd found, I didn't think I'd have to—" He choked back a sob. "After I telegraphed you, I came straight back here to make sure nothing happened to the bodies. I stayed all night. I want to do everything I can to help you find this butcher."

"Staying here must have been difficult," Jake said.

"The Carsons are at the back of the house, in the washroom. They were good people." On the verge of breaking down completely, he choked out, "David and Martha were my friends."

Sam sat the sheriff down at the kitchen table. "I'm sorry for your loss, Sheriff. It's probably best if you stay here while Marshal Jacobs and I take a look around."

Jake tried not to think of his parents as he examined the area, forcing himself to inspect the bodies, looking for anything that might be a clue. There had to be something. He was repulsed to find that the woman's breasts had been removed. She had been brutalized inside and out. He thought of his mother and father and swallowed the primal scream that threatened to erupt.

Taking a shallow breath, Jake bridled his anger and continued his inspection of the slaughter. He and Sam studied and restudied the bodies and the room. Each tried to ignore the overpowering smell of death and the increasing number of carrion flies surrounding them.

The Carsons sat on the floor across from each other with a washtub between their hollowed-out bodies. It was filled with their blood, innards, and clothes. Mrs. Carson had a washboard in front of her, and a bloody shirt clasped in her hand.

"He must have killed and gutted them one at a time in the wash-tub. Then posed them like it was wash day," Sam said, struggling to maintain his objectivity. "It looks like he moved them around several times. What the hell was he doing, looking for the right spot? And how did he kill two people without any sign of a fight? Everything's in place. There's no sign of a struggle. Barely any blood on the floor."

"Maybe they knew him, and they let him in, and then he bush-whacks them?" Jake posited.

Well, we know it wasn't Tiny. He's physically unable to do this." Sam squatted beside one body, then the other, gingerly feeling the back of their heads. He looked up at Jake. "No lumps."

Jake shook his head. "Let's take another look." And for the third time, they inspected the room and its contents.

"Jake, I didn't notice it before, but something is sticking out of the corner of Mrs. Carson's mouth."

Jake forced himself to look. Her lips were barely parted. Sam was right. There was something there.

Sam carefully pushed back her upper lip. "It's a finger, and it's stuffed into the space where her canine tooth should be." Sam inspected both of her hands and saw that one of her little fingers was missing. He turned to her husband and inspected his hands as well. His little finger was gone and was also in a gap where his canine tooth should have been. "Has anyone ever reported this at any of the other murders?"

"No. Even the doctor in Clay Springs had nothing about this in his notes. Maybe this is a one-time thing? But what does it mean? Does he collect canine teeth? And why shove the finger in their mouth? And why the little fingers? I've been looking for something, and now that we've found it, I can't begin to imagine how it can help." Jake thought of his parents, and his control began to slip.

Sam saw it and grabbed his arm. "Let's get out of here, Jake. We need to talk to the sheriff."

Jake and Sam sat across the table from the sheriff. In the middle of the table was a box tied with a satin ribbon, and under the bow was a folded piece of stationery.

"I didn't see this yesterday," Sheriff Waters said, pushing the box across the table. It was on the washstand over behind the door. It's addressed to you, Marshal."

The minute he saw the package, he knew it was for him and knew what it was. Jake touched the package, his hands shaking. He pulled the ribbon off and unfolded the stationery. He read the note and handed it to Sam.

*"Another souvenir for your collection. I hope you enjoyed meeting the Carsons. I know I did. They are a lovely couple and very hospitable. Till next time, Marshal."*

Jake opened the package, pulling back a scrap of material. It was the woman's missing parts. He looked at Sam and nodded. They had both suspected. Jake didn't show the sheriff.

"Sheriff, was there anything different about yesterday? Anything at all? Anything?" Jake asked.

The sheriff thought for a while before replying. "No, except for Tiny coming through. Nothing I can think of."

"Nothing at all? The slightest thing could make a difference."

"Well, Dr. Sumner was here yesterday."

Jake looked at Sam. Then turned back to the sheriff, "Quinn Sumner was here yesterday?"

The sheriff nodded. "He was here bright and early yesterday. He stayed for maybe an hour or so, passing out those little toothbrushes of his, trying to drum up business. Pulled a tooth for old man Handlin and lit out."

Sam turned to Jake, "There's nothing more we can do here. If we leave now, we can be back home before dark. Thank you, Sheriff, you've been a big help, and be assured we're doing everything possible to find this killer." Sam rose from the table and started for the door.

Jake looked at the sheriff, seeing his grief and sharing in it. "He killed my parents, so I understand what you're feeling. I want to find him as badly as you do."

"Marshal?" Jake turned back. "When you find him, tear him to pieces and kill him slow."

Jake and Sam mounted their horses and headed for Grant's Crossing. They rode hard, but halfway home, Jake raised his hand, signaling for them to stop. "The horses need a break."

"How's the head?" Sam asked as they led the horses to a nearby stream

"Not too good, but not as bad as when we were in the sheriff's office." Jake paused. "The headache started yesterday, but I don't remember exactly when."

"It's been getting worse since yesterday?"

"Yeah, but none of my alarms went off, so I didn't think much about it. I figured it was just a plain old headache."

A wave of horror slammed through Jake's body. "Sam, it started right after I ran into Quinn coming out of Grant's office. That's when it started. Why didn't I see it? He's been after Winnie ever since she got home, and she told me he was beginning to scare her."

"We'll be home soon, and we can find out what's happening."

"Sam, he's after Winnie. I would bet my life on it."

"If you're sure it's Quinn, let's go straight to his house." Sam saw the fear and concern in Jake's eyes. "Quinn doesn't want to hurt her, Jake. He wants to marry her."

Jake took no solace in Sam's words. If Sumner was after Winnie, they had to find him, and they had to find him fast.

## CHAPTER 73

# WE WILL HUNT TOGETHER

Leaving the Carmichael Café after lunch, Kat and Mary both cautioned Winnie to get Logan to ride with her, but she insisted she could take care of herself. "I know how to handle a gun," she assured them, "and there's always a pistol in my saddle holster, loaded and in easy reach."

Mary and Kat watched her mount up and ride out of town. "Let's find Logan," Kat said. "Whether she likes it or not, she shouldn't ride alone."

"Maybe we're overreacting. Winnie has always been able to take care of herself," Mary said, trying to convince herself.

Kat held up her still splinted arm. "I've always been able to take care of myself, too. Until I couldn't. Sometimes things happen."

"Ooooh, you're right, Kat," Mary said, wringing her hands and watching as Winnie's dust settled in the street. "It's better safe than sorry."

"I'll find Logan," Kat said. "You get home. You look flushed, and it's a long walk back to your house." Kat frowned, looking closer at Mary. "Maybe you should see Coop. Make sure you're all right."

"I'm fine. Go. Go find Logan," Mary said, rubbing her rounded belly.

Kat hurried up the street, but Logan wasn't in the marshal's office. She ran across the street to the livery. "John, has Logan been here to get his horse?"

"No, I haven't seen him, and Aggie is still in her stall. What's wrong?"

"It's Winnie. I think she's in trouble. I can't find Logan, and I don't have time to search the town for him."

John tossed his hammer onto the workbench and ripped his leather blacksmithing apron over his head. "I'll get our horses."

"If she stops at Picnic Table, we might catch up with her."

Winnie did stop at Picnic Table Hill, as was her habit. When she was small, her dad told her it was a good place to rest the horses, but Winnie knew it was something much deeper than that. There was something special about this place…something spiritual. When you were here, there was an unexplainable connection to the All-Powerful Creator and the universe.

She sat on one of the flat-topped boulders, leaning back on her hands, basking in the warmth of the late afternoon sun. A gentle breeze ruffled her hair. She was thinking about Jake and all that needed to be done for the wedding. She wanted a simple wedding but smiled, knowing her father would never let that happen. Winnie felt for the ring Jake had given her. It was gone. She panicked but then remembered she had put it on Mary's windowsill when she washed her hands.

As she stood to leave, thinking she would have to be more careful in the future she heard a noise behind her.

"Winnie?"

She didn't have to see him to know it was Quinn. She spun around, "Why are you following me?"

"I want to talk to you." He would give her one last chance.

"We have nothing to talk about, Quinn. You need to leave me alone. I'm going to marry Jake. Whatever you thought could happen between us…never will. And if you follow me to the ranch, you'll wish you hadn't."

She spun away, turning her back on him, and moved toward Ember, but strong arms grabbed her from behind. "Let me go," she screamed, struggling to break free. "Let me go." She tried to scream, but a cloth held tightly over her nose and mouth muffled her screams. She held her breath, bucking and lurching to free herself.

"You can't hold your breath forever. Breathe, my love. That's right, darling," Sumner said, feeling her gasp for air. "Breathe deep." Her struggles ceased, and she went limp in his arms.

The next thing she knew, she was standing, looking at Quinn. Everything was hazy, and the more she tried to focus, the more nauseated she became. She couldn't move, but she didn't seem to care. She thought she should care and should fight, but her body wouldn't respond.

"Get on your horse," Sumner said, half-carrying Winnie to Ember's side. "Go on, get mounted. We have much to do to prepare for our wedding night. And don't worry about Deputy Logan showing up to ruin everything. I knocked him out and drugged him. He won't be waking up anytime soon, if ever. Not much of a bodyguard."

She mounted Ember with Sumner's help. She wanted to kick out at him but couldn't. "Where are we going?" Winnie's voice sounded like an echo in her head.

"Home, Winnie. We're going home. You'll love it there. The beautiful house and the gardens will be our world to share. You won't be able to leave for a while. Not until I know I can trust you, but you'll have everything you need, and I'll spend every moment I can with you."

Winnie looked at him and smiled. She knew she smiled but didn't know why. All she wanted to do was to tear into him. He hadn't seen the pistol in her saddle holster. If she could move her hand closer—

They rode slowly, keeping off the main roads. When they reached Quinn's plantation house, he dismounted and put his horse in the stable. "I'm sorry, Winnie, but I can't take you to your room as planned. I'm afraid the marshal and your friends may show up any time now to rescue you."

Winnie could feel control returning. She sat quietly on her horse, tilting her head slightly and keeping her face blank, trying to hide the fact from Sumner. He took Ember's reins and led her out of the stable through the forested area behind his house.

"I lost control this morning when Kat told me you were marrying Jake. I reacted badly." He paused and looked at the dazed woman sitting astride her horse. "After I had time to think, I realized you were teasing Jake, and I was the one you truly wanted."

Just as he finished his sentence, Winnie kicked out at him and pulled her pistol, but she was too slow. He dodged and yanked her off Ember's back. They fell to the ground, and he wrestled her into submission, taking the pistol from her hand. Breathing heavily, he straddled her. An ugly smile split his handsome face. "That was very naughty of you, Winnie." Holding her wrists in one hand, he slapped her. "You must never try to hurt me or run away." He slapped her. "I'm not going to punish you this time," he said, slapping her. "Your life here will be different, and you must learn how to conduct yourself. I will allow for a few mistakes."

He smiled his most beguiling smile, and his eyes softened. "You look concerned, my darling, but don't be. I'll teach you everything you need to know." He wrapped a handful of hair around his hand, thinking how soft and beautiful it was. It smelled like strawberries. He yanked hard and pulled her face to his. The smile was gone, and his eyes burned into hers. "Never disobey me, Winnie, and never try to hurt me. Never."

His voice softened. "I don't want to punish you, but you must learn to do exactly as I say. There will come a time, Winnie, when you will beg for my attention and enjoy pleasuring me."

While he was talking, he pulled a hanky and a corked bottle from his coat pocket. He pulled the cork with his teeth and doused the hanky, tossing the bottle aside. Winnie struggled to escape, turning her head away from the cloth he was pressing over her nose and mouth, but her bucking and flailing only aroused him.

He smiled down at her. "Your advances are most pleasing, but shame on you for being such a tease. There'll be time for this when we're properly married. Taking a handful of hair to control her, he leaned down and kissed her. It was a rough kiss that split her lip, and the tang of her blood on his lips stoked his desire. He could hardly resist taking her, but she had to be cleansed first.

"We are going to be so happy, Winnie. I promise you we will." Quinn pulled her up roughly and pushed her in front of him. She stumbled and careened from side to side. She could move, but the fight had left her. She was his puppet. He grabbed her arm and jerked her beside him. "I have a secret place right down by the river. No one will ever find us there."

## CHAPTER 74

# THE POWER

"Here we are," Quinn said, proudly opening a trap door camouflaged to look like the forest floor. "Be careful, my love. The steps are quite steep, and we've already had one tumble." Once she was down, he pulled the door back into place.

Quinn led her to a chair near a small square table. Both the table and chair were anchored in large rough slabs of concrete. He cuffed her wrists tightly to the arms of the chair, and then kneeling, he snapped shackles around her ankles. His hands trailed up her long legs. He could feel the muscles, and soon he would feel them wrapped around him, pulling him in, draining him. He sighed laying his head in her lap, breathing in the smell of her.

He knelt there for only a moment. "Not yet," he said, resisting temptation. He looked into her face with adoration. "You're so soft, and yet I know you to be strong." She would be hard to break, even with drugs, but she would be worth it. She would make a wonderful bed partner, and he would teach her to hunt. She would be better than his mother ever had been.

"I have to leave you for a few moments to send Ember on her way home. If they find her here, they'll know you're close by, and that will never do." He started up the steps and then turned to admire his bride-to-be with a covetous smile. She was his now, and he could mold her into whatever he desired.

He climbed to the top step and slightly lifted the hatch, glancing through the narrow slit, making sure all was clear. He thought of his mother and how she had enjoyed hunting with him. She was unable to hunt with him now, and he missed her, but Winnie would take her place. Yes, Winnie would hunt with him. Perhaps when they were married, he would change her name to Emma. Yes, he would call her Emma, after his mother.

Ember was by the river where they'd left her. He led her to the road and slapped her with his whip. She would head home, and there would be no proof that Winnie was here.

He returned to the cavern and went directly to his workbench. He selected a knife and walked in front of Winnie, testing the sharpness of the blade with the pad of his thumb."

Winnie struggled as he came at her with the knife but couldn't move more than a fraction of an inch. A scream died in her throat as she passed out.

She woke with him splashing water in her face and slapping her. She opened her eyes and looked blankly into his smiling face, his dark eyes inspecting her. She didn't remember anything. "Quinn? You're hurting me."

"I need you awake so we can prepare for our wedding."

What? Where are we?"

"We're in my workshop. You fainted at the sight of my knife, but it was only to cut away your clothes. I would never hurt you, Winnie, I love you."

Winnie tried to move, to shake herself loose from the chair, but her hands and feet wouldn't move. Were the chains that tight, or was it the drug? Her head throbbed, and nausea threatened to spill the contents of her stomach.

She heard him moving about behind her. She couldn't see what he was doing, but he was humming and mumbling to himself. She fell in and out of a haze, hearing the drone of his voice…far away, then closer. Occasionally, he passed by the chair she was chained to and caressed her neck and her breasts. Naked, cold, and panic-stricken, she squeezed her eyes shut, trying to block out what was happening.

She sensed him in front of her and slowly opened her eyes. She flinched at the sight of his naked body. He smiled at what he thought to be her desire. "I am so glad the sight of my body excites you."

"I'm repulsed at the sight of you," she muttered, slurring the words.

He looked down at her, his face turning an ugly crimson red, his fists clenching and unclenching at his sides. "Don't ever say that." He slapped her, leaving a bright red handprint on her cheek.

He put his hands on her thighs, staring at her longingly. "Tell me you love me, Winnie. I know you do, but I need to hear you say it."

"I love Jake, and I'm going to marry him." Her voice was emotionless and soft.

Quinn dug his fingers into her thighs. "Tell me you love me."

She looked at him blankly, unable to comprehend what was happening. "Quinn, you're hurting me. Why are you hurting me?"

"Winnie," he said, pushing her knees apart and kneeling between them, "I don't want to hurt you, but you must tell me you love me." He waited, but she didn't answer. He rose to his feet and backhanded her. Then he whispered in her ear, "Winnie, I won't ask you again. Tell me you love me."

She gasped as he dug his fingers into her shoulders. "No."

His hands closed around her neck, choking her. She had braced herself for another slap, not this. "Tell me you love me," he growled.

His rage-distorted face was inches from her ear, and she could feel his spittle pelting her face and neck.

She could hardly breathe but managed to choke out a weak, "I love you."

He released her neck. "Now, that wasn't so hard, was it? Tell me again. This time, say I love you, Quinn, darling."

Winnie was still choking, gasping for air, unable to speak. He was impatient to hear the words and backhanded her, splitting her lower lip. His eyes cleared. He was enthralled by the trickle of blood running down her chin onto her neck and between her breasts. His heart raced, and his breathing accelerated. He wanted to lick it. To taste her life. But first and most important, he needed to teach her what would be expected from his wife. She needed to be broke like a horse and trained for his bit and his saddle. He raised his arm, ready to deliver a devastating blow, but her words stopped him.

"I love you, Quinn, darling," she rasped out.

"Oh, Winnie. I love you, too, but if this marriage is going to be successful, you must remember one rule…always do as I say. If not, you will be punished, and I guarantee you that each punishment will be harsher than the last. Do you understand?"

"I understand," she whimpered, barely able to speak.

"And do you love me?"

"Yes, Quinn darling, I love you," she spat out through tears, still choking from his stranglehold.

"Will you do anything I ask of you?"

"Yes."

"Yes, what?" he demanded with a frown.

"Yes, Quinn…darling. I will do anything you ask."

"Well, now that we have that settled, let's proceed with the wedding preparations. First, you must be cleansed of all remnants of your previous life. A sweat lodge would be more effective, but a good scrubbing will have to do. It's symbolic of a fresh start, and once you've been cleansed, you will be worthy to receive me."

He went behind her. Something metal clinked against something glass, and she heard a faint scratching like a pen on paper. "I didn't mention it before, he said conversationally, "but an underground stream flows through here. You can't see it from where you're sitting, but it is perfect for bathing. It's not too wide and slow-moving. I use it often when working with my friends."

"While I finish mixing this formula, I'm going to share a secret with you. It hasn't been officially announced, but I know you won't say a thing. Your husband-to-be had dinner with the territorial governor, and it went quite well. The food and drink were exceptional, but the power in that room sizzled. Five of the most powerful men in the territory were seated around that dining table."

He came around in front of Winnie, holding a syringe. "All my fawning servility and sycophantic groveling with that half-witted imbecile of a governor have paid off. When he runs for reelection this fall, he wants me as his running mate. Me. Imagine it. I will be a heartbeat away from being governor of the territory. Just a heartbeat away. And when the governor dies unexpectedly, you will be my first lady.

"I wish I could trust you," he said, pressing the plunger of the syringe until a thread of liquid shot into the air." She flinched at the sight but knew it was pointless to struggle.

"I've made the previous doses light enough so we could get acquainted, but now I'm going to make you a little more agreeable. I've been working on this formula for years studying and experimenting with different plants and cacti and the effects of combining them with medicinal drugs." He chuckled, "Some of my experiments have had appalling but interesting results. It's taken time, but now I have the perfect combination. With the right dosage, I can control you completely. You will willingly do anything I say. I hope in time the drugs won't be necessary, but that will be up to you." He jabbed the needle into her hip. "Let's see how you react."

There was the slightest sting and a moment of clarity before she tumbled backward into a well of darkness, sinking deeper and deeper until there was nothing.

## CHAPTER 75

# CLEANSING RITUAL

When she woke, her arms were pulled tightly over her head, and she was dangling in cold water up to her waist. She vaguely remembered him saying something about a stream before he drugged her. Her head throbbed, and her mouth felt like she'd swallowed a bale of wool. Quinn stood beside her in the stream, soaping her with a stiff-bristled brush.

He dumped a bucket of water over her head, rinsing away the soap. Sputtering and choking, hanging from the iron bar, she struggled, the shackles cutting deep into her wrists.

Quinn grabbed her, holding her firmly against his naked body. "Stop struggling, Winnie. You'll only hurt yourself." At his voice, she went limp. He continued to embrace her, nuzzling her neck and nipping at her ear. She wanted to pull away. She wanted to scream, but nothing happened.

Still holding her close, rubbing himself against her leg, he murmured in her ear, "I am having trouble waiting, Winnie," he said, pushing his erection between her thighs. "But I have found anticipation to be quite an aphrodisiac." His hot breath defiled her neck. "I can't wait much longer, my love," he said, backing away from her.

She let out a deep breath. She could see more of the cavern from here, and her eyes searched for a way out. The ceiling was a dark tangle of roots from the plants and trees growing overhead, and the walls were solid rock and dirt, but there was a steep stairway along one of the walls, leading to where, she didn't know, but it could be her way out.

She saw part of a workbench with syringes and vials scattered about and a long table. The kind Coop had in his operating room. The drug still had a hold on her, and she was having trouble focusing. There appeared to be long blond hair hanging from a peg on the wall. Perhaps her eyes were playing tricks on her. She blinked several times, trying to focus. It was a scalp, still bright with blood. Her eyes fell shut, and she drifted into oblivion.

She woke to Quinn's soapy hands washing and fondling her, massaging her breasts, and his fingers wandering to places they shouldn't, dipping into her. She wanted to lash out, but her mind had no connection to her body.

"Kiss me, Winnie. Kiss me like a bride who wants her husband."

She shook so hard her teeth rattled, but the drug still controlled her. She kissed him, deep and long.

The shackles rattled with her efforts to resist, but the drug was stronger than her will. *This is only the beginning*, she thought and made no effort to stop the tears. She had no choice. She would obey him in everything. The drug would make sure of that.

"How sweet. A bashful bride. All shivery and afraid on her wedding night. Or is it excitement? I'll be gentle, Emma. You're mine now, and I won't hurt you. But you must do everything I ask of you." His eyes were black as coal and blazed with feral lust. "Everything, Emma… everything."

*Why is he calling me Emma?* She wanted to scream, but no one would hear her. She had to pull herself together and think, but her thoughts were random and chaotic. If only he would stop drugging her. If he stopped, maybe she could think rationally. She grasped for a sane thought, but there were none within her reach. Fear clutched her insides, and bile rose in her throat. What if Quinn kept her in this state of limbo? Knowing but able only to respond to his commands. What if she were never found? It was hopeless.

She wept for the life with Jake that she would never know and for the horrible life stretching before her with Quinn. She scolded herself for crying. Tears wouldn't cure anything. She pushed away the fear and the tears. Jake would find her. She wouldn't abandon hope. She couldn't.

Quinn finished scrubbing her for the third time, his ravenous eyes devouring her body. "I shall never tire of looking at you and making love to you. You will bear me a dozen sons." He put his cheek on her belly, imagining his seed growing there. "And we shall hunt together. You'll learn to enjoy it as my mother did. She fought me at first, but after a cup of special tea and getting her hands bloody, she hunted with an exuberance I hadn't expected. We worked together on Jake's parents. One of my best efforts. They were such a sweet couple and strong-spirited. Those are the best kind, but they begged. They all do."

Winnie's stomach lurched. Sumner was the man Jake had been hunting. How could she have been so blind? Even in her drugged state, how could she not realize Sumner was the killer Jake had been hunting? The man standing beside her had slaughtered Jake's parents. A blade of fear slashed through her, and she choked back a gag. His voice was droning in her ears, but she didn't understand what he was saying. Anger and hatred melted the fear. How could she have been attracted to this monster? What had she seen in him?

She struggled in her restraints. Or she thought she did. If only she could get to him.

"I have to go for a while, but I don't want to leave you hanging here like a side of beef. You'll be more comfortable back in your chair." He wrote something in his book and picked up a syringe from the workbench. "This will calm you and help with the headache."

"Quinn, darling, please don't drug me again. And I'm terribly cold. Could I have a blanket?"

His eyes turned dark, and his handsome face went grotesque with displeasure. *The drug must be wearing off,* he thought.

The unexpected punch to her side spun her around on the iron bar. Winnie gasped, wondering if her ribs were cracked. The manacles cut deeper into her wrists, and blood ran down her arms.

"If I want you to speak, I will give you permission, and I will not cover your body." His eyes and face softened. "I want to look at you and touch you whenever I want."

He ran his hands down her sides and over her hips. "You'll enjoy this drug. It's different from the others," he said, jamming the needle into her hip. "You'll see wondrously strange things, and you'll want to sing and dance, and," Sumner said, smiling at his bride adoringly, "you'll be desperate to make love to me."

He winched her out of the water and swung the bar around until her feet dangled over dry ground. He could tell she was already in that wonderfully dreamy place where sleep wasn't sleep, dreams weren't dreams, and life wasn't real.

She tried to fight it, but she had no chance. The drug won easily, and she swooned into an odd place filled with riotous colors and weird oddities that made no sense. She was wearing her beautiful green dress and dancing with the devil. It was a beautiful waltz.

Quinn unchained her from the bar and carried her lovingly back to the chair. "You think your marshal will find you, but he won't," Sumner said, reattaching her chains and caressing her thighs as he rose. "No one ever will." He kissed her, and her lips responded. Her arms encircled his neck, and her moans of desire inflamed his primal lust. He wanted her. She'd been cleansed, but there had been no ceremony, and his mother wasn't there.

"Soon, my darling, soon," he said, gently pulling her arms from around his neck. "I'll be back soon with Mother. She will be witness to the ceremony and the consummation of our marriage." He dressed quickly. He had to head off anyone who might be looking for her. And he was sure someone was.

He suspected they had known for some time that she was missing, and unless Kat was an idiot, they probably suspected him. But he would play innocent, a man sitting on his veranda taking in the evening air as he so often did. *I may even offer to help them look for her,* he thought with a smirk. *Now that would be something, me out searching for her?*

CHAPTER 76

# THE SCHOOL BELL

Lorene was taking laundry off the line but stopped to watch two riders barreling down the road toward her. Kat and John rode in at a full gallop, their horses skidding to a stop.

"Lorene, is Winnie here?"

"No, we thought she was in town with you and Mary."

"She's missing. Where's Grant?"

Lorene ran to the huge school bell beside the house and pulled ferociously on the wheel. The clapper swinging back and forth sent heavy chimes resounding across the valley. "This is our emergency signal," Lorene said. "Grant and the men will come running." Before she got the words out of her mouth, Grant was running toward the house with a dozen ranch hands close behind him.

"What's wrong?" he hollered.

"Winnie's missing, and I think Quinn may have kidnapped her," Kat said. Her horse pawed the ground and shook his head, rattling the bridle. He sensed the human panic and was eager to run.

"Lorene, start ringing that bell nonstop," Grant hollered on his way back toward the stable. "We need to shake everyone out. Come on, men, let's get saddled up."

John rode to the corral, joining the additional men who were gathering there. "Saddle up," Grant hollered to them as he raced past.

Linc ran into the stable. "What's happened?"

"Winnie is missing, and Kat thinks Sumner kidnapped her. Get the men organized," Grant said, slinging his saddle over his horse.

Within minutes, two dozen men were saddled and ready to go. Grant sized up the men in front of him. "We believe Quinn Sumner has kidnapped my daughter. I intend to tear his place down board by board until we find her and then tear him apart limb by limb. If any of you want out. Now's the time to stand down."

No one moved. "Let's ride," Grant hollered.

Kat and Lorene watched as the men galloped over the hill and out of sight, leaving only a cloud of dust hanging in the air behind them.

Kat was having trouble controlling her horse. "I'll ride back to town and find Logan. He needs to know Winnie is missing. I only hope he's okay."

## CHAPTER 77

# A PAINFUL VISION

Sam and Jake were within five miles of Sumner's place when Jake pulled up in the middle of the road. "Sam, my head. We need to stop." They sat in the middle of the road, long shadows stretching behind them as the sun sank low on the western horizon, Jake sat quietly in his saddle, his eyes closed. He wanted to scream.

From somewhere, a faint voice, no, it wasn't a voice, told him what to do. *"Relax, breathe, see."* That's what he…heard?

Sam sat silently beside him. Jake was white as a ghost and swayed in his saddle. Sam had never seen Jake like this before and wondered if he should do something. But what?

Jake heard it again…*breathe, relax, see*. He didn't understand, but the knowing kept repeating itself. He let his mind go, and the pain and the icy fingers squeezing his chest were gone. There was a strong, earthy smell, and then Winnie was right there in front of him, shackled to a chair. Tangled roots hung over her head, reaching down, grabbing at her. He heard moving water and felt a cold dampness. No, he didn't feel it, Winnie felt it. Then, as suddenly as the vision came, it was gone. He tried to bring it back, but he had no control. There was nothing.

"Winnie," he whispered. Then he glanced at Sam. "Winnie's in trouble, Sam. I saw her. She's chained somewhere. Maybe in a cave of some kind. It was dark, and I heard water. We have to find her."

"We still headed for Sumner's place?"

"You bet we are," Jake yelled, slamming his legs against Drach's sides. Drach reared and stretched into a gallop, with Pal right behind him.

Leaning low over Drach's withers, flying through the gathering dusk, all Jake could think about was Winnie and wondering what Sumner had done with her. He was sick with desperation. It wasn't the pounding of his horse's hooves that he heard as they rode toward Sumner's place; it was the pounding of hate and anger.

## CHAPTER 78

# THE GOVERNOR SHALL HEAR OF THIS

Jake jumped from his horse's back as Drach skidded to a halt in front of Sumner's house. He saw Quinn on the veranda and bounded up the steps. His jaw set and a frown pulling his eyebrows low over his eyes as he ran toward him.

"Where is she?" Jake yelled, grabbing Sumner by the collar and pushing him against the house. "Where's Winnie?"

"Marshal, please release me. How would I know where Winnie is? She's your woman." Quinn couldn't help but smirk.

Jake tightened his hold. "Tell me where she is," he hissed, anger eating at his control.

"I have no idea where she is. Why would I? I'm not her keeper."

"You lying son-of-a-bitch," Jake said, his face inches from Sumner's. "I know you have her," he growled, pulling his gun and shoving the barrel under Sumner's chin. Jake's voice was low and guttural as he pulled back the hammer. "Tell me where she is, or I'll put a bullet in your brain."

"Deputy, get this man off me," Sumner said, recognizing the danger he was in.

"I'm going to kill you," Jake said, his whole body tensed, ready to pull the trigger.

"Don't," Sam said, placing a hand on Jake's shoulder."

Sam's quiet voice shattered Jake's primal need to kill his enemy. Sucking air into his lungs, Jake eased the hammer down, but he didn't take the gun from beneath Sumner's chin.

"Marshal," Sumner said, awkwardly trying to smile. "I'd appreciate it if you'd point your gun elsewhere."

Jake pushed the barrel of his gun harder into the soft flesh under Sumner's chin. "Just because it isn't cocked doesn't mean I won't shoot you. What have you done with her?"

"I don't know what—"

Jake thumbed back the hammer. "Try again. Maybe you didn't understand the question. Where's Winnie?"

"Jake," Sam said. "We're wasting time. He isn't going to tell us anything. Let's search the house. We may find something helpful."

Jake hesitantly released his hold on Sumner.

"You don't have a warrant to search my home," Sumner smirked, straightening his shirt and trying to maintain his composure. "If you don't have a search warrant, you can't enter my home."

"Who's gonna stop us?" Jake said, slamming his 45 Colt into its holster. Then he slammed his fist into Sumner's face, knocking him to the floor.

Sumner sat up slowly, spitting out blood and bits of his precious white teeth. "My teeth," he screamed, pushing himself to his feet. "You can't use me as a punching bag. I've done nothing wrong, and I don't know where Winnie is."

Jake hit him again, flicking his hand with the pain. Sumner was prostrate on the veranda floor, groaning, blood running from his mouth and nose. Spitting out blood and more bits of tooth, he floundered, laboring to get to his feet.

"Are you deaf as well as incompetent? I've told you over and over that I don't know where Winnie is." Sumner could barely form the words. "I'm a law-abiding citizen, for God's sake."

Jake was about to take another swing at Sumner, but Sam stepped between them. "Let me handle this."

Jake hesitated, rubbing his damaged hand, then nodded.

"Quinn Sumner, you are under arrest for kidnapping and assaulting a U.S. Marshal. Please put your hands behind your back," Sam said, pulling handcuffs from his belt. Quinn resisted, and Sam backhanded him, knocking him halfway down the length of the veranda.

"Resisting arrest isn't the smartest thing to do, Doctor Sumner," Sam said.

Quinn tried to get to his feet. "You can't possibly have proof of me doing anything wrong. The governor and mayor will vouch for me."

"I don't care if the President of the United States vouches for you," Sam said in a calm voice. "We have proof," Sam lied, pulling Quinn to his feet. "Now, put your hands behind your back."

Sumner struggled to get free of Sam's grip. "Stay out of my house, you ignorant cretins."

"Cretins?" Sam said, handing him over to Jake. "Hang on to him while I get a rope."

"You can't hang me," Sumner screamed, twisting to escape Jake's hold.

Sam fetched the rope from his saddle and hogtied Sumner, throwing the end of the rope over a beam of the covered veranda. He pulled Quinn up until he was swinging five feet off the ground.

"Now, you stay here while we search your house and the grounds," Sam said, giving Sumner a forceful spin as he walked away.

Jake watched Sumner spinning helplessly. "Get me down. You hear me? Get me down. The governor will hear of this. You'll be in jail for this outrage." Sumner tried to sound righteous, but it was difficult to do while spinning dizzily in the air.

Jake and Sam hurried into the house. They didn't expect to find Winnie there but hoped to find something that would tell them where she was or the proof Sam had lied about having.

"Let's check his bedroom first," Jake said, heading for the sweeping staircase.

## CHAPTER 79

# ARTEM?

Starting up the stairs, they heard a weak voice. "Artem, is that you?"

Sam pulled his gun and slowly opened the door. An elderly woman was propped up in bed, looking at them with glazed eyes. They assumed it was Quinn's mother.

"No, Mrs. Sumner, it's Marshal Jacobs and Deputy Watkins. Maybe you can help us. We're looking for Winnifred Grant, and we think she might be somewhere here on the property."

"Hmmm, we have many friends, but I don't recall a Winnifred. Have you seen Artem? He should be home at any time."

"No, ma'am, we didn't. Do you know where your son might hide someone if he didn't want them found?"

"He has a secret place in his bureau, behind the glove boxes. He has all kinds of keepsakes his friends have given him over the years. If you help me out of bed, I'll show you."

She guided them to Quinn's room and went to his dresser. "He fixed hiding spots behind these drawers," she said, pulling one of the glove boxes out and laying it to the side. Then she reached in bringing out a cloth bag.

Jake took the bag from her hand and emptied the contents on the dresser top. There were too many teeth to count. All of them were canines. The other bag was the same. A shiver ran down his spine as he realized that Sumner was the killer, he'd been searching for. He flinched at the thought that two of the teeth belonged to his parents. He wanted to scream, and to kill the monster, but first he had to find Winnie All he could think of was what he might have done to her.

They heard a door in the hallway open and spun around with guns drawn. A large woman was bent over and gingerly balancing herself against the doorframe. Her robe hung open, exposing bloody slashes, old scars, and bite marks. Her fingers had all been broken or dislocated, one hanging precariously as if only the skin kept it from falling to the floor. They could only wonder what she had endured and what kept her on her feet.

"Is Emma all right?" she asked, and for the first time, they looked directly at her bruised and swollen face. "I'm Carol…I care for Emma," she slurred through a broken jaw and swollen lips as she collapsed onto the floor.

Jake watched as Sam squatted beside her, checking for a pulse. "I don't know how, but she's alive."

"We'll take care of her later. Right now, we need to find Winnie," Jake raged with fear and anger at the sight of Carol. *What has he done to Winnie? Where is she?*

Jake turned to Mrs. Sumner with all the kindness he could muster and asked her gently, "Is there somewhere your son might hide something bigger, like Artem or someone my size?"

"I'm looking for Artem. Have you seen him? Who are you?"

He continued patiently, "I may know where Artem is, but you will have to help me find the way. I've forgotten how to get there, but

I remember that it's dark and damp, and there's the sound of running or dripping water. If only I could remember, I would take you to him."

She gasped, "He must be in the cavern. Oh, no. If he is in the cavern, it means he's been bad, and Quinn will punish him. Was he chained when you saw him?"

"Yes, Mrs. Sumner, he was chained, but Quinn wasn't with him. If we hurry, we can save him."

"Is that Carol? Carol, why are you sleeping on the floor? What a silly place to take a nap. Don't you think? Are we going to get Artem?"

"Yes, we are going for Artem." Sam swept Mrs. Sumner into his arms and ran down the stairs and out the front door. "Which way, Mrs. Sumner, which way do we go."

"That way," she said, pointing to the right. "I'm coming, Artem. I'm coming, my love." It wasn't much of a yell, but Quinn heard it.

Swinging back and forth in mid-air, he fought against his restraints, screaming at his mother. She was going to lead them to the cavern and Winnie. How could he have been so stupid? He should have killed her weeks ago. She was worthless. He screamed vile obscenities at the top of his lungs. His desperate attempts to free himself caused him to spin erratically and the ropes to tighten.

"You'll pay for this. You'll all pay. I'll kill you all."

Mrs. Sumner directed them to the hidden doorway leading to Quinn's underground cavern. Sam set her down gently as Jake lifted the hatch. There wasn't much light, but enough to make out the steps. Jake started down carefully, unsure of his footing. When he saw Winnie, he leaped down the last few steps, running to her.

"Sam, she's here. We've found her."

Halfway down the steps, Sam saw Jake in the dim light, frantically trying to unchain her. Sam grabbed a blanket from the cot and threw it to Jake. "Here, wrap this around her."

"She's breathing, Sam. She's alive."

"Jake, calm down and help me look for the keys to the shackles. They have to be here. I doubt he has them on him." Sam saw the syringes on the worktable and held one of them up for Jake to see. "She's been drugged."

Jake was excited at finding Winnie, and so was he, but right now, they needed to be lawmen and get Winnie out of this hole in the ground.

Mrs. Sumner stood at the bottom of the stairs, her eyes wide with excitement. Quinn had left her a present. She hadn't been to the workroom in a long time, but vivid memories flashed through her mind. Going to the workbench, she selected her favorite knife and pulled Quinn's 45 from the drawer. She didn't know who those strange men were and she didn't trust them.

Standing in front of her present, she threw off the blanket and poked it with the tip of her knife. It raised its head and looked at her. *What strange eyes it has*, she thought.

"Got 'em," Sam yelled, turning to toss the keys to Jake. "Jake," he hollered. Jake saw Mrs. Sumner at the same time.

Mrs. Sumner saw them starting toward her. She grabbed Quinn's gun in both hands and leveled it at them. "What have you done with Artem? You said he was here?" She looked longingly at her present, and Jake took a step forward toward her.

"Back away, or I'll kill you," she said, pointing the gun at them. Her arthritic fingers and wrist made it difficult to hold the gun leveled at them. Jake saw the weakness and started toward her. "Stay away," she screamed, "or I'll kill it." She pointed the gun at Winnie. "If you've hurt Artem I'll kill you."

"We haven't hurt him. Put the gun down, and we'll take you to him."

"You're lying to me. I don't trust you." She took a step back, and Jake saw Winnie. A trickle of blood running down each of her arms from wounds on her shoulders.

"What have you done to her?"

"I only poked it a bit. Quinn gets angry if I go too fast. He says it's better nice and slow." She took another step back, trying to keep the gun aimed at Winnie's head, but her hand was hurting and about to give out. Jake saw her wince and rushed at her.

"Stop," she barked, putting the barrel of the gun against Winnie's head. "I've never shot one of our pets before. It will spoil all the fun, but I'll do it."

Sam hadn't moved. "Mrs. Sumner?"

Her eyes darted between the two men.

"I found Artem. He's over here."

"I don't see him. You're lying to me."

"Quinn hurt him, and he needs you." Sam motioned to a dark corner of the cavern. "Can't you hear him calling for you?"

Her arm dropped to her side. "Artem? I'm coming," she said, racing for the corner, but Jake grabbed her from behind, twisting the gun from her hand. She fought to get away. Arms swinging, she twisted and thrashed, screaming for Artem. Exhausted, she slumped into Jake's arms like a rag doll. "Artem," she whimpered, "Artem."

Jake handed Mrs. Sumner to Sam and unlocked Winnie with shaking hands. She fell into his arms, blinking awake. "Jake?" she whispered. "I knew you'd come." She smiled weakly and passed out.

Jake checked her shoulders. The cuts were shallow and had already quit bleeding. Wrapping the blanket around Winnie, he carried her up the steps. Sam followed with Mrs. Sumner slung over his shoulder.

The trapdoor slammed shut behind them as they started back to the house. "You take care of Winnie," Sam said, "and I'll handle Sumner."

"No, Sam. Sumner is mine."

"I was afraid you'd say that. What have you got in mind?"

"I don't know. Maybe cut out his heart and feed it to the pigs."

"Can't say as I'd blame you, but it's probably not a good idea, *Marshal* Jacobs," Sam emphasized.

Jake scowled at Sam. "I know what you're telling me, Deputy Watkins."

When they were within sight of the house, they saw Carol bending over Quinn with a knife in her hand.

"Good God, she's killed him," Sam said, lowering Mrs. Sumner to the ground.

But Sumner was getting to his feet. The housekeeper had cut him loose. After everything he had done to her, she had freed him.

Jake settled Winnie on a nearby garden bench. "Sam, stay with Winnie." He didn't want to leave her, but the vile creature had to be dealt with.

Sumner saw Jake and pulled Carol in front of him, a knife at her throat. "Don't come any closer," he said, backing toward the stable. "You know I'll kill her."

"Let her go."

"I don't think so." Sumner motioned to the bench where Sam stood watch over Winnie. "I see you found what you were looking for. Take your filthy whore and get off my property."

"That's not how it works, Sumner. Put down the knife," Jake said, taking a step forward.

"Stay where you are. I'm telling you, Marshal, my knife is sharp, and her throat will slice like butter."

Jake saw a trickle of blood dripping down Carol's neck. He couldn't take a chance on getting her killed. As fast as he was, he knew he couldn't draw and shoot before the knife would fulfill Sumner's threat.

Carol reached for Sumner's hand, causing him to fumble briefly before throwing her to the ground. That gave Jake an instant to act. He charged at the man, taking him to the ground, the knife flying from Sumner's hands. Jake landed two punches before Sumner surrendered.

"I've had enough, Marshal," he said. "I surrender." But a rage burned inside. He'd been attacked in his own home, his life destroyed. His mother had turned on him, Winnie was lost to him, and the idea of hanging did not appeal.

The stoop-shouldered, defeated man, who had surrendered, turned into a demon fighting for his life. He lowered his head and plowed into Jake, knocking them both to the ground.

Quinn's hand pawed the ground, searching frantically for the knife, but no luck. Then his hand connected and he swung it at Jake. Jake blocked Quinn's arm and shoved him away. They rolled to their feet, circling.

"You want me to shoot him?" Sam hollered.

"No, he's mine. He's going to hang."

"Marshal, you will not be taking me in." Sumner lunged, slicing Jake's arm. The pain sent Jake off balance and Sumner hurled himself at Jake, taking him to the ground. Sumner raised the knife, ready to thrust into Jake's heart. Jake rolled out of the way, and the blade struck the ground. Sumner howled in fury.

Jake pulled himself up, facing Quinn, blood running down his arm. Quinn's eyes turned black as a raven's and his heart raced. He had been on the brink of exhaustion, but the sight of blood triggered a demonic fierceness in Sumner. He came at Jake, slashing wildly. The knife ripped down Jake's ribcage, and blood soaked the side of Jake's shirt.

Quinn had never fought for blood before, and he roared. He was thirsty for it. He remembered the Shaman telling him how his ancestors would rip the still-beating heart from an enemy's chest and eat it to steal their strength. That's what he wanted. An evil smile darkened his face as he imagined Jake dead at his feet and holding his heart up in victory. He would kill Jake and steal his strength. He would become Jake. Then Winnie would come to his bed willingly. He lunged wildly at Jake. Jake sidestepped the thrust and grabbed Sumner's wrist. He twisted it hard and pulled the knife from his hand. He threw the weapon as far as he could and slammed his fist into Sumner's face, knocking him out.

Jake stood over the man, catching his breath, and then pulled him up to face him. "It's over, Sumner. You're under arrest, and you'll hang for all the lives you've taken."

"I'm not going to hang, and you aren't arresting me. You're going to die with a bullet in your back."

"Artem?" Jake heard Mrs. Sumner's voice behind him.

His mother had no gun, but the distraction gave Quinn an opportunity to break free and run for the woods, but Jake was fast and recaptured him before he cleared the expanse of lawn.

"Need any help?" Sam asked. He knew this was Jake's fight and had held back.

"No, Sam. This asshole is mine."

"There was time, Jacobs…before you got here." Sumner's voice was like an echo. "I had her, and she liked it. She couldn't get enough of my cock." He laughed, choking on the blood running down his throat. "Oh, and I bet you'd want to know that your parents begged for their lives. Your mother was pitiful, begging, doing everything I asked, thinking that would save them. I had them both, Jacobs, and they begged for more."

Jake shook his head and turned back to Winnie, thinking Sumner was finished talking. "Tie him up, Sam."

Sam bent down to pick up a piece of rope. Sumner doubled over with a groan as if in pain and pulled a knife from a hidden scabbard in his boot. He came up slashing and caught Sam in the thigh. Sam staggered back, surprised by the unexpected attack.

"Jake," Sam yelled.

Quinn's arm was back, ready to throw the knife. Jake spun, drew his gun, and dropped smoothly onto his haunches. He shot Sumner between the eyes. The back of Sumner's head exploded, and the knife fell harmlessly from his fingers.

"Is he dead?" Jake asked Sam, as he moved to Winnie's side.

"Yep."

"How's your leg?"

"It's just a graze," Sam said, joining Jake.

"You?" Sam asked, seeing the blood on Jake's shirt.

"Same. Just a couple of scratches."

"The bastard went down hard," Sam said.

"He did have gristle."

"Jake, I hear riders. There's a lot of them. Get Winnie and get back in the trees."

Jake gathered Winnie into his arms and hurried into the shadows. Sam pulled his gun and backed into the protective cover of the trees alongside Jake. He didn't think Sumner had any hired thugs on his payroll, but they couldn't take the chance.

Sam let out a deep breath when he saw Grant and his crew come thundering around the corner. Grant saw Jake carrying Winnie from the shadows. "Is she alive?" he yelled, flying off his horse.

"She's alive, Grant. She's been drugged, but her breathing is even, and she's starting to come around."

Grant looked at his daughter's limp form and pale face. "I'll kill the bastard," he seethed. "Where is he?"

"He's over there, but you're too late. I put a bullet in his head."

"Good," Grant said, looking from Sam to Jake and seeing the blood. "I see he put up a fight. You boys all right."

"He was the killer, Grant. The one who killed my parents and all the others. He admitted to killing them. God only knows what he might have done to Winnie if we hadn't found her."

"Sumner, huh?" Grant said, shaking his head. "I never liked the man, but who would have thought he could be such a monster."

"I would have enjoyed seeing him thrash about at the end of a rope, but I'm glad he forced me to put him down."

Winnie squirmed, and her eyes blinked open. She searched Jake's face, her eyes tearing. "I thought it was a dream," she whispered, "but it *is* you."

She turned to see Sam and her dad, and smiled. "You found me. You're all so beautiful," she murmured softly before her eyes fluttered shut.

"Jake, let's get her into town and have Coop take a look at her. Let's make sure she isn't injured," Grant wiped his hand down his face and motioned to his foreman. "Linc, take a couple of men down to the stable and hitch up a carriage."

"I saw some vials, medicine bottles, and a notebook of some sort down in the cavern," Sam said. "I'm going after them. The information might help Coop figure out what drugs he gave her."

By the time Sam returned with a saddlebag filled with a wide variety of bottles, Linc and the two men were returning with a carriage. Sam handed a tattered notebook and the saddlebags to Grant. "Maybe Coop can figure out something useful to do with this stuff."

Grant turned to Jake. "What do you want to do with Sumner's body? The men can take him to the undertakers on their way to town if you want."

Jake nodded, not taking his eyes off Winnie. "We need to find the housekeeper and Mrs. Sumner before we leave. They need to see the doctor, too."

Grant looked up at his crew. "You heard the marshal. Round up the strays and haul them and Sumner into town. And as long as you're in town, you might as well stay the night. Tell Lars to give you rooms at the hotel and tell Kat I've got your drinks covered."

They thanked Grant and spread out, looking for Mrs. Sumner and her caregiver.

"There's at least a dozen horses in the stable needing to be tended to," Linc said.

Grant stood with his thumbs hooked over his gun belt, watching the men as they scattered through the woods. "Send a man down in the morning to take care of the place and see what needs to be done."

Sam tied Pal and Drach to the back of the carriage and hopped gingerly into the driver's seat, favoring his injured leg.

Grant took Winnie from Jake and held her in his arms. "Jake, get in, and I'll hand her up to you. Let's get her comfortable for the ride into town."

"Daddy?" Winnie whispered, putting her arms around his neck with a happy sigh. Grant was a man of remarkable strength and control, but that one little word brought tears to his eyes.

"I'm here, Winnie," he said, blinking back his tears.

The trip into town took thirty minutes but seemed like hours. Winnie was in and out and talking nonsense, but Jake kept talking to her. She nestled her head on his shoulder and felt his warmth and the rumbling of his voice as he spoke to her. She didn't know what he was saying but she wasn't dreaming. He found her, and she was safe.

"Jake? Where are we?" She mumbled, not moving.

"We're close to town. We're taking you to see Coop."

She abruptly sat up, and Jake pulled her tight against his side. "I was so afraid I'd lost you," he said clumsily.

Winnie turned to him and put her arms around his neck, pulling his face close to hers, and after intense inspection, smiled. "It is you. I was afraid maybe—" She put her lips gently against his. "I'd know your lips anywhere." She kissed him repeatedly, hugging him tight.

She pulled away in sudden panic. "Where's Quinn? Where is he?"

"He's dead, Winnie. He can't hurt you or anyone else ever again."

Winnie sat up straight. "Thank God, he's dead."

A chill shot through her as she remembered the bloody scalp hanging on the wall. She began to shake and slumped against Jake, realizing for the first time how close she'd come to death.

Sam reined the team to a stop in front of Coop's office and jumped down. Jake climbed from the carriage, fussing over Winnie like a mother hen. He tucked the blanket around Winnie and carried her into Coop's office.

"Set her on the end of the table," Coop instructed Jake, motioning to one of the examination rooms. "Grant tells me his men will be along with Quinn's mother and housekeeper. Said they were both in bad shape."

Jake stood beside the table, his arm around Winnie's shoulders. "Will she be all right, Doc?"

Winnie's eyes flew open clear for the first time. "Jake," she said, grabbing his hand. "I'm going to be fine."

Coop looked at Winnie with a smile. "Jake, I need you to wait outside. She's awake now, and I want to talk to her alone."

Jake looked from Winnie to Coop, trying to decide if he wanted to leave her.

"Marshal Jacobs, she's safe here. Go."

Coop closed the door behind Jake. "I seldom have trouble getting a man to wait outside. They're usually eager to escape." Coop smiled, motioning to the blanket. "And, as a general rule, I have a considerable amount of trouble getting a woman to shed even one piece of clothing. Never had one come to me wrapped in a blanket before."

Winnie gave him a weak smile and swayed a little. "Very funny, Doc," Winnie emphasized the word Doc, knowing he hated it. Coop smiled, glad to see she hadn't lost her spunk.

"You caused quite a stir today. Tell me what happened."

"It's only been a day?" She asked in disbelief.

"Not even a full day. Drugs can distort your perception of time, and he used quite a variety on you. Your dad brought in some samples and a diary of his experiments. He was a clever bastard…and kept detailed records. According to his notes, everything he gave you he'd created from natural ingredients. The effects should wear off in a day or two with no permanent damage." Coop handed her a glass of water. "Here, drink this."

"I've seen some bizarre things, and my senses have been…exaggerated." She was thirsty and drank down the glass of water. "I'll be glad to have this all behind me."

Jenny knocked and peeked in the door. "Your dad, Kat, Sam, and Jake are all outside waiting for you." She tossed a wrapped bundle to Coop. "These are for you, Winnie. Sam got Steven out of bed to get you something to wear besides that blanket."

Winnie looked at the blanket wrapped around her and smiled at Jenny. "I can't imagine why he thought I needed anything else."

"Jenny, see to Jake and Sam. They might need stitches," Coop said.

"Already done, and they whined like babies." Jenny closed the door leaving Winnie and Coop alone.

Winnie gasped, "Logan? Where's Logan? Quinn told me he drugged him, and he'd never wake up."

"He's at the boarding house, and Mrs. Murphy is tending to him. He'll be fine," Coop said.

"So, Winnie, start from the beginning and tell me everything. What you decide to share with me or anyone else is up to you."

"I don't remember a lot, but if I wouldn't do as he asked, he slapped me, and once, when I spoke out of turn, he punched me in the side. I guess the worst was when he choked me. I thought I was going to die. I couldn't breathe. Thank heavens Jake and Sam came for me when they did. Quinn kept talking about our wedding night and consummating our vows, but he didn't." Tears filled her eyes, and a hot flush crawled up her neck

Coop offered her more water and waited while she emptied the glass.

After examining her, he pronounced her unharmed. "You'll have a few bruises, and those abrasions on your wrists will take a while to heal, but there will be no scars as reminders. You may experience some dizziness until the drugs wear off."

She thanked him, and he left the room to let her get dressed. Sam and Steven had chosen well, the soft cotton dress was slightly oversized and slipped easily over her head, and the slippers were soft and perfect.

Coop knocked and entered after Winnie's acknowledgment. "You look much better. The blanket was not a good fashion choice."

"I feel much better, but a hot bath and the softest sponge I can find will do wonders."

Coop escorted her out, steadying her with his arm. "Drink lots of water and remember, I'm always here for you. Never hesitate."

"Glad you're all right," Sam said, giving Winnie a hug.

"Thanks, Sam," Winnie said as Jake helped her into the front seat of the carriage. Sam untied Pal and waved to them as they headed to the hotel, followed by Grant on his buckskin horse.

## CHAPTER 80

# CAN'T RESIST

Sam and Kat stood alone in front of Coop's office. "Kat?"

"Hmmm?"

Sam looked at her with a wry smile. "I need a drink. A real drink."

"Whiskey?"

He nodded. "Sounds about right."

"I know a place."

When they were in front of Kat's Place, she took his hand to stop him from entering. "I know a better place," she said, leading him to the back of the building and up a hidden stairway to her private apartment.

"Have a seat, and I'll pour."

Sam took a seat on the sofa and looked at his surroundings. He had never been in her apartment. Few people had. The furnishings fit her. If he hadn't known this was her home, he would have suspected as much. The furnishings were simple and understated but elegant. Not overly feminine, but not masculine, the kind of furniture you weren't afraid to use.

Kat handed him a crystal glass and sat across from him on a love-seat, her legs folded beneath her. They sipped the whiskey in comfortable silence. Each combing through the details of a strange day.

Kat got up and silently took their glasses for a refill. She handed one to Sam with a quiet sigh. "How do you think Jake will get along now Sumner is dead, and his search is over? He's been obsessed with this for a long time."

"He'll be fine. He'll never forget, but he'll be fine. It's like carrying a hundred-pound bag of flour on your shoulder and then shifting to a fifty-pound bag. The weight is still there, but way more tolerable. In time, I reckon it'll become more like a twenty-pound bag and maybe someday like ten, but what he saw as a young boy will be with him for the rest of his life." Sam threw back the whiskey and held his glass out to Kat. "Mind?"

"Of course not." She went to the sideboard to refill their glasses. "I don't often see you drink anything but soda or an occasional beer."

"I've always been afraid I'd like whiskey too much and end up like my dad."

Kat scoffed, "He could drink a lot all right, and when he was drunk, he turned into a whole lot of ugly. Bear tossed him out more times than I care to count."

Sam snorted, "If he could manage to stagger home, Mom and I would run and hide. If we didn't, we'd each get a thrashing. We'd wait for him to pass out before leaving our hidey-hole. Come morning, we were forgotten. All he wanted was a drink."

Sam emptied his glass. "I can't count the number of times his belt stung my back. I hated the man."

Kat refilled his glass and left the decanter on the side table. She handed him his drink and sat beside him.

"I'm sorry, Sam. I've taken some beatings myself and know how it hurts your soul. The headmaster at the orphanage whipped his belt out of his pant loops more than once and in the parlor house…where I worked…some of the men liked to rough a gal up first."

"I didn't know you were a..."

"Whore?"

"I'm sorry."

"Don't be. If I hadn't been there, I wouldn't be here. I'm not ashamed of what I did, but it was a terrible time in my life and best left in the past."

Sam pulled her into his arms, and she nestled into his comforting embrace. They sat sipping the whiskey and enjoying the shared comfort. A warm, tingling sensation that had nothing to do with friendship or the whiskey spread through Sam's body. He got up; it was time to leave. Kat put her hand on his arm to stop him.

"It's been a rough day, Kat, and we're both on edge. He looked at his empty glass. "The whiskey is working against our common sense. This wouldn't be the smartest thing to do. It will change how we are, and I like the way we are."

"It will change us only if we let it," she said, looking up at him, her eyes bright with desire. "Sam," She breathed out his name in a sigh. "I know how to satisfy a man." She placed a delicate hand on his cheek. "I can please you in ways you can't begin to imagine."

"We'd regret it, Kat," he said, bringing his lips down to meet hers with a hunger that had been brewing for years. Then slowly he pulled away. "We'd regret it."

Kat walked him to the door, and they lingered there, knowing they should say goodnight but not wanting to. Sam leaned down for a long, deep kiss. They finally pulled away from each other. "I should go," Sam said. "Before we do have something to regret."

# CHAPTER 81

# THE NIGHTMARE'S OVER

Winnie was settled in her hotel room, dressed in the plain cotton nightgown that Sam had provided. The warm bath had worked miracles. She was feeling better by the minute as she snuggled into an overstuffed chair with her legs folded beneath her.

*How could we not know Quinn was the killer? How could I have been attracted to him?* She shivered, remembering the kiss on the hotel porch and how she had wanted more. She had been such a fool…so naive.

\* \* \*

Grant and Jake had gone to the hotel dining room for a drink, waiting for Winnie to finish her bath. She wished they would return.

Jake looked across the table at Grant. "I was beginning to think I'd never find my monster, and I still can't believe Sumner was the killer. He was a snob and as arrogant as the day is long, but he seemed decent enough until he got the notion to court Winnie. He was right here, under my nose, the whole time. No wonder he was so self-righteous and smug. He must have thought me a fool."

"He had everyone buffaloed, but you caught him and saved my daughter. I couldn't be more proud of you. If we'd lost her, I doubt I could have survived." Grant cleared his throat, pushing back emotion.

"I always thought I'd kill him slow and make him suffer," Jake said, "like his victims did. I imagined it a thousand different times, but when it came down to it, I wanted to bring him in to face a judge and jury. But in the end, I didn't mind putting a bullet in his head."

"Is it over, Jake, or is there hate stuck in your craw?"

Jake sighed. "It's over, Grant. But I'll never be able to completely close the door on what he did. It will always be there. Waiting."

"When it knocks, don't answer," Grant said, rising from the table. "Let's go see if Winnie is finished with her bath. I need at least one more hug before I can turn in for the night."

Sitting in her room, Winnie felt safe enough but alone. *Where are they?* She fidgeted and was considering getting dressed to go looking for them. When they knocked, she jumped but ran to the door, throwing herself into her father's arms. Then she grabbed Jake and hugged them both. She ended up in Jake's arms holding tight to him.

Grant laughed, "Guess I'm being replaced." He grinned at the dismay on Winnie's face. "That's how it works, Winnie."

She smiled at her dad but clung to Jake.

"Linc left for the ranch a little earlier. He said he wanted to get home tonight and would tell Lorene you're safe. I'll head out early tomorrow. I doubt you two will need me for anything more tonight, so I'll say goodnight."

Grant left, closing the door behind him, knowing his daughter was safe with Jake.

Winnie spoke softly, "Jake, you need to know everything he did to me, and I need to tell it."

She told him what she could remember, and when she finished, she said, "I knew I had to stay strong and wait for an opportunity to escape. I knew you wouldn't stop looking for me."

"You were right. I wouldn't have stopped looking for you, ever."

"I have something for you, Winnie. John dropped it off when he stopped by to check on you." He pulled her ring from his vest pocket.

Winnie gasped, "My ring. I left it at Mary's. I can't imagine what Sumner would have done with it." Jake slipped it on her finger and wrapped her in his arms, kissing her softly.

Winnie led Jake to her bed. "Stay with me tonight. I don't want to be alone."

At his side and cradled in his arms, she was safe. She was where she belonged. He would do anything for her. Jake kissed the top of her head. "I love you," he whispered, and they fell into a deep sleep. The nightmare was over.

Read what's next in the *Grant's Crossing Series*!
Here's the first chapter of *Marshal's Dilemma*.

# MARSHAL'S DILEMMA

## CHAPTER 1

# IT'S A MORGAN

The gunman lay sprawled halfway off the boardwalk, the trigger guard of his pistol barely clinging to his index finger. The man had fancied himself one of the fastest gunmen in the West, but United States Marshal William Jacobs was faster.

Marshal Jacobs approached the man, watching for any movement. He kicked the weapon from the dead man's hand and squatted on his heels beside the body; he emptied the gunfighter's pockets searching for identification. He found none.

The marshal stood and looked across the gathering crowd. "Anyone know him?"

Ross Meadows, owner of the saddlery shop, pushed his way forward. "I don't know him, Jake, I mean Marshal Jacobs, but I saw him ride in. He stopped and sat on his horse, staring at your office. Then, he went into Kat's Place." Ross motioned to a nearby hitching rail. "That's his horse over there."

Jake looked to where Ross had motioned and slowly walked to the animal. He spoke softly to the chestnut horse, running his hands down his neck. The horse had bloody cuts and scars covering his body, which helped quell any remorse Jake was feeling about killing the bastard.

Sam Watkins, Jake's deputy, had heard the pop of gunfire and came running. "What happened?" he said, "You hurt, Marshal?"

"Nope. I stepped out of the office, heard a holler from across the street, looked over, and he drew on me."

Jake gently removed the dead man's saddlebags from the horse, while Sam examined the horse's injuries. "How could anyone mistreat an animal like this?" Sam said, checking the horse's withers and legs and running his hands down his neck and chest. "Jake, this here is a Morgan," Sam said, looking across the saddle. "You find anything?"

"A wad of money and the usual items. Nothing to tell who he is. There's no bill of sale for the horse, and our four-legged friend isn't wearing a brand…probably stolen before the owner had time to mark him."

Sam walked to the boardwalk where the dead man hung off the side. Blood still oozed from the hole in his chest and dripped from the rough edges of the boardwalk into the street. He touched the man's neck, checking for a pulse. "Someone get Doc Cooper. Might as well get Bones, too."

Most of the curious on-lookers had moved away, and Jake suggested to the stragglers that they do the same.

"We have a dodger on this man," Sam said as he stood. "I don't remember his name, but I remember the face. He's a hired gun."

"That could explain the wad of money in his saddlebag. Think he was after me?"

"I doubt it. I'm more inclined to think he wanted to take down the man who out-gunned Russel Fitz and Graham Bryson. That would add a lot of value to his gun hand. The money could be a coincidence."

"Could be. That was quite a bit ago, though," Jake said, reluctantly remembering having to shoot the men when they challenged him to a gunfight. He had never killed anyone before that. Fitz and Bryson were the first, and it had taken a toll on him.

"Like it or not, Jake, you've got a reputation."

Jake's skill with a gun came from years of practicing. He and Sam had been sworn enemies up until they were ten, but became friends as they learned how they could work together. As teens, they were always trying to outdraw, outshoot, and out-twirl one another. Sam still pivoted his Colt into his holster out of lifelong habit.

Sam unhitched the Morgan. "I'll take him to the livery and have John look him over and fix him up. Didn't deserve to be treated that way; poor thing. You want the saddlebags and bedroll?"

"Yeah, leave those here."

Leading the horse up Bridge Street, Sam met Dr. Cooper. "Heard gunfire. Since you're here, I'm guessing it was Marshal Jacobs. Hope Jake is in better shape than that horse. Tell John I can help if he needs me."

"Jake's fine, but the gunman needs Bones."

"Well, I appreciate your diagnosis, Doctor Watkins, but I'll be the one to say if he needs the undertaker or not." Coop grunted sarcastically, "Every yahoo thinks they're a doctor."

Sam smiled and listened as Coop walked away muttering. He grabbed the horse's reins and continued walking.

Up the street and across from the marshal's office, Russel Walters, President of Fair Valley Bank, watched from his office window… disappointed. He hated wasting all that money.

www.ingramcontent.com/pod-product-compliance
Lightning Source LLC
Chambersburg PA
CBHW060221030726
47499CB00004B/1141